JAMES DREADFUL

AND THE
TOMB OF FORGOTTEN SECRETS

BOOK TWO OF THE
DREADFUL SERIES

ALAN CREED

CREED PUBLISHING

James Dreadful and the Tomb of Forgotten Secrets.
Copyright © 2021 by Alan Creed.

ISBN (paperback) 978-1-7357809-2-4
ISBN (ebook) 978-1-7357809-3-1

Cover design by germancreative
Interior design by Aaxel Author Services

To my dad, Leroy,
for supporting my writing
and for believing in me.

TABLE OF CONTENTS

1

A Mortal Breakfast

The fire wasn't hot.

Yet the ship burned.

The mizzen cracked under the strain of the flames and tilted. The tortured wood moaned. A flurry of sparks, reflecting over the boiling water of the lagoon, danced frenzied in the chilled dawn air, and whirled over the gunwale, some lighting on the wood there and turning to ash. The others glinted off the underside of fish, jostled by the scalding water, floating belly-up.

James was spent of screams.

His wide eyes were fixed on the glinting misericorde between the fingers of the gruesomely burnt specter, whose crisp skull shone through the charred flesh like a face through a melted plastic bag. The man threw a portion of his cloak aside, sending a spiral of crackling sparks into the smoky air like fireflies, revealing a belted scabbard glittering with silver chasing and minute specks of flame. The pommel of his sword glowed like a harvest moon as he placed his palm on it and leaned forward, a tiny beard scintillating with gnat-sized embers on his burnt-black chin.

Rekenhowler.

He held the dagger clasped between his fingers like a surgeon and slid the end along James's cheek, then down his neck and to his shoulder, the one visible eyeball watching him with crafty humor. "Hmmmmmm," he breathed, sending a stream of smoke from his nostrils—a stream that produced a cloud in front of James's face. "It can't always be a lazy day in hell. But I figure I'll just run it through yer eyeball—blade's *shit* for skinnin'. Bloody misericorde. Couldn't yeh have a better one at hand, yeh clotter?"

James was only marginally aware of his own frantic breaths—the sweat gathering in beads on his forehead, the striking of his heart, like breakers waxing in a storm. He wanted to close his eyes, but he dared not take them off the nightmare leering over him. After what seemed like a minute, he noticed the grotesque face had turned aside, looking at something out of his peripheral. James couldn't move; the terror had locked his muscles. But he turned his head a little, trying not to take his eyes off the dagger. Still, he was able to notice something small standing on the table near his face, shouting like a mouse.

"*Wait!*" it was screaming.

"Wha's this?" Rekenhowler growled. The misericorde was tapping a rapid staccato against James's left cheek.

"I said *wait* because you need him, you *idiot!*" the small voice shouted again.

It was Quizlow.

Rekenhowler gave a laugh, his desiccated lips like the skin of a cooked apple, shooting out a thick rivulet of smoke. The tip of the misericorde nicked James's cheek slightly, and a thin dribble of blood swelled and ran hot into his ear. "*Idiot?*" His eye tightened with cruel irony, and then he drove the misericorde forward. "*Idiot?*"

James screamed. He thought his face had been skewered. But a moment later, he saw the dagger had instead pierced the table beside his ear where the drops of blood had splattered.

"Idiot—d'ja call me an idiot?" In a movement that struck like a viper, Rekenhowler seized the gnome in a tar-black hand. The gnome—about four inches high, his neatly combed hair parted in the middle, and the tiny rivet spectacles resting on his nose—looked about as threatening as a cotton mouse. Yet, as Rekenhowler's hand slowly squeezed against his minuscule frame and his lungs deflated, he still managed to keep his composure.

"*You* are *an idiot!*" the gnome wheezed, his voice gradually shrinking.

Rekenhowler's one eye thinned with rancor, its oily black membrane of eyelid skin folding over the bloodshot eyeball. "I'm'a split you open like a pea—"

"Because that's the son of Jack!" the gnome half gasped, half squeaked.

My father, James thought. But even his now-deceased father, whom Rekenhowler used to serve, was not going to help him. *I told Rekenhowler who I was, but that just made it worse!* Indeed, even after James had told him who he was, the monster had only laughed. *"I hated that sombitch!"*

"*I know that, yeh vermin,*" Rekenhowler growled now.

"And as I understand, you—have—unfinished business with—*him!*"

Rekenhowler's one eye squinted more as he stared at the tiny being in his hand. "And how the bloody hell would yeh know that? Who are yeh?"

"I—knew James's mother."

James wasn't sure what she had to do with this monstrosity, but it seemed to draw the demon's attention. Rekenhowler's one fleshy eyeball stared past Quizlow to focus on James's face, his iris dilating with consideration. "Penelope Farrow," he crooned, and let loose a smooth current of smoke through lips puckered with a sneer. "How's the bloody dame?"

"She's—she's well," Quizlow lied. "And she—"

"Yer a bleedin' liar," Rekenhowler snarled. "She's dead as a bleedin' coffin nail."

Quizlow looked nonplussed, and for a moment he was speechless. "Er—how do you—"

"Hahahahahaha." Rekenhowler flicked his burnt eyelid, which was singed with flecks of embers glittering on its tarred folds. "Think she'd ever let 'er bleedin' son call me, yeh fornicatin' puck? Oh, she *loooooved* me, she did. 'Specially when I offered teh spend the night with her in Jack's stead—heh heh. 'N' Jack was a bit of a renegade—styled himself the 'Dark Lord.' But Dark Lord or not, that shrill woman had a clutch on 'is stones, she did.

"Me name can't be written—the letters turn to smoke if yeh try. It can only roll off the tongue. And it was a Dreadful's tongue me name rolled off of, that I'll wager. No other. Over her dead body would that name be spoke again." He leaned closer. "But here's where I made meself bloody clear teh Jack when he was alive. 'Don't bloody call me again, yeh fetcher. I'll slide a knife under yer skin and make sailcloth outta it.'" He sat down in the one chair at the table and folded his arms. "So yeh can imagine how I felt when I heard it a li'l while 'go."

"But James didn't summon you," Quizlow said. "I assure you—he—didn't—"

"A Dreadful summoned me to serve. Them's the only ones that can call me name."

But I didn't, James thought. And that was the truth. It was the crow. He had thought surely that this terribly rotted corpse the Ring Witch had summoned to bring him back to the Hut would take him and drag him back into the swamp. But before she could, the crow, which was standing on the railing of the boat, had said the name: *Rekenhowler.*

"I don't bloody serve *no one*!" Rekenhowler growled. "It seems yeh mortals can't get that through yer thick pates. So, I'm'a make an example—startin' with *him.*"

Finding his voice, James croaked, "What'd my father promise?" His mouth was dry; the voice seemed to die halfway out of his throat. "*Icundoit.*"

Rekenhowler turned his eye toward him. "*Youcndoit?*" he growled, his eye widening with derision.

"Q-Q-Quizlow said y-y-you—"

"He can," Quizlow said. "Jack never fulfilled his promise. So, now that obligation goes to his son."

Rekenhowler looked at the gnome, then at James, who was soaked with sweat and tears running down his soot-caked cheeks. He laughed. "Yeh think this little runt can fulfill a promise left unfulfilled by the *Dark Lord*?" He leaned closer to James, pulling the tar-black muscles and flesh clinging to his skull into a grin. "What do yeh say, darlin'? Think we oughtta tie the knot? Yer not really my type."

"What is it?" James asked.

"Don'tcha mean—*whassit*?" the monstrosity ridiculed.

"Excuse me, but—formalities," Quizlow said abruptly.

Rekenhowler dropped the gnome on the table, and he finally gasped for air. Then the man let go of James and stood up from his chair. "Fo'mality, eh?" he drawled, and unleashed a spate of laughter. Smoke clouds surrounded him. He stepped away from the table and began pacing back and forth, muttering, "I'd given up on it. But it just might work. The Dark Lord's heir." He halted and scratched the stubble on his burnt chin.

James gripped the table, then stood on wobbly legs. He eyed the misericorde still jammed in the table.

"Can't expect much from this runt, though," the monster drawled on. "The Dark Lord's seed is frail. But maybe that's the Farrow in 'im. So, he's a wolf crossed with a pig—and now this is the little piglet here."

James grabbed the misericorde and held it in his hands, staring at Rekenhowler. Only impulse guided his nerves. For the first time, he noticed Cat and Igvard just off to his peripheral right. Cat—the thirteen-year-old boy, and native of Suniria—was stricken with fear, a characteristic James was not accustomed to seeing in his hickory-colored face. His wild, crisp hair was turning gray with the ash floating lazily in the air, and his wide, purple eyes were still fixed on Rekenhowler, though they switched to James with blank, speechless terror. The loosened halyards had coiled around his torso and legs like snakes, and tiny wisps of fire flickered on the fabric, blackening it, but somehow not burning him.

Igvard, James's estranged uncle, was beside him, pulling at the ropes that had also bound him. He'd figured out that the fire wouldn't burn him because as he worked at them, his fingers passed through the flame without flinching. Every now and again, he looked up at Rekenhowler with eyes alert with adrenaline. Sweat rolled down his forehead, blotting eyes James had come to distrust, and ash had also collected in his fashionable beard and long, black hair he kept in a ponytail.

Rekenhowler laughed to himself, and finally said, "It's a one in a million chance."

James looked at the monstrous being and thought, *Jack wouldn't be scared. He's the Dark Lord. And this monster served him!* It gave him the bit of balls he needed, and he steeled himself and acted. He launched himself at the demon and shouted, *"Die!"* and shoved the misericorde straight into Rekenhowler's chest as he turned around to face Quizlow.

Rekenhowler puffed smoke out of his mouth in a chuckle, and then shoved James to the deck like he was shoving a toddler, before confronting Quizlow. "How can I expect any sort of promise from a bloody shit-for-brains like this?" he asked, gesturing at James. He leaned forward into the gnome's face. "But I trust yeh'll bear full 'sponsibility?"

"Yes," the gnome said, nervously eyeing James as he climbed to his knees.

"Well then, let's put it in ink. But you see here," Rekenhowler growled. "His old man cheated me by dyin', 'cause I waited too damn long. Won't make the same mistake twice."

"Course not," Quizlow allowed.

Rekenhowler gave a smile again and turned to regard James. "Very well, then." He pulled the misericorde out of his chest and slipped it into his belt. Then he crouched beside James, still on his knees by the table, and said, "Cheers, mate. This is our betrothal," and he blew a smoke ring out of his mouth. The ring floated across the deck, crackling with fire, and the halyards binding Igvard and Cat came undone. Like snakes, they fell to the deck, smoking, and burned until a small pile of ash and charcoal lay on the wood. Rekenhowler stood, then sat in the chair, dropping one arm over the back of it to look at James. "Well, I've a contract to make with yeh. Or are yeh gon' squat there all day, honeybunch?" He spat on the deck, and his spit fizzled, ignited, and turned into an old, charred chair, with hundreds of embers sparkling in the wood like specks of starlight. *"Sit, fetcher."*

Slowly, James climbed to his feet, as though expecting Rekenhowler to pay him back in kind for the stabbing. Then he stood looking stupidly at the chair, unsure if it would burn him. The demon grinned and then clapped his hands together. The chair whizzed around behind James and knocked him off his feet. He sat so hard on it his teeth rattled. Then it raced up to the table. "M'boy," Rekenhowler said, and he placed a cordial hand on James's shoulder, making him flinch. "Was gon' flay yeh, then was gonna stab yeh, but as yer li'l button-headed friend here said, yeh have the means of fulfillin' a promise yer father once owed me." He leaned forward, and James recoiled, but Rekenhowler grabbed his arm and pulled him closer. "S' let's get ready teh tie the knot, shall we? And make bloody sure yeh don't die before yeh fulfill yer oath. 'Cause in this contract, yeh don't get off by dyin'. I'm gon' own yer *soul*, see?"

James started, "What do I have to—"

"Don' worry 'bout that jus' yet," Rekenhowler interrupted.

Then he turned around in his chair, and to the ship, cried, "Oi, shipmates. We've a journey ahead. Sunlight on our skinn't faces, salt dryin' on our bones 'n' ligaments, tendons 'n' cartilage. Git her out teh sea, yeh whimperin' shellbacks! Yeh know the procedure—she only sails if yeh tease the bitch. Play with her riggings, pluck at her ratlin's. She's a lute with no strings, but she sings all the same!"

At once, they heard moans coming from somewhere belowdecks.

Cat, who was still transfixed where he stood, turned around, his eyes wide with fear.

The hatch opened. Smoke poured out, and something emerged. Fire blossomed from burnt skin, licking and cracking on bone-thin arms and legs. The thing climbed out onto the deck. Smoke wafted from flesh hissing with white smoke. Where its eyes had been, there burned only holes. Their throats wheezed and sighed, scathed by fire.

"Gurn," growled Rekenhowler, as more of the burning men climbed out, bringing with them a gassy pong of rotting flesh smoldering on embers. "It ain't so bad livin' an eternity with yer clothes melted into yer arse, back, and limbs. Just try not teh leave yer skin on the ratlin's when you g' up 'em, though."

The *Persephone* had begun to drift in the lagoon as the early morning breeze pushed her away from the shoreline. The roar of the fire still raged; the mizzen toppled over into the water, hissing and sending up clouds of steam and smoke with its sails. Parts of the bulwark cracked and split, but the ship continued to stay steady on the water. Now, one of the apparitions went to the helm to steer the ship; others went to work the riggings.

Satisfied, Rekenhowler turned back to the table. He pulled the misericorde from his belt, stabbed it into the table, and looked at the gnome. "Now that we're on such dear terms, yeh can call me what me friends call me—the ones I've skinn't, o' course—*Stray*."

"That's—er—generous of you," Quizlow said.

"Hadwin, where are yeh, yeh bloody marrow!" Stray roared. And then he turned and looked at James, drumming his grease-slick fingernails on the wood while blowing a spark out of his nostril.

A moment later, something stepped out of the smoke from the hatch. It looked like a silhouette of a person at first, but then James shuddered, wanting to avert his eyes. The creature did not appear human. It was bone-thin, like the other horrors, but it had no flesh at all. Acidic soil had stripped at its bones, making them brittle and yellowed, with fractures of walnut brown. "Ah, here he is, me scribe. But if yeh can call 'em that I can name me anal warts the same—the worthless bit o' graveyard dross," Stray growled, continuing to drum his fingernails. "I need a contract. Written on human skin and drawn up in the blood of that piece of trash under the ground—*Cthalis*." He turned to look at James. "He's Satan to yeh, clotter." He snorted. "If yeh break a contract written in Satan's Blood, yer bloody eyeballs'll melt. Howdya like that?"

"Oh," Hadwin said in a servile tone. "I'm sorry, but I'm afraid we don't have any more eyeball-meltin' Satan's Blood ink, Stray."

"What the bloody hell?" Stray growled and spat on the table. Mucous and saliva foamed on the wood, and a quiet blue flame hovered over the spit. A moment later, a greasy, charcoal-black quill floated out of it, with only its edges fringed by wispy, gray smoke. Stray picked the quill up and tapped it on the table twice before giving it a shake over his crusted fingertip. A drop of pitch fluid dripped onto it. He then placed his finger on his black tongue, which sent smoke and ash flurrying across the table. "Wha's this?"

"Oh—plain old ordinary *lampblack*, sir," Hadwin said.

The snarl from Stray sounded more like a cougar's as it rose in his throat. *"Lampblack?"*

"Well, we've been drafting your memoirs, sir, using Satan's Blood, because you wanted anyone who read it to have their eyeballs melt. You've lived a long, exciting life—full of so many verbs and adjectives, sir. You wanted lots of gory descriptions. One such description went on for *pages*, sir. Anyway, that is the trouble with being immortal and wanting to write your gratuitously gory memoirs. It's painstaking work. And though it's full of murder—it's also murder on the *inkpot*. So, in short, we're all out. Although, we could begin an ink-making—"

"Shut yer bung hole, yeh fornicatin' tosspot," growled Stray. He set the quill down and spat on the table. Again, fire burst from it, and a blank parchment appeared out of the smoke and flame, all rolled up. "Hang it. Very bloody well, I need yeh to draft a contract fer young Dreadful here." He stood up from the chair and stretched and looked around. Hadwin sat in his place, took the quill up, and began scratching away furiously.

For the first time, Stray looked at Igvard and Cat. "Suppose yeh can have breakfast while yeh wait. This could take a while."

***

It was a strange breakfast. No one actually said they wanted it, and no one wanted to eat. Stray said he wanted to watch them "et" something. It was funny to watch people "et" since he hadn't had to "et" in over a hundred years. He sat on a keg on the other side of the table, leaned against the gunwale, and propped his booted feet on the table, occasionally shouting at his sailors, who scrambled around the *Persephone* howling in pain. "Shet yer fornicatin' bung holes!" he said, and growled that their howls were getting old and tiresome. "You've been torches for a decade at least, so yeh should be used teh the fire ticklin' yer bones by now!" Then, for kicks, he spat, and two more skeletons appeared, each one holding a tray of something a "mortal might nibble on." There was hot beer, crumpets, sunny-side up eggs, and sausages—all of which might have been good if they hadn't been burned black.

Igvard knelt stiffly at the table, occasionally looking at the demon, who continued to shout curses at the sailors from time to time. Meanwhile, Quizlow, who'd been given a teacup, a saucer, and a large crumpet, managed to take a sip of the hot drink out of politeness, before addressing the demon again, even as Hadwin continued to scratch out the contract. "Mr. Stray, perhaps we should go over the—"

"Not now," interrupted Stray, turning back from his distraction. "Stuff yer bleedin' faces."

Both Cat and Igvard, still wearing stripes of soot from where the ropes had bound them, nibbled at the crumpets and sipped at the tea. They appeared too terrified to refuse. James just looked at his crumpet, turning it over and over in his clammy hands, and watched the skeleton scratch away on the parchment. He did, however, take a sip from the tea, letting the drink wet his parched lips.

Finally, Cat said, "Sir—er, Mr. Stray, are we still your h-hostages?"

"You got someplace to be, boy?" growled Stray, who'd resumed drumming his fingertips on the table. "Or—I shouldn't be so rude. Lagoon's yours to swim in, shipmate. Fancy boilin' water?" He leaned toward Cat. "I'm not the kind teh give yeh simple liberties just 'cause I let yeh sip some bloody tea, yeh clot. James here will buy yer freedom by acceptin' a contract that would put yeh in me employment. Then yeh can fetch somethin' for me."

"What am I fetching?" James asked, putting the teacup down.

"Just be concerned about the fetchin' part fer now," Stray said.

James looked at Quizlow. "But—I want to know what it is."

"Now, now," the demon growled, leaning forward. "First yeh gotta *ink*."

"But," James said, "how can I sign without knowing—"

"Yer clever, boy. Yer father was clever. And I hate clever clotters— think they're cleverer than I," Stray snapped.

"James," Igvard said warningly. He looked at Stray. "He'll sign it."

James and Cat looked at Igvard, but just then, Hadwin, who was sitting at the end of the table, chuckled. "Oh, Stray. You might as well tell 'em. They'll—"

"Ink whatever I bloody tell 'em teh ink," Stray said. "Shet yer stinkin' bung hole, yeh marrow."

Hadwin went back to scrawling on the parchment, mumbling to himself, and even picked up James's crumpet and took a bite from it. He continued to scribble away as he munched, and the burnt crumbs fell through his mouth onto the parchment.

Quizlow had wandered over to the parchment, and then shook his head. "It's in Cthalic," he said.

"Ah—the chief gab of the Underworld," mused Stray. "Don't worry, I'll give yeh the run of it when it's complete. But it's no big deal. Yer father had lots of stuff locked away in that place he called the—the—"

"Tomb of Forgotten Secrets," Igvard finished.

Stray snapped his fingers. "Yes—the Tomb of Secrets." The snap, however, had unintentionally triggered a jinx, which caught Igvard's mustache on fire. Igvard quickly slapped at it with his hand.

"What's there?" James asked. "What's there that you want?"

"Galajitar."

It was Quizlow who spoke, as he stood looking over the parchment

Hadwin was furiously writing on.

Stray looked up, amused. "So yeh can read Cthalic," he murmured, narrowing his one eye in displeasure.

James looked at Quizlow, shocked, and remembered what his grandfather had said about the gnome the night they returned to Nobrocoso. He was small, but clever, and an intermediary between demons and mortals. *Well, that comes in handy when you're dealing with undead mercenaries*, he thought.

But on that same night, he also recalled that his grandfather had tried to keep the secret about the book from Quizlow since he had asked James to come with him alone into the woods behind his house. *So, Quizlow knows about Galajitar—my father's secret grimoire.* Certainly, he would have known that James and his grandfather were bringing it with them when they were leaving Earth—the place his grandpa Arthur and Quizlow had called Urrd. Yet he gave no indication that he knew.

Until now.

He looked at Stray. "You want—"

"Yer father's old tome—*yes*," Stray confirmed.

James felt his heart sink. It would have been fine if the evil goblin named Wizizorkus hadn't stolen it right before his grandfather died as they were plummeting thirty thousand feet through the sky. How would they get it back from him? That creature was *impossibly* powerful.

"Is that it?" Cat said. "We can get that, right?"

James looked at him. Of course Cat didn't know anything about of that. James had only met him afterward. He'd ended up sharing a cell in an Arupan dungeon with him after Quizlow had inadvertently wished them out of a giant narwhal's mouth into a desert city where magic was forbidden.

"What is it, anyway?" Cat probed.

"It's a book," Stray said, looking at James. "A book that taught the Dark Lord his secrets."

James started, "What do you want with—"

"What I want with the book's me own goddamn business, yeh clotter," Stray snarled.

Hadwin finished the contract and put down the quill. Then he blew on it, an action as ineffective as him trying to eat, since nothing came out of his mouth. "Oh," he said. "I forgot. I don't have lungs!" He held it up and tried to shake the crumbed ink dry, but a breeze caught it and blew it overboard.

Stray snapped, and the parchment zipped into his fingers. "'Ow many times, yeh bloody—" He pulled the sword from his scabbard and lopped off Hadwin's skull. It bounced across the deck and landed in a bucket of boiling water a swabber was scrubbing the deck with.

As Hadwin stood, pawing the air, and went groping for his skull, Stray said, "Thar—she's writ. Now—" He took James's teacup and saucer and chucked it over the gunwale into the lagoon before he could take another sip. "'Nough o' that silly business. 'T ain't a soiree. But—thought 'twas rather cute teh watch. Yeh clotters are entertainin'. Either teh skin, or teh watch yeh do that—heh-heh! Here, mate. Yeh can sign the bottom." He leaned forward and dropped the quill on the table in front of James.

James looked up at him. "What—so I—"

"Yeh can bloody go free, buttercup. That's what yeh'll get. Otherwise, I rip off yer face with me fingernails. Done that once." He looked over to Hadwin stumbling about. "Yeh put that in me memoirs, yeh marrow?"

Still shaking, James reached for the quill.

"No deal."

It was Quizlow again, and he was standing before Stray, his arms folded, and looking confident.

"Whaddya mean 'no'? Look at this li'l kidney bean with 'is arms folded. 'No deal'? Are yeh drunk on neckler piss, yeh bleedin' leprechaun?"

"I meant what I said. James will *not* sign the contract, and he will *not* acquire Galajitar's tome for you. He's under no obligation to sign any—"

Stray pulled the misericorde out of the table so fast, James didn't see his hand move. The misericorde gleamed in the sunlight peeking through the trees, and then he reached for James. But before he could touch him, his hand stopped an inch from his neck.

"See?" Quizlow said, a little hesitantly. "You can't harm the boy now. Once the contract is complete, threatening a signatory to sign is illegal—according to Underworld laws."

James stared at Stray's finger stopped an inch from his throat. He couldn't have been more pleased to have Quizlow on his side, but he hoped the gnome had not just gambled with his jugular. Yes, his grandfather did mention he was an intermediary between demons and mortals, but he also said his allegiances could seem *ambiguous*.

"Ah, yes," Hadwin said as he returned to the table, placing his skull firmly on his neck. "I could have told you that, Stray, but you wanted me to 'shet my bung hole,' as you so kindly put it, so—"

Again, Stray whacked his skull off. This time, it flew all the way to the forecastle.

"Yeh tricked me," the demon growled, glaring at Quizlow.

"I'm only following the laws of your realm," Quizlow said, though he couldn't hide the uneasiness in his tone. "Your laws limit your powers in our realm. No arm-twisting when it comes to contracts. Seems all the time in Under has made you a bit rusty on the legal stuff here."

"It has, hasn't it? And those *are* the laws," Stray snarled. "But maybe that won't be forever, *mortal*."

"As long as Cthalis sits the throne down there in Under it will be. The Architects negotiated those rules so your kind won't run amok in our realm and Cthalis agreed to them because he's stuck in the nether."

"Oh, yeh li'l kidney bean, I'm gonna—" Stray stood up so violently, he knocked the table forward a couple inches. Then, with a ferocious growl, sent a spell of roaring fire from his mouth. He stormed across the deck, and the temperature rose, the air around Stray shimmering with heat waves. James felt the hairs on his body rise. The planks beneath Stray's feet glowed with flame, turning flecks of it to charcoal.

Quizlow's done it now, James thought, panicking. *He's gonna cook us all to death!*

But Stray's boiling wrath cooled, and he turned and approached the table, a new smile on his burnt skin. He sat again and put his boots on the table once more. "Well, then," he said after a moment of contemplation, "still's the matter of you gettin' somethin'. 'M I right?" he growled, looking at James.

"What?" Igvard asked, now emboldened by the demon's powerlessness.

"I know yer silly mortal affairs are none of me business, but I understand yer after a thief."

"How do you know that?" James asked, feeling bolder and sitting forward.

"How d'yeh think I was summoned? Heard me name said, and the seal was broken. Pulls me into this realm. But I *hear*, buttercup. I know yer mercenaries mutinied against yeh and decided to run off with somethin' of value. Now, I can help yeh get it back. Me men—they're good fighters. Don't mind their moanin'. They cry all the time because o' the pain. But they fight. I can sail this ship teh the island and get yer precious jewel back. Yeh get me what's in this tomb place that's—er—*somewhere* and we'll call it even."

Igvard looked at James. "James, that's—that's a good—"

"Terrible deal," Quizlow finished, giving Igvard a nasty look. "James is to fetch you a powerful weapon in exchange for this service? No. And I'm sure this book will break some seal binding you to Cthalis's realm so you can rampage freely in ours—"

"That's not why I want the book," Stray growled. "I want the book to *destroy* him."

"*Him?*" James inquired.

"Galajitar," Stray said. "The book is not what it seems. It's a he—and he's a bloody sorcerer."

"And by destroying the book, you break your curse?" James said.

"Nay," growled the apparition. "Galajitar is the only one who can break the curse on me. And I'll let hell freeze o'er 'fore I'll let anyone make me mortal again. Mind yeh, I *like* who I am. No existential crisis here.

"So, do we have a deal? Hell, I'll even throw in these Boneheads fer free." He sat back and looked at Hadwin, who was coming back, fixing his skull to his neck once more. "Matter o' fact, I'll let yeh have 'em with or without. *Take* 'em. I wanna get rid of 'em. They're nitwits, and they make burnin' in the netherworld into'erable. And burnin' in the netherworld shouldn't be into'erable."

"Are they useful?" James asked.

Stray gestured at one of the skeletons holding a tray. "This one's name is Digfred. That one's Moffat. They'll serve yeh tea and crumpets on a sinkin' ship. Does that answer yer fornicatin' question, yeh bleedin' fool?"

"I object," Digfred said. "I am not useless!" And just to demonstrate this, he began to do something that resembled a tap dance. As he did, Moffat bowed and said, "I'll delightedly break all two hundred of my bones in good, conscientious effort to serve you, Your Excellency."

Digfred tripped over his feet and fell, smashing the tray over Igvard's head and splashing tea on him.

Igvard jumped up and fell over Moffat, who stumbled backward and collapsed with his face in the bucket of boiling water.

"*No.*" This time it was James who said it. He looked at Igvard, then Quizlow.

"What?" Stray said.

"I said 'no.'"

Stray rose from the table, blowing out another stream of smoke.

"I say that," James said, rising, "because the book is not in the Tomb of Secrets. It's *gone.*"

"Agreed," Quizlow said. "It was taken by the goblin Wizizorkus."

"I don't care," Stray growled. "I didn't tell yeh it'd be easy. I said *git* it."

"And I won't," James said, standing up straight. He felt a wave of confidence surging through him now—now that he knew the demon couldn't touch him.

Stray stared at him for a moment with that one organic eyeball, a barbed wire of smile flickering through his cheek. Then he turned to his shipmates. "Aye, sea dogs!" he barked. It was like the report of a shotgun going off. "Gurn—git back teh Under where yeh belong 'n' leave this goddammed ship be. This bitch goes no farther under me command till this contract's inked one James bloody *Dreadful*." He turned back to James, the lines pulled taut in the burnt skin over his faceplate—*rage*. "See, boy. Now yer stranded at sea, *miles* from shore, and no rowboats teh git yeh anywhere. Try sailin' her with no shellbacks, yeh bleedin' spawn o' a swine herder. Yeh won't git her to Sarvelok—nay. But after yeh've been stuck at sea fer days, piggie-boy, and the sea worms be gnawin' at the hull, and the bilge be full o' seawater, and these Boneheads are drivin' yeh mad"—he cocked a thumb at the skeletons—"yeh'll be callin' me back teh ink that scrap o' human skin as sure as burn's me middle name."

All of a sudden, there was a blinding flash, and all the fires went out on the ship. The sailors gave shrieks and turned into streaming columns of smoke.

Stray himself gave a howl like a dog, and then turned into smoke that blew away in the wind.

The *Persephone* moaned and smoldered, and beneath the dark clouds, her tortured wood snapped back in place. Cracks and charred boards and planks creaked and vanished—and beneath the veneer of soot and sparkling veins glittering like melted ore, was the old boat, as though she hadn't been touched by hellfire—or the curse of Stray.

2

A SKELETON CREW

"No deal?"

James couldn't tell what was more surreal: the fact that the boat had been a burning inferno for the early part of the morning, releasing streams of smoke into the air, and yet had continued to sail, or that all of that had vanished just as quickly as it had started, leaving almost no sign that it had happened. He would not have believed it had all happened if it wasn't for the ash in their hair—or the puncture on his cheek that had clotted by now. Further, he felt a strange disconnect with himself. *I was just chatting with...* His grandfather talking about the three-headed hound came back to him; he remembered having felt a chill in his spine. *But I didn't know what or who he was.* His grandpa had said his father owed him a debt, and he had implied that the dog would someday call on him to collect.

"No deal?" His uncle was clutching the ratlines on the starboard side and looking at Quizlow, who was still standing on the table. Igvard's cheeks had gone slightly flushed, his eyes sparkling with fresh anger.

Quizlow was looking at him with calm assurance, however, before he walked across the table where a blotch of ink had splattered, and dabbed at it with his foot. "Are you finished, Igvard?"

James was barely paying attention. He had seen a lot of amazing things:

flying carpets, teleportation, a falling house, and some dreadful witchcraft. But Stray. That was a new type of wild. A new type of nightmare.

His skin crawled, and his memory flared: An image of the charred figure holding the misericorde, threatening to impale him with the pointy thing.

He sat still on the bed. Cat had done the same and was ruffling his crisp hair that had now begun to form knots. Ash poured out in clouds. His tunic was still blackened by the bands the halyards had left on him, but where the halyards had touched his hickory skin remained unblemished. Certainly, the hot sparks in the halyards would have scorched his skin and left blisters. It was some strange magic—maybe an illusion? A very real one—where the smoke drifted like ghosts, and the fire was as hot as lucid dream-fire. But we're both OK, he thought, looking at Cat. We got through this. Realizing he, too, was covered in ash, James ran his fingers along his forearm, scoured the powdery flakes tangled in the hairs there, and brushed them from his long walnut-colored hair. He stood and went to the standing mirror by the gunwale. It was still there, like the bed, and furniture decorating the deck, left by the ogres who'd looted his uncle's castle back in Cades. *Where I belong*, he thought. *Where I should be.* He stared at himself now. Dried tears had left tracks in the thin film on his cheeks, and the whites of his citrine eyes were red, the bags puckering the skin below them making him look like a sobbing child instead of the fourteen-year-old son of the Dark Lord. *I am nothing like my father Jack.* An unpleasant memory of himself crying made him ball his fists. He saw his tremulous fingers dig into his palms at his sides in the looking glass. But that was a good thing, he supposed. His father Jack was the Dark Lord after all.

"I can't believe I—I was, like, talking with that—that thing—Rek—" James had started to say the name, but bit his tongue. No, don't say it. Don't ever! His stomach cramped with fear.

"You told Cthalis's pup to go fetch 'is pecker," Cat said, looking at him and gave a small, nervous laugh. "Gorblimey—that was wild. Didn't think you had balls like that, kid."

"You seriously think we should have bartered with James's soul?" Quizlow was saying over at the table.

Igvard folded his arms and pursed his lips, staring at Quizlow. Then he turned his attention toward James. He was about to speak, when Quizlow cut him off. "Don't look at him." Quizlow went to the edge of the table looking fiercely at the man. "You Dreadfuls have a habit of playing with fire. I'd just managed to trick Stray into invalidating his deal, and you wanted to strike another with him?"

"You got into bed with Dreadfuls, Quizlow!" Igvard retorted, rounding on the small figure.

For once, James could agree with his uncle—and he had no love for the man. Not more than a week ago, his uncle Igvard had kidnapped him and Cat from the Faugs castle under the impression his band of ogre pirates were working for him hoping they could deliver Jack's heir to the Dreadful witches in the Realm of Shadows. He discovered, however, that the ogres in fact weren't working for him when they stole the enchanted stone—Roseheart—his mother had left him in her will. But James would have never believed that Quizlow, who'd promised he'd return to James and Cat, after leaving them at the Faugs castle, had been working for the Dreadful witches—called Gralls—supplying them with information about the Spell-guardianship his mother had bound him, his grandfather, and uncle Oskar, through a ritual some eleven years ago. It would allow all three of them to enter the place James's Dark Lord father had discovered his greatest weapons—the Tomb of Forgotten Secrets.

"Yeah," Igvard continued. "I heard about you. You play with fire just as well as we do. Didn't you just try to sell the child out to the Dreadfuls? So, don't pretend you have this child's well-being at heart."

Hearing his uncle call him a child made his blood boil. "Am I some sort of pawn in your twisted little game?" James challenged, glaring at him. He was reserving most of his animosity for his uncle, however. It was he who had started everything by kidnapping them. "First you want to sell me out—then you accuse Quizlow of doing the same thing? Oh, that's rich!"

Cat suddenly sniggered, and James turned, somewhat surprised. "Don't pretend you're shocked, James," he said. "This dirtbag has been trying to upsell you the moment he laid eyes on you back in that castle, so it's not news to you that he's a dirtbag. But then you went and chose him, remember?"

He was right, of course. After the Ring Witch had awakened the enchanted stone and it had turned into a mockingbird, the enchanted creature did what nobody expected her to do. She put them all to sleep with a song—all so she could go with the ogres. Later, James had been the first to awaken, and he had a chance to go with the uncle from his mother's side of the family—the king of Scofirr—or go with Igvard, his kidnapper. Stupidly, he'd chosen Igvard.

Igvard's nostrils flared with annoyance as he regarded Cat briefly. The child had become a prickly splinter in his finger ever since they left the swamp, and Cat had hassled him about his dodgy behavior ever since. "I only want to reclaim what's yours," Igvard said, looking at James. "Oskar—that horrid brother of mine—"

"Don't lie to me," James cried, turning to him. He stepped toward his uncle menacingly, imagining he had the same ominous persona of his father. Right now, he wanted to pummel this stupid man's face. Did he really think he'd forget that Igvard wanted to use him to get his hands on the inheritance his father had left him? "I chose you only because I knew you the longest."

Igvard smiled wryly. "Well—said as much a week ago, didn't I?"

"Don't flatter yourself," James retorted remembering how Igvard had warned him about his horrible relatives. It was a pathetic reason, and it made him feel uneasy inside, but it was true.

"He's a pathetic, dishonest opportunist, so his motives are clear," Cat said with a simper. James had always found the simper disconcerting, but this time it was spot-on, and he could do nothing but agree. "And it's easier to trust what you understand."

"Well," Quizlow said, "if that's true, you make a fine point. But it doesn't excuse his treachery."

"No, it doesn't," James decided. He stared his uncle in the eyes and folded his arms. "For instance—you kidnapped us out of spite. You betrayed your brother Oskar, and your father, too. Why?" He knew it wasn't just his uncle's greed that made him bring them to the Realm of Shadows. Only a week ago, he'd sensed a deep-set resentment in the man as he sat in the chair of the castle's great hall, scowling at the past.

Igvard looked flummoxed, chewing his lip. "I saw the way you talked about your grandfather," he said at last, averting his eyes. "That was the man who abandoned me." He walked toward the gunwale and ran his hand through the ash dusting his hair. "Many years ago, when we were just teenagers, my brother Jack betrayed me. Left me to face the curse of the witches after I'd helped him escape the Hut. Betrayal is all I know, James. I grew up a snake."

He thought that Igvard meant an invertebrate, which described him perfectly. But then he realized his uncle meant the symbol of the witches, which was officially the Grootslang—the giant snake named Snafligul he'd seen in the witches' hall last night, and the tattoo all Dreadfuls had magically burned into the backs of their necks. But maybe it was both.

Quizlow looked at James. "You see now that this man will take you for all you're worth."

"Of course I do," James said.

"I wronged you—yes," Igvard admitted. "But don't expect me to apologize for what I am. I am your blood, like it or not."

"Go to hell," James said.

"You saw your relatives," his uncle continued. "We're Dreadfuls. That's what we are."

"You're right," James said. As much as he wanted to deny his uncle any kind of dignity, he admitted that he was pretty normal for having grown up with that bunch of degenerates. "But I can't trust you."

"You understand where I come from," Igvard said lowering his voice.

"Doesn't mean you get a pass," James said. "Fool me once, shame on you."

His uncle was not familiar with the saying, it seemed, because he offered up only a stoic shrug. "You're stuck with me whether you like it or not," Igvard said. "Trust me or don't, it makes no diff—"

But Cat suddenly poked James in the shoulder, and said, "Look!"

The sound of his voice made the hairs on James's back bristle. He imagined when he turned, he'd see that blistering, charred face of his father's mercenary leering at him again out of a curtain of smoke. But instead, he turned to see Hadwin strolling back from the quarterdeck, followed by Digfred and Moffat.

"Ship's weathered," Hadwin was saying. "I bet the rats go back some sixty generations, not to mention that the sails have mold on 'em."

"And did those pirates raid an old lady's bedchamber?" Moffat added as he clacked behind him carrying a candle tree. "And what's this mirror doing here? And this four-poster bed's completely mildewed. And there's an antique nightstand that looked like an ogre gnawed on it out of boredom."

Digfred, meanwhile, was rummaging through a dresser and pulled out a pair of smallclothes before holding it up to his body. "What do you think? Will it cover me pelvis?"

"What are you still doing here?" James demanded.

Igvard stepped toward them. "Oh, come now, James, don't be daft," he drawled in a tone tight with sarcasm. "Do you think Stray—Cthalis's right-hand man—would leave without planting informants?"

James looked at his uncle, then back at Hadwin, whose jaw had dropped, and then shut repeatedly, in what he now began to interpret as an attempt at laughter. "Hahahahahaha! Informants? Do you hear that, Digfred? Moffat? We're informants!"

"I think you are," James said. "You're his informants. Well, tell him we don't want you."

"His?" said Digfred. "Let's play a game of pronouns, shall we? Perhaps you're referring to Lord Skull-Splitter of Cairn Peaks."

"I had to work in the marrow mines under lord Maggot-Melvin Doom-Bringer," Moffat said. "Is that the 'he' you're referencing?"

"You know what he means," Cat said.

"Oh," Hadwin said, slapping his faceplate. "How doltish. He means Cthalis. Or maybe he means the boy's—uh"—he pointed a loose fingerbone at James—"late father." He tried to snap his fingerbone, but it fell off with a crack and clattered on the deck.

"Jack Dreadful!" Digfred supplied as Hadwin stooped to pick it up.

James pulled the misericorde from the table and advanced on the three of them. He didn't know what he'd do with it, but he felt it made him look more intimidating. "Tell me why you're really here—now!"

"Oi, we surrender, mate," Hadwin said, holding his hands up. But his voice did not betray the slightest bit of the emotion he feigned. "You don't recall, I suppose, that our tormenter—"

"That's Cthalis's stray mutt," Digfred interjected.

"—was kind enough to offer you our free services?"

"Services?" James echoed. Now that he said it, he did recall hearing Stray say something of the sort, but he didn't think he meant it—not after they rejected his offer. "He was serious?"

"Stray is always serious," Hadwin said. "Although I prefer to think he did it out of the kindness of that crispy organ above his ribs, which, I daresay, hasn't struck a rhythm in well over a hundred years."

"They cannot be trusted." It was Quizlow who spoke now, still standing on the table with a suspicious, yet stern expression.

"Shucks," Hadwin said. "That was what Stray said, too. See, he was under the impression we were reporting to that ole bum on the chair of skulls. Y'know—Cthalis. Stray didn't like the idea of us breathin' down his neck. Mind you, Stray likes to spend his time drinkin' in Bofslat and wastin' Mr. Brimstone's eternity." He sat at the table. "Yer father gave him more work than he'd had in a long time as he sought those Armagods."

James knew he was referencing the stones his father had searched for and died trying to keep from the hands of a mysterious enemy—Cowl.

"Wait"—James went to the table, his fingers playing with the misericorde's thin blade—"you knew my father Jack?"

Hadwin turned his head, an action that gave a creak, and said, "Oh, who do you think invited us aboard? Yer father was the captain of this tub when ole Stray wasn't the helmsman."

"We were Jack's slaves," Digfred said.

"His slaves?" Cat repeated dubiously.

"Well," Hadwin went on, "he acquired us on one of his voyages and put us to work. Jack used Stray on occasions because he was bloody useful. But that came at a cost. Each time ole Stray would grumble more and more, and he'd get under Jack's skin. You see, Stray don't like doing anyone's bidding. And I think he was tryin' to get something on ole Cthalis because he wanted that—that—"

"Book," James finished.

"Yes—the one called Galajitar. Personally, I think Stray is tryin' to find a way to break Cthalis's hold on him. Or maybe it's the book that binds him—I don't know. All I know is that the book was mighty important to him, and when Jack still refused to turn it over, Stray told him not to summon him again unless he had the book for him. But Jack didn't fear him. And so just to spite ole Stray, he put a rather sinister curse on the ship."

"What kind of curse?" James asked.

Hadwin gave that same peculiar laugh, moving his jaws first before the sound came out. "Well—us."

"You?" Igvard said, scowling at him.

"Us," Moffat said, sitting on a barrel. "So, it wasn't Cthalis who stuck us here, it was your father. But because of this curse, we are unable to return to the Underworld and go about our deaths. We must follow the soul of the *Persephone* wherever she goes."

"Although I believe we are able to walk about three or more miles from where the vessel has dropped anchor in this realm—I'm not entirely sure," Digfred said.

"But no matter how many times and how many ways Stray tries to dispatch us—" Hadwin began.

"We always come back," finished Digfred. "Whether we are mauled to itty-bitty pieces, or burned to a heap of cinders—"

"We always come back," finished Moffat.

Hadwin gave his strange laugh again and turned to the other two, clacking his fingers on his femoral bone. "They believe we spy for Stray." They all broke out in chuckles, and Hadwin turned his head fully around. "We're actually honored you'd think we could have the resolve—"

"Not to mention wits," added Digfred.

"Or care," growled Moffat.

"To perform the task of informing."

"OK," James said. "If Stray really wanted to be rid of you, why didn't he just leave you on the deck like this before? Why bring you along to wherever he goes?"

"To the Underworld, you mean?" Digfred said. "He can only come to this realm when a Dreadful says his name, and he can only leave us in the charge of another Dreadful."

"Yes," Quizlow said, folding his arms. "That is something I'd like to put to you. Who called Stray's name?"

It had been a nagging question for the longest time, and now James turned to focus on Hadwin, whose head had turned fully around to look at Quizlow.

"Why—the son of Jack," Hadwin said, drumming his fingers on the table and looking at James. "And he wasn't too pleased to hear—"

"Me?" James felt a chill run along his spine, but stared accusingly at the skeleton, nonetheless. "I did not call him! How could I? I didn't know his name!"

"Really?" Hadwin said, and the skeletons laughed. "Well, ole Stray was sailin' his ship on the netherworld lake headin' for Lern to spend some of the heads he'd severed at Decapitator's—and was even winnin' a game of Skalp with a flesh hunter—"

"He had us entertainin' him by jugglin' five of his severed heads, which he had set on fire—" inputted Digfred.

"Every time we dropped one, we had to wear our feet on our hands, and hands on our feet, and sing a ballad of his choice while we served his guests a porridge made of bablit brains by holding the tray in our teeth," Moffat pitched in.

"Yes—he was havin' fun," said Hadwin. "Anyway, he was winnin' when he hears his name called by a Dreadful, which really, really irked him."

"Because he said, 'Thought all 'em Dreadfuls who'd say me name were as dead as coffin nails. Gon' reach down 'n' pull this one's balls outta his mouth and shove it in Cthalis's bloody eyehole next I see 'im fer makin' me do business with the li'l shit,'" supplied Moffat.

James looked at Cat, and then back at Hadwin. "But it was a crow that said his name. A crow."

"Crow, eh?" Digfred said.

Igvard looked grimly at Quizlow, then at James, before nodding.

"Do any of you Dreadfuls have shapeshiftin' abilities?" the skeleton asked.

James didn't need to look at Igvard to see that his face had gone a shade of moon white. "Yes," Igvard said, lowering his voice.

"Mangler," James breathed. Of all the most grotesque relatives he'd met in Coven's Hall last night, the most frightening had been the man locked in the Iron Maiden. A man who screamed and laughed, as he bled from the spikes puncturing his flesh, like a madman. But that was because he was a madman. His uncle Cledenhyn had told him that they locked him up because he liked to bite, and that the pain kept him from changing form. Of course, before they'd run out of the Coven's Hall, it appeared Mangler had been set free by one of the ogres.

"So," Quizlow said, "it was Mangler."

"He knew Stray's secret name," Igvard said. He ushered Hadwin out of the chair and sat, fingers smoothing over the thick stubble growing on his jaws as he contemplated. "There was a rumor—I heard it when I was in Estyrmor many years ago—that Mangler had been set free from the notorious asylum Istalador by my brother Jack. That was some—what—fifteen years ago? Sixteen?"

James stared at his uncle, who gazed intently at Quizlow now as though looking for clarification. Quizlow only shrugged. "I wasn't a part of Jack's inner circle at that time. I didn't hear about this."

"Mangler," Digfred said as he walked around the table, holding the ladies' smallclothes. "Does he mean—"

Hadwin nodded so furiously, his head fell askew, and he had to fix it on his neckbone. "Mangler Dreadful—indeed. The day we came into Jack's service, there was a man who sometimes went by that name. Oh—Jack called him"—he snapped his fingers—"Sigurd."

"Sigurd Dreadful," Igvard said, "was one of the most feared Dreadfuls. Even the Grall witches feared him. He bit, he clawed, he murdered indiscriminately. He was called 'the Mangler' because he terrorized the citizens of Yorkhelm for years before he was captured and sentenced to death. But they could not keep him imprisoned. He'd always escape."

"Makes sense—he's a shapeshifter," James pointed out. "And you say my father released him from this asylum Ist—"

"Istalador," Igvard supplied. "Yes, I'd even heard news of the man's escape back then. Apparently, he was captured again—I think it was shortly after your father died." Igvard looked at James.

"This fellow—I wasn't aware he was such a decent man," Hadwin said.

"He makes werewolves look tame," Igvard snapped.

"Like I said—sounds charming."

"Just the type I'd like to sit and have a cup of ale for a chinwag," Digfred said.

"I'd swap tales of torture and dismemberment with him if I could," dreamed Moffat.

"Anyway, he was this lad's father's—er, what do you call it? Ah yes, he was a guide for this—er—tomb thing," Hadwin said. "They wanted to go to a tomb, or—"

"You mean the Tomb of Forgotten Secrets?" James said.

"Oh!" Hadwin slapped his hand against his hard brow. "There's that look! These faces are simply glowing with realization, like they invented the bloody astrolabe. 'It's the Tomb of Forgotten Secrets,' they're all thinking."

James turned to look at Quizlow, who was also fondling his boyish jaws with his fingers and a pensive expression. The Tomb of Forgotten Secrets was the legacy his father had left him. And though he was sure it was filled with his father's dark secrets, it was also said to have loads of Wizard's Gold—something that had also caught his greedy uncle Igvard's attention.

Igvard grabbed Hadwin by the cranium. "Do you know where it is?" The skull came off in his hand, but Hadwin continued to speak all the same.

"Oh, the Tomb of Forgotten Secrets? Jack was lookin' for it all right, and we went along for the journey."

"Can you take us there?" Cat asked.

But Quizlow stamped his foot—a noise that sounded like a finger tapping the table, but the action still caught James's eye. "Stop," he said, his face getting red with exasperation. "None of this has any importance." He looked at James. "Because you're not going."

"Why not?" James's protest almost came too quickly as he stared at the gnome.

"Have you forgotten? You have no Spell-guardian, and you're not near old enough to take on such an—an obligation. For now, our only objective is to return to Cades where you are to stay."

James glared at Quizlow but said nothing. He was right, after all. He was only supposed to go to the Tomb of Forgotten Secrets under the guidance of his Spell-guardians, which at present, he didn't have. He wanted to protest, but he could only sigh in frustration. If Oskar was the only remaining Spell-guardian, where was he? And why hadn't he come to take him into his charge? "Fine," James snapped. "We'll do that, then!"

3
ADRIFT

The shoreline had long melted into the distance and the water was all they could see for miles in every direction. It was quite a situation they were in, and James had to recount several times how they'd managed to get into it.

Had he made the right decision?

There was no way I was going to stay in Estyrmor to grow up with Grall witches like my father, he thought. He did not regret leaving, but he felt he should have foreseen that the witches would somehow retaliate. *But I didn't think they'd summon Mother Orla!* Mother Orla, the original Grall, whose body remained decomposing in the swamp. He still did not understand what had happened after that. He remembered seeing that nightmarish creature shuffling up the gangplank. He thought she would grab him and drag him screaming back into the marsh.

But then there was that crow.

Mangler.

Rekenhowler, he'd said.

And that was when the burning man came. Mother Orla fled into the swamp, and fire took over the ship.

Now looking at the sea, he saw there wasn't a chance of sailing back—not with only three able-bodied shipmates.

Still, Cat, who had the most sailing experience, wasn't about to give up. "Right now, we're dead down wind," he said, looking up at the telltales flapping against the wind from the backstay. He studied the sails with intense scrutiny. "If we want to get back, we'll have to tack, which would require us to move the sails windward to bear away and then switch the sails to the leeward side." He ran his hands through his knotted hair, scrunching up his face as beads of perspiration gathered on his forehead. "I dunno. Does anyone know how to work rigging?"

The answer was no. Igvard had done little more than drink and complain when Formandible had captained the *Persephone* from Cades, and though he'd spent many of his days traveling the seas, he'd been only a passenger and didn't know the difference between shrouds and halyards. Cat was the only one with sailing knowledge, but his memories were yellowed around the edges and frayed like old sailcloth, since he hadn't sailed with his father since he was eight.

Still, he thought they should try, and he and James walked back and forth studying the riggings with some help from Quizlow sitting on James's shoulder. Meanwhile, Hadwin gave Igvard a basic understanding of ship sailing, explaining that to sail back straight into the wind would "put them in irons," and that they'd have to zigzag, or "tack," to get back to shore, as Cat had described earlier.

James figured the Boneheads would know sailing since they'd spent their deaths aboard the *Persephone*, but he thought they'd be more useful. They weren't. He learned that it was an impossible task for a bunch of "wickedly unqualified bos'ns," as they called themselves, to man a boat. For one, they weren't men. They were *bones*. And pulling on the riggings was nonsense—the shrouds slipped right through their tightly clutched phalanges every time. At other times, they bumped into furniture, tripped over the swabber's bucket, or fell down the quarterdeck's steps losing "metacarpals," "fibulae," or "clavicles," all of which scattered over the deck.

By the time they'd realized it was useless, night had fallen, and they'd drifted some fifteen nautical miles farther out to sea. Igvard retired to the poop cabin to rifle through charts, Quizlow went scrounging for crumbs to make a meal (since the ogres had taken the gnomes Igvard had brought on their first journey), and the Boneheads went searching for the pieces of themselves in the starlight.

James wanted time to reflect on the day, and after Quizlow used his gnome magic to make rye bread sandwiches with cheese, beans, and beef (making the food grow out of the crumbs like thick sponges), James and Cat snatched up theirs, hungry as they were, and scrambled up the ratlines to the crow's nest where they could look out at the night sea and eat.

"What a day," Cat said as he swung his leg over, and climbed into the barrel with James, the already half-eaten sandwich clasped in his fist. "Just this morning—ash floating through the air." He had brought a wineskin with him, which he now passed to James. James had turned around to look out across the water with the monocular he'd swiped from Igvard in the poop cabin. "I've seen magic, but—" He paused, and prodded James in the ribs. "You still owe me an explanation. A real honest-to-the-gods explanation."

"About...?" James could tell Cat was still pissed at him.

Cat slapped the monocular down. *"About?"* In the moonlight, he threw his hands up in frustration. "About why we're stuck with this lunkhead uncle of yours. Why *that* whoreson?"

James raised the monocular again. "You saw my relatives back in Estyrmor." Last night was a horror he wouldn't soon forget. After Igvard had conjured the very *real* specter of the Ring Witch in the Faugs' great hall, so he could inform her they would be attending the Spell-guardian ceremony, he'd had a great deal of anxiety about seeing his Dreadful relatives. And they had not disappointed his fears. One of the witches was a penanggalan, a witch whose head came off and floated in the air. Her husband was a Dreadful, but he more resembled a mutated pig-goblin, and he'd tried to eat James. But he was sure Cat was wondering why he hadn't chosen Cledenhyn—the Viking-like uncle from his mother's side.

He was from a warlike clan of Seabeards—and he was the king of the Neptune Isles, and had a stronghold in Scofirr.

"You don't understand," James said, looking at Cat. "I wanted to choose Cledenhyn. But Roseheart—she chose Gunter. Why? I dunno."

"And you trusted her?" Cat asked.

He thought back to the mockingbird. She had given the Dreadfuls a lashing with her sinister tongue. He had trusted her—up until she chose Gunter. *Well*, he thought, *we later decided it wasn't Gunter she'd chosen, but the man who'd hired him. My other uncle. Oskar.*

"I trusted my mother," James said. "And I still do. She chose Oskar for my Spell-guardian. So, really, Roseheart *didn't* betray me."

Cat folded his arms and put his elbows on the rim of the barrel. "Well, I think I trust Hadwin and his cronies more. I also don't trust that— y'know—Quizlow."

"I trust Quizlow," James said absently. "He came through, didn't he?" And he was quite thankful for that, though he realized he'd never expressed his gratitude. After the gnome had told him he was going back home to the Faugs, James had given him the cold shoulder. How could Quizlow expect him to have all these adventures, and then expect him to just go home and sit around for four years? Of course, he knew that this was what he was *supposed* to do. It had all been planned by his Spell-guardians. When he came to Nobrocoso, he was only to go directly to the Faugs, where his uncle lived, and stay there and train as a sorcerer with that book Galajitar under his Spell-guardians' guidance. He supposed Quizlow would have come around from time to time to see how things were going and to give them news.

But after he'd come to Arupa—that Arabian-like realm where he met Catwyn—stole the Glutton's flying carpet right out from under his fat blobfish-looking nose, flown across Nobrocoso, got captured by ogres, then dragged to the Realm of Shadows to meet his Dreadful relatives, escaped them, only to face his father's hellfire servant—Stray—how the *hell* was he supposed to stay put after *that*? Still, he came very close to being skinned alive by the horror—with that one grotesque organic eyeball. How close that fiery man's misericorde came to his face! He felt a finger of fear creep up his back just thinking about what would have happened had Quizlow just froze and done nothing.

What a horrid way to have died in this twisted fairy-tale world! he thought.

"Yes, he did," Cat allowed. "But somehow, I feel that's more worrisome."

James looked at him. "What do you mean?"

"He knows an awful lot about dark sorceries—necromancies. In my land, consorting with demons is abominable. Why does he know such things?"

"I dunno." He looked up at Cat. "He knew my father?"

"And yet you trust him?"

In a flash of memory, he saw Stray reaching for his neck. Had Quizlow known that little trick would work? "Maybe he knows those things so he can deal with demons like Stray."

"That's a naïve way of looking at it," Cat grumbled.

James thought of something. "About my uncle—if I'd chosen Cledenhyn, we'd be sailing to Scofirr now." He wasn't sure what it'd be like there.

"Your mother's home," Cat pointed out.

"I don't want to go there," he said distractedly. He admitted it would have been interesting to see his mother's relatives—how she'd grown up. Maybe someday he would. But now he wanted to find Oskar...and Roseheart. "We have to find Roseheart."

"Cledenhyn would have used his raiders to find her. He wanted her, too, y'know."

"I suppose so," James reasoned. But instinct told him the Seabeards were not what he needed right now.

～

They slept on a bearskin under the stars. He'd found out the first night on the sea when they'd left the Faugs that he couldn't sleep in the bed the ogres had brought from the castle. They'd hit a turbulent spell of water one night and he was thrown off and tumbled bruisingly into the gunwale. The bearskin was the one he'd brought downstairs to lay on the flagstone floor of his uncle's great hall. Sag Lips had taken it, grunting that it was a good pelt, and had hung it up belowdecks in the crew's cabin beside a pile of sacks. Now, James shared the skin with Cat, who curled up beside him. It was still difficult to sleep on with the boat rocking on each tuck of the sea. On his first voyage, it had been far worse since it had been his first time. He hadn't gotten seasick, but sleeping on a heaving ship was challenging. Especially after the bruises from being knocked about all day, and rubbing against sunburned skin as he shifted for a good position. He'd spent many a sleepless night trying to keep from rolling—or wondering if a rat would chew off his face.

Now he was more used to it, and he'd found a spot against the gunwale. His body rocked rhythmically against Cat's as the warm night air rifled with their rough-spun clothing. The mice—not rats—he'd gotten used to, and no longer feared. The sounds of them scampering around in the dark was almost as soothing as hearing the gentle notes of the water plucking at the hull. As hard as it was—life at sea—he felt it didn't detract from his experience. Rather, he felt his soul strengthen, tempered by the element of water and wind.

I don't want to go back to the Faugs. He did not know where his uncle Oskar was—he was some mystery at the end of a long journey. But he didn't want to return to the Faugs.

When morning came, Quizlow tasked him to catch one of the mice they'd heard last night.

"Don't *you* usually do that?" James asked sleepily.

"It took me over a day to find a mouse when I was trying to rescue you in Akhret," Quizlow said as he was parceling out crumbs on the table, preparing to make breakfast with his "boggart magic" as Cat called it. "I had to trade some things with them to barter my way into their mischief. And then they took me to some smalls—only after I'd bought their trust. Here, I'd have to run around the boat trying to find one and it's much harder for me to get around. And right now, I'm busy making you breakfast."

"Fine," James said, not realizing how much work it had taken the gnome to find a mouse. He felt a small stab of guilt for not having asked about it. "OK, I'll get Cat to help," he said, a little sheepishly. Quizlow just *ptsh*ed him as he headed for the hatch leading belowdecks.

It took a good part of the morning to catch one, running around barefooted with a fishing net, stumbling against the constantly moving sole. But in the end, they caught one living in a grain sack over which James had found the bearskin. After they'd brought it to Quizlow, they sat at the table and ate breakfast, which was sandwiches again. Igvard had brought up a half barrel of ale from the crew's cabin and some tankards, and James and Cat ate and drank the ale, belching pleasantly and feeling the warm sun on their skin. Quizlow sat beside the mouse and spoke to it in tiny, squeaky gibberish James and Cat thought was funny. It was a female white-foot mouse with a twitchy pink nose that sniffed at the crumbs and bits of grain he offered her. Occasionally, Quizlow shared tidbits of information about the mouse with them. As it turned out, she was part of a family of mice that went back several generations, and none of them even knew what a human was—or a gnome. He'd named her Fowlsey.

"I'm not going back," James said at last, rubbing the crumbs off his fingers, and giving some of them to Quizlow's new pet. "To the Faugs, I mean."

Cat had just finished wolfing down his sandwich, and he looked at Quizlow to see his reaction.

Quizlow did not seem surprised, however, even as he looked up from the mouse. "Might I presume you've been afflicted with a strong case of wanderlust?" he asked absently as he offered the mouse another bit of rye.

"No," James said. He got up and walked over to the gunwale and stood, arms folded. "My mom wanted me to stay there until I was eighteen, learning—" He gestured at nothing. "But what can I learn cooped up there? I want to see the world. And right now, I want to see what my uncle Oskar's up to. Besides, I'll learn much more traveling."

"And," Cat said, standing up and going to stand beside James, "you've got some balls telling him to go back to that place. Last time you told him to stay put, you left him there where he—*we*—were kidnapped by seafaring monsters. We could have been eaten—*devoured*."

"He was insolent," Igvard said as he strolled over to the table from the quarterdeck and picked up a sandwich. "That's why Formandible almost ate him."

James could smell liquor on the man's breath and made a face at him. He was about to give him the rude goblin gesture, when another voice spoke up. "A virtue among young lads, insolence is." It was Hadwin. He had climbed halfway up the ratlines where he appeared to be taking in the view of the sea. James hadn't even noticed him there—his bones kind of blended in with the ropes. Now he was moving, scratching the back of his skull and yawning. "Had a son in Under. He was too polite—you know, being new to the whole dead thing."

Igvard looked up at him and frowned. "Where's Tweedledee and Tweedledum?" he asked.

"If you're referring to my undead brethren, they're down in the hold playing Doskhr. I just want to enjoy the sunshine."

"What's Doskhr?" Cat asked.

"A card game they play in Under," Hadwin explained.

Quizlow turned his attention back to James. "You have every reason to be upset with me for that, James. But remember that that was out of my control."

"I liked it when you just accepted responsibility for what you did," James said, coming away from the gunwale. "Getting involved with the Wozigod—that was on you."

"They are not the enemy," Quizlow insisted.

"You're still saying that even after they left you," he cried, pointing at him, "to the Gralls?" Surely the gnome couldn't forget how he ended up serving the witches. It was the Wozigod, which as he recalled was a bunch of wizards, that ordered him to spy on the witches. But once the Ring Witch had found out, she cursed him and turned him into her own informant. Quizlow had had to explain that this was the only reason he never returned to the Faugs—because the witches had him snooping around in the Wozigod archives trying to find a way to undermine the Spell-guardian magic his mother had used to bind him to Roseheart.

"You know, you're sounding a lot like your father," Quizlow said quietly.

James looked at Igvard; there was a simper in the corner of his uncle's mouth. "He's right. My brother was hotheaded and distrustful of the Wozigod," Igvard agreed.

"But I suppose I'm being a bit unfair," Quizlow admitted. "You only seem to have heard of them when you learned they were trying to kill you."

When James thought about it, that was the only thing he knew about them. Sure, his grandpa had agreed that they were "the good guys," but that didn't give him much of a perspective considering they were after him. "What do they do?"

"They are the seat of power in Nobrocoso, and their headquarters are in the northwest in Yofhemgad," Cat said.

"Over a thousand years ago, a confederation of sorcerers came together to defend the world from dark magic," Quizlow told him.

"Prior to that, the Architects had ruled the world," Igvard added.

"Who are the Architects?" James asked.

"They're an old race that no longer exists," Cat said. "Like the djinn, whose blood my ancestors have running in their veins."

"The Architects made the Magic Stones," Igvard explained, "as well as other powerful magics that still remain in this world."

"You could say they were the forebears of this realm," continued Quizlow, "who carved it out and ruled it. But that was a very long time ago. For thousands of years, wizards and common men have fought to possess artifacts and weapons of the Architects—like the Magic Stones. And there were many dark ages and wars."

"And that's why the Wozigod came to be?" James inferred.

"Yes," Quizlow said. "And kings and emperors have all pledged support to the Wozigod's cause over the centuries. They've since grown to become the ruling power in the realm. And for the most part they've kept the peace between men, monsters, and magical beings."

"Some would argue that," Igvard challenged.

"I don't doubt they would," Quizlow allowed. "I know a few species would disagree with their ways."

"*Strongly* disagree," Cat added.

"Like who?" James asked.

"Like the goblins who attacked my homeland," Cat pointed out. "And the ogres—"

"Who were shut off from the world by a magical stone wall called the Symplegades," Igvard said. "This surrounds their entire island."

"When I was in Arupa," James recounted, "that fat man—the Glutton—was hosting a midnosh for a bunch of goblins and—"

"Gluffors, Gejvuds, and Gasfan slavers," Quizlow supplied, "yes—remember, I was there. They are all part of what is known as the High Seas Syndicate, who united to expel the Wozigod from the region. They were led by Grisledor, who originally started out with small-time piracy, and styled his outfit the Black Flag Company. They later brought all the raiders, separatists, and slavers together and made the accord in Arngor, Dores. They called themselves the High Seas Syndicate because they are essentially stateless. No kings truly wanted to wage war against the Wozigod. That changed over time, however, when things heated up."

"Right," James said, remembering what Cat had told him about it when they were hanging out in the Faugs.

"That's right," Cat said, "and many of the countries, like Gluffos, have supported Cabalus in the invasion of my country and sold us into thralldom."

"You were not yet born when your father and Grisledor championed the voices of these oppressed countries," Igvard said, looking at James, "and led a war against the Wozigod's dominion."

James didn't know how to digest all of this. He wasn't sure who was the good guy and who was the bad guy, but he remembered being in Arupa under the Glutton's rule and finding it quite unpleasant. "So, my father supported them—the High Seas Syndicate?"

"We grew up as Dreadfuls," Igvard said. "We didn't share the views of the Wozigod." He folded his arms. "Remember, our kind—the Dreadfuls—were born in the Realm of Shadows after Gralls and the like had been chased to that dark corner of the land—all advocated by the Wozigod."

"What about Oskar?" James asked.

"He joined the Wozigod because he was a traitor," Igvard said darkly.

Quizlow treated this retort with casual indifference, though he looked, for a moment, like he was about to clear his throat and object to it.

"Why?" James said, channeling the gnome's sentiment. "Because he didn't choose to join this High Seas Syndicate?"

"Oh, so a few words, and now you're all *for* the Wozigod?" Igvard challenged.

"No," James snapped, angered by the trap his uncle had laid. "But my mother made him my Spellfather." His tone turned caustic as he eyed the man with annoyance. He'd heard Igvard had been turned down by his mother to become his Spellfather. Apparently, she didn't trust him either. He wasn't surprised.

"Well, Oskar *was* your Spellfather, anyway." It was Cat who spoke now—not Igvard. He was folding his arms, but occasionally, he'd pull a knot out of his hair as he looked at James. "Didn't he tell the ogre mercenaries to leave you behind?"

James hadn't really thought about that—not until now. If Oskar had hired mercenaries to steal the fayling, why didn't they take him, too? "Dunno—probably Formandible's mistake." It was easy to blame the brutish pirate. The large, smelly ogre was distant, cruel, and unintelligent.

"No—Formandible wouldn't make that mistake," Igvard said, sitting at the table and wiping away the mouse droppings before setting his sandwich down.

"But Oskar didn't even know I'd returned," James pointed out.

"Oh, come off it, James," Quizlow said as he walked the length of the table, the mouse following him, sniffing at his clothes. "Where do you think he's been all this time? He's been plotting this long before you returned to Nobrocoso."

"No, Oskar wouldn't do—"

"Oh—so you know my brother, do you? Last time you met him you were—what—*three*?" Igvard snapped, pouring himself a tankard of ale from the barrel on the table. "One thing you should know about Dreadfuls, James, is that we're capable of *anything*—my brother included."

James looked at Quizlow, but just then, Hadwin, who was still sitting on the ratlines, said, "Might I add somethin'?"

Igvard looked up at him and glowered. "Are we still listening to Stray's spy?" he asked, before knocking back his drink.

"Go on," Quizlow permitted.

"I can sort of piece together what you fellas are talkin' about." He hopped down, came over to the table, then stretched and yawned. One of his ribs fell off and bounced on the table, which scared the mouse, and he picked it up and scratched his sternum with it ("Don't have a belly button") before fixing it back in place. "Well," he said at length. "If I wasn't mistaken, Stray let slip last night that you won't get this boat to Sarvelok. So—ahem!—so I think that's where this uncle of yours might be."

Cat, who was now balancing on the gunwale, said. "I wasn't sure why he'd said that—*what*?"

"He let that slip because he wanted to let you know where Formandible and his crew were heading," Hadwin said, yawning again while reaching for one of the slices of bread on the table.

"Sarvelok?" Igvard said, smacking his hand away. "Why would they be heading to Sarvelok? Why not head to the island where Tomb of Forgotten Secrets is?"

"What's Sarvelok?" James asked, and looked at Quizlow, who appeared lost in thought.

"Sarvelok was Grisledor's impenetrable island," Cat said, "fortified by steep mountains—"

"And a sea monster," Quizlow said.

James looked at everyone hesitantly. "What kind of sea monster?"

"The kind that would keep you out," Igvard said.

"It's known as a charybdis," Quizlow explained.

James contemplated this. "And what exactly is *that*?" It was not one of the mythical monsters he'd heard about in school, but he supposed he didn't pay much attention.

"My father told me how in the old days, merchants from Dores and the Cabanes would sail all the way around Brobdingrag to reach the East just to avoid the Seventh Sea, now known as Sarvelok's Sea," Cat said. "It was because a great charybdis, whose mouth was as wide as a canyon, would suck the sea down a throat full of knife-sharp teeth—teeth that were larger than a galley."

"That was when it was untamed—later the Tritons, an ancient merman race, captured the beast and held it captive beneath an island. They named the beast Sarvelok."

"So, it lives under an island?" James asked.

"Yes—the island Sarvelok," Igvard said. "The island is named after the beast."

"There were entry points on all four sides of the island," Quizlow went on. "All lead the sea straight into the island's interior through doors shaped like heads.

"In the later years, the island was taken over by Grisledor and used as his operational hub. With high, steep mountains surrounding the island, it was impossible to reach by ship without being sucked inside the great mountain.

"But that was before the great battle fought by the Wozigod to put an end to Grisledor's reign of terror," Quizlow explained further, lowering his voice.

James could tell by the sudden silence that something terrible had happened there. Some sort of historic moment. Cat had slipped his feet to the deck and was folding his arms, while his uncle rubbed a finger under his nostrils, sniffing loudly, before turning to gaze out over the water. Quizlow put a hand on the rim of Igvard's tankard and walked around it slowly, before looking up at James.

"What happened there?"

"That was the day your father crushed the island," Hadwin said, bringing his fist into the palm of his other hand.

"And betrayed the Wozigod," Igvard added, "by striking their fleet during the battle." He picked up the tankard Quizlow was leaning against, letting him stumble, and took a long draught before continuing. "My dear brother was supposed to have made a pact with the Wozigod through an intermediary."

"My predecessor," Quizlow supplied. "He was also a gnome. His name was Buschwaddle."

"Yes," Igvard said. "Anyway, the arrangement was that he'd help the Wozigod defeat Grisledor."

"My dad was after the Magic Stones called Armagods, right?" James said, realizing he didn't have a clear picture of the whole conflict aside from the bits and pieces his grandfather had told him.

"After your father formed the cabal of sorcerers to find and use the Armagods," Quizlow began, "Grisledor betrayed your father and took the Poseidon Stone. But your father fought back and beat Grisledor to the rest of the hidden Armagods—then wielded them against him."

"But Grisledor was on a rampage," Igvard said. "He sacked the world's largest bank with his Archridge—a tower that floated on the sea. Drowned cities, and his raids, including levies from the High Seas Syndicate, sprawled across the globe. He even launched an attack against the seat of power—Yofhemgad."

"He had to be stopped," Quizlow said.

"And my father stopped him?" James asked, almost hopeful. He knew it was a stupid question. Igvard had said that it had ended with his father betraying the Wozigod.

"Originally, my brother Jack had sided with Grisledor—against the Wozigod. Against their empire," Igvard said. "He wanted to strike at the seat of power in Yofhemgad. But Jack's and Grisledor's infighting turned the focus of the conflict away from the Wozigod."

"Hence, the secretly formed pact with Yofhemgad," Quizlow said. "He was to strike at Grisledor in Sarvelok and put an end to Grisledor's carnage."

James turned his focus back to Hadwin, who was strolling over to the table. "And that's when your father had the brilliant plan to strike them both," Hadwin said with his usual insatiable bloodlust.

James looked at Quizlow, who was staring at Hadwin with a darkened scowl. But when his eyes met James's, he nodded. "He was armed with three of the Armagods—Vayu, Tatenen, and Vulcana. And despite assuring Buschwaddle that he would help and not attack the Wozigod, your father—wielding the Magic Stones of air, fire, and earth—brought down a storm of meteors from the sky and struck Sarvelok *and* the Wozigod fleet together. He wreaked havoc on both sides. It smashed the mountain's interior tunnels in and buried about three-fourths of Grisledor's notorious lair. But it wreaked destruction on the Wozigod's great fleet, too. The betrayal shook the Wozigod to the foundation. With my mentor among those buried there, all communication was cut off from Jack, and Yofhemgad issued a *shiqudu* against him and his family—a kill on sight order."

"It wasn't all for nothing," Igvard said, turning to face James. "Grisledor's Third Fleet vanished from the sea as well as his notorious Archridge tower. Word was that it'd sunk into the sea."

"A sea that boiled," Cat added. "I remember hearing tales of boiled corpses washing up on the shores."

"How?" James asked, the color in his face slowly waning.

"Your father was on a rampage," Quizlow said, his eyes turning glassy as he paced the table. "We don't know what triggered him, but he was out for blood. In his search for Grisledor—he used Vulcana to burn towns and cities. Turned deserts into glass. Boiled the sea." James knew they were not intending to shame him, yet he felt he couldn't look at any of them. "Your father's attack crippled Sarvelok, however, and the Scathra could no longer launch attacks from the place anymore. The rash of sea raids stopped—but at what cost?" Quizlow said.

"And now it appears to be the place the ogres are going to rendezvous with your uncle," Hadwin pointed out.

James had to shut his eyes for a moment before shaking his head. He wanted to rid himself of the images he was now seeing—his father on a murderous rampage. The death and destruction left in his wake. And now his uncle was going there? For what reason? He looked up at Quizlow. "Why's he there?"

"Dunno," Quizlow said, and sat down on the table pensively. His mouse came to him, whiskers twitching. Igvard leaned forward to prop up his chin with tented fingers, but James just stared at Quizlow. *What does he think about me? What do* people *think of me?* He felt a chill slide through his skin, like a cold finger of seawater that had leaped over the gunwale. He realized now why his grandfather had shielded him from the truth of his father. It was burdensome to hear. Quizlow, however, had almost appeared stoic about telling him. *He was angry my grandfather hadn't told me all the details.* He pushed it out of his mind. It was too ugly to look at for long—to dwell on.

For a time, the only sounds were of the boat drifting through the water, the gulls circling overhead.

"Well, what do you think is there at Sarvelok?" Igvard asked at last, looking at Quizlow.

"The Scathra raiders who once served Grisledor," Quizlow answered.

"They know about the Tomb of Forgotten Secrets."

Igvard frowned. "How?"

"Oskar told me long ago that before Penelope died, she revealed to him that when Jack was betraying the Wozigod, Grisledor had wanted her to lead him to the Tomb of Forgotten Secrets."

"She did," James confirmed, raising his eyes toward him. He remembered that story Arthur had told him while sitting in his attic when they were back in Urrd.

Quizlow met his gaze. A ghost of guilt must have passed through his small eyes, because he turned his attention quickly toward Fowlsey. He supposed it wasn't easy telling a fourteen-year-old that his father was a mass murderer. "She obeyed—but only to lead him into a trap." The gnome stood and left the mouse to walk along the table, contemplating the whole matter, before shaking his head. "You see, when Grisledor entered the Tomb of Secrets, he brought the Scathra raiders with him. But Penelope had failed to warn Grisledor of the curse until it was too late. She fled before Grisledor could understand what she'd done, but she wasn't fast enough to escape the poisoned knife he threw at her." Quizlow seemed lost in thought now as he was pacing.

"Anyway, only a few of the Scathra survived the curse and fled the island of the tomb with Grisledor—and briefly returned to the annihilated Sarvelok. He was last spotted sailing northeast. Then Jack found him and destroyed the *Lloraham* ship with Grisledor on her."

James was watching Quizlow intently as he spoke. When the gnome didn't continue, he gave a snort. "So, they—"

But Igvard beat him to the punch. "Know how to get there, and what awaits them inside."

"So, he made a deal with them," Cat surmised.

James looked from Cat to Igvard, then to Quizlow. *First my father, now my uncle's a traitor?* He didn't believe it. He *wouldn't* believe it. "This is all just...speculation!" he shouted, clenching his fists. Then he realized something and laughed. "And besides, the Grall witches couldn't use the fayling without me." It was the reason his Dreadful relatives had all tried to curry favor with him at the ceremony to determine his next Spell-guardian. The fayling—the magical key to opening the Tomb of Forgotten Secrets—could only be used if James was present. "So, it's just a pretty rock to my uncle, too, isn't it?"

But Quizlow just shook his head. "Ever wonder why the Wozigod wanted to obtain the fayling?" he asked.

"Why?"

"They know secrets the Gralls don't. There are other ways of getting her to work."

James glared at him. "So, you lied to that old witch? There *are* ways around my mother's magic?"

"I would never let those witches enter the Tomb of Secrets," Quizlow said. "Of course I lied to her!"

"Is anyone considering the fact that the ogres might have betrayed Oskar?" Cat asked.

"They couldn't," Quizlow said, turning to him. "Remember that Roseheart said she knows intentions? She wouldn't go with the ogres if they had no intention of delivering her to the rightful Spell-guardian."

James didn't want to hear any more. He felt as though an even heavier weight was pressing down on him. *No, I don't believe Oskar betrayed me.* Part of it was his commitment to believing in his mother. Ever since he'd seen her portrait in the Faugs, he'd remembered that haunting look— that *knowing* look. She knew everything. And he trusted her. Especially now that he no longer could see his father as the hero he grew up believing he was. *No,* he thought, *she would not entrust my well-being to a traitor.* He looked at Quizlow. "We have to find out what Oskar is up to. We have to go—"

"To Sarvelok?" Igvard said, raising an eyebrow. He looked slightly amused at the mere suggestion.

"We have to!"

"And what about the raiders still living there?" Cat asked.

James stared at him. "There are Scathra still there?"

"They stopped launching raids," Igvard said, "but they didn't leave. The sea monster keeps them safe from any more attacks. Once this ship gets into Sarvelok's Sea, we'll get sucked inside the mountain."

"Besides," Cat said, "you probably haven't noticed, but"—he gestured at the deck—"we don't have a *crew*."

James looked down and thought, *Well, there are other means.* But he didn't say this. Instead, he felt anger and frustration boiling up inside him. Maybe his desire to find Oskar was simply him longing for another fatherly figure to fill the void in his life, and this man, whom his mother trusted, was the final person he thought he could trust—even admire.

I want to know the truth.

He didn't believe Igvard and his smugness, or Quizlow, who was too trusting of the Wozigod, or Cat, who had given up relying on anyone and was determined to stay on his own.

"No," Quizlow said. "This changes nothing. Whether your uncle has betrayed you or not is unimportant."

"But it *should* concern you if he's a traitor!" James shot back.

Quizlow was silent, his face an expressionless mask. "It bothers me more than you know," he said at last. "You forget that I saw him only months ago, right before he sent me off to get you in Urrd. I didn't see any sign that he was plotting something—that he was thinking of stealing your inheritance. But there's nothing we can do."

"There isn't, huh?" James muttered.

"I won't hear any more about it," Quizlow said at last, and he jumped onto his mouse and leaped off the table. In a streak, he was off, breaking in his new mount.

When Igvard had gone back to the bow to look out at the sea, James turned to look at Cat. "I *can't* let it go." He sat at the table and banged his head on it. "Oskar is up to something, and I want to know what it is."

Cat gave a hefty sigh. "You know, I'd feel more comforted if you just wanted to know that there's at least *one* good Dreadful in your family left.

That I can get behind. What your father has in this Tomb of Forgotten Secrets—maybe it doesn't belong in the hands of a fourteen-year-old boy."

James snorted. "You're starting to sound like *Quizlow*."

"Well, what are you gonna do about it, Prince?"

4

AN OLD FRIEND

He found her in an old sack stashed in the crew's cabin. Light filtered in through the porthole, illuminating the cabin full of sacks, barrels, a table, and a dozen or so chairs. Nets hung from the ceiling, and the sole was stained with tar, salt, and wine. Most of the stuff the ogres had collected from the Faugs had been tossed into this corner, alongside a barrel with a candle melted on its head. James was sitting on it now, balancing on the chime. He had been sorting through the sacks all afternoon while munching away on another of Quizlow's rye sandwiches until a bright bit of fabric poked through along with the beautiful gold frills like richly spun hair. He pulled her out, immediately recognizing the lavish tree-of-life design. Another nest of mice had been behind the sack, and they had chewed a hole in the Hessian fabric, which also contained old brass candlesticks tarnished with verdigris, and the tapestry Cat had wrapped his naked buttocks in what seemed like a lifetime ago. Mouse droppings rained out of the carpet along with bits of grain and a few dust bunnies. The cabin had been damp, and any other fabric would have mildewed, but the carpet remained unblemished and as beautiful and sleek as ever.

"So, you still have her."

James spun around and looked down to find Quizlow on the sole of the cabin. The mouse allowed him to appear in places quickly and discreetly to James's irritation. "Yes," he said, placing her in his lap. "She doesn't fly, though."

On Fowlsey's back, Quizlow sprang up onto the barrel's head and climbed off beside the candle stub. He wrapped his tiny hand around the blackened wick. "Flying carpets are known to be fickle, James. Your father was the only one who truly seemed to understand them. But there were times when even he took boats or rode horses."

Now Quizlow put his own small hand on the silky frills and then looked up at James. "As dangerous as it is beautiful," he said. "But don't tell Igvard about it."

It had never occurred to him to tell Igvard about the flying carpet—not even to explain why he thought he could fly the rug that night at the Faugs when Formandible had told his fellow ogres to bind him. Cat was right, Igvard's motives were easy enough to see. He wanted wealth, and James could see little stopping him from seizing the carpet and trying to sell her on some foreign market. If he recalled correctly, the Glutton had said she was worth more than his palace. *Maybe I should sell her*, he thought, though the idea was fleeting. Not even all the gold in the world would make him give up something so priceless—so unique. But he couldn't help but feel that there was another reason he didn't want to admit. *Of course, my dad used one.* It gave him an uncomfortable prickle to think about it.

He told Quizlow how he'd found her again on a ledge below the window in one of the Faugs' chambers after he had left them, and how he'd practiced flying her—first around the great hall, and then outdoors. He could see—even in the light filtering in through the porthole—that Quizlow didn't approve, but he did not speak as he sat on the candle stub, only listened, while occasionally watching his face. Finally, James recounted the experience he had that fateful night when he was flying— after his fight with Cat—and she just stopped, and he fell into the moonlit water. Quizlow's eyes snapped up at his face, and his own had gone slightly wan in the shifting noon light coming through the porthole. "She—*it* just stopped?"

"Yes," James said, noting the refusal to use the gender pronoun. It seemed evident Quizlow had an aversion to the carpet.

Quizlow hesitated as he thought about it carefully. Then he said, "Try it now."

James stared at him in disbelief. "You want me to—"

"Call its name."

James ran his hand along the fabric contemplatively. Then he regarded her with some anxiety. At last, he stood, and brought her over to the table. He unfurled her across the splintered oakwood tabletop. Quizlow had scurried off the barrel on his mouse, dashed across the sole, leaped onto a chair, and then the table, all in a flash. He had broken the mouse in quickly.

James had plopped himself down in a chair and smoothed out the wrinkles. He leaned close; he could smell that same sweet floral incense coming from her like a lady's perfume. He eyed Quizlow, who had dismounted, before focusing on her. Then, quietly, he whispered, "Rimbecella." It was a smooth tone, but he said it plaintively, not the way he had come to address her during the days he had taken her into the skies above the Faugs—a time when he felt he owned her like a steed he'd tamed from the wild land. He waited, watching for even the slightest movement, but after a minute, he knew his call had fallen on deaf ears—did magic carpets have ears? James sat upright. If only he knew what his father knew of the—the creatures.

"It's for the best," Quizlow said, looking at him, his face expressing a subtle hint of relief. "If it had—well I don't think a fourteen-year-old should have that kind of power."

James frowned. "You sound like Cat."

"I sound like—*hey!*" But Quizlow stopped suddenly and leaped back with a small, startled gasp.

James, who had turned to stare out the porthole, looked at him, before his eyes fell on a corner of the carpet, which seemed to have partially lifted, as though tousled by a draft. He stood up and craned forward, eyes widening in disbelief. "Rimbecella?" he said again.

Now the front half of her rose, as though in response. James felt a shiver slink down his spine, making his back break out in gooseflesh. She levitated off the tabletop, eerie ripples dancing through her colorful fabric. Her frilled edges hovered weightlessly in the air.

"Ho—man!" James exclaimed. "She's—"

"Unbelievable," Quizlow breathed.

James touched her; her cloth felt warm with the life of a furry animal. He kept his hand there, running his palm back and forth, until he felt a small ticking. Or pulsing. *She's alive*, he thought with excitement. He hadn't felt the pulse before. Probably because he'd only been interested in flying her. How silly of him to not to have listened to her. He looked at Quizlow. "We're not stranded at sea anymore," he said triumphantly. "I can fly!"

But Quizlow's face was grave once more. "Not ever," he said. He turned his eyes up toward his. "And I expressly *forbid* it."

James felt his nostrils flare. "Why?" He couldn't understand the small man sometimes. "I can fly her...just like my dad. I—"

"You can fly her like Jack, eh?" Quizlow said, raising his eyebrows sharply and leaning against the beating fur of his mouse's back. "Do you think you're Jack?" he asked in a cold voice.

James sighed, lowering his eyes to the table. He hadn't meant to say that. It sort of just came out.

"Now," the gnome continued, mindless of his chagrin, "you told me she failed you. Not once, but *twice*."

"That was because she—I—" James started. But he couldn't give an answer why. He simply didn't know why.

"Regardless of *why*," Quizlow interrupted him sternly. The man might have been no taller than James's anklebone, but he could project authority when he wanted. And he wanted to now—with his penetrating gaze. "One should not play with lightning while standing in water."

He sighed, and for a moment, James felt like he was receiving a lecture from his History teacher Mr. Carbonaro once more.

"You were cursed the instant you touched her, James."

"What do you mean *cursed*?" he demanded, his tone crackling with indignation.

"You are Jack Dreadful's son," Quizlow said calmly. "Here in Nobrocoso, that name carries fear. I thought you would have—" He lowered his voice. "After what you'd heard today about him and—"

"I heard enough," he snapped, not looking at the gnome.

"James."

He raised his eyes at the tiny man, blinking back shame he was trying to hide.

"If the people of Qo'atyn or Ermefol saw you flying that carpet—a boy with long, flowing hair, and sparkling citrine eyes...." He paused, his own eyes filling with raw emotion again. "The scars your father left behind have not healed—not even after fourteen years. That memory, James, will remain in this land, and the people will not forget. They will not forget the reek of burning flesh, or the seas filled with bloated corpses, blackened and eaten by fish. The ash falling from the skies, covering everything in a film of wintery gray. The people walking through streets, their bodies covered in ash. And fires burning for weeks, like a curse on the land. Houses turned to charcoal, soot raining from scorched trees. The charred figure of a mother with a child in her arms—"

"Stop." James felt his nostrils tingle with disgrace. A visceral pain in his stomach seemed to make his lips tremble. "Please stop."

"Yes," Quizlow said, seeing the look in his eyes. "He did it on a flying carpet. That was why rumors flew that he had a dragon. A dark silhouette in the sky filled with ash flying on a carpet with an Armagod that spewed *fire*." Quizlow was silent for a long time as the boat creaked, the nets with sacks swaying overhead. The mouse scuttled across the table, sniffing at a crumb. "*That* image, James. Do you want to be *that*?"

"No."

"She *is* a curse."

James looked down at the carpet by his knuckles.

"Your father has made her a symbol of death. And those who see you fly her will only remember that."

James didn't speak.

"Curious," Quizlow said after a while. "Where did you learn to fly her?" James raised his eyes a bit, but Quizlow gave an understanding nod. "The *book*." It wasn't a question. "The book your grandfather gave his life for."

James stared at him. He didn't know what he meant by that. It seemed absurd. But Quizlow was pacing up and down the table now, the grave expression still on his face.

"What do you mean?"

"Let's go back to that night when your grandfather sent us from Urrd prematurely, remember that?"

James nodded, but scrunched up his forehead. "We had to escape that evil goblin Wizizorkus."

"Precisely. But would it be wrong to assume that Wizizorkus was only after the book?"

James thought back to the night in Paris the first time he had come across the goblin creature. *I've been waiting all these years for your father's dark secrets. Now, tell me, boy. Where did you bury it?* "He wanted the book," James allowed.

"Yes," Quizlow established. "And if your grandfather had given up the book, wouldn't the goblin have left us alone?"

"You don't know that!"

"But I do," Quizlow said. "He was not after you."

It hadn't occurred to him to simply let the evil goblin have the book. But he supposed he'd been brainwashed by years of fairy tales and stories where you didn't just hand the powerful weapon to the evil villain. Bad things tended to happen when you did that. "Well," James said, realizing that this wouldn't have made a sound argument, "Grandpa said that Mom wanted me to become what Dad failed to become." He recalled his grandfather standing with him in the woods that evening as he was getting mosquito bites on his ankles. "She wanted me to become a great sorcerer. She entrusted Arthur to do that. And I could only become as great as my dad if I had—"

"His reading material—yes," Quizlow finished.

"How did *you* know about the book?" He had been meaning to ask Quizlow about it ever since he brought it up with Stray. "My grandfather wanted to keep it from you."

"I picked up on that," Quizlow said quietly. "Arthur shared your father's views about not trusting the Wozigod. I don't blame him, since they'd sent assassins after you."

"Did they know about Galajitar?"

"Buschwaddle was passing information about Jack to the Wozigod," Quizlow said, a bit uncomfortably. James supposed this was highly sensitive intelligence he was sharing with him. He supposed Quizlow was telling him this because he wanted to gain more of his trust. "So, they knew about the book."

"Maybe my father had a right not to trust this Buschwaddle," James responded.

"Your mother trusted Buschwaddle, and she also trusted me," Quizlow said, almost pouting. "She had your well-being in mind more than your father or grandfather ever did, James. And I was fond of Penelope."

"Really? What was she like?" His voice softened when he asked, and he felt a gentle tug on his heartstrings as he looked down at the gnome.

Quizlow walked along the table, pensive. "She was a wonderful woman, James. Adventurous, caring."

"Run-of-the-mill description," James said flatly.

"OK—I only remember that she scolded me once in Arngor," Quizlow added, a secret grin livening up his face.

"Where's that?"

"It's in Dores, which is near Logres—the High Seas Syndicate had their accord—"

"Right, right."

"Your father stayed at a beautiful villa there, and Buschwaddle and I would often go there to meet with Jack. I would bring Buschwaddle's luggage and take his notes and feed our mounts while he consulted with your father.

"Anyway, she scolded me for casting a spell that was quite powerful. I'd taken it out of Buschwaddle's bag, and I'd thought it was a moving spell. But it made quite a disruption and a mess. Playing with magic." He looked at James. "And then some twelve years later your grandfather wanted you to do the same. Do you remember that night in his attic, when we were in Urrd—or your Earth—right before we came here?"

"How could I not?" He could never forget that first time he cast a spell and set his grandfather's pants on fire. He'd felt like such a klutz.

"The fire I was hoping we wouldn't have to put out was the one started when he brought that horrid book with us back to this land. Luckily the goblin took it. And I say good riddance to it."

"But Grandpa wanted me to learn from it—from Galajitar."

"*That's* the fire, James. I told you two to not play with it. And I meant it. And since your mother entrusted your well-being to me, my discretion counts for something." He paused and then smiled. "Actually, that was a lie. She entrusted your well-being to Buschwaddle—my mentor. She had hoped the Wozigod wouldn't put a *shiqudu* on your head. But then Buschwaddle died in the Siege of Sarvelok, and that oath went to me.

"I tried my best to convince the Wozigod you weren't a threat, but your father... Your mother wants you to right his wrongs. But she isn't here. And you," he said, poking James in the arm, "are too young for Galajitar. Too young to have lost your mother, father, and grandfather—" For a moment he looked away, and when he turned back, his voice was quieter. "To the notion of greatness. You shouldn't have to face your father's legacy, or to take on the onus of changing his image.

"What you need is to return home and live those days out serenely. Gain the wisdom of responsible people who care for you. Be yourself."

James just snorted. He wished Quizlow didn't have to end with something corny. "Well, Oskar is my Spellfather, so—"

"Forget him!"

"Then who's going to take his place?" James growled mutinously. *"You?"*

Quizlow just gave a laugh and then looked at the carpet. "No, James. Not me. But at any rate, put her away, and don't tell any more people about her. You don't have to live down, or *up* to anything. But remember what I said."

"You expressly forbid it?"

"I do."

5

SIMPLE MAGIC

Igvard had been trying to plot a course all morning, but with little success. Quizlow sat astride his mouse, which stalked across the table on the poop deck nibbling at crumbs, while Cat was leaning against the gunwale, teasing the torn flesh of his ear as he looked off toward a bunch of peaks in the distance, his purple eyes sparkling. James just stood by the table with his arms folded, not knowing whether he wanted to pitch in to the conversation or not. They figured if they kept the ship on course heading northeast, they could reach Arupa in several weeks. "We'll have to steer the ship in shifts," Igvard was saying, while holding the wheel. James had lent Igvard his magic compass Orbis after a bit of an issue Igvard had with the old rusty one he'd found in the hold. James had not wanted to because he didn't trust the man. Quizlow had given his father's magic compass—Orbis—to him the night they left for Nobrocoso, and he was sure that—like he suspected he'd do with Rimbecella—his dodgy uncle would hold on to it, and later sell it for a good chunk of gold when he got a chance. Even when James handed it over, he saw the man's eyes probing the beautiful object in his hand and run a questing finger over the Grootslang design before flicking it open. But James had no choice. As it turned out, plotting a course was not intuitive, and Cat was not much help either. He'd only done some sailing with his father and had not listened very attentively when his old man talked about plotting courses. Sailing wasn't Quizlow's expertise either. Boats had never really interested him since he spent more time flying on birds and riding mice. He could speak innumerous different fowl and rodent languages, and he had bragged once that he had advanced degrees in the geometric probabilities in kinomancy, which meant he could land them right on an X from one world to another, but he knew nothing about plotting a boat's course. He put forth his own input, nevertheless. "Well, when plotting, first you'll need to be sure our route doesn't take us into waters too shallow, or through rocks or sandbars. And I'm sure we'll have to compensate because the magnetic pole doesn't sit exactly at the geographic pole, so the calculations you're making will be off by a few hundred miles."

It was only enough to frustrate Igvard, but that was why James had to offer up his father's compass, because it was magic—not magnetic. Still, he felt a sting of annoyance when he saw how comfortably Igvard put it around his neck.

As Igvard turned the wheel, James could hear the sheaves and pulleys sighing below as the tiller ropes stretched tautly. "After today, I'm going to take the night shift. You and Cat can take over during the day."

"Couldn't we get the Boneheads to pitch in?" Cat asked. James agreed with Cat that steering the ship all day would become tedious. Cat had already explained that the wind was blowing them due north and they had little room for changing course without moving the sails. If they tried to go west without doing that, they would become too unstable and possibly capsize. The only sure course was northeast, which would lead them to Arupa. That was the soundest plan, since they could hire a crew to take them home from there.

"I'm not sure if they're capable of anything," Igvard said of their undead passengers. It made sense that he didn't want to leave their lives in the hands of the Boneheads, so James left it at that.

"It might interest you to know that on the course the wind is currently blowing us, we'll probably be passing the outskirts of the Sea of the

Abyss," Quizlow pointed out, dismounting Fowlsey to walk across the chart. "Very dangerous."

"We can't plot a course around it without going too close to the Centrennial Belt."

As James understood, the Centrennial Belt was a trailing archipelago of raider territories. One such island—the Scowl—was the birthplace of Grisledor, too, and the hub of most of the world's seafaring hostiles. It was wise to give the whole region a wide berth. "But heading too east will simply take us straight into the heart of the Abyss," Igvard finished. "So, we'll have to take our chances with the outskirting Storm Seas."

James fidgeted uncomfortably. "Isn't the Abyss the sea we first landed when we came to Nobrocoso?" he asked, looking at Quizlow. He remembered now that he had bad dreams about that night he left Urrd. The Magic Stone—that could transport them across worlds—didn't just take them from Urrd, it had taken the whole *house* from Urrd. His grandfather had decided to use it a minute before midnight, despite Quizlow's warning, because Wizizorkus was imminently close to capturing them. And that was how he died. Falling through the sky. Quizlow had barely gotten them out of that situation alive.

"Several months ago—yes," Quizlow finished. Even his voice betrayed a slight discomfort when he said it, and James remembered that he'd blamed himself for coming up short on traveling wishes because of a past indiscretion.

"I've never steered a ship before," James said.

"You'll get the hang of it, skipper," Igvard said, and looked at Cat. "Ask him."

"It's time for you to learn," Quizlow agreed.

During their time on the *Persephone*, it seemed that Quizlow and Igvard had come to terms with one another. Quizlow was the more diplomatic; he seemed to understand that it would be more practical if they were on the same page. And he supposed Igvard saw Quizlow as another adult whom he could confer with about—well—*adult* things. He also noticed that Igvard had begun to respect Quizlow's opinion more. He wasn't sure how he felt about that. On one hand, it was good they were getting along. On the other, it felt like an old friend fraternizing with his enemy.

"We're gonna want to try to avoid the Sea of the Abyss," Igvard was saying, "without straying into the Eleventh Sea."

"Because that's raider territory," James confirmed.

"Of course, any day the winds could change," Quizlow said, "in which case, we'd have little agency over the matter."

"The wind could stop, too," Igvard added.

James looked at him. His uncle was smelling, well—*ripe*—by now. The poor man hadn't changed that white argyle-patterned doublet since the night they first found him sleeping in the chair by the fire in his uncle's great hall. He wore his long hair loose, and he'd tried to shave this morning with a blunted knife while using the standing looking glass the ogres had brought aboard from the castle. His jaw was covered in nicks, bumps, and patches of bristly hairs. Now, he massaged the skin there and looked out at the sea uncomfortably. *Just let it grow out, you moron*, James thought. But it seemed his uncle was used to trimming his beard.

The lateen-rigged sail with the device of a red bat flapped violently behind him as he removed his hand from the chart and set his tankard on top of it to keep it from blowing away.

"I'm more concerned about the Storm Seas," Quizlow warned.

James frowned at him. "Couldn't we hit a storm anywhere?"

"Of course," Quizlow said. "But what we're heading for is—"

"One of the many Storm Seas that outskirt the Sea of the Abyss," Igvard finished.

"What's a Storm Sea?"

Igvard looked up with bloodshot eyes. He'd been drinking an awful lot lately. The ogres had left half a keg of their liquor aboard. James and Cat had tried it once, and it tasted like "goblin piss" as Cat had put it. Still, Igvard had developed a liking for it, but that wasn't a shock. On the night he'd arrived with his band of seafaring ogres, they'd watched him eat a disgusting fish head casserole. "What's it sound like?" he snarled, turning back to looking at the sea.

James gave his uncle a nasty look, then left, climbing down the stairs from the poop deck, Cat following.

"Those are enchanted seas with raging thunderstorms," Cat explained as they headed midship. "My father said there are seas like that scattered all over the world."

"Where's the Boneheads?" James asked. He wanted a distraction. It was of his opinion that if the Boneheads had come along with them on his first voyage at sea, the trip would have been more interesting. Instead, Cat and he had had to endure the smelly seafaring ogres as they prowled about the deck, spitting and carving superstitious runes in the larch planks. The Boneheads, contrarily, didn't have smelly bodily functions, and James and Cat thought it was funny whenever one of them made wisecracks. Quizlow still didn't trust them, but he had to admit they were good sources of information about the Under.

He didn't know where the other two Boneheads were, but they found Moffat midship reclining on the four-poster bed—not at all minding the mildewed blankets—as he tried to read one of the books taken from the Faugs. Gunter had taken several of them with him when they departed Strangeshadow Lagoon, but had left this one—probably because it had been rained on, and a bit of gull turd stuck the pages forty-eight and forty-nine together.

"Oi, Moffat," James said as he approached the bed, "can you show us how to swordfight?"

Moffat was holding the book almost up to his nose hole trying to read a word. "I've told yeh before, swingin' a sword makes me more nauseous than a bad case of the seasick," he said as he struggled to turn a page. Without skin, or finger oil, he couldn't turn just one page, only a few dozen at a time—and only if he managed to hook one of his phalanges into the leaves.

Cat licked his finger and turned the page for him, but Moffat showed no gratitude.

"It's a shame," James said, folding his arms. "You'd be useful in a fight."

"Think so?" Moffat said, looking up.

"You don't think?"

"You clotters are all the same," he muttered, shaking his head. "Whassa matter? Can't fight your own battles?"

"What's a clotter?" Cat asked.

"I'll give you three guesses," Moffat said.

"You mean like blood clots?" James ventured.

"Was about to have a gander at that dome o' yours. Reckon there's a snippet o' gray stuff in there." He set the book aside. "Now, if I was a big bag of blood like you, I'd be afraid to play with sharp pointy things. But not you clotters. No, you like to make all these sharp pointy things, and you love to play with 'em. So—maybe you should find a sharp pointy thing to play with and let me be."

"I thought you were made for fighting," Cat said.

"Oh, did you? That's mighty kind of you. Well, to put it frankly, we are. Only, it's not our cup of bonemeal tea anymore. Back in the day, I really enjoyed comin' to the Land of Up to poke at you clotters."

"Why can't you poke clotters now?" James asked.

"Your father was a bit cleverer than you it seems," Moffat said. "He noticed the bloodlust in our eyeholes and didn't trust us. If we could fight for him, we could also slit his throat while he slept."

Cat frowned. "I thought death mages bound you with spells to prevent you from doing that."

"We were granted our liberties," Moffat said.

"Why?" Cat asked.

"We all belong to Cthalis," Moffat further explained, "but once we're released from him, we can do as we please in the Land of Up. Jack knew this and had to restrict our capabilities, or we'd do 'im in. So, he put a lasting curse on us so that the very thought of killin' made us sick."

"So, he made you pacifists?" James laughed.

"I imagine if I castrated you I'd laugh, too," Moffat said.

"So, you can't kill us, right?" Cat said hesitantly.

"No," he said, sighing gloomily. "And it gives me a heavy heart that I can't." He leaned forward, rubbing his phalanges together. James could only imagine the expression he'd have if he had a face. "Sometimes, though, I fantasize that I go to you while you're sleepin'. You'd wake to a tap on your shoulder. When you opened your eyes, you'd find me standin' over you...and I'd be wearin' Cat's *skin*," he sneered, jabbing his thumb at Cat.

"You're creepy," James said.

"That's what we do to clotters like you in the Underworld. We wear human skin like the way you'd wear a wolf's pelt. Oh, I'd be stylish, mate." He leaned back on the bed and put one leg over the other. "Being creepy is truly a compliment. I'd fail in my deathlong purpose if I wasn't a creep. But, oh, I can just imagine you wakin' up—eyes buggin' out—" Moffat cried out, imitating a woman's scream. Then he was laughing, falling back on the bed.

"But you can't do any of that," James said, slightly unnerved, "so shut up. You don't scare us."

"Ah, you're no fun," Moffat growled.

"Could you at least show us what to do with a sword?" Cat asked. "We should know how to defend ourselves."

"Show you?" Moffat tapped at his chin with a curious index.

"You won't have to do violence," Cat said. "You're just showing us footwork and fighting poses and—"

Moffat gave it some more thought and then sat up. "Ah—bugger it. Could be fun. Bored to shit right now." He stood and stretched, then went over to the cauldron beside the bed and rapped his knuckles on the rim. "Oi, think you fellas can teach these blood sacks a thing or two about the ole sword ballet?"

James was wondering what he was doing, when a metallic voice replied, "Whaddya want?" A moment later, Digfred rose out of the cauldron, placing his skull on his neck and yawning. Hadwin came up after him, but then ducked back down, apparently looking for something, because his skull banged up against the iron sides of the cauldron.

"What are you two doing in *there*?" Cat asked, trying to suppress a laugh.

"*Was* nappin'," Digfred said, looking down at Hadwin. "Oi, that's *mine*, yeh whinging shellback!"

"You need to sleep?" James looked doubtful.

"Course we do," Moffat said. "Keeps our bones nice and sturdy."

"Stupid clotters don't know what it takes to keep an ole marrow together," Hadwin's grumbling voice rang from inside the cauldron.

"That's right," Digfred said. "Our bones got limitations. And we've been around for *ages*. It's not like deadin' in the Underworld."

"How do you keep your bones together?" Cat asked.

"The magic in the Underworld holds our bones together. But since we're far away from it, we need to rest."

"Is it really, like, horrible, being dead?" James asked, his curiosity piqued.

"I find death *more* enjoyable," Hadwin's voice said from inside the cauldron.

"I always thought eating, sleeping, and breathing stopped when you died," James said.

"Nah—we don't have to breathe or any of that nonsense," Digfred clarified. "Breathing is rather *ridiculous*. All that time you spend filling those bleedin' bags in your chests just to push it out again. And you gotta do it all *day*! It must get tiring. Much easier to just be dead and have no breath at all!

"And then there's the whole deal with chamber pots," Digfred went on. "You spend so much time squattin' on that bloody pot. You could be loppin' off someone's bean or spillin' someone's bloody organs. But no— three times a day, you gotta squat on a pot. A bloody waste."

Cat thought about it and then looked at James. "Wish I was a marrow."

James just snorted. "So, you never said why you sleep in a cauldron."

"It's so me bones don't get lost. Fallin' apart's a real pain," Digfred said. "A bone goes missin' and I've to go lookin' for it next morn if someone comes along 'n' kicks it. After a while, it finds its way back to me, but for a bloody long time, I've to hop around lookin'."

Hadwin finally came up holding a bone and said, "Is this yours or mine, mate?"

Digfred began examining it, then shook his head.

"Anyway," Moffat said, sitting back down on the bed, "these clotters want to learn the dance of death."

"An atrocity in the makin'," Hadwin grumbled. "But I'd like to partake, even if it makes me queasy." He climbed out of the cauldron, fastening his wrist and flexing his phalanges, before tossing the bone back into the cauldron. "Y'know, I saw a blade belowdecks. An old, rusted estoc the ogres must have thought was a toothpick because they left it behind. I'll fetch that." Hadwin went belowdecks and returned a few minutes later carrying a baldric scabbard with a rusted sword in it.

James took it from him, drawing the rusted blade from the sheath and letting the baldric fall to the deck. "I suppose this'll do," he said, examining the edgeless blade.

"That's not a sword fighting weapon, mate," Cat said. "That's an estoc—it's made for piercing heavy armor."

"Well, it's something," James said as Cat came over and took it from him and made a thrusting motion with it.

Cat eyed Hadwin. "You really know how to use it?"

Hadwin took the sword from him and James noticed how the hilt seemed to cling to his hand. "Ah, the feel of a hilt in me hands." He made a jabbing motion in the air. "Oh, it already gives me a skullache. Well, let's see."

Moffat wasn't joking when he'd said it could be fun. Hadwin gave James a broom and told him to defend himself. But there was really nothing to defend against. Whatever curse Jack had put on him, it made him as clumsy as he always was—but now he was clumsy wielding a sword. On his first demonstration, he tripped over his own feet and impaled himself with the pommel, which wasn't hard if you don't have a chest. "Oh, my thorax's been dislodged," he complained, rolling over and fingering the bone.

Digfred had a go at it as well, but his attempt was ill-fated even before he climbed out of the cauldron. His foot caught on the rim and he stumbled and hit the bed. "There goes my patella," he moaned, looking down at his knee. Then he took up the broom and swung it like a claymore and, roaring, hit Hadwin's head. It bounced off the ratlines, struck the mirror Igvard used to shave at every morning, and cracked it. Hadwin, however, continued to charge forward, swinging left and right, until Cat and James had to jump out of the way.

But Digfred grabbed on to the ratlines and climbed out of Hadwin's path. "Oi, yeh missed me, yeh clumsy marrow!"

Quizlow came up along the gunwale to see what the hubbub was about and watched with growing disapproval. "What's going on?" he demanded at last, as the headless skeleton fell on the deck, losing his phalanges, and Digfred fell on top of him. Together, sword lying forgotten on the deck, the two of them squabbled over whose bones belonged to whom.

"They're teaching us how to use a sword," Cat said, stooping to retrieve the estoc.

James shrugged. "I dunno. It has some educational value. We're learning all about their bones," he muttered, thumbing at Hadwin, who was beating Digfred over the skull with his tibia to get him to give up his middle phalange before they both sprawled out on the deck, nauseous from the violence.

"Don't be ridiculous," Quizlow said. "If you're going to learn anything, it should involve magic."

James looked at Quizlow. He didn't expect to hear that from him. Back when they were sitting in his grandpa's attic, he had been against James learning any kind of magic. "Do you think I could learn?" he asked hopefully.

Quizlow sighed, watching the two skeletons return to fighting over their foot phalanges. "It could save your life someday," he ventured. "But there isn't a proper mentor who can teach you."

"What about Igvard?" James asked, looking toward the helm where his uncle was steering the ship.

"He never could do magic," Quizlow said.

"You mean he's a whorp?" His grandfather had told him that a whorp was a fake wizard.

"Like your grandfather," Quizlow said.

Cat was practicing a few thrusts with the estoc on his own when he looked at James. "Well, *I* could give you some pointers." He picked the baldric up and sheathed the sword. "When I was in Akhret, I couldn't do much magic. I'd get caught by the pjjin if I did, so I didn't get much practice."

That is no surprise, James thought, remembering that the pjjin were those meerkat-like creatures that could sniff out magic and often would chase down wizards, shrieking.

"I assume Dreadful magic is different," Quizlow pointed out. "Since you're a Jalfar, your magic is mostly inherent from your djinn ancestry, so you couldn't teach James anything."

"That's true," Cat said. "And our spells were only to help focus magic we already had. Most of them came from ancient djinn words. Words have power in them." He looked at James. "But James can understand all forms of language. Maybe he can understand all forms of spells and learn to focus his magic the same way."

James looked at Quizlow. "Is that true?"

"It makes sense. Jack had a talent for picking up foreign and old magics. It might have something to do with his ability to understand tongues."

Cat handed Moffat the baldric. "Here, put it on."

Moffat slid the baldric over a shoulder and Cat went to stand several feet away from him before looking at James, who hopped up on the gunwale to watch. "I used my *haas* to protect myself from the Fahreen as I ran from them in the streets."

James raised his hand, before realizing how silly he looked. *What am I—in school?* "Hey, Cat—that's like telekinesis, isn't it?"

Cat just looked at him and scrunched up his face, before shrugging. "Uh—not familiar with *that* word, but it's a mover spell."

"That's what I—I meant," James murmured.

"Well—sometimes, if I got cornered, I'd have to use another version of *haas*." And he raised his hand and muttered, "*Faal*."

Nothing happened.

Cat shut his eyes and then muttered it again. *"Faal."*

This time, the estoc bolted from the scabbard, flew a foot through the air, and fell clattering on the deck.

Moffat looked down at it and scratched his chin curiously.

Quizlow seemed impressed as he sat astride Fowlsey—he even clapped his hands, which made a tiny clicking sound. "Very good," he said. "That's a useful spell."

"Well," Cat said, looking sheepish. "It was supposed to fly into my hand, but—"

"Still, that was impressive. It could give you a few seconds to get away," Quizlow said.

"So, it's a disarming spell," James confirmed, a little disappointed. "I thought it'd knock him over."

"I can only do that when I'm not trying," Cat said, and James remembered the story he'd told him when they'd first met—how he'd inadvertently knocked down a grocer who'd hit him in the face with a broom. "It's like when you're frightened, and you get a surge of adrenaline."

Cat continued to try. By now, Hadwin and Digfred stood watching, having sorted their bones out. Two times, the estoc flew from Moffat's scabbard, but it fell short of Cat—even when he lunged forward to catch it. "In order to catch it, you've gotta use *ruun*. That's control. But I can't do *ruun* much." It was lucky for him the estoc had an edgeless blade, because Cat finally caught the blade after a particularly strong *faal* sent it cartwheeling through the air. He got better at it for a while—until after an hour, when the sword began to just clatter at his feet again. It was midday by that point, and everyone had gone except James, who'd taken up the baldric so Cat could practice on him.

"You try it now."

"I dunno," James said. The whole idea of performing magic was exciting, but he remembered that even when he had Quizlow's magic notes he couldn't cast a spell properly. He wasn't sure if casting a spell on a rusty sword made to pierce plate armor was wise for a beginning lesson. "Maybe I should try something safer."

"No," Cat said. "When I was on the streets, I learned in real situations. I didn't have a teacher. Just my own wits—and an angry guardsman who'd lost his turban. Now—" Cat strapped the leather baldric around his shoulder and put his hand on the pommel of the sword. "First say it. Feel it on your tongue—*faal*."

"*Faal*." He tried to say it like Cat did, which sounded like *fawl*.

"Now—close your eyes."

James obeyed.

"What does the word feel like?"

He didn't know. "*Faal*," he said. He said it again and again.

"Now," Cat said slowly.

James opened his eyes, ready to cast.

"What's the word mean?"

"What?" This caught him unawares.

"What's the first thing that comes to mind?"

"Uh—power?"

Cat smiled. "Yes," he said. "Power is what you tap into. Now, what else does it mean?"

"Force?"

"Yes, and there are three forces of *haas*, each one more complex than the last. The first is *haas*—push. The other is *faal*—pull. The last is *ruun*—hold. It is the strongest. You must hold the force. It takes a highly trained

Jalfar mage to hold force, which allows you to manipulate an object in the air."

"That's why you just let it fly?"

"Yes," Cat admitted. "But my kind are the best at moving objects using bursts of *haas* to throw stones."

"It was a rock caster who almost killed your father," James heard Quizlow say. The gnome had come up on them again to see how they were doing.

"You mean the Qo'atyni assassins?" James asked.

"The assassins were recruited from Suniria," Cat said, "and they used *haas* to hurl stones from their hands. The stones can fly faster than arrows."

"Lemme see you do it, James," Quizlow said, climbing off his mouse and fixing his pants, which had rode up on him.

James looked at Cat, trying to imagine him as the city watch coming at him with a curved talwar. Then he said, "*Faal!*"

Nothing.

"Try not saying it at first," Cat coached. "Thinking's more important. Focus on the hilt, like you're pulling it, and then transfer that feeling to the word. At last, when you want power, use a jolt of emotion, like fear, or anger. But spells don't always need these to be powerful. *Skill* can substitute for emotion."

"Why do *you* say it, then?"

"More power when you say it. However, you have to visualize it first."

James tried it again and again, to no avail.

Quizlow went to make a midday meal as James worked at it, focusing on the hilt of the estoc. His brow glistened with beads of perspiration and his mouth grew parched from trying.

"Maybe a break?" James said at last.

But even after lunch, he had no success. It was only after he'd sat down on a barrel to watch Cat do it again, casting *faal* on the baldric lying on the deck, that he recalled his first true lesson with magic. He was back at his grandfather's home, standing beside the tree where the book had been buried when he had heard the mysterious voice emanating from the tree. But he discovered later that the voice was Galajitar's—speaking directly into his mind. *Magic must come from a wizard's heart, not his head*, the tome had said. *And certainly not his hands!*

After he'd taken a draught of water from the skin, he stood up again to confront Cat wearing the baldric. "Now," Cat said. "Disarm me. Say it now—*faal!*"

This time James stopped looking at the hilt. Instead, he looked at Cat's face.

Magic is instinctive. Never control.

He breathed deeply and then looked out at the horizon behind Cat. *Control, by not controlling*, he thought. It was a contradiction, and very hard to grasp. But he recalled his first time with Rimbecella—how he'd had to relax and still his mind. *You're letting go of your mind and just feeling.*

He didn't focus on the task, nor did he look at the estoc. He just thought of Oskar and his betrayal, and a spark of anger suddenly tore through him.

"Go 'head," Cat prompted. "Eyes on the hilt and—"

The word he said was barely a whisper off his lips.

"Faal."

He was only aware that something had happened when he felt the sword nick the lobe of his ear. A flash of silver had shot past his cheek grazing it with the quillon.

Cat stood there with his mouth hanging open, his eyes wide. A moment later, there was a splash.

James turned in the direction of the sound. "What?"

Cat raced past him to the stern and looked over the side. "You—you—" He was at a loss for words.

"Well, that's just great," a voice said, and James turned to look at Moffat, who'd been watching them silently on the stairs of the quarterdeck. "That was the only bloody sword on the ship, and you just *faal*ed it into the sea, skipper. Now we'll have to fight with teeth and foul language!"

Baffled, James went to the stern where Cat was. "I made it do *that?*"

Cat looked at him. "OK, the object is to *disarm* someone. Not to slice your bloody head off!"

When Quizlow heard about it, he agreed with Cat that this wasn't a success. "Magic you can't control is as dangerous as a fire you can't put out. But keep practicing."

To James, however, only one thing mattered:

He was finally doing magic!

6
CAT'S STORY

Even after several days, James had made little progress in his training. So little, in fact, that he'd begun to grow bored of it. At first, making things move was exhilarating. It gave him a sense of power and control—even if it wasn't the magic he was controlling. Knowing that he could do something made him feel giddy inside. Kind of like discovering that he could fly Rimbecella all over again. But after three days, the exhilaration had begun to wear off. After breakfast on the third morning, he tried to make the flagon he'd drunk from fly into his hand. It didn't budge. Three days of practice and he still couldn't even make his cup move! This soon led to him giving up on it, and he found himself retiring to the starboard to stare off at the water, his mind tired from all the concentrating. (He knew he wasn't supposed to concentrate, but even doing *that* took concentration.)

As per his uncle's instructions, James finally learned how to steer the ship—with Cat's help. Cat would sit beside him with Orbis in his hand and remind him when he was veering off course. Meanwhile, he'd talk about the places he'd been with his father. This always took James's mind off the tedious task. He'd heard about the Floating City of Yu and about the flying ships there, so Cat told him all about it—every single detail. The Floating City was in Imiriz, which was much farther northeast, and was just that—a city atop a floating island. It had been enchanted thousands of years ago by an unknown race, and as far as anyone knew, it would continue to float for another thousand years.

Excited to tell James more, Cat went on to share his knowledge of other places, like the city of Bajchipu. Bajchipu was a place near Keyrlodun—not far south of Imiriz. There were elephant-like creatures the size of mountains called Bajchipu with gemstones growing on their backs, and sprawling, ancient cities had been built on their backs to harvest these rare gemstones. The creatures strode slowly along the coasts on their fat legs, and wealthy Nevrbejans lived in the metropolis. They were strange, wealthy rhinoceros-looking people who drank salt water and sea-grape wine.

James continued to listen with the same sense of wonder he had had before, though it still seemed peculiar that Cat would not tell him any more about what had happened to his parents. Cat had only told him that his parents were dead, and that was the end of it. James admitted that he hadn't actually talked to Cat about his own grandfather's death either, and supposed that if he brought it up, maybe Cat would reveal more. So, he told him about it—how the old man had died when Quizlow's spell had been blocked by that horrible goblin and the house they were falling in tore apart. Cat was quiet for a while, listening. James felt it was good to finally get it off his chest.

"What about you?"

Cat was sitting on the table in front of him with his feet on the chair, his head lowered as he twisted his crisp locks between index and thumb. Now he raised his eyes at him, a look crossed with confusion and scorn. "Your steering's shit, Prince. Now what are you gettin' at?"

"Your story."

"My *story*?"

He could already sense Cat's downcast mood; the cloud of reluctance. He wasn't sure why, but Cat insisted his past remain a mystery. "My steering's not shit," James said, eyeing the compass in Cat's palm with one hand on the wheel.

"Few months ago, while we were hunting, I'd said I wanted to be a smuggler," Cat said, ignoring him. "Suppose that after a time on the street smugglin's all you know." At first James thought he was changing the subject, but then he realized he'd just found something he could talk about—something he considered part of his *story*. Cat cleared his throat and sat up.

"I can understand that," James replied. He recalled it had actually been over a week ago they were in Cades when he'd talked about the smuggling thing, but it did *feel* like months. "You were rich," he remembered. "You had an uncle who was a trader." That was about all he knew. He didn't know why, but he swore Cat just flinched when he said that. When he looked up, Cat had resumed his casual demeanor, however.

"That's right. My uncle's ship was *Glassfire*. Someday, I'd like to return to Troblos," he said coolly.

"Where's that?"

"Suniria's capital. It's the largest trading port in the country. We exported a lot of exotic commodities from Suniria to the world."

He imagined Cat walking with his uncle in this Troblos place and felt a great sense of wonder steal through him, awakening more pockets of mysteries. "What was it like there—your homeland?"

"Beautiful, diverse, populated." Those adjectives poured off his tongue like a litany, but there was also a sadness there. "Not anymore. The stink of goblins spoils the land, and I hear Gluffors have gone there to ravage the resources and food.

"If I do return, I'd be spearheading a fleet of Jalfar spellcasters, the hulls of our lapstrake boats enchanted to deflect magic." He had a whimsical tone now. "We'd land on the beachhead, and I'd charge through the breakers crashing on our shore, seafoam at my knees as I cast sacred fire behind my shield—a shield with the family device engraved on it.

"One day, you'll go there with me. There's the Olbi—the bronze statues of the goddess with nine teats that sit in the village centers. They were enchanted thousands of years ago by our ancestral djinn to produce muulu milk for all eternity. No babes go hungry in our land."

"Uh—wow?" He wasn't sure what to say of a goddess statue with nine teats.

"And then there's our national treasure—the tuutuns. They are bronze balls that pulsate with sunlight from inside. They grow on squat spidery trees, and if you eat them, you are filled with courage for an hour. We used it as a secret weapon for centuries. Legend has it that our djinn ancestors died in a fight against their enemy, the bronze-skinned Cucculio."

"Who's that?"

"Some call them Afreet—the beasts from the Underworld. Anyway, it was said that when our ancestors died, their blood fertilized the soil, and the fruit trees grew. When our people ate them, a sacred fire burst from their hearts and they used it against the Cucculio and turned them to stone. Their hideous statues are strewn across our land now. And that fire we cast—it would later become our *igra*."

"Do you think I could ever cast *igra*?" James asked hopefully.

"You don't have the djinn blood in you, friend. But you were able to do *haas*, so...dunno."

"What's your name—your family name?" He felt a small pang of chagrin when he realized that this was the first time he'd asked the question.

Cat brooded over this for a moment, before finally saying, "I'm of the Pymat descendants. My forefathers were members of the Gyreben Cloth Consortium operating in the Fifth and Sixth Seas, and we have a lot of old money and friends in high places. My dad had wealthy associates of the consortium in Grucci with vast palaces with gemstone walls and gold baths."

"Why didn't you tell me this before?" James asked. "I could have flown you to Grucci on the flying carpet after we left the Glutton's palace."

"And miss all this?" Cat said. "Besides, like I told you before, I prefer being on my own. The goblins have a lot of power in the East with crime syndicates that run the shadow markets, abduction rings, and assassinations. I was told not to ever go there without my uncle's guards. Anyway—" Cat looked away, and James noticed the discomfort in him.

"How'd you end up in Arupa?"

Cat let out a lengthy sigh before staring out to sea. "I was traveling with my mother in Arupa when the invasion occurred in Suniria—the goblins' invasion." It seemed as though Cat had been waiting for the question; his response came quicker than James anticipated. "My father had died a year before from food poisoning when he was in Wu'al, so my mother was taking over the business. She and I were meeting with associates of the Gyreben Cloth Consortium in Lakravia—a port city in Arupa—when we were ambushed by the Glutton's Shaziri—his goblin snatchers. They had crossbows and throwing knives. They killed our guards and tried to take us hostage for ransom, but my mother and I escaped."

James stared at him with an expression of disbelief.

"I remember fleeing down an alley with her as his Shaziri chased us, stumbling through lean-tos, smashing into vendors, knocking over plates, and once sending a bowl of water in a shopkeeper's hand flying into the air. He shouted at me, but then a goblin's quarrel caught him in the face right through the eye, and he went down. The shoppers screamed and ran, and my mother cast a spell and the bazaar burst into flames. Hidden in the smoke and crowd, we fled, me coughing—and seeing that man's face with the quarrel sticking out of it for the rest of my life."

"You were just eight?"

Cat nodded. "We got away and found my uncle. He said he could smuggle us out of Lakravia. He had dealings with some of the goblin clans and knew who to bribe. My mother thought we could trust him.

"But...when we were about to sail away, we were boarded by goblin warlocks. The leader commanded them to stun the Suniri whore and take her alive. But my mother, she drew a zulfiqar—cast *igra*, and said, 'Only one sorcery can subdue a Jalfar—and that is death!' And like she said, the stuns did not harm her, and she slew four of them before the goblin leader threw a knife at her and curved it through the air with a spell and got her. She screamed and went down, and the leader ran her through with his blade in his fury. I saw the flame on her zulfiqar go out. My uncle was apologizing to me. Said they had his family. I stabbed him and jumped over the side into the water. The goblins jumped to the side and loosed crossbow bolts at me, but I swam away underwater. They thought I was dead and gave up."

James's felt his body tingling in awe as he looked at him. "Shit, Cat, you're like—" He was at a loss for words.

Cat just snorted and shrugged.

"I mean, you were like, *eight*," James said.

"I don't know what became of my uncle—whether he lived or not—but I was unable to leave Arupa," Cat went on. "Later I learned that they'd invaded my country. I was homeless. If they'd caught me, they would have sold me into slavery, like they did with many of my people in Suniria. So, that was how I ended up on the streets of Akhret."

James stood at the helm staring off at the sea. Cat was silent. "That was—I can't imagine what you've been through, Cat," he said sadly.

He was just eight when he experienced that, he thought. *I was just five when my grandfather burned down his house with me inside, but that was nothing in comparison. He watched his own mother murdered in front of him! And his uncle betrayed him.*

He knew now why Cat had jumped when he mentioned his uncle. *I'd said his uncle was a trader. It probably sounded like I said his uncle was a traitor. Which he is. What is it with uncles and treachery?* He supposed Igvard's treachery reminded him of his own uncle's, which was why he was so touchy about it. And no wonder he didn't want to go to Grucci. *No wonder he wants to stay with me.*

"Hey," Cat said, "now you know. I don't like talkin' about it."

"You've been through hell," James said. "Screw your uncle. You didn't deserve that. Nobody deserves that."

"Now you know why I don't trust your uncle Igvard—or that other one," Cat muttered.

"I don't blame you," James said. "And you're smart to be distrustful." *And maybe that should be a lesson for me as well,* he thought. *From now on, I'm not gonna trust anyone.*

Well, except Cat.

7

THE ENCHANTED SEA

Cat was right about his steering. It *was* shit. He found he wasn't paying much attention to the steering at all, and after they'd drifted off course, Igvard came up, and following a brief argument, it was decided that they should use the Boneheads after all. This was against Quizlow's judgment (and this created a bit of friction between the two), but Igvard said that they should allow it—or at least give it a try—and Quizlow couldn't argue with that in the end. This was a relief to both James and Cat. But after the next couple of days with Digfred at the wheel, James ended up just moping around the deck. He thought a lot about what Cat had said—it certainly gave him insight into the boy's motives. Why he didn't want to stick around at the Faugs when Oskar was going to turn up. Why he didn't trust Quizlow. Why he seemed to want to be alone and trust no one.

But he seems to trust me.

The days slipped by. James hadn't noticed how long his hair had gotten until Quizlow said something about it, and Igvard offered to cut it for him with a knife. His uncle hadn't been able to get the shut-eye he needed in the daytime, because it was too warm and stuffy belowdecks, and the Boneheads were noisy in the cabins, so the lack of sleep had taken a toll on him: the skin below his eyes were puffy, and redness outlined them with a bit of blush at the tip of his nose. Cutting James's hair was something to do, and maybe even an olive branch of some sort, which was odd, because he was more irritable than usual. But James passed on it either way, and instead used a piece of twine to tie it into a ponytail.

Cat, in the meantime, had gotten better at *faal*. He could pull the knife Igvard let him use out of the table and catch it. But even he had limitations to his commitment. Like James, he grew bored, and decided he needed to do something else. He supposed this was why it was necessary to have a mentor—someone who could instill discipline in them. They couldn't stay focused long enough on their training.

It was Quizlow who suggested they do something more exerting. They were spending too much time inactive. "You're young teenagers. You need exercise."

"Exercise?" James grumbled.

Cat was close to going mad with cabin fever by now, so they ended up substituting their practicing *faal* for trying to do pullups on the poop deck's rail. Quizlow was glad to motivate them into building their strength, but the Boneheads just chortled at the sight of it. "Their scrawny bones don't have the meat to go the mile," Moffat sniped. "What they need's a bloody claymore to swing about—tone up those puny limbs."

"Shut your bung hole," Cat told him.

But they ended up settling for pushups instead since neither of them could properly do a pullup.

By the eighth day at sea, Quizlow decided to go on a food-scavenging mission and sent all the mice he could find to search the boat for old crumbs and bits of desiccated food. It would make their meals more interesting, he thought, and raise their morale a bit. He and his mice eventually turned up a stash of goodies scattered around the old ship: an old shriveled-up blueberry, bits of rye, a braid of garlic, old dusty beans, grains of rice, and a very rotten bit of lettuce. With all the scraps he'd found, he spread them all out on the table and set to work. The blueberry was the juiciest of them. All he needed was water, and it wasn't long before Quizlow was muttering some strange gibberish, and the old, shriveled knob of fruit miraculously swelled into a full, round ball the size of a dime before it burst in two, then three, then four...

Soon three dozen delicious blueberries were rolling around on the table. It did raise their morale—at least for a day.

But by the ninth, it had plummeted again. The sun had dodged behind the clouds, and the wind had slowed. James had gone up into the crow's nest in hopes of spotting land. Cat had joined him after a few sets of pushups, and narrowly escaped Moffat's disparaging remarks about his "flimsy arms" to tell him what he'd overheard Quizlow and Igvard talking about. "They're saying we're heading for less gentle waters," he warned.

"What do you mean?" James asked, feeling a twinge of anxiety in his stomach.

"We're passing the outskirts of the Sea of Abyss. Your uncle didn't want to chance sailing too close to the Centrennial Belt. But there are all kinds of wild things in the Abyss. Sea monsters, underwater volcanoes that shoot spears of lightning-ice from below, some seas that boil for miles around with enchanted fires that burst from underwater, and, of course, the Poisoned Sea."

The Poisoned Sea happened the next morning—which was the tenth day they were at sea.

James awoke beside Cat, his nose twitching from an acrid odor in the air, and heard Digfred clacking across the deck and stomping his foot, trying to fix his calcaneus, which wasn't behaving properly. By now, James had begun to learn what many of the bones were, and the calcaneus was in the heel of his foot, which was probably why he was trying to stomp it back in place. "G'mornin', yeh clotter," he said, and took off his skull and tipped it at him. "The sea's like a ripe plum today."

"Ripe plum?" James rolled over, jumped to his feet, and rushed over to the larboard, waking Cat in the process.

Just as Digfred had said, the sea was purple as far as the eye could see. And in the distance, a set of peaks rose like sharp spikes, silhouetted against a crisp backdrop of a wisteria and salmon sunrise. From the peaks frothed greenish smoke glinting with a thick eggplant tinge melting across the sky.

"What stinks?" Cat asked, coming up beside him. "Oh—whoa." He leaned on James's shoulder, yawning. "See that glowing purple light in the distance?" he said, pointing toward the water that seemed to glimmer like amethysts. "That's where the ice volcanoes are. When they burst under the poison, it shoots out of the sea in frosted geysers with lightning trapped in the ice, and it rains icicles and glacial fragments for miles around. Passing boats can be impaled. The violet lightning is trapped in the ice crystals. Beautiful, but deadly once it melts."

"Iced lightning?" James said dubiously. "Are we headed there?"

"No," Digfred said. "Hadwin's steering us clear of that delightful place."

Hadwin at the wheel was a terrible idea, since the other day he had dropped the monocular into the sea while he was trying to spy a school of flying fish. ("Oh—look! Flying fish—*ooops!*")

"It's a shame. I'd like to see icicles raining from the sky," Moffat said as he sauntered past, looking out at the horizon. "I'm curious as to whether they'd impale your heads. Still, there's more pleasure yet to come. Look to the fore—it's fast approaching, and I daresay, it's inescapable at this point."

James and Cat hurried to the bow of the ship where they could see a darkness far off on the horizon. Every few seconds they could see a flicker of bluish-lilac light glinting in the clouds.

The Storm Sea.

~

The *Persephone* sailed all day through the outskirts of the Abyss. James could see the poison flowing from volcanoes in the distance, which sent molten sangria-hued glass rolling down their sides. Porous vents in the mountains sent out clover-green gasses into the air, which mixed with the salmon sun pouring through pinkish-mauve clouds. Glass islands rose from the sea like jagged knives, and when he looked down into the water—sometimes a shade of eggplant—he saw it boiling. The fumes would not be toxic, not until they went closer to the volcanoes, but it smelt like the air of a subway station.

Soon, the Poisoned Sea faded behind them, and all was calm. But they could still see the dark clouds on the horizon lit with quivering sparks. Seeing the storm clouds in the distance decided James. Cat had told him that in a storm, they'd have to batten down the hatches, but without knowledge on how to work the rigging, the prospects of surviving the storm was slim. Quizlow scampered about worriedly, as Igvard, who'd taken over the wheel, did his best to navigate. But as the day wore on, they drew nearer and nearer to the thunderheads flickering with lightning.

"I want to use her." James had taken Cat aside and told him—against Quizlow's wishes—about what he'd discovered about Rimbecella.

To his surprise, Cat already knew. He leaned against the gunwale and looked toward the Storm Sea, scratching his head. A small scowl on the corner of his face told James something was annoying him. "Y'know we've been at sea for eleven days. In all that time, you never thought to tell me about her till now."

James stared at him, but Cat refused to look at him. "What do you mean? What's this about?"

Cat turned to face him now. "All that time I was talking to you—y'know, about traveling places—I was sure you'd tell me about her. And here I thought we weren't keeping secrets."

"That's not true," James said, feeling his hackles rise. "You never opted to tell me about your parents."

Cat looked at him, a scornful laugh catching in his throat. But the inflection of it betrayed a darker tone. "Ah, Prince, but you see, that's not the same."

"How do you figure?" James said, raising his eyebrows while trying to suppress his indignation.

"'Cause I'll elect to talk about the scars in my life when I choose—not you." He leaned against the gunwale, fastening his fingers over his stomach and fixed James with a distrustful scowl. "But Quizlow had to tell me about her for me to find out. Thought we were mates."

"Quizlow?" James grumbled. He looked around for the gnome whom he always could identify as the blur scurrying across the deck on four legs. "He was the one who told me *not* to tell anyone."

"You see, that's the thing," Cat said. "You listened to *him*. I didn't think you trusted him more than me. If you didn't, you'd tell me, anyway."

James sat on a nearby barrel. "What's the big deal?"

Cat just looked at him. "Trust isn't a big deal?"

"I trust you." And he meant it. There were times when he felt Cat was the *only* person he could trust.

"Doesn't seem like it. When he told us to stay put at your uncle's place—you didn't listen."

In truth, James didn't know why he didn't tell Cat.

Yes, you do, he thought.

Deep down inside, he knew.

Cat had never seemed to like her. He remembered how Cat had leaped away from her when she came to life back when they were in the Faugs castle. He was afraid of her. But there was also something else. He *resented* her. It had been the cause of their conflict that night he had fallen off of her. He'd become more drawn to her those days leading up to the incident, flying her every day. His interactions with Cat had diminished as he became more obsessed with the freedom—the power she gave him. Cat had ultimately decided he wanted to leave—get on with his life.

James bit his tongue to prevent himself from a stinging riposte. "I didn't think it'd make any difference to you."

Cat knit his eyebrows. "Well, Quizlow, turns out, doesn't trust you. Sort of like the way you don't trust me. That's why he asked me to keep her safe."

"What?" James stood up, hands on his hips. "What do you mean 'keep her safe'? Where is she?"

Cat chuckled and looked away. "What I said, Prince. Safe."

"I don't believe you."

But five minutes later, he was rummaging through the sack where he'd last stored her, only to find her gone. He rounded on him now. Cat was standing behind him, arms folded, rolling his eyes toward the ceiling. "Where?" he demanded.

"Told you where, Prince."

He hated when Cat called him that, and Cat knew it. Cat had chosen that as his nickname the night he was shoved into James's dungeon cell. He said it was because he had such smooth hands and looked spoiled.

Cat walked over to the porthole now to look out at the approaching thunderheads. "If it were up to me, I'd chuck her in the sea." He turned around. "Back at the castle you weren't yourself around her."

"What does that mean?" James growled, kicking a sack. "You don't know me!"

But Cat just laughed. "I had you pegged when I first met you, milk. Always thinkin' about runnin' off. Well, it's flyin' off, actually. Now we're heading into a storm, and you just want to fly off and—"

"I wasn't going to do that!" James retorted.

"Oh, you'd never do that, huh?" Cat said, staring at him. "What was the plan, then—tell me."

He hadn't figured it out yet. Whenever there was danger, it was compulsory that he thought of flying Rimbecella. It was an instinct.

He supposed that was the instinct his father had as well. It was like she'd become a part of him—like another arm, or leg.

But I wasn't going to fly off and leave them to their fate! "That day I rescued us from that palace," he said at last, "you had no problem with *that.*"

"So, you're going to fly us to safety," Cat said. "Or as far as you can go before you lose control and fall into the sea, is that it? No, I'll take my chances on the *Persephone.*"

It struck him as odd that Quizlow would not trust him all of a sudden. "What did you say to him?" he demanded, his suspicion slowly melting into accusation.

"Quizlow?" Cat said, noting his tone and frowning.

"Why doesn't he trust me?"

"You told him how you found her again at the castle, and he wanted to know what you were like when you had her," Cat said. "So I told him."

"And what'd you tell him?"

"The *truth*," Cat said. "You're a complete arse when you have her." He scowled, and his voice bristled with sarcasm as he added, "So, Prince. If I tell you where she is, are you gonna fly off again with her?"

James felt his face flush with anger, and he stepped toward him, but Cat shoved him away. "Please, you couldn't throw a punch if I wound your hand up for you. Scab your knuckles a few times," he said, pushing past James, "I'll present my face for you to bloody when *that* day comes." And with that, he stepped out of the cabin.

~

James found Quizlow at the helm where Igvard was steering the ship. By now, the wind had picked up quite a bit, and his uncle's loose hair clapped in front of his vision. James strode up to the table and slammed his fist on it. "Where is she?"

Quizlow looked up at him. Fowlsey moved skittishly about the table. "There isn't time for this," he said with mild irritation.

By now, they'd reached a small metropolis of peaks rising from the sea, and Igvard was doing his best to navigate around them, even as the sky grew darker. The sea also had come to life, with waves bashing against the hull violently, scaring Fowlsey.

James looked at his uncle, and then back at Quizlow. He didn't care if his uncle was here. "If there's a way we can get out of this, we should—"

"Pick me up," Quizlow shouted at him. Apparently, he did care if

Igvard overheard about Rimbecella.

"What?"

Quizlow didn't repeat himself, but he did make a gesture with his thumb, and James reached down and plucked him from the table and placed him on his shoulder. Quizlow gave a tiny whistle—a pitch practically for dog ears—and Fowlsey perked up. "Belowdecks," Quizlow shouted. "So you can hear!"

He was right. With the wind whistling in his ears, he could barely hear the gnome's tiny voice. He left the poop deck, Fowlsey following, and climbed down belowdecks. Once in the crew's cabin, James set him on the table. "So, what's going on now? You don't trust me?" he snapped. "Why'd you have Cat—"

"Hide your precious flying carpet?" Quizlow finished. "Why? Were you thinking about taking her for a spin in the storm?"

"No, I—I—" he stammered. "We might be—"

"If we come to that," Quizlow said, smoothing his ruffled hair, "then by all means, I'll tell you where she's hidden. Then you can fly off."

"Don't be ridiculous!" James cried. "I wasn't thinking about abandoning you. I flew us all to safety before."

"There were only two of you then. Now there's your uncle. What about him?" Quizlow inquired.

"I'll think of something," he said.

Quizlow sat on the table, even as Fowlsey leaped up onto it from a chair, and scurried over to him, sniffing. "What Cat told me of your time in the Faugs—it was a little disappointing to hear. But I don't blame you. I blame your grandfather."

"Why?"

"He was perhaps not the best choice for a Spellfather. Your mother only saw a man willing to make up for his failure with his own three sons. But in my opinion, you shouldn't be allowed a second chance at parenting. If he was a bad father, he'll make a bad grandfather."

"That's not true—" He stopped himself in his stubborn anger, bit his lower lip, and looked down at the sole. In the growing darkness, he suspected Quizlow was taking his silence for concession on the matter. He was right. James sighed. "He was not a good grandfather," he allowed, "but his heart was in the right place."

"But it didn't help you much, did it?" Quizlow said. "You were a child. A heart in the right place is like a road of good intentions. When Arthur had Jack, he had no intention of being a bad father."

"Are you saying I was raised bad?"

Quizlow laughed. "You were raised by Bradys, if I can recall. And they didn't do a half-bad job. You grew up like a child should—a bit spoiled, but—"

"Spoiled?"

"—you quickly grew out of it after you spent a week in a dungeon. That builds character, I suppose. Anyway," he went on, without giving James time to respond, "I've decided you won't return to the Faugs."

James felt the boat rock and gripped the table to steady himself. "I won't?"

"I thought that after you'd lived a sheltered life in Urrd—y'know, a comfortable bedroom, TV, pet millipede, a vegan diet—"

James scrunched up his face, wondering if Arthur had told him all about it after he'd run out of the Paris shop what felt like a year ago.

"—it'd be a bit harsh for you to live a life in Scofirr. I'm just telling you why I had thought you should return to the Faugs castle. If you didn't go back, your alternative was living with your uncle Cledenhyn, who holds sway over most of the Neptune Isles. You'd sail through the ruins of Ihmoftha hunting for relics and fighting mongolors—those winged, fire-spitting monkeys. You'd war against the Watawa sea tribes for territorial control of the Red Neptune Sea, and raid Hajalbar coastal towns."

"OK," James said, feeling that it didn't sound *awful*—well, except maybe the raiding part.

"But I've reconsidered. Cledenhyn is a reasonable man, and I heard he's a decent king who doesn't drink overmuch. Buschwaddle—my mentor—

attended Jack's wedding to your mother, and he met the Farrows there. Beards are boisterous singers who favor axes, longboats, and wind charms, though you might have to ink your skin with tattoos of squid and sea lions. But family is important to them." Quizlow looked at him, gauging his reaction.

"Are you joking?" He wasn't quite sure.

"I'm serious," Quizlow said. "This isn't twenty-first-century Urrd. Your old world is fiction and fairy tale now. You'll hunt whale, cast fireballs at goblin plunderers, and learn to roar like a Pzuukian berserker."

James offered up a droll grin, still curious as to what Quizlow's motive was. "Why did you change your mind?"

"Jack did not really have a place he could call home. Nor did he have a father. It was my mistake to leave you alone and not expect you to grow impatient. It should not have been a surprise that you became attached to—to Rimbecella." The boat shook and he stumbled. James sat to steady himself. "It will, perhaps, be an answer to that aching wanderlust in your blood. Your father had that and died as alone as the ghostly moon."

James thought about Uncle Cledenhyn. Perhaps Quizlow was right. *Clever that he should think to replace Oskar with him.* But did it really make him stop thinking about what he was stealing?

The boat gave another violent lurch, and James tumbled out of his chair. Quizlow slid to the edge of the table, and Fowlsey leaped off and scurried for a corner. But Quizlow whistled and called her back. "That sounded like we hit something—scraped the hull. I'd better go and check."

When Fowlsey leaped back onto the tabletop, Quizlow hopped on her back. "Don't be angry at Cat. He didn't want to hide her from you, but he said you were not yourself around her. He was only looking out for you." He started to leave, but then added, "He's not such a bad kid, either—that Cat." Then he sprang from the table and vanished through the doorway.

8

MOFFAT THE DRUNK

Looking out the porthole, James saw that the wind had picked up significantly, and the clouds were all overcast. In the distance, the flashes of lightning were getting closer, and the *Persephone* rocked spasmodically as breakers belted her hull. James fought to balance himself; planks creaked overhead, and the sails boffing loudly against the wind in thunderous claps. *If we survive this storm, there's a life for me in Scofirr.* He wasn't sure, however, if that's what he wanted. Certainly, it was more interesting than sitting around in an abandoned castle on a remote island for four more years. He wasn't so sure about raiding coastal villages, and he still wondered if Quizlow was joking when he said that. *He can be facetious sometimes. Maybe he thinks that I'll change my mind and decide to return to the Faugs. Can a mellow, twenty-first-century all-American boy cut it as a spellcasting Viking?*

He wondered if Cat would come with him if he decided to go that path. Or maybe he would just run off to become a smuggler? But was a smuggler such a bad idea? Cat had said he could make a fortune smuggling Wizard Glass into Skystar. Cat and he had talked about it some more a few times while steering the boat and there was something provocative about it. Skystar's capital—Threbal—was the trading hub of the world. They could slip in at night by carpet, bypassing customs, and bring the glass to the fences there for dozens of urlans. Cat had told them that an urlan—Skylar's currency—could buy a huge meal for both of them as well as pay for a night at a luxurious inn.

He heard Cat's voice coming from the cabin across from his and saw light flickering from inside. The Boneheads were in there making japes.

"Can I play?" he heard Cat ask.

James left the porthole and stumbled across the rocking cabin, hitting his head on the nets and dangling hides, crossed the narrow corridor, and found himself standing in the doorway of the well-lit cabin, where Digfred and Hadwin were sitting on crates. Cat sat with them on a barrel of half-empty ogre rum.

Digfred looked up and said, "Oi, it's fetcher!"

Both Hadwin and Digfred laughed, and Cat gave a hoot. James felt his face darken, but Cat said, "Don't gimme that look, fetcher. What—can't take a jab?"

"Yes, little scrawny-arms here said you was a fetcher," Digfred said. "Now look at 'is face. Yer not gonna get all mawkish on us, are yeh, fetcher? Was just tellin' me mate here how boats use teh make me seasick. But I'ven't hurled in a hundred years, at least. Yer not gonna make me hurl, are yeh? That'd really be a shame, wouldn't it?"

"I'm not gonna get—mawkish," James said. "Whatever that means."

"It looks like this," Hadwin said, and he put his fists to his eyeholes and rubbed them. "Sometimes snot will dribble through your bleedin' nostrils—bloody disgusting. But that's a clotter for yeh."

"No," James said as Cat laughed, and slapped him on the shoulder.

"Good, 'cause if yeh can't take a sally," sniggered Hadwin, "then you can't expect to pack a punch someday. Imagine what barbs will fly at you when people see you flying that bloody rug of yers?"

James stared at Cat. "You told *them*?"

"No," Cat said.

"Oh—we may not have eyes, but we're not deaf and dumb," Digfred said.

"Clotters have those silly organs and they can still be blind, see?" Hadwin said, turning to Digfred. "In't *that* ironic?"

"Yes, we know about your bloody rug," Digfred said. "But it's no surprise. You're Jack's son. He likes rugs. It runs in the family."

Cat just giggled, and then hunkered down on his heels in front of the crate. "Can I play?" he asked again, watching as Digfred upended a sack full of foot bones on the table.

"You've a pecker, yeh tosspot. Go play with that," Hadwin said, flicking his hand at him.

"Oi—just take it in the other cabin," said Digfred.

"'Sides, do yeh even bloody know how to play Lub'n, yeh clot?" Hadwin inquired. "Orn't you a fleshy? Well, it's not a game for fleshies."

"I've played Lub'n with my dad," Cat protested. "Goblins play it, too."

"Oh, goblins play it," Digfred mimicked in a high falsetto.

"I heard," Hadwin said, "that they boil the bones of their enemies down to nothing, and then make them dance with old goblin hexes. But that's not the dead way."

"Really?" James said, curious.

"You mark bones, and then try to stack them with your mark," Cat explained. "But you have to knock the bones of your opponent's mark out of the stack and add them to yours without making it fall. You each take turns. The more bones you have, the harder you have to concentrate to keep the stack from falling."

"We use our own bones," Hadwin said. "And we don't *mark* 'em."

"But I can make them dance," Cat said. "I can *haas*."

"Stick yer *haas* up yer arse," Hadwin said. "Yer not *haas*ing with my metatarsals. My talus, navicular, and cuboid are still sore from this mornin' when I fell off the yard arm."

James folded his arms. "How do you know so much about your bones? Did you go to school?"

"If you're in the Underworld, you've gotta know your bones, clot," Hadwin said, knocking a bone to the sole. He got down on his hands and knees to look for it.

"Ayuh, gotta know your bones, mate," Digfred said. "In Under, our parts don't magically appear on us after a day or two. Your father cursed us so that this happens to us. You know—made us pretty unbreakable. So, if we lose a piece in Under—and get too far away—we lose that part."

"Then we have to go to a bones bazaar and buy our pieces," Hadwin explained. "And if yeh don't know what you're missin', or what it's called, you're gonna—"

"Please, suh," Digfred said, still groping on the sole and slapping his hands together, pleading, "can yeh spare a fibula? I've been crawlin' for a week!"

He climbed back onto his crate with the bone part, and they began mixing the bones together.

"It sounds rough living in the netherworld," James said at last, as the boat rocked, and he stumbled against the wall. The bone pieces rolled, but both the Boneheads scooped their arms around the table to keep them from falling.

"Ayuh, but we don't *live*, mate. We *dead*. It's quite literally a verb—because it's not the end, just the beginning of a new death," Hadwin said. He looked up. "But Jack, he was gonna make it better for us. Our death in the dead world."

James looked at him. "He was?"

"Ayuh. He was secretly workin' for Cthalis—our Underworld king—didn't yeh know?" Digfred asked.

Cat looked at James; James just gaped at Digfred. "He *was*?"

The two Boneheads snickered. "Oh, I suppose yeh *don't* know. But you never wondered why he was sailin' in Cthalis's ship and using Stray?" Digfred asked.

It hadn't occurred to him why his father would have such weapons. "What was he doing for this Cthalis?"

"Take a guess," Hadwin asked.

Cat looked at James. "You mean, the Magic Stones," he said.

"This one's as canny as a crow," Hadwin said. "He was fetchin' the stones for Cthalis, mate. Even yer father was a fetcher. But he was a proper Dark Lord, too. You should be proud. He sent many souls to Under."

"I bet you were great slaves," James said acidly.

"Oh, we didn't enjoy it as much as yer father enjoyed being Cthalis's bloody concubine," Hadwin ridiculed. "But we could've. Prior to Jack, we had a necromancer who charged us with protecting a king's ancient tomb in a mountain that guarded the Forbidden Sea. It was the Symplegades—one of many we're told. Anyway, they close off the Forbidden Sea, and the keystones that were enchanted to open them were in our tomb. We were to guard it with our deaths. But then one day, this clotter turns up sneakin' around our tomb."

"We were playin' ole F'zzensprot (that's shootin' arrows through our rib cages without hittin' a bone) in Nabayoon—that's a place in Under—when we get the tingly feelin' and our souls are plucked out of our skeletons, and our bones end up in this tomb in the good ole Up—swords and maces stuck to our bloody phalanges with that worm magic."

"Oh," Hadwin groaned, "we'd been summoned to kill someone. Boy, I was all excited. I missed the musical sound of intestines splatterin' at my victims' feet, heads springin' gracefully off shoulders with those dead crazy eyeballs, and limbs goin' *spluck, spluck*, fallin' on the ground, fingers idly grippin' the buckler or sword hilt. Oh, what pleasure for my empty skull!"

"Oh, I'd feel nostalgic," Digfred said, "if the very thought of it didn't fill me with nausea now."

"Anyway, your father showed up wearing these silly rivet spectacles—"

James looked at him, and suddenly, he recalled his grandfather saying, *Your father wore these when he ran into some undead cutthroats once.*

"You're the ones my father used his specs on!" he cried.

Digfred lifted his head. "Us? Oh, you're mistaken, fetcher. He thought those spectacles worked on us, but we got our orders from Cthalis. 'Don't harm the fetcher!' Well—he didn't *say* 'fetcher,' but he said it with the inflection, y'see. Anyway, we were to open the Symplegades for him so they could get their boat through into the Forbidden Sea. So, Moffat, he's all like, 'Oh, well that's bloody imbecilic!' So, he gets all sarcastic with yer old man, and he gets on his knees and he started genuflecting to that ole clot, he did! He wanted to gut him, but noooooo—Jack was the—er—concubine of the ole maggoty king of Under! So, he figured he should genuflect, which he did *beautifully*."

"He *did* genuflect rather beautifully," allowed Hadwin. "And your father took off his specs like—'what the bloody hell?'" Digfred laughed and then stopped. "He didn't actually say 'what the bloody hell.' It was just like the way he *was*," he explained, tickling his chin.

"Anyway, Moffat was being such a marrow, Jack caught on—what with him genuflectin' everywhere yer old man went. 'Oh yes, Your Majesty,'" Hadwin said. "'I'll delightedly break all two hundred of my bones in conscientious effort to serve you, Your Majesty.' I think Jack realized that he was being sardonic then, and that we weren't a litter of silly whelps. He realized then we were dangerous, cursed us, and made us afraid of violence, which was just about the meanest thing a man can do to undead marrows like us."

"After that," Digfred continued, "it was swabber, swabber, swabber—and go fetch, yeh mangy marrow filth! Alas—gone are our days of slicin' open adventurers to gawk at their organs, and boilin' their bones! I do enjoy the sight of blood and organs with no bodies, severed limbs and loose and frayed arteries splashing hot, lovely blood all over our cold, old bones."

Cat stared fondly at him. "If I had a mother, you'd frighten the willies into her. I love you! And I aspire to be as depraved as you marrows one day!"

Hadwin just waved his hand at him. "You'll have plenty of time when you're dead, yeh clot. But Moffat's havin' the hardest time of all of us."

"Oh yes," agreed Digfred. "He loved his days of loppin' off heads with his ax. Found an old ax in the hold and was tryin' to imagine what it looked like with hair and blood on it, but it made him sick. What's that word I said? Ayuh—*ambivalent*. He's in the hold now lookin' for sauce, the ole ambivalent tosspot."

"What?" James said in disbelief.

Hadwin mimed drinking. "Gulp, gulp."

"He drinks?" Cat said.

"Sadly, he never could give up the ole poison...in life or in death," Digfred explained.

James scowled. "How can he—"

"Likes the way the wet tickles his sternum, he does," Hadwin told them.

"First week after Jack did the curse on us Moffat took up the vice," Digfred said. "And Jack did everything he could to get him to give up the nasty practice. He didn't like Moffat wasting the sauce—or splattering it all over the deck as he moped about, whinin' about wantin' to see brains and blood with little bits of hair mixed in. Jack got so annoyed, he even hid his head for a few weeks, knocking it off every morning."

"But the ole boozer just poured it on his ribs. Said it was right about where his liver used to be," Hadwin said.

"Oh, he *does* miss that liver," Digfred said.

"Poisonin' it, anyway," Hadwin added.

"Ironically, Moffat didn't mind at all serving your father. Even if he couldn't go cuttin' off heads. He believed your father was magnificent. Full of destruction. He was passionate about world domination." Digfred sighed histrionically. "He might not be able to split someone's head open, but Jack did enough of *that*."

"Unfortunately, he can't say the same about you," Hadwin continued. "'What a waste of the Dark Lord's seed,' he says. 'The boy is a bit of a mooncalf. I've half a mind to sink this ship, but the screams would fill me with nausea.'"

"Pity. You know, Stray thought he was helpin' you by leavin' us aboard. But Moffat—he won't do it. No, sir. ''Em li'l clotters can go to hell. Jus' keep 'em outta mine. I won't tell 'em the *Persephone*'s secret. So, we can just sail straight into that storm and capsize for all I—'" But before he could finish, Hadwin had slapped Digfred across the face, before cringing at the violence.

"Oi—shet your bung hole," Hadwin said. "'E said not to speak of it."

"Speak of what?" James demanded, looking from Digfred to Hadwin.

"Dunno," Cat said. "Sounds like they're holding out on you."

"Oh, nothing," Hadwin said. "Digfred runs his mouth like a little crake."

"I talk a lot of slag. Me mum says I've a mouth for the mines of Doira where there are a lot of slag-talkin' marrows with phantom tongues that lick the Underworld privies."

Cat smiled. "Oh, you're not as coy as you think." He turned to James. "This one's a dolt, James."

"Hey, dolt," James said, looking at Digfred. "Out with it. What's Moffat hiding?"

"Out with what?" Digfred asked politely.

"OK," Cat said. "Quizlow said there's some laws you must obey in the Under. So, you've gotta answer us."

"Yeah," James said.

"That's a pile of shit," Digfred said. "But I'm sorry, you'll have to be more specific. I can't answer what I wasn't asked."

"What's Moffat not telling me?" James put to him.

"Oh, *that* question," Digfred said. "Well, Moffat isn't telling you that he—"

"He's a drinkin' problem," Hadwin finished.

"Yes, that's it."

"That wasn't it," James growled.

"Oh, but it *was*," insisted Digfred.

"You didn't want him to say something," Cat said, jabbing his finger in Digfred's face.

"The boy thinks he's gonna make us slip up. Like we'd mention how this tub of splinters can fl—"

Suddenly, Hadwin pulled his leg off, and with a skillful swing, sent Digfred's skull flying from his neck. "I said, shet yer bung hole!"

James ducked as the skull flew over his head, bounced off the wall, and fell rolling across the sole into a heap of sacks as Hadwin moaned of a skullache. James looked at him as he was trying to brace himself up on the crate with his one leg. "It's about the *Persephone*?"

"Oh dear," Digfred's head said. "I've gone and spilled the bonemeal tea."

"Moffat won't say nothin' about it," Hadwin said.

"That's right," Digfred continued. "He'd ruther see her on the bottom of the sea. He'll never tell you about her magic."

Hadwin swiped a finger around in his eyehole and moaned. "Oh *boy*."

"Magic?" Cat said. "What magic?"

"The magic Jack did in the storm—" Digfred continued.

But before he could finish, Hadwin had punted his skull right out of the cabin, using the leg in his hands, and it landed between barrels and crates. "Oh dear, all that violence has made me sick. Now I'd better sit down before my bones fall apart from nausea," he moaned.

James grabbed Cat by the forearm tightly, his eyes wide with sudden excitement. "The *Persephone*! She has other powers!"

Cat jumped up. "He's in the hold," he said.

James followed him out into the corridor, ducking below an oscillating candle lantern, its perforated metal shining dancing stars of light on the crates, barrels, and the overhead hanging cobwebbed nets. "The magic in the storm?" James said. "What does that mean?"

Above, the wind struck incessantly at the weathered sails making them snap loosely like ill-tempered flails, and the *Persephone* tilted forward, causing them to grab on to the walls as they made their way back to the hold.

When they barged through the door, they saw that the cabin was cluttered with old sacks and piles of crates of all sizes and shapes. There were forestays and mainstay sheets rolled up and hanging from the ceiling, baskets of hooks, netted bags with corroding fairleads and pole rings, and old chests, some filled with rusted chainplates and halyard sheaves. Cat had paused in the threshold, his hand on the jamb, sweeping the cabin with his eyes. A single lantern hanging from a hook creaked as the boat shifted, showering the hold with seesawing light. The wind buffeted against the porthole window. "Moffat?" he called out.

They heard a chuckle over in the corner behind a stack of rectangular crates and barrels, and James stepped into the hold. He could smell a faint coconut odor wafting through the stale air, along with mildew and old molding food. Light spilled in through the porthole; the larch beneath their feet creaked loudly as they treaded softly, and the sound of the tiller ropes reeving through pulleys and sheaves could be heard through the wood.

Something seemed wrong, but James couldn't quite place what it was. Cat stepped over old sacks, toward the source of the chuckle, James at his heels. He paused momentarily, the light of the swinging lantern brushing his hair, then he turned his head toward James with a curious expression—a splattering sound had sifted through the noise of the storm. James looked down and saw runnels of whiskey rolling across the sole, gathering in scattered barley from a ripped sack and rushes. Squeaks told him that a mischief of mice was occupying the corner of the hold, and he spotted several of them scurrying away, light glinting off their tiny chitinous eyes.

Edging around the crates, they found Moffat sitting on the sole, an old, stained bottle of whiskey in his hand. He lifted it to his mouth and took a swig. Liquor poured through his jaw, then splashed down his rib cage and splattered the floor. "Gulp, gulp, gulp," he articulated, throwing his head back. "Petroire—a vintage brand. Made by dwarves. Those little fetchers know how to make a good sauce. And your uncle didn't even know it was here!"

"*Moffat,*" James said.

"You've an indicting tone," Moffat accused as he took another swig. "Ah—*that* hits the spot."

"What spot?" Cat asked, watching the whiskey saturate his spine and pelvis.

"The *spot*," clarified the skeleton. "Get out! You're not welcome here, yeh clotter," he slurred with a well-placed hiccup. "You're a disgrace to the Dreadful name."

"You watch how you talk to your master," Cat said, stepping forward in a puddle of whiskey.

"Master?" Moffat choked out. "He's no master of mine." He sat up and threw the bottle at them. They ducked, and it struck the wall, as thunder broke overhead. Pale light from the storm bled through the porthole. "'E's a *mountebank*. And don't you forget it, yeh clotter. You'll go down with this ship—glup, glup, glup!"

"You know about the magic on my dad's boat," James growled. "*Tell me.*"

"I know," Moffat growled back. "I know lots of things. I know because I was there when your father made that journey to the island. We were in a storm like this one." He gave a laugh, and then stood up, teetering on his feet. "And ole Stray was there—yes! Jack thought Stray had betrayed him, sailed them straight into the Storm Seas. But then—" He picked up another bottle, uncorked it with some effort, and threw his head back, dropping the cork at his feet. "Gulp, gulp, gulp!" Whiskey splashed over his mandibles and washed down his body. He arched backward.

James's eyes narrowed; he leaped forward and grabbed the bottle. "Put that down—"

Moffat tried to hold on, but James had the better hold on it—that was until Moffat kicked him. Then the bottle fell, and rolled across the sole, even as the boat shifted violently to one side, throwing James and Cat into a pile of sacks.

"Oh bloody hell," moaned Moffat, holding his head. "That kick'll cost me. I'm gonna vomit."

James steadied himself as the boat rocked again, and he grabbed on to the net hanging loose overhead. The bottle, meanwhile, had rolled back into the corner where there was a pewter plate and a flagon, along with a pile of crumbs that mice were sniffing around. Still hanging on to the net, he looked at Moffat, who was trying to get his knees under him to stand. "Who're you feeding?"

"Who?" growled Moffat, looking over at the plate. "Feedin' the rats," he snarled. "It's a pastime."

"On a plate?"

Moffat brought his knees up, squatted, and then sat, turning around to face them. "Ha ha—the stupid boy thinks he's clever as a crow!" He rubbed his hands together and laughed. "Well, it's over, mate. Sorry—I'm pissing drunk. Can't keep a bloody secret."

James exchanged glances with Cat. Then turned his attention back to the skeleton. "Who're you talking to?" he demanded.

But at that moment he was aware of a shadow in the hold with them, and Cat grabbed him by the shoulder and shouted, "Look!"

It was a large rat, but it was only large because it was growing by the second. James and Cat stepped back. Moffat stood up and laughed. He laughed so hard, he sat down again in the corner and one of his ribs came off as he knocked his head on the wall in the corner.

The rat's fur transformed into pale, liver-spotted skin, and James realized, suddenly, that a naked man was squatting on all fours on the sole.

9

SECRETS BENEATH A CREAKY LANTERN

His skin was covered in scabbed wounds, and his hair, greasy and as white as bull thistle, reached the small of his back. His thick, white beard, with flecks of black and silver, touched the floor.

The man crept forward, sniffing the sole with bluish-white, stubby nostrils, and his fingers, ending in long, mustard-colored nails—gnarled and friable—grazed the planks feverishly. A pinkish-blue tongue emerged from his mouth with a stream of sticky drool, and lapped at the spilled whiskey on the sole, while a hand threw a greasy curtain of knotted hair from his butchered face. He wrenched his head around suddenly to look at the two of them. A bloodshot eye stared with animal ferocity, a deep bestial growl festering in his throat.

James felt his skin crawl; he backed away from the man but slipped on the first bottle Moffat had thrown. He grabbed Cat to stop his fall, and they both tumbled to the sole, Cat's hand pulling down the swaying net overhead.

The man leaped, a second growl escaping him like a cougar, and he was on them in a second, pinning James to the planks. "James Drrrrrrreadful." His guttural voice was an awl scratching on a rusted iron breastplate. His breath smelled as though his mouth had been corked for decades. His black, decayed gums had strangled the chips of whey and carob teeth in his mouth, and his lips were cracked with fissures of blood and flakes of dried skin collecting beads of saliva like dew on a fern's frond.

James grabbed the bottle under his leg and tried to strike his assailant with it, but the man's hand shot out and wrestled it from his fingers, then smashed it on the sole. Shards of glass danced in the swaying lantern beams as a crack of thunder sliced overhead. The sole maneuvered beneath him, the *Persephone* offering up a creaky protest.

Cat was struggling in the net, but the wild man sprang away, grabbed him, and pulled him to his chest and thrust the broken bottle to his throat. "Scream, and I'll slash his neck, boy!"

James fell mute, his heart beating wildly. He could hear Moffat giggling over by the crates as he reached for another bottle of whiskey.

"What do you want?" James breathed, feeling his lips turning dry with fear. Only a whisper emerged. His feet were tangled in the net. On his hands, he moved backward, eyeing the glint of sharp glass in the light.

For a moment, the man crouched there, the bottle's broken neck poised over a wide-eyed Cat's carotid artery. Then, quite suddenly, the muscles around his jaw turned up in what James realized, with incredulity, was a smile. He opened his mouth, and a soft wheeze came out. "A—a decent ba-ha-hath," he said, with a chuckle. His voice croaked, half dying on its journey out. Then he let Cat go. "Apologies, young Dreadful. Sometimes, it's hard to remember that I'm h-human."

Cat pulled away and faced the man, balling his fist, but the old man laughed again and sat on a barrel. "'T's why they call me Mangler. I sometimes have a tendency to *bite*."

James glowered at him. "Wait, you're the one who—who said Stray's name. His *real* name."

A glimmer sparkled in Sigurd's eye as he cracked a smile. Abruptly, his pale, naked body shrank to the sole and turned midnight black. Feathers folded out of his back, and from his head distended a crisp, black beak. With a flap, he leaped up onto the crate. "*James Drrrrrrreadful,*" the crow squawked.

James kicked the net from his legs, his hands grabbing for purchase.

The crow gave a deep, strange chortle, before the naked man took form again, crouching on the crate. He sprang to the sole, nimble as a feline.

"You're a shapeshifter," James said.

"Told you he was brains," Moffat said, holding his bottle of whiskey.

Sigurd turned to Moffat and said, "Gimme." Moffat had uncorked it with his teeth, but now he reluctantly handed it over to Sigurd, who took it and drank. He turned back to James. "Had to ensure that you didn't fall into the hands of the Dreadfuls," he explained, and he turned and snatched up a pair of rough-spun pants balled up on the sole. He stumbled as the ship rocked, and braced himself against the crates, before sliding his leg through a hole. "That was why I called Stray." He turned to Moffat. "Got any food?"

Moffat aimed a thumb at the corner where the rats were nibbling crumbs on the plate. "Yer furry mates are gluttons, Whiskers."

Sigurd threw the bottle at him, and it bounced off his thick skull. "Then get me a plate, yeh marrow!"

Moffat grabbed his skull and stood up, indignant. "This is how I'm treated for caterin' to you and keepin' your secret?"

"But yeh didn't, did yeh?" growled Sigurd. "Now gimme some food!"

As the ship tossed over a wave's crest, Moffat stumbled for the door, muttering, and kicking bottles. He hit his head on the swinging lantern and cursed, before finding it.

Sigurd turned back to James.

"But why would you try to stop them? You're one of them."

Sigurd was running his fingers over the hideous scabbed wounds, some of them still oozing with pus. "I'd promised your mother," he said, raising his eyes to look at him, "when I last saw her alive." He looked out the porthole at the storm, and staggered toward it, balancing himself on the overhanging net, before stopping before it. "That was the day she asked me to be your Spell-guardian."

James stared at him, bewildered. "What?"

Sigurd turned to stare at him. "Not lyin', boy. Chose me before she chose your uncle Oskar."

"If you were his mother's choice for Spell-guardian," Cat said, "why'd you hide from us the whole time?"

Sigurd chuckled and gave a wheezing cough. "When people see me, they tend to run instead of listen."

"Why were you stowing away?" James asked.

"Was hoping you'd take me to Cades."

"You can turn into a crow," Cat pointed out. "Can't you just fly away?"

"Had to stay put for a bit," Sigurd growled. "The spikes in that rusted cabinet made me frail. I'd lost a lot of blood. I needed to eat and rest. But now that I see you—figured I'd tell you somethin'."

"About what?"

"You wanted to know about her—the *Persephone*, didn't you? You accused Moffat of knowin' somethin'—"

"You know about the boat?" James asked.

"Course I do. I went with your father and mother on their first journey."

"To the Tomb of Forgotten Secrets?"

"Aye, that place."

"How does the magic work?"

"You wish."

"Like a Suniri Lamp?"

"Not quite," Sigurd said, facing James. "Once she reaches the heart of a storm, she'll take you to the place you want but fear to go most." He snorted. "Course that's just a fancy way of sayin' she takes you where you wish to go most. Just sounds more mysterious the other way. We all fear what we want the most. We fear that it might not be what we expect it to be."

"And where is that?" James asked.

"Right now—Sarvelok," the old man said.

"Because that's where my uncle is."

"He has Roseheart. You can't get into the Tomb of Forgotten Secrets without it," Sigurd agreed. He sat on a sack, lifted his leg, and plucked a shard of glass from the arch of his foot. Blood rolled thickly between his fingers as he tossed it away. "Your mother and I formed a fellowship ever since that day I went there with her and your father."

James looked at Cat; Cat hadn't taken his eyes off of Sigurd, however.

"It was Stray who sailed the ship—*this* ship," Sigurd said, plucking at a scab on his arm. "He sailed her straight into a storm. A storm not unlike this one. That was how we got there."

"What was my dad looking for?" James asked.

"Something that would help him locate the stones. But he found Galajitar instead—and something else." Sigurd looked out the porthole. "I turned it down." He picked up an old blanket off the sole. It was full of mouse droppings and bits of rushes. "The charge of Spell-guardianship," he elaborated, before he looked at James. "I had no desire to return to that accursed place."

"Why?"

"The *something else*. Not a something, though—*someone*. Her name was Miasharun. Penelope called her the Lady of the Tomb."

"The Lady of the Tomb." James tried to recall if he'd heard the name before. He had no recollection of it.

"Jack had gone into an inner sanctum and returned a short while later. Penelope sensed danger because she warned me to flee. When I looked at your father, I knew his intentions were to kill me. Miasharun's orders, I believe." He chuckled and drank from the bottle. "Your mother would later tell me that Jack believed I'd seen too much. But I know it was *her* idea—the Lady of the Tomb's."

"What do you mean too much?" Cat asked.

"The Tomb of Forgotten Secrets," Sigurd said. "The place where the world's most dangerous secrets are laid to rest...and forgotten. If one should feast their eyes upon that place...death is the only cure for such knowledge."

"How did you escape?" James asked.

"Turned into a bird and triggered an enchanted trap that sent a sandstorm into the mountain. I hoped your old man would be buried." He leaned back and folded his arms, the bottle pressed against his sinewy forearm, smiling. "He wasn't. I flew out of the narrow window and escaped. But Jack had unleashed a terror upon the world."

"She sounds dangerous," Cat said.

"She is," Sigurd agreed, stepping toward James. "Nevertheless, she is your father's legacy to you. And you should find her."

"Why?" James asked. It wasn't the first time someone had told him he should dabble with something dark and mysterious against his better judgment. When he held Galajitar in his own hands that night he called it, he'd asked his grandfather the same question. *Why should I seek the same magic that had corrupted my father?* The answer had been that his mother Penelope had wanted him to be what his father had *not* been. A champion of magic—but with moral fiber. "My father used the book Galajitar and look what happened to him. He also used those stones—and that made him a monster. Now you're telling me that he also had Mia-shrun—and she's evil, too. So why—"

"Don't be so naive," Sigurd growled. "There is no *good* magic, boy! Magic can be good. Magic can be evil. But you must learn how to wield it while walking that fine line. That's why you need a Spell-guardian."

James massaged his eyebrows with his hands while shaking his head, conflicted. Confused. Finally, he looked up at Sigurd. "Could *you* be my Spell-guardian?"

"Think I'd reconsider, eh?" he asked, raising a wary eye. "No." He frowned. "I'm too unstable. Like your father." He sighed. Then fixed James with penetrating eyes. "But I wouldn't believe everything the world says about your old man."

"What?" James said, glaring at him.

Just then, however, Moffat entered the hold, grumbling, and holding a plate of wet bread and cheese.

Sigurd grabbed it and shoved the food in his mouth hungrily. *"Breb'f foggy.*"

"Soggy's all we got."

"You lyin'—"

But Moffat just gave him a goblin's curse using his middle finger and stumbled out again.

"There are some things you oughtta know about your old man," Sigurd went on, turning back to James and swallowing. "He told your mother about a man who hid in the shadows and could control those who used the Armagods. His name was *Cowl*."

James knew that name. His grandfather had told him that he was the one who had mind-slaved Jack after he'd obtained the Armagods. It was the reason Jack had destroyed the Armagods with his sword—because he knew that once he was fully under Cowl's control, Cowl would win. He'd have control of Jack *and* the Armagods.

"Who *is* Cowl?" He was hoping Sigurd could answer him better than his grandpa.

"Your father knew him best, but he was only ever a mystery, James. He mentioned seeing him throughout his life—especially when he was searchin' for the stones. Sometimes, he'd spy him on a street. A cowled figure who'd disappear when he tried to pursue him. Another time when he was in the swamps in the Realm of Shadows. Always with the cowl hidin' his face. Thus, the name.

"Only after Jack had begun to acquire the Armagods did Jack realize that he was fallin' under the control of that dark force. But Jack couldn't stop usin' them, could he? Not when he was in a war with Grisledor. Not when the power of those stones was so addictin'."

"Are you saying," James said, stepping toward him, "that my father was being mind-slaved *before* he became the Dark Lord?"

"Jack alleged he was being manipulated for some time, according to your mother."

James folded his arms. "Why wouldn't she tell Arthur, then? Wouldn't he want to know if his son was a monster or not?"

"It would hurt him the most if she told him this, only to find out later it wasn't true. Jack could have been lyin' to her. She wanted proof of it before she'd say anything."

"So, Jack might *not* have committed those atrocities himself," Cat breathed beside him.

James didn't know what to think. It was too much for him to process, and he sat on the crate and stared out the porthole. *No*, he thought. *I won't believe it—not yet*. He remembered the dark image of the man with the citrine eyes. The man in the robe, the long black hair. *Is it possible that Cowl was possessing my father even when he went on his murderous rampages?*

"I suspect that Jack knew that only death would free him from the curse of Cowl." Sigurd smiled ironically. "And Miasharun returned to the tomb after he died, where she has slept for over a decade. And she'll awaken only when Jack's heir sets foot inside it."

"Me?"

"*You*, James." Sigurd fixed him with that penetrating gaze again. "But he is after her, too. That's why you must find her first."

"Cowl?"

"He was after your father, wasn't he?" Sigurd growled. "Your mother saw everything that night using her clairvoyance. She saw your father destroy the Armagods and die. But she did *not* see the face of Cowl. She told me, however, that your father's soul was safe with the Lady of the Tomb. So I'd imagine that it is still there in the Tomb of Forgotten Secrets."

James gaped at him. "My father's soul?" A crash of thunder shook the *Persephone*, and James grabbed on to the net overhead, as the vessel rose on a great crest before plummeting.

Sigurd let go of him for balance.

James felt his stomach in his mouth, and fell, his fingers twirling in the net. "You're lying!" he shouted.

"The day Jack discovered her, he pledged his soul to her. And his soul she took. Your mother knew this before she died. She said she was sure Cowl knew it, too. She feared Cowl would find Miasharun—and possess the soul of the Jack. That is why you must find her first. Do not let Cowl possess the power that made your father invincible, James!"

A power that made his father invincible was tempting. He could use a power like that to protect himself against the enemies he was accumulating. But it wasn't what he cared about most.

If she has my father's soul, then maybe I could finally face him. And I could find out if my father was Cowl's pawn...or if he was truly evil.

"It's your decision, James. But you must make it soon. We are almost at the eye of the storm. You can either go home, or you can find out who your father was."

*I could wish for home, yet she—*Persephone—*knows what I truly want. She'll only listen to my heart.* "But the *Persephone* will take me there either way, won't she?"

"You always have a choice, James. I trapped your father in the Tomb of Forgotten Secrets when he was commanded to kill me, but he escaped, didn't he? I'm sure you can escape a boat on the sea. But *will* you?"

He means the carpet. The curiosity was burning inside him. *I have to know if I'm a mirror image of my father—if I'm following in his footsteps. I have to know if the darkness is in me, too. I have to know if I'm destined to become the Dark Lord.*

"I'm going." He didn't say this to Sigurd, however.

He said it to Cat.

Cat sighed, but there was a mischievous light in his eyes all the same. "Under the tablecloth of that gastric menace's table, I said something to you. Remember what it was, Prince?" As the sole shifted beneath their feet, his fingers clutched the net tightly, but he leaned toward him fixing his violet eyes on him. "'I want in.'" He leaned toward him. "If you can prove your father was not the monster everyone thought he was, I'm with you. I'm *always* with you."

James looked at Sigurd.

"Blood is strong, young Dreadful," Sigurd said. "Catharsis is stronger yet. You hope to find a mirror there. A mirror you shall find." He stuffed the rest of the soggy bread into his mouth and almost swallowed it without chewing. "You've a journey ahead. But count me out. I've met the Lady of the Tomb once. She's a real *bitch*." He tossed the plate at Moffat's feet and then headed for the door.

A wave struck the hull with such impact that James and Cat tumbled to the sole. But before Sigurd could fall, he had turned into a silver gull, and flapped around the cabin. He perched atop the forestay sheets hanging from the ceiling long enough to say, "Farewell, Drrrrrrreadful." And then he was gone through the door.

10

THROUGH THE EYE

By the time they had clambered out of the hatch, the storm had subsided. The sun had swum out of tumultuous clouds and was glimmering off the polished crests of the sea, and wet sails cracked in the wind scattering droplets like fans of iridescent gemstones. Sunlight splashed off the glistening cloth; water drizzled from riggings. The *Persephone* moaned, her planks talking like old, harassed bones as a warm, humid odor of wet rotted wood washed through air.

Still, surrounding the eye of the storm, the sea continued to rage and send frothing breakers into the glittery waters under the sun. Lightning winked around them, igniting from thick thunderheads smoldering like furious morphing shapes.

A caw caused James to look up; the gull had flown from the hatch and was now circling the *Persephone*. Suddenly, it shot straight into the sun, rays bouncing off its wings that gleamed like ghostly diamonds.

"Yeh can't reef the sails, mate," Hadwin was calling to his uncle, who was pulling on a sheet as he stared up at the sails. "Yeh don't bloody know what you're doin'. Besides yeh need to bring her head to wind for that."

Igvard had been hoping they could do something about the sails, which were causing too much instability. The *Persephone* had been heeling dangerously toward the starboard side, but now that the storm had let up, she was more balanced. It wouldn't be for long, though. Frustrated, he tied the sheet back around the horn cleat and looked at Hadwin. "What do we do, then?" he growled, exasperated.

"Don't ask me," Hadwin said. "I'm just tellin' you you're not doin' shit with that, mate, so stop pretendin' you're a bloody shellback."

"I've an idea," Quizlow said. Riding Fowlsey, he splashed through a puddle of water as he rushed past James. "Move everything over to the larboard." He was referring to the bed and the furniture that had slid across the deck during the storm. "It'll give us some balance. Might be fruitless, but it's worth a try."

"Maybe." Igvard looked doubtful, then cast a glance over at the boys, fixing his wet curtain of hair into a ponytail. "You two, get that stuff over to this side, quick."

The wind was still whistling, giving a high-pitched song as it blew over the larboard. "And Hadwin, go steer the boat; turn her west away from the wind." His eyes were glassy and turning red from salt water, and shades of salmon ghosted his cheeks.

James turned in a full circle, the cold wind whipping against him as he took everything in, before he stopped to look at Cat. "What the heck. We're heading straight into the eye. We should just let the magic do its thing," he said. He didn't know *what* would happen. When would the *Persephone's* magic work? Or did he have to think of his destination like the Suniri Lamp? Whatever it was, it was better than heaving furniture across the deck and hoping that the ship wouldn't capsize when the storm started up again.

"Dunno," Cat said. "I mean what if—"

"Come on, you two!" Igvard shouted. "Move!" He was struggling to move the bed that had slammed up against the mainsail's mast.

The *Persephone* rose on a crest; James stumbled across the heaving deck as he made his way toward his uncle.

Moffat had just come up from belowdecks and he and Digfred were fighting to keep their poise as they splashed through water gushing over their ankles. "Something bad is about to happen," Digfred was saying. "I can feel it in my bones." He wrapped bony fingers around the post of the bed when he reached Igvard. "Of course, I don't have anything *but* bones...but that makes them quite intuitive."

"We're balancing the ship out," Igvard was barking through the clap of the mainsails in the wind, as he shoved the bed up to the gunwale.

James rushed toward Igvard and grabbed on to the triple deadeyes' lanyards. "Forget it," he said.

"What do you mean by that?" Quizlow shouted.

"Don't worry about that now," Cat said, clinging to the lanyards alongside James and looking up at the clewlines and buntlines on the sails. "Those sails are gonna sink us, and we don't know how to reef them. She'll capsize for sure when we clear the eye, even if we do this."

"None of this matters, anyway," James said. "The *Persephone's* magic needs the storm."

"What?" Igvard rumbled, facing him. "Didja hit your head, or something? What're you rambling on about?"

James ignored him and looked down at Quizlow near his feet. "Quizlow, I know you said we should go to Scofirr, but—I'm changing the narrative. We're going to where Oskar is."

"James, that's an order!" his uncle barked furiously, grabbing his arm.

James shook free. "You don't give me orders!"

"It's a bloody mutiny," Cat snarled.

"James," Quizlow said. "What's going on?"

James stooped and plucked him off Fowlsey's back. "Sigurd was below; he told me what I have to do. We must go to Sarvelok to find Oskar."

Igvard, who had wrapped his hand around the shroud, looked at James in incredulity. "*What?*"

"He was here on the ship with us," Cat explained.

"Did you know my mother proposed to make him my Spellfather?" James asked Quizlow. "You must have known. You were there when she made Arthur and Oskar my guardians."

"No," Quizlow said. "I never saw him then, and—wait—are you telling me that Sigurd was—"

"He was," Cat said. "We just talked to him."

Igvard gripped the gunwale for better support. "He was here the whole time?" His forehead crumpled in confusion.

"He was disguised as a rat, and Moffat was taking care of him in the hold," James said, looking toward the skeletons who had wandered off. He held Quizlow up on his palm. "But you knew about *her*, didn't you?" He was intentionally vague; he wanted to know if Quizlow knew who he meant.

Quizlow looked at him blankly. *"Her?"*

He was cold, the wind was whipping his ponytail against his neck, and water was dripping on his head from the sails and running down his face, but James was oblivious to it all. He fixed his eyes on Quizlow's with a petrifying stare. The gnome was trying his patience now—he knew who *she* was. "The Lady of the Tomb."

Igvard's wet cloak clapped loudly against the wind as he moved away from the gunwale, grasping the ratlines and causing a shower of water droplets to fall on his already soaked head. "She is only a myth, James," he said darkly.

"No," James said obstinately.

Quizlow looked at James quietly. He was standing on James's palm looking small and subordinate, but his expression did not betray that he felt inferior. "He told you this?"

"Answer me."

Quizlow walked along his palm. *"Yes."*

James felt his face turn stoic. "All right," he said, more calmly, "and you didn't think to tell me that"—he hesitated, breathing deeply—"she has my father's soul trapped in the Tomb of Forgotten Secrets with her?"

Quizlow just stared up at him, almost sadly now. "James, your father is not there. And even if he was—"

"You had no right to keep that knowledge from me."

"I had every right to," Quizlow said sharply. "She is not some plaything like"—he nudged his head toward the amulet around Igvard's neck—"or your—" He caught himself before saying it—Rimbecella.

"Wait," Igvard said, looking at Quizlow. "Are you saying she's real?"

"Is it that surprising?" Quizlow asked him, without turning around. "Most of Jack's possessions were otherworldly—things of myths."

"It's not that," Igvard said. "It's just that nobody has ever laid eyes on this—this lady."

"Except Penelope," Quizlow said.

"And Sigurd," James added.

Igvard looked nonplussed.

Quizlow turned to regard James again. "I had every right to keep that knowledge from you because I took on the burden to protect you, James. And I was protecting you from her. You are not ready for her. Like Galajitar, she is very dangerous."

"*Stop telling me I'm not ready!*" James roared, his nostrils dilating with fury.

The wind had picked up, whistling through the sails, but James barely felt it as they scooped it up, hurtling the *Persephone* forward.

"Look!" Cat suddenly cried.

The clouds, swirling around the storm's eye, were suddenly closing around the open sunlit sky.

And then it came. A white-gray funnel descending from the clouds that were scraping across the firmament. It struck down in the sea like a crack of lightning, and at once, the wind picked up very turbulently. It howled, sucking at both foresails and mainsails so violently James was thrown off his feet. Quizlow went flying to the deck, as a deluge of water struck the hull, rocking them.

James found himself rolling head over heels as the icy sea engulfed him on all sides. He tumbled toward the quarterdeck as a bubbling, wrathful sea foamed over the gunwale. His mind was numb, as well as his body. He reached out to grab something—anything. It was the gunwale he caught, and he pulled himself up, just as the *Persephone* dipped forward and he looked down. The four-poster bed danced cartwheels toward the bow before hurtling into the spuming sea along with the cauldron, the mirror, and the nightstand. When the bow came up again, his knees buckled beneath him. The mainsails flapping in the gale had become a roar in his ears as torrential rain—made fluorescent blue from lightning—burst from the sky.

"Grab on to something!" he heard his uncle—who was just a silhouette against a flare of Saint Elmo's fire—scream.

Gripping the gunwale for his life, James edged his way midship, but stopped as a wave exploded against the hull and suffused him in ice. He opened his mouth to scream and swallowed liquid salt. His eyes stung as though ground glass smothered his sight, and slivers of sunlight passed across his vision, shooting ghost rainbows onto his retina before he went blind.

A sudden violent movement wrenched his fingers free, and he slammed to the deck, drowning beneath the weight of the sea. He felt the *Persephone* change direction vehemently and opened his eyes. The waterspout was on top of them—a knot of wind and vapor, like an alloy serpent dancing over the surface. Wind vibrated the sails; a thick frenzied cloud churned overhead. Lightning streaked sideways and crashed into the mast. Sparks rained, catching in bursts of water, and an orange patch of flame extinguished immediately, but was followed by another spate of Saint Elmo's fire spiraling madly from the mast. A galaxy of fireflies—blue and white—darted quickly through the air before being swallowed up by the hungry sea. Then he was thrown, and he struck something, and all went dark.

11
AND INTO THE MOUTH

He didn't know where he was. He knew only that his head ached. His whole *body* ached, in fact, but mostly his head. He moaned, opening his eyes. Daylight, like beaded diamonds on rays, threaded into them sending throbbing pangs to his forehead.

"Wake up!"

A small wave washing over the deck had clapped against the gunwale before washing back toward him. It splashed his face and filled his mouth with a fresh taste of salt. He coughed and sat up, hearing his ears pop.

"Hello?" A hard finger nudged his shoulder as he rolled onto his knees, feeling warm water run from his hair down his neck and shoulders. A coppery taste was filling his mouth. He wiped his face. Blood streamed from his nose, staining his wet tunic. His knees burned, and as he got his feet beneath him, he saw bloodstains on his pants. He felt as though he'd been skinned raw; there were splinters jutting from his elbows. One of his fingers pulsed with intense pain, and he saw a fingernail on his index peeled grotesquely back.

"Hello!"

He spied a chair lying sideways on the deck, half-submerged in water that was washing over his ankles like a breaker from the sea. His ear had been immersed in the water, so his hearing made everything sound far off.

Squinting, he turned toward the voice to see a shape silhouetted against a bright blue sky with a hot sun bearing down on him.

"Oh, I forgot your skull is full of meat. Your brain is probably mush right now—apologies."

James felt someone tap his head again, and he spun around. It was Digfred.

"Just wanted to tell you that I'm missing the humerus on my left arm, and three phalanges on my right hand," he said, "so if you happen to come across one of those, I'd—"

"Where are we?" He stumbled, splashing through water. A dead mouse floated past, and the chair washed toward the starboard. He barely listened, however, as Digfred gave him an account of what he saw:

"Well, there was this big thing that went whoosh, and then"—he whistled—"we landed—*kerplunk!* Then I lost my ulna and fibula and those others I mentioned, so I'm trying to find them. But I bet Moffat picked mine up. He does that all the time—"

His vision was returning. The light was so bright, his photoreceptors were still adjusting, but he could make out tall shapes on both sides of the boat. He rubbed his eyes and squinted harder. He knew his eyes were red because it stung to open them, and he staggered toward the gunwale, where he could hear voices. "Cat?"

"James?"

His friend was holding on to the ratlines. He looked in bad shape, too, with his knotted hair covered in beads of glittery water, and blood streaming from his mouth and dangling off his face in streams. "You're up."

"Thanks for checking on me."

"I poked you and you moaned. But then I saw this." Cat pointed at what looked like a mountainous wall in front of him.

James grabbed on to the gunwale as he felt the *Persephone* rise and fall on a crest of water; there was hardly any wind, but she was still moving quick. Now he could see the tall shapes on both sides of the boat were the steep walls of a gorge. "Where are we?"

"The Grasp." It was Quizlow's voice, and James looked toward it and saw Fowlsey spring nimbly from the ratlines onto the gunwale, before scampering toward them. The mouse's fur was sticking up wetly, but Quizlow was the worse for wear. His maroon doublet and padded hose clung to him, glistening in the sun, and he squinted horribly, though James couldn't tell if it was because of the brightness, or his missing rivet spectacles.

"Where's Igvard?" James asked.

"He's at the helm trying to keep us from hitting rocks," Quizlow answered.

"You said we're in the Grasp?" Cat asked. "What's that mean?"

But Quizlow was looking accusingly at James. "How'd we get here? What were you telling me before? You said we were going to—"

"Sarvelok," James finished, looking up at the towering precipices. The gorge must have risen some three hundred or more feet above sea level. He spied trees clinging to bluffs, small caves, and an occasional crumbling watchtower. "The *Persephone* is magic," he said. "My father used her to travel across the seas. He used her to get to the Tomb of Forgotten Secrets."

"And you took us here?" Quizlow inquired.

"I—I dunno. I guess." This was the place he feared the most, apparently. But it was also the place he wanted to be.

They heard the hull grind suddenly against stone—they were too close to the side of the gorge. Water flashed in the air, and Fowlsey sprang from the gunwale. Quizlow and the mouse fell in the water that had washed across the midship deck toward them. James tried to scoop him out of the sudsy water, but he himself lost his balance. Cat managed to grab him and yank him back onto his feet.

As Fowlsey scrambled away from the water, James plucked Quizlow off her back and set the furious gnome on his left shoulder.

"I still don't know what you did." His voice came loudly in his ear now. "How did you know about the *Persephone* and the storm?"

James wasn't sure if he had been responsible for moving the ship. He didn't have a clear image before they departed the Storm Sea—the way he did when using the Suniri Lamp. He'd never been here before, so he wouldn't have known where to land the *Persephone*. This had to be something else... or was it somehow Stray, still manipulating the *Persephone*?

"We told you—*Sigurd*," Cat said. "He told us it would take James to the place he wanted but feared to go."

Quizlow's forehead creased with confusion—and impatience. But Cat explained everything the old man had told them in the hold, and as Quizlow listened, his face grew livid. "Are you daft?" he asked at last.

"To be honest, I don't know if it was me or not," James snapped, turning his head, almost forgetting Quizlow was holding on to his ear. The gnome had to let go, or he'd fall off his shoulder. James could still only barely make out Quizlow's silhouette, which made it difficult to argue with him. Though he couldn't see his face, he could still tell he was flustered. "She would have brought us here even if I'd wanted to go home!"

But the gnome was not convinced. "I don't know if you are responsible for this," he said, though plainly his tone suggested he was certain he was, "but clearly you don't understand the dire situation we're—"

"You lied to me," James countered. "You never told me about Miasharun."

"What does that have to do with anything?"

"You're never—forthcoming."

"Because you're too rash, James," Quizlow shouted, finally losing his temper. "You don't want me to tell you you're not ready, but you don't think about consequences!"

"But I don't have a choice, do I?" James cried. "I came back to this land because you brought me here—you! My grandfather died because you brought us back too soon. Then you abandoned me—not once, but twice!" He couldn't argue with Quizlow like this, so he picked up a barrel floating in the water, plucked him from his shoulder and set him on it. "Twice!" he said again, for emphasis, as the ship rocked, throwing him against the gunwale. "From the moment you stepped into my life, you've been giving me"—he reached for the amulet around his neck, but grasped nothing, before realizing his uncle had it—"my dad's stuff. I found Rimbecella and flew her to escape my execution. No, you don't get to tell me I'm not ready. My father had many enemies. I *have* to be."

Quizlow didn't speak for a moment, and James turned his back on him, putting his aching elbows on the gunwale. "We're following Formandible's band," he growled. "I'm hoping they're going to Oskar. That's where the *Persephone*'s magic took us. *She* knows."

"You're wrong."

James turned around to look at the gnome standing on the barrel.

"That's where *he* took us."

James folded his arms arrogantly. "What do you mean?"

"Stray wanted us to come here, James," Cat said.

"You're sort of right," Digfred, who'd overheard them, said. He was crawling around on his hands and knees still looking for his phalanges. "Stray wanted you here—but so did Sigurd. And Sigurd told us to steer the ship toward the Storm Sea as much as we could so you could get here."

"Why would he want that?" Quizlow demanded.

"He said James would find his destiny...or some tripe," Digfred said. "But *I* did it just for the excitement."

"Well, we'll find more than we can bear," Quizlow said, turning back to James. "Because you brought us straight into the Grasp."

"What's the Grasp?" James asked, but he saw Quizlow had already turned toward the bow.

James did the same and saw the mountain ahead of them for the first time. His mouth went dry. They were heading straight for three stone faces carved out of the mountainside. The foremost face had a tall mouth opened so high its bulbous scoria-stone cheeks overlayed the hooded eyes so that the eyes almost resembled hidden pockets lit with large pitch-filled braziers. He could see they were hollows for lookouts, and their faint orange glows glimmered off the stone of the algae-stained tear troughs.

Its sinister nostrils looked scaly, and the nasal bridge stretched long, its domes flaring open, sending forth gray smoke. And then the mouth. The mouth was a great iron and wood door that lowered like a drawbridge—a drawbridge that was larger than any he'd ever seen. The upper and lower jaws had sword-like incisors, dappled mossy green from algae. The other faces—one on each side of the head—were crumbling in many parts, showing the inner iron frameworks beneath, and a collapsing scaffolding structure around them showed where work had once started.

He didn't need to ask what it was. He remembered what Cat had said about this terrible place. It was the graveyard of half the Wozigod's fleet, and home of thousands of Scathra raiders—not to mention the horrendous sea monster.

"*This* is the Grasp," Quizlow said. "We're in a gorge being funneled into Sarvelok's Maw. Unless we can fly, there is no way out. Is this what you had in mind, *James*?"

James shook his head. *I could fly us out*, he thought. But where would they go, even if he flew them all one at a time? They'd be trapped here on the island without a boat.

He looked down into the frothing seawater now moving more rapidly. Shipwrecks scattered along the steep rocks, boards, old torn sails trailing in the water from splintered masts and yard arms.

"Yet it was what you wanted," Quizlow said. "And here we are." He looked at James. "Will you call him now? Will you call Stray?"

Cat stared at James expectantly.

"This is what he wanted, but I—I—no! I don't know what's ahead, but I *won't* call him." James gripped on to the gunwale defiantly and clenched his teeth. *"So—we're going in!"*

"Oh boy," Cat said, and he grabbed onto the deadeyes' lanyards for dear life.

James imagined the charybdis beneath the island sucking the sea into its belly. The closer they came, the harder the water rushed. By now he could hear the roar of the water crashing against the shoals near Sarvelok's

Maw.

"Igvard!" Cat shouted toward the helm. "It's useless now! Just—brace yourself!"

As Cat said, now it was useless to steer the *Persephone*. The water was pulling them along so violently she was beginning to spin. Igvard had let go of the wheel and lumbered down the stairs to the quarterdeck, grasping the gunwale.

The *Persephone* rose and fell on the water like a seesaw, and the Boneheads moaned and fell over, grabbing on to whatever they could.

James edged his way to the bow, and as the ship rose again, prow-first, his legs buckled under him as a wash of seawater burst over the gunwale. The mouth of Sarvelok was very close now, with hanging seaweed visible under the nasal base, as well as hairline fractures in the stone. The jaw-door was gigantic. Great, rusted chains—each link the size of a human torso—controlled the lowering of the deck. As they came near this, the mouth sucked them suddenly forward. Water smashed against the rocks beside the jaw-door, where the debris of shipwrecks had clustered. The water flowing over the fangs frothed and boiled with activity. Small eddies whirled spastically, and spray glittered in the slanted rays over the bluffs of the gorge.

Cat huddled, gripping the lanyards with both hands, and squeezed his eyes shut. Water erupted over the sides, foamed in his face, and suds glistened like pearls off his shaggy, black hair. The *Persephone* rose high and then plunged like a rollercoaster going down.

Hadwin came stumbling up from belowdecks, a pewter plate with a heel of rye bread in his hand, and a slice of cheese stuck through his finger like a ring. "Oi, what'cha doin, yeh silly clotters?" he cried. But a surge of water struck him, washing the bread off his plate. "What's this about? Can't an ole marrow get a bit o' grub 'thout gettin' knocked to bits?"

Igvard screamed, "Brace yourselves—we're hittin' the Maw!"

The mouth-shaped door loomed in front of them, and the *Persephone* rose again, her masts coming dangerously close to the iron teeth overhead.

Seawater caromed from the sides of the mouth and erupted over the gunwale. James felt he'd been swallowed by the sea and doused in iciness. He gripped the gunwale desperately as he felt the deck smash up against his legs. The ship vaulted upward, then the prow plummeted with a crash that shook like the end of the world and rattled his teeth. James fell forward, his hands wrenched loose from the gunwale. He skidded across the forecastle. His skinned elbows and knees were already raw from before—now they screamed with renewed pain as the salt water scourged them.

Hadwin, meanwhile, had fallen into a pile of bones, the plate he'd been holding flying into the air.

The hull scraped on the bottom row of teeth, and then the *Persephone* stopped, suddenly caught, grinding.

"That's gotta be bad!" Hadwin's skull bubbled as it rolled around in the water.

Digfred and Moffat, however, were trying to crawl after their missing bones.

James grabbed on to the gunwale again, panting, and Cat clawed his way to the side. "*Igvard!*" James cried, looking around for his uncle. Quizlow was nowhere to be seen. "*We're stuck!*"

His uncle was still midship holding on to the ratlines tightly and trying to weather the storm of water, his doublet plastered to his skin, his hair matted around his face, covering his eyes. "I know!" Igvard shouted, shaking his head.

The water had rushed down to the prow and washed overboard by now, along with the table, the barrel, and everything else.

Meanwhile, Hadwin had begun to connect himself slowly, crawling toward limbs and phalanges. "Oh—so we've decided to visit some murderous raiders. Wished someone would'a told me. Doesn't matter. I'll be happy to serve a new master when they stick your heads on pikes outside to collect flies!"

Something moaned. Vibrations shivered through the planks beneath their feet. James looked up and saw what appeared to be a murder-hole opening in the ceiling where the hard palate would be. That part was made of wooden beams and rusted iron frameworks, which dripped dirty, coppery water. He didn't see a face, but he heard rumbling noises overhead mingling with the crash of water flooding off the boat from the bow.

"What's up there?" Cat shouted.

James could not answer him. Ahead, all they could see was darkness, though it was possible to make out the silhouettes of catwalks and a canal that led farther inside from the outside light.

Suddenly, they heard *clink-clink-clink*, and James looked around to the side. The colossal, russet chain links were beginning to move, lifting against the pressure of the sea rushing over it.

"We're not going to make it!" Cat cried, clutching the gunwale close to James. "Look, they're closing the door already!"

Laboriously, the chains were reaving through hawseholes one link at a time, and they could feel the deck shifting beneath their feet. Deep inside, a groan wailed, like a prehistoric creature. James felt his skin bristle beneath a frigid layer of goosebumps from the cold. He looked at Igvard, fighting to hold on, and saw that the stern of the *Persephone* was rising out of the water, her boards moaning strenuously under the strain. The teeth were clamped firmly into her keel. One of the masts touched the top of the mouth's door and cracked.

"It'll snap us in half!" Igvard shouted.

James felt they had reached forty-five degrees by now; the sea behind them was crashing violently into the lower jaw, splashing water through the sides of it.

"Oh my," Hadwin cried. "I just got my bones back together. Now I'm gonna get crushed. I'd jump overboard, but I can't swim!"

All at once, the ship's hull came loose and the boat slid forward, down, down, down, and crashed into the water. Her hull scraped the bottom, creaking, wood protesting from the sea's abuse. Next, they were hurtling forward into the canal. The jaws of the door closed faster now, with the great teeth blocking out most of the light. And then they were in darkness, speeding along with the flow of the sea.

"We're heading down now!" Cat cried. "Only death's ahead!"

James feared he was right. He feared they would keep going until they came to that pit at the end of it. A pit as massive as a large moon crater full of broken, glass-sharp teeth, and then go down into it, transom, mast, sails and all, torn into splinters and bits of jetsam, frothing on the way to a stomach.

But instead, they came to a sudden stop, crashing into what looked—in the light filtering in through the gaps of the teeth—like a steel portcullis.

12
DEAD SILENCE

He could hear the slowing of the water, the sound of the *Persephone*'s insides creaking, and her bowsprit jousting against the portcullis. Inside the dark canal, the sounds echoed. James crouched wetly against the gunwale and listened. He was waiting for them to come—the raiders. *Where are they?* It was cold and clammy. He could smell algae, mustiness, and wet wood. He wished there was light. After a while in the dark he could see more: Silhouettes of the mast and sails. Shadows of the riggings. Cat, who was still clinging to the deadeyes' lanyards.

"Cat?"

"James." The boy let go tentatively and crept toward him, his feet sloshing through water. He could hear him sniffling and spitting. Watching him walk made him think of Quizlow, who had disappeared when they were swept into the mountain. "We need light," James said, keeping his voice low.

Cat cleared his throat, then called, "*Igvard!*"

"Shush!" James hissed.

"Why?" Cat said. "It's not like they don't know we're here."

Igvard stumbled toward them, running his hand along the gunwale. "Any broken bones?" his voice came through the dark.

"Not sure," James replied. To tell the truth, he was hurting all over, and possibly suffering a concussion. He was afraid to see the state he was in. Maybe the dark was best. "Where's Quizlow?" He imagined the gnome could have been washed overboard when they'd nearly capsized, and he felt a stab of panic mixed with guilt. He should have put him somewhere safe before the chaos started. He didn't realize just how much he relied on the small's advice.

"We can't find him without light," his uncle said.

Moving slowly, they sloshed through the water. James could see much better now because his eyes had adjusted. He found the soggy book Hadwin had been reading, a broken chair, and a half-submerged bucket. He was terrified that he'd find the gnome floating facedown in the shallow water, but he'd found only a dead mouse, which he was thankful to learn was too small to be Fowlsey.

Is this my fault? He couldn't help but feel responsible. If the ship was anything like a Suniri Lamp, he might have just wished them to their doom. *And if Quizlow had drowned...* He pushed the thought from his mind and resolved to search for him. *Maybe he's belowdecks.*

Cat had the same idea, because he headed down the hatch first. James followed and stood beside him in ankle-deep water. Carefully, they sloshed through it, listening to the incessant dripping from the planks above. He noticed Cat was limping and holding on to the wall as he went.

"You all right?"

"Sprain, I think."

"Let's hope you don't have to run."

Cat gave a chuckle in the dark and sneezed. James bumped his head on something, realized it was the lantern, and unhooked it. Cat reached out for it, judging where it was by the creak. It was too dark to see. Then he held it up and muttered, "*Igra.*" A flash lit up inside the glass before quickly extinguishing again.

"Gettin' better," James pointed out, remembering when he last used the spell while they huddled in his uncle's great hall.

"It's wet," Cat said.

James looked off into the dark. "Quizlow!"

"Igra." Several more tries, and a small blue flame lit in the smoke-stained glass, before turning yellow, casting light and shadows everywhere. Gleams glanced off the water, like quartzes dancing on a coat of chainmail.

Suddenly, they felt the sole shift underfoot; James grabbed the wall. Water rolled astarboard.

"What's that?" Cat whispered. A flurry of activity came suddenly from farther down the corridor from the hold. He held up the lantern. A mischief was swimming through the water toward them.

"James!" His uncle's footsteps creaked on the planks overhead. "Cat, come out of there!"

James ignored him and moved toward the mice. The boat moaned again, shifting, and he swore he felt water swelling around his ankles, creeping up his legs.

"This water's not all from over the side," Cat realized.

"Yes," James said. "We hit a tooth coming in. We're sinking." That meant, of course, there was no leaving Sarvelok. Not on the *Persephone,* anyway. His mind went immediately to the carpet, and he looked around, remembering that Cat had hid her. He was about to ask about it, when they heard a small cry from the mischief. James rushed forward just out of the light and saw the gnome—one arm slung over Fowlsey's neck, as he kicked to stay afloat. Apparently, he couldn't ride the mouse in the water without drowning her.

Quizlow let go, just as James scooped him out of the water. Another moan, and the sole shifted sending a rippling wave sloshing into storage barrels. Scurrying behind the others because of her burden, Fowlsey was swept under.

"Fowlsey!" James shouted.

Quizlow was coughing. "They're coming in through the hull! Get out!"

Seconds later, they heard a squeak. Fowlsey had just surfaced to paddle through the wave, when she was snatched back under by a silvery shape darting through the murky water. Moments later, a scaly fish fin flapped out, sparkling in the light, and a dark cloud, like red wine, seeped through the water by his feet.

James retreated with Cat, who almost dropped the lantern.

"Get out!" Cat cried.

Up they went, all the while Quizlow held on to James's earlobe, sputtering and coughing.

"What's down there?" James cried as he climbed out. He swore the angle of the deck was different now.

"Skinners," Quizlow informed them, sounding devastated. "Poor Fowlsey!"

"We have greater concerns," James said.

"Hey," Cat said. "A little more sensitivity."

"I shouldn't've—" Quizlow started.

"Where're they coming from?" James asked.

"There's a large hole in the hull," Quizlow said. "But—we're almost on the bottom already. We can't sink much lower."

"Are you sure?" Cat asked.

Quizlow wasn't sure. He didn't know how deep the canal went in truth.

"What are skinners?" James asked. He figured the name was self-explanatory, but he was hoping the name was more macabre than it sounded.

It wasn't.

"Carnivorous fish," Quizlow said.

"Now, now, let us be more definitive—they like to eat *skin*," Moffat said delicately as he limped toward them. "Ah—a *lantern*. That can help me find my fibula."

But Cat moved the lamp away from Moffat's outstretched hand. "I'm not relinquishing my light for your bloody fibula."

Moffat put his hands on his hips, and James could imagine he was scowling fiercely at him. "Oh, I suppose I can wait a few hours when the boat is on the bottom and you're nothing but a pile of bones. I'll have the lamp from you then—you'll see." Moffat turned to the other two, still looking for their pieces, and said, "Oi, let's go belowdecks where we can finally get some tranquility. I think skinners make *delightful* company." The three Boneheads climbed down the hatch, Hadwin holding the metacarpal he'd found in his mouth until he could identify who it belonged to.

Igvard went to the hatch and called, "Bring us the other lantern in the hold, will you?"

But Digfred, who was the last one down, only gave him a goblin curse gesture with his middle finger. Only he hadn't put it on yet.

~

"Gimme the lantern." His uncle was holding his hand out to Cat.

Cat forfeited it, and both James and he followed Igvard up the deck to the larboard—now tilted at about a hundred and seventy degrees. On this side, a ghost of some structure was visible above them, and he held the lamp farther out to see deeper into the cavern. He looked down first; James and Cat mirroring his actions. The water was a murky mystery, but James thought he could see small grayish forms rippling through the wavering slivers of light. *Skinners*, he thought, feeling an unpleasantness in his stomach.

Overhead, the catwalks James had glimpsed earlier were there. They were made from frayed-looking rope and were crusting with mud and hanging bits of seaweed. Currently, there was no sign of the feared raiders crossing to the tunnels where they led. Igvard looked at Quizlow standing on James's shoulder. "What do you know of this place?"

"Not as much as I'd like," the gnome replied. "See if there's something around."

Igvard began to walk along the gunwale holding the lamp out as far as he could. James and Cat followed. Igvard halted midship, one foot on the stairs to the quarterdeck, and pointed. Quizlow pulled on James's earlobe for him to stop. James did, and Quizlow leaned forward and squinted.

135

He couldn't see, so James said, "There's a tunnel in the wall there, but it's blocked by—"

"Portcullis," Cat contributed.

"This is our prison," Igvard observed.

James was sizing up the surroundings. He figured they could maybe reach the rope catwalks from atop the crow's nest, but it was still quite a distance. Yet, even if they could, how far could they go in the lair swarming with raiders?

Eventually, Igvard found the broken chair and set the lantern on it, pulling it toward the side, then sat down tiredly on the deck, his back against the gunwale. James and Cat did the same.

Quizlow hopped down onto the chair and looked at James. "How're you two?"

"Not dead," James said. He felt Igvard take his chin in hand to examine a gash on the side of his face.

"He's right."

"Not what I asked," Quizlow snapped, but Igvard only fixed his bloodshot eyes on him disinterestedly.

"It's not going to matter soon. Maybe you can talk some sense into my brother."

"Do we know if he's here?" Cat put to them. He stood and walked alongside the gunwale looking into the darkness. "We're working on inference here."

"He is," James said confidently. "Why else did the *Persephone* bring me here?" Yes, Sigurd had wanted him to come here, but he didn't guide the ship here. The ship seemed to have a mind of her own—a mind that knew his.

But maybe it wasn't her. Maybe it was Stray. He'd said we'd need him sooner or later. Well, he couldn't make me sign his evil contract—not unless we needed him. And what better way to make us need him than to send us into the dragon's den—or in this case, the sea monster's den?

"Let us presume we cannot rely on my brother," Igvard was saying, looking at James. He turned to Quizlow. "Tell me what you know of this place. Surely your predecessor told you something."

"He died before he ever returned with firsthand intelligence from this place. But we received intelligence from his informants. He'd sent dozens of them here, almost all of whom died—either before the siege, or during."

"So, he had many informants working under him?" Cat asked.

"Buschwaddle was very familiar with the species of waterbirds in the region and had made an agreement with the guillemot's flock leader living in the Galajzectcaran archipelago mountains. Many of his spies took off from the bluffs there and rode in baskets strapped to their snow-white breasts and brought them to this place. The first ones infiltrated Sarvelok's mouse population where they painstakingly mapped out the rocks and defenses for months. They sent messages back to the Wozigod." Quizlow sat, folded his legs up, and wrapped his arms around his knees, staring into the lantern's smoky wet glass. "Buschwaddle wanted to go there himself to close down the network when he learned of the invasion. The Wozigod did not give him much time; there were complications, and the fleet had already arrived by the time he got there."

He looked up at James. "I never got a chance to thoroughly peruse the maps they'd made of the routes, but many informants were captured and killed to give us this information. Their names would never make it into the history books. Those who sacrificed their lives to map this location."

"And the invasion failed, anyway," Cat pointed out.

Quizlow cleared his throat and stood up. "Nevertheless, the vital information returned to the Wozigod. I know from what I've seen of it that these canals go for miles inside the mountain, and they learned that the water flow is controlled by the charybdis."

They heard a creak above them. Igvard picked up the lantern and shined it around looking for the source of the noise, but only the echoes remained.

Quizlow ignored this and continued. "The sea monster brings the water in during feeding. That can last up to fourteen days—maybe longer.

Of course, they can close the door altogether at any time to stop the water flowing in. The doors used to open on four sides of the island, but after the invasion, a large part of the tunnels was destroyed, so there's only one now."

"How did *that* information become available after the spies left?" Igvard asked.

"The last of the spies that survived the disaster left here after the invasion with the news to the Wozigod. The Wozigod were satisfied to know that the Scathra were no longer a threat to the world. Since the sea monster was still too dangerous, they left this place alone. And without Buschwaddle's connections, they were unable to send more spies. Buschwaddle was well-connected in this region."

"So, there's only one way out," Igvard said. "Through this—" He gestured toward the way they had come. "But how do we open it?"

"Spies had discovered a large sanctum where the Tritons—who built this place—worshipped her," Quizlow said.

"Did they chain her to the island?" Cat asked.

"No," Quizlow said with a laugh. "For a creature that size only an addiction can imprison it."

"*Drugs?*" James said in disbelief.

"An 'ambrosia' as the natives called it—but it's really a fungal opiate known as Tears of the Sea. At least a ton of the opiate is needed. It used to be farmed in Qoxipreconia, but then they began to cultivate it here. As long as she is fed the opiate, she remains here digesting and regurgitating the sea." Quizlow stood up and paced around the chair, even as the *Persephone* moaned again, and James swore he could feel the incline steepen. "What spies learned about this sanctum was that they kept a kettle of poison there. Enough to kill a city, really. But it was only enough to make the sea monster sick. There is a well in the sanctum over the cavern covered with a lid, and a kettle of poison is released by use of a lever."

Cat scratched his chin curiously. "And the creature gets sick and—"

"Sicks up all the water she swallowed," James finished.

"Are you saying that is our only way out?" Igvard asked. "You expect us to slip past the Scathra raiders and find this sanctum? We have no maps or—"

"It'd be far more difficult than you could possibly imagine," Quizlow said with an ironic smile. "There was a reason why only gnomes could be spies in Sarvelok. Scathra are distinguishable by their black sclera, fangs, and turned up, flattened nostrils where their gills are. They're almost completely human except for their webbed feet and taloned hands, and a slightly grayish, yellowish tinge to their skin. Undoubtedly, they'd spot anyone else unlike them in their corridors. They are also formidable fighters, so you can't expect to fight your way through."

"But I'm not asking *you* to do it."

"*You?*" A little while ago, James had feared the worst of the gnome. It hadn't occurred to him just how dangerous the world was to such a small person. Now the prospect of hearing about him scampering about a dangerous place full of hostile people gave him anxiety. "Out of the question, Quizlow. Even if you could find this place, how—"

"There's a network of mice living here who once belonged to my predecessor's spy ring," Quizlow said quickly. "I'll locate them; they'll know the network of tunnels here."

"Still, how are we going to get out of here without a boat?" Igvard asked. "Remember, this one's sinking."

"There's a shipyard full of boats," Quizlow pointed out. "I'm sure there's some boat we could find small enough for the three of you to handle."

"What about that well?" Cat asked. "Can you open it?"

Quizlow walked away, his hands behind his back. "I'll think of something," he said.

He usually did.

~

Whether this was the plan or not, Quizlow never officially said. Like always, he was making it up as he went along. He was tiny, but his mind worked twice as hard. As they sat in the dark around the light (occasionally hearing the Boneheads laughing down in the hold over Lub'n—and a scrap of light told them they'd found the lantern Igvard wanted) Quizlow continued to inform them of all the intelligence he'd learned. He told them that they were most likely to be taken captive by the raiders and not fed to the charybdis. The Scathra didn't have resources, and so relied on captured ships as much as possible since they'd stopped raiding. Their ship would be redirected through the waterways to a main shipyard that had survived the attack. This shipyard was vast, and it was where they repaired their fleets of ships. The layout of the place was impressive—industrial even.

"You'll have to get off this boat," Igvard said after Quizlow had prepared them for what was to come. "But I don't see how. The water is infested with skinners."

Quizlow, however, had been formulating a makeshift plan—even as he was making them sandwiches from the crumbs they found in Cat's pocket. James wasn't sure he had much stock in Quizlow's plans. He hadn't planned much further than springing him and Cat loose when they were rotting away in the Glutton's dungeon almost two months ago. James had had to improvise just a little—and they ended up escaping on the fat king's prized magic carpet.

About how he'd get off the boat, Quizlow hadn't thought much more ahead of finding a mouse. Once again, he gave that task to James and Cat. It had saddened him that Fowlsey had been killed in such a horrible way, and James was under the impression Quizlow would have attended a funeral for the rodent if there was time. He was particular about them finding a relative of Fowlsey's—partially because Fowlsey was such a good mount, and also so that he could pass on his condolences to the family, but James thought this was absurd. Not mourning a mouse—finding a relative.

"How will we know a relative?" Cat quipped.

"Shape of their ears and head, style of whiskers—Fowlsey's cream white underside was mostly hidden by her yellowish-brown, tinted, fur overcoat—oh never mind. I can tell who her relatives were simply by the antic way they twitch their tails."

It was not hard to find mice, since many of them had come up from belowdecks to escape the flooding. Using the lantern, James and Cat cornered one, and Cat grabbed it with his hands. It was a *he*, Quizlow informed them later on, but not a relative. He nurtured him—and quickly named him Hatset after a mouse he knew in Cockaigne where he grew up. "He was young but grew fat quickly because my family cooked a lot of *jnoot*, which was his favorite meal. That's rice pudding with *iwa* cheese and crusted topping. He ended up fat and slow. I was late to small school a lot."

"You went to small school?" Cat asked.

"We learned how to speak the tongue of smalls and understand them. We rely heavily on them—it is quite necessary for my kind." He climbed on Hatset's sodden back and played with his ears. It troubled him he did not have a saddle with a tether. He didn't like pulling on their ears—especially when he needed to go fast. He often heard them squeal in pain, but it was necessary if they were in danger.

"I'll have to rely on Hatset's ability to find other mice," he said. "Once I do that, I'll have to convince them to help." Without his spectacles, however, this would be difficult.

"What about the Boneheads?" Cat asked. "Maybe they can help. They can go through the water without worrying about having their skin stripped off."

Quizlow told him to bring this up next time he saw them. He was being facetious, of course. But when the Boneheads came up for some "chew" (they were wasting Quizlow's bread and cheese, but it was the only way to get them out of the hold where they were playing Lub'n), Hadwin giggled a short haw-haw that went through his nose hole. "Oh, *hail* no. I'll lose my scapula for sure, and who'll find it for me—*you*, yeh clotter? I hate waitin' for my bones to find their way back to me. It's the whole phantom limb thing for bloody hours, and I sometimes fall on my arse if I forget it's not there! Go away, fetcher!"

It didn't matter, because by now Quizlow had come up with a plan. "Bring me a ceramic bowl and a wooden ladle," he said.

They managed to bribe Digfred with sandwiches into going belowdecks for the items, and once he had them, Quizlow looked over the larboard with skepticism. "Water's still enough. If you place Hatset and me in it, I can paddle through the portcullis we saw in the side. From there, I can get up on the docks and get into the lair. Then I'll try to establish contact with the mischief."

James had to admit that this was a very daring adventure for Quizlow. Without his glasses he could barely see in the dark, and if the water began to move abruptly, the dish would capsize. It was dangerous. He wanted to tell him not to do it, but he knew Quizlow would hear nothing of it.

"What do we do in the meantime?" Cat asked.

"You'll be captured," Quizlow said as he wrapped a blueberry in a piece of cloth and tied it with twine fiber. This was not for him to eat, but to entice the mice living in the lair. "The Scathra speak Marslan so you'll mostly understand them if you can understand heavy slang. It is highly likely you'll be interrogated, however." He looked up at James and met his eyes, squinting with unpleasantness. "If you feared the interrogation methods in Argolhum…" He paused and looked away. "You'll gain nothing by holding out. Tell them about Oskar. That will save you."

"Wouldn't it be best to say we were just caught sailing through—" James started.

"Sure, that would work much better," Quizlow said testily without giving him time to finish. "Realizing that you're of no import, they'd throw you to the skinners." He turned his eyes toward James now. "Let me make myself clear. You must convince them that you are *very* important. They won't hurt you if you are. Or rather, they won't *kill* you." He continued to struggle with the bundle of cloth as he tried to knot the twine fiber and muttered a charm under his breath that made the twine looser and more flexible. James had never seen him do this before. Despite it being such an insignificant charm, it seemed very useful. *He's always so resourceful*, he thought. *We're in good hands*. It made him feel safer, Quizlow's warning notwithstanding. It made him wonder more about the gnome's life and his many capabilities, which seemed endless. He wished he'd learned more about him while they'd been sailing for over a week. But he'd been too busy avoiding him and treating him like an overbearing parent. "If Oskar—or Formandible's band—are coming, they'll most likely spare you until they arrive," Quizlow assured.

"You don't think they'd have arrived yet?" Igvard asked.

"If Oskar were here, he would have come to us by now. It's been two hours at least."

"What do you suppose they're waiting for?" Igvard growled. "This waiting's unbearable."

James couldn't agree more. The echoes and clanks in the dark were unnerving, but the long, unremitting silence was torturous.

"Nobody's been this way in a long time is my guess," Quizlow said. "They have no discipline. They nearly closed the door on us when we were halfway through. They probably don't know how—or don't have enough of them—to work the waterways anymore. Maybe I can reverse the flow before they figure it all out." He looked at Oskar impatiently. "Use your observational skills—this place has not been fully functional in over a decade. That dilapidated scaffolding on the face shows they haven't even attempted to maintain this place."

"One thing," Igvard said. "If they don't open that door, will it flood the lair?"

"It will," Quizlow said, finally tying the knot. "So, they'll have to open the main door to let us out. Now"—he looked at the man—"let's get this over with." He strapped the blueberry to his back, tying another knot around his torso.

"Why not cheese?" James asked.

Quizlow snorted. "Mice hate cheese," he said. "In fact, in Suelene, there is a whole movement of smalls protesting this pigeonholing idea."

"I heard," Cat said sarcastically. "They stopped going into mousetraps until they found a better substitute."

Quizlow scowled at him.

The *Persephone* was no longer level on the water so there was no cautious way to use the gangplank. Instead, they went to the starboard side where the water had risen up the side of the hull, and using a splintered oar, Igvard placed the ceramic bowl with the ladle on the oar's spoon and set it gently in the water. Next, Cat held out a long piece of twine and dangled it over the ceramic bowl floating on the placid surface. Sitting astride Hatset's back, Quizlow had the mouse leap onto the twine and Hatset shimmied down and landed delicately in the ceramic bowl with the ladle in it.

"How long will this take?" James called. He figured Quizlow could at least give an estimate, given he'd been in similar situations before.

Quizlow made himself comfortable in the ceramic bowl, but he had to be careful. The water was about an inch from the rim. "Give me a week," he called back.

As Quizlow began paddling away, making sure to stay away from the bowl's edge so as not to tip it, James and Cat exchanged looks of horror. "*A week?*" they said together.

But the gnome had already vanished in the dark.

13

THE SHIPYARD

Igvard had inspected the scrapes on James's elbow and decided he needed care. He gave Cat the task of tearing up an old tunic, and now he was wrapping James's elbow in a plaid strip after dousing it in the Petroire whiskey Moffat had brought up from the hold, making James wince. His uncle eyed him suspiciously. "You know an awful lot about my brother's magic."

"Whaddya mean?"

Igvard ran a hand along the stubble growing on his jaw and frowned. "Sigurd told you about the *Persephone*'s magic, and the Lady of the Tomb. But I'm guessing my father told you about the grimoire."

James didn't look at his uncle as he sat on the one remaining barrel. He could sense the man's silent displeasure in the way he tugged the makeshift bandage tightly over his arm. But he couldn't tell exactly what it was in his voice. Was it envy? Or perhaps something worse—fear disguised as scorn?

"He didn't tell me much." And that was true. That night Arthur told him to summon the book from beneath the tree, he'd told him only that they were playing with wildfire. He did not tell him anything more. *But that's why I had Spell-guardians. They'd teach me what I needed to know.*

Only he had no Spell-guardians now.

Well, there's one. And he's due to arrive here any day...

Igvard poured whiskey over his knee and James winced again, glowering at him. "Arthur was not forthright with us or himself."

James assumed he was talking about how Arthur had believed that it was his wife who'd been responsible for the witchcraft in their family when it was instead his own past. Arthur had admitted as much to James but had left out certain details. Like how he'd abandoned his children, leaving them to poverty—and for Jack and Igvard to be captured by raiders.

"It is no revelation to me that Arthur failed to tell you about the other things. You were blindsided by them." He snorted and took a swig of the whiskey. "He was not even a *decent* father."

James didn't know what to say about that. Even Quizlow had said this was true, and he'd been friends with Arthur.

"But I never would've thought that you'd have a connection with Jack's magic. Should've seen it coming, though. Arthur never said a word to you about his son, so you grew up thinking he was some sort of hero. Am I right?"

James glared at him, and Igvard just snorted again, his mouth forming a sneer, and he took another draught from the bottle. "You two are very much alike—your father and you."

"That's not true," he blurted angrily. James knew that his mother was to blame for Igvard's contempt. On the day she had chosen his Spell-guardians, she had looked into Igvard's eyes before deciding to pass him up. But it was no surprise. There had been a lot of darkness in his life. Only a week or so ago, his aunt-in-law revealed that when Igvard and Jack were teenagers, they had lived in the swamplands with the Dreadful witches. Igvard had helped Jack escape them, but only at the cost of himself getting caught. He paid dearly for it—and with no help from his brother Jack. His aunt-in-law had said that he'd been turned into a lizard for two whole years.

And if you add on top of this that Arthur had run out on him when he was a child... For the first time, James felt a small pang of pity for Igvard. *Explains his bitterness toward me. My mother, father,* and *grandfather never thought much of him, while they all sacrificed the world for me.*

Igvard folded his arms and looked at Cat, who had done a shabby job bandaging his own knees and was crouching against the mast taking a swig of whiskey to dullen the pain.

James thought he should do the same and gestured for the bottle in Igvard's hand.

"My brother was all rage and stubbornness," Igvard said, handing him the bottle. "And he hated Father. Penelope was the only one who could stop Jack from killing him when he turned up in Arngor. I'd heard the story from Oskar."

James took a swig of the vintage whiskey. It burned pleasantly in his mouth.

"My brother Jack was horribly injured once and had to recuperate there in a beautiful villa by the sea. That was when Arthur first showed up since he'd left us."

"Why'd he leave?" James asked as he took another swig. He remembered Arthur had told him that he wanted to deny his roots, and Igvard had told him, on their first encounter, that Arthur had left after he discovered his children had unnatural powers. But neither had painted a clear enough picture of his grandfather—or his motive.

"The fool denied the curse in his own blood," Igvard said. "Blamed it on our mother instead—and wanted nothing to do with us." When James looked confused, he elaborated. "Well," he went on with a lengthy sigh, "Arthur was found by the Storms—a childless couple one night when he was about five. The couple raised him as their own and denied the fact that the night they found him, Wicards had been looking for a mysterious boy who'd fallen off a raft crossing the Mistglow River with his mother. The Wicards had just killed her and claimed she was a Dreadful witch."

James felt a small chill go through him as he recounted that Wicards were witch hunters—and that his uncle Oskar had once belonged to them.

"Because the Storms denied it, Arthur denied it as well. He did not believe his blood had the curse of witchcraft in it. The Grootslang tattoo on the back of Arthur's neck had been burned off with magic before they found him, so this made it easier to deny who he was. And it was important to deny it, because the couple feared the citizens of the village they lived by would do something horrible to their little boy if they suspected he was born of witches—particularly the Dreadfuls. Without the tattoo he could blend in."

James rubbed the back of his neck unconsciously where the symbol of the mythical snake was; Igvard noticed and smiled. "She wasn't just fleeing the Wicards that night, I believe."

"The Gralls?" Cat guessed, as he listened in on the conversation.

"Whatever it was, Arthur's mother was keen that her son was not seen as a Grall before she died," Igvard said.

"But many years later, *Jack* was born. Oskar was born before him, but *he* showed no sign of the dark arts. I was born afterward, but *I* showed no sign either. It was only *Jack*."

"What'd he do?" James asked.

Igvard took the bottle from him and took another draught from it. "We lived in Morswin—a province in Heartstar. Crimson mud homes with gardens on their roofs. Smalls lived in mouseholes, Gejvuds owned the local pubs, and goblin bravos and Pzuukian pirates frequented the city streets along with Arstaglian and Greguci chagla spice and cloth traders who brought their barges in to port. But we also lived next to Morrfir, and many of the witch spawn had migrated into Wyrmst and the fens there. So, it was common to find people in Morswin with bloodlines that led back to witches, or other abominations. Luckily, we were all born without the telltale mark of Dreadful on the backs of our necks, and the witchcraft seemed gone from our blood."

"But it wasn't," James guessed, meeting his uncle's eyes.

"Gralls have a tendency to play with dead things," Igvard went on, his voice turning chilly after he'd had another drink and wiped his mouth. "Your father was no different. He had a rather unhealthy fascination with death, in fact. Worm magic, the people in Morswin called it. I watched him practice it with his girlfriend." He squatted on the deck, set the bottle down, and rubbed his hands together for warmth.

Seeing his uncle do this reminded him how cold he was. Now that the adrenaline was gone, his blood was cooling, and his nose was starting to run from the chill.

"But it was that pjjin that got him in trouble. It belonged to the local pub owner. It had died, and Jack brought its carcass home one day." Igvard rubbed a hand along his bristled jaw. "And I'll be damned if it wasn't walking the next."

James shared an uncomfortable glance with Cat, and then turned back to his uncle. "So, he could bring animals back to life?"

"Life? No. Never life. It was attracting flies and maggots." He knocked back another drink, and then sort of laughed as he sat on the deck and wrapped his arms around his ankles, still holding the bottle's neck. "Arthur found out. He was furious. Had it killed, burned. Buried its ashes deep in a hole he made Jack dig far on the outskirts of the city.

"But he wasn't as furious at Jack as he was at Mother. Belinda. Her kind—he'd said. Her *kind*."

"What do you mean her kind?"

"Like I said, Morswin was full of bloodlines with witchcraft in it. And Belinda was from Wyrmst."

"But he married her," James said.

"He said she deceived him," Igvard explained, focusing his gold eyes on James. "He didn't know she had wretch blood in her until one day a brother of hers with ancient witch tattoos showed up asking for coin.

"After the pjjin incident, the dreaded witch mark on Jack's nape started to show. At first it looked like a faded birthmark. But after time, it became much darker and more distinguishable—to our horror. He had tampered with the dark Dreadful magic, and now it had marked him. Defiled him. This horrified Father so much he left her—left us. We were poor before— Arthur being a ratcatcher. But now we could barely scrape a living. We had to move to the outskirts and live in a lean-to near frog hags and wretch children.

"Then one day—the Sha'haren goblin sea raiders came and sacked the city there and ran off with my brother and me to sell as slaves. I never saw Mother again."

He knew the story from there: Jack and Igvard had met Grisledor, who recognized the Dreadful ink on Jack's neck and had sent them both to the Realm of Shadows with Catpernica—the matronly witch James had met in Estyrmor. Grisledor was distantly related to Dreadfuls as it turned out. "So, Arthur just left you to fend for yourselves?" James asked. He didn't know what to think about that. It didn't sound like the Arthur he had known.

"Arthur did not know his true parents," Igvard went on gravely. "And the skin on his nape was scorched, so the mark wasn't seen. It was easier for him to deny it came from him."

"Where did he go?"

"Why should I care where the whoreson went?" Igvard snapped, and James could hear the resentment clearly in his tone. He must have seen James's eyes narrow because he gave a mock smile. "Oh, but he was touched by your mother's kindness, wasn't he? An angel who saw the good in him. I bet Penelope made him see himself. She taught him—like she did Jack— that our name was great. She unleashed Jack. She inspired Arthur."

He could not say it wasn't true. When he thought back to Arthur living in Urrd, he remembered how he'd wanted to be the greatest sorcerer in the world. But Igvard didn't know this. He eyed his uncle. "Nothing came of it. He was never great."

"No—and yet your mother saw fit to name him and the traitor Oskar your Spell-guardians. One thing you should learn from all this, James, is that treachery is as rife in your family as is evil."

"I'll keep that in mind," James said.

～

At least two more hours passed. The canal was cold and silent with the occasional noise of dripping from the ceiling or from the sails. There was also the trickle of water, and the sound of mice as they scrambled underfoot with their wet fur spiking up. James went to look for a blanket belowdecks but stopped several rungs down when he saw the water would come up to his knees. He called Digfred, who waded toward him from the hold gripping the lantern. It was a surreal moment—seeing the skeleton coming toward him with that light glimmering off his skull. It looked nightmarish. But an instant later, the skeleton stopped to giggle, because a fish was tickling his cuboid. James didn't know whether to laugh or scream. Instead, he snapped, "Can you get us a blanket or not?" Digfred waded into one of the cabins and came out with a soaked blanket. "Will this do, you silly clot?"

That was when he heard the godawful sound of the portcullises rising.

"Cat!" James heard his uncle shout. "Get over here with the lamp!"

Forgetting the blanket, James and Cat hurried toward the bow where Igvard stood. The man snatched the light from him and held it forward. The noise was almost deafening, and it made James's blood run cold.

Another sound overlaid the first—but this came from behind. It was the main door opening once more to let the sea flood into the canal.

James and Cat rushed to the gunwale and held on, and shortly afterward, a wave struck them, pushing the *Persephone*, laden with seawater, forward. Only a starlit sky shone outside Sarvelok's Maw; night had fallen by now.

The boat was heavier and lower in the water, but she pressed her bowsprit into the rising portcullis, catching in the lattices and clacking on each one until it slid past the rusted spikes at the bottom. The spikes dripped murky, muddied water as the *Persephone* was swept forward.

Igvard swore; the stern of the ship had pulled up somewhat before they were thrust along. They ducked; the portcullis was rising too slowly. James could hear the old pulleys turning above, the chains clinking through them, the steel screeching like a banshee in the jamb's grooves. "It's going up too slowly," Igvard said.

James saw they'd never make it before the sails and mast crashed into them, and he was right. As the bowsprit lanced forward, the *Persephone* was swept partially through, but the sails struck the rising latticed threshold. For a moment, they were caught there, the foremast sighing as the stern floated around, striking the walls. And then, finally, the gate came clear, and the water from the sea washed them suddenly forward. Igvard held the lantern in front, a grave expression etched into the aging skin of his face, adding ruin to the sandbags beneath his eyes. As they moved along, they heard the murder-hole hatches opening up in the stone ceiling and torches shone through. They caught glimpses of nothing more of their captors except their shadows.

The canal turned and branched off in two directions up ahead, and James spied a closed floodgate. This time, it wasn't a portcullis, but an iron door that had descended, and Igvard's lantern showed sprawling designs of rust over the same cast-iron face of Sarvelok carved into the mountain. They followed the water, hearing another portcullis rising ahead of them, slowly, like the last. This time, they cleared it in time. The walls here were older and speckled with moonmilk and creeping designs of algae and calcite. The roar of moving water was everywhere now, echoing through tunnels that branched out and led deeper into the island's mountain. Every now and again, they heard a deep growl of something untold, perhaps at the center of the canals.

Sarvelok.

The air grew staler and icy. Limestone and dolomite deposits crept from the ceiling, and the lantern made frostwork visible overhead. There were no more murder-holes here, only stalactites and bats fluttering out of the light.

Before long, another source of light appeared, and they saw a number of braziers up ahead that sat on plinths built into the walls. When they came closer, James could see the plinths were large ugly statues with tongues hanging out and bulbous eyes caked in salt and algae—they were holding the braziers. The smell of burning pitch greeted their nostrils.

Beyond this, a vast cavern of an undetermined size opened before them, its walls glittering with bioluminescence from mushrooms.

Cat gasped, "Look!" And he pointed to the large, dark shapes dangling in the air, up, up, toward a height that made James dizzy to see—a height with no end.

"This must be the central mountain," Igvard observed.

James felt his mouth drop open. He realized what he was seeing could not be real, yet it was. This, undoubtedly, was the shipyard Quizlow spoke of, only the dozens of these ships were dangling from chains so large he'd only seen ones like them on aircraft carrier anchors. The chains were linked to some twenty or more very large cranes at various levels poking out of the sides of the mountain's interior walls some three hundred feet up. A network of catwalks and caves dotted these walls, lit with the luminous mushrooms—blue, purple, and green. When he looked more closely at the ships, he noticed that they were of all sorts, and they were all hanging at different heights from one another. Some were in clusters, others alone, but all their hulls glistened with the same swaths of liplike mushrooms that were on the cavern walls, like glittery coral reefs on sunken ships. He had no doubt these were the Tears of the Sea Quizlow had told them about.

Some of the boats shook with interior activities and were lit up with lanterns. Rope bridges connected them vertically, horizontally, and diagonally, and they spied silhouettes of people climbing around on the boats, or agilely scampering along rope ladders.

The *Persephone* coasted into the cavern, and the iron floodgates screeched shut behind them, cutting off the flow of water—and any notion of escape. To their left, they saw a spit of land cluttered with piles of loot from raids. It had been flooded, and wooden planks had been thrown down to form walkways through the mud. There were also piers, and two wooden fifteen-foot-tall towers constructed on them, mounted with ballistae armed with quarrels the size of spears.

The cavern was vast, so much so they could not see where it went or ended—there were only the towers of plunder rising like a strange, ancient forest of stacked rotting boxes and chests. The ground broke off in the water farther down the spit like an archipelago, with small towers of crates, or old furniture submerged in shallow water. A tumbledown jetty, with upturned and broken planks, connected the spit to the island—and they saw that this island was composed almost entirely of loot. But it was not just *one* island. The jetty led off toward others, all of them piled with loot, more loot, and still *more* loot—and all lit with glittering lantern lights.

The water continued, but the *Persephone* had come to a slow drift.

Then out of the dark they heard a whir of flying projectiles. *Clank, clank, clank*—grappling hooks, loosed from the ballistae, sailed over the gunwale and struck the planks before their thin ropes dragged them back to latch on to the larboard gunwale.

James and Cat gave yelps of fright and scrambled away from them, and seconds later, stunted shadows shimmied across the ropes, squawking. They had come from the wooden towers constructed on the docks. In moments, a dozen of them had leaped over the gunwale. Some launched themselves onto the yard arms, or the boom, others the shrouds and mainstays. They shrieked and gesticulated, their tiny, furry fists clasping knives.

One landed beside James holding a gilded stiletto, and with a skillful flick of its hand, cut at him. James folded backward, balancing on his heels to avoid having his stomach slashed, but fell. Another landed behind him, and shrieked, pointing a saber at his face. As he rolled over and put his knees beneath him, the creature jumped at him wielding the sabre, and shrieked again.

"Stop! I surrender!" he shouted, raising his hands in forfeiture.

The creature hesitated, watching him through squinting black eyes. That was when he noticed that its whole body was covered in fur—that it had a long, curling tail. *"What?"* He turned to see if the others were the same; dozens more had come aboard. Knives flashed in the lantern light in Igvard's hand. "Cat, are you seeing this?" he cried.

Indeed, they were all the same.

Igvard dropped his weapon, surrendering. He was pressed up against the gunwale, a half-dozen daggers threatening him.

Cat, meanwhile, was crouched in a corner, looking around for an escape route, but finding none.

"What's this?" James heard his uncle say. "This is—ridiculous. They're all—"

"*Monkeys*," Cat finished.

14

THE PIRATES OF SARVELOK

Yet they were pirates. That much James was certain of. They had tattoos, and piercings, and some wore strange leather gambesons sized for children. Others wore kettle lids with strips of eyeleted leather rove through holes on their heads. And still others had hideous scars, or put-out eyes, or nicks in their ears.

One—a large, black-furred spider monkey—climbed over the gunwale, snarling, followed by a smaller one carrying an old candle lamp with its tail. It gestured at the monkeys standing around them, and some of the creatures prodded their three captives forward with their knives. The large one snatched the lantern from the smaller one's tail and lifted it to peer into their faces. His own held crude features: A gruesome scar stretched to his furred cheek, which was pinkish where the fur was gone. He had an eye blanketed in a film like an egg white, and his right nostril had been cut away, revealing the ugly flesh beneath.

It—*he*—James realized it was a he—pointed at Igvard first, raising a flail, and prodded him on the shoulder. Then he pointed to the ship, and threw his hands up, scowling, and making the hairs around his nose flare like the legs of a spider.

Igvard's face was blank, a reaction that seemed to rankle the creature, because his frown deepened.

156

Cat said quickly, "He wants to know where the rest of our crew is. *No—just us.*"

The commanding monkey turned to him, but Igvard stepped forward. "Are you in charge here?"

The commander ignored him and gave a hoarse grunt in his throat. At that moment, however, another monkey leaped onto the gunwale. For a moment, they exchanged guttural sounds in their throats, but then the newcomer leaped down onto the deck, and then waved to shadowy silhouettes standing on the pier's wooden towers. The creatures there squawked in response, and James looked over toward the towers and saw them turning capstans. The grappling hooks clinked tightly on the gunwales. Ropes snapped taut. Slowly, the *Persephone* was reeled in toward the spit of land.

The commander put his flail in his mouth, grabbed a knife from one of his lackeys, then sprang onto the gunwale and sawed through the forestay sheet, cutting off a length of rope. He tossed it to one of the monkeys, who took it and tied Igvard's wrists in an overhand knot. The others did the same to James and Cat. By then, the *Persephone* was close enough to the towers, and boarding bridges were released and fell across her larboard's gunwale. The commander issued a series of shrieks, and James felt the tips of daggers prod his backside. Wrists bound, they climbed up onto the bridge and crossed over to the tower, flanked by their captors.

Igvard led the way, bound hands on his head. They had to walk down a ramp and step onto the planks covering the soft, wet earth. James paused momentarily to take in his surroundings. They were standing beneath towers of chests and crates—mostly chests: Rectangular chests banded in brass. Flat-topped ones made from Dalbergia wood. Painted ones. Pines with black hasps and strange designs. Jade-painted metal with copper hinges. Old red ones with rusted hinges. Some opened and spilling corroded bronze coins onto the wood platforms. Others were turned on their sides, looking battered and beaten from the aggravated freebooters that had tried to get inside.

Monkeys surrounded them clasping their ornate knives. They crouched behind barrels, or were perched on the towers of treasure boxes, lanterns hanging on their tails. Of them, two were squatting on top of a tower of chests fussing over a gold coin. When Igvard passed, one of them—with a badly cut face—hissed, leaped down in front of him, and spat at Igvard's feet. Then he grabbed a pilum leaning against a lamppost and gestured at them to follow.

They did, striding across the creaking wooden planks, water squishing underfoot, as their previous commanding monkey flanked them with his barrel of aggressive combatants.

Still limping, Cat hung back a bit for James to catch up, and whispered, "Whaddya think happened to 'em?"

"Dunno," James replied as they weaved through cluttered paths of loot: piles of moldy books, dozens of chairs, a divan, sideboards, and a chifforobe. "I've never seen a Scathra sea raider before. So—"

"Well, they're human, as Quizlow said," Cat told him. "*Mostly*. They can breathe underwater. That is pretty much the only difference, so the fur and tail is very—*new*."

James tried to think back to what his grandfather had told him about the raiders Grisledor had led. They had been a formidable force striking fear across Nobrocoso. Certainly, they couldn't have done so as monkeys. "Why did they stop attacking after the war?" he whispered. "I mean, they were pretty—" One of the monkeys prodded him with the tip of a knife, and James lowered his voice. "They'd all but dominated the world."

"The war crippled them," Cat whispered back, putting a hand on James's shoulder to steady himself as he hobbled along. "But that wouldn't have *transformed* them."

Noises from above made him look up at the boats there. It reminded him of a planetarium—only with boats hovering in the air instead of planets in the solar system. The monkeys had returned to their duties there, scampering across the ladders. "No," James said, and stumbled over a plank that was sticking up. "But maybe it had something to do with the

Tomb of Secrets." Cat's scrunched-up face was his only response, and it was only visible in the light of a lantern hanging from a polearm sticking out of a stack of crates. They passed clothes hanging from lines overhead, trying to dry in the moist air. James continued. "When Grisledor went there, his men got cursed. Only Grisledor escaped."

"A curse?"

Negotiating through a path of furniture, boxes, and large chests—some filled with gleaming gold bars, others with jewels—they came to a large opening in all of the loot. The first thing he saw was an old ship lying on her side, a giant chain pooled around its transom. Skeletons hung from the gunwale with frayed, greasy ropes tied around their necks, while their feet struck against the portholes. He realized that they must have reached the other side of the spit because he could see the water behind it, as well as stacks of chairs, some colorfully designed cassoni, and a dozen or so bahuts filled with exotic clothes. There was also a bunch of oil paintings leaning against barrels, and a number of chests with their lids opened. More than a dozen monkeys were rifling through them beside a table with an oil lamp and a monkey who sat in a chair holding a quill. But what caught James's eye were the other isles of loot far across the cavern, and the hundreds of pinprick lights from lanterns. Several of these isles had heaps of plunder that rose so high they were like small mountains.

This is their stash, he thought. *This is where it all went, isn't it? They've been stacking it up for over a decade!* The whole cavern was a treasure trove. Possibly the largest in the world.

The monkey with the pilum stopped and prodded Igvard toward the table with the simian bookkeeper. The creature wore a pair of spectacles and was squawking at the dozen monkeys rummaging through coffers. Two were squatting on the table over one, examining its contents, while the bookkeeper wrote on a long scroll unraveled to the planks.

"Think they understand us?" James asked, noticing a dozen monkeys seated around another table and looking as though they were built for combat. They were playing cards and drinking whiskey from bottles out of a crate, their spears and crossbows leaning against the table.

All of a sudden, the commanding monkey made a loud shriek toward the table as he hobbled up to the front, and one of the combatants playing cards—a Rhesus monkey with a helmet and a gambeson—leaped from his chair, grabbing his spear. The others threw their cards down and followed suit.

The commander had gotten the attention of the bookkeeper, who stopped and looked up at Igvard, then James and Cat.

The troop of larger monkeys came over, lowering their spears and scowling in the lantern light.

For a moment, the monkey who'd led them over grunted and barked at the bookkeeper. Then several spear-wielders seized James, Igvard, and Cat. Grunting, they went through their pockets, patting them up and down. One found James's amulet Orbis around Igvard's neck and snatched it off—and confiscated the knife, too.

Damn, James thought. He wished he'd thought to hide the compass. Now it was too late.

They dropped the items on the table, and the bookkeeper began to examine them carefully. After several minutes of inspection, the one at the table grabbed the lantern, hopped off, and walked up to Igvard, looking at his face. He looked at James and Cat, too, then gabbed to the one in charge, gesticulating passionately.

"Whaddya think they're sayin'?" Cat whispered in James's ear.

But before he could answer, they heard someone laughing.

Hadwin, Digfred, and Moffat were walking across the planks, following several monkeys. Digfred was carrying his head, but it appeared Moffat had found all his parts because he was no longer limping. Hadwin, however, was talking to one of the monkeys. "Oh, what a marvelous place you have here. Damp, moldy—but the decoration makes up for that."

James's jaw dropped. The monkey leading them gave a hoot and grabbed a crown from a nearby stash and showed him.

"Oi—look at this, Digfred," Hadwin said. "He's showing me his bloody loot. Truly adorable."

Igvard turned around at the sound of Hadwin's voice and said, "Give us a hand with these baboons, will you, mates?"

The spider monkey snarled and grabbed Igvard's beard. Then, yanking his face down, gave a deep-throated growl, his one black eye squinting at him. A knife flashed in the light of the lantern, then stopped, poised over Igvard's throat. "*Kshuhaaa-uh!*" the furred creature sneered in a strange irregular pitch, his throat laboring to form vowels. Furious at his ineffective vocals, he struck Igvard across the cheek with the pommel of the knife.

Igvard stumbled to the ground, blood forming from a gash on his jaw. Several of the hirsute freebooters from the card game struck him with the butts of their spears until he scrambled to his feet again, clutching his face.

"*Mates,*" Digfred said as he stepped into the lantern light still holding his head under his arms. "He called us *mates.*"

"What were some of the other things he called us?" Hadwin asked. "Let's think."

"*Mooncalves,*" Moffat offered.

"*Numbskulls,*" Hadwin added.

"*Spies,*" Moffat said.

"Well," Digfred snorted. "Regardless of the appalling treatment we endured under your charge, I shall nonetheless acquiesce." And with that, he let go of his skull, which fell to the ground, and wrenched his hand off, before tossing it at Igvard's feet. "There you go, mate," the skull said at his feet. "I gave you a *hand*—all the bloody phalanges attached and everything. Now shove off!"

The bookkeeper gave a shriek and threw his ink pot at Igvard, which hit him in the arm and splattered ink on his face. Rubbing his jaw, Igvard looked at him as the creature pointed in the direction of their ship.

"That's our ship," Igvard confirmed.

The monkey threw up his hands.

"We were"—Igvard paused and wiped the ink from his face—"were lost at sea. Our crew abandoned us when—"

"Hey!" James elbowed him. He remembered that Quizlow had insisted that they tell the truth. They were here for Oskar.

"Oh, come on," Digfred said, having picked up his head and hand, and walked up to the table. "They may be monkeys, but they aren't monkey-brained." He set his skull on the table and put his hand back on.

The bookkeeper looked at Digfred, then rose on his hind legs and pointed straight at Igvard, before looking back at Digfred.

"Yes, he's lying," Digfred's head said. The headless skeleton leaned against the table, putting his hand on it, and turned his head to look at the scroll the monkey had been scratching on in ink, and said, "They're here to find the boy's uncle. They believe he's come here."

The monkey gesticulated wildly at Digfred, screeching.

"Don't know, mate. Yeah, I think they're a bunch of clots, too. What's that? It's what we call fleshies who don't use the rotting meat wastin' all that space in their skulls."

The bookkeeper hooted laughter, and the other freebooters surrounding them joined in.

"Anyway," Digfred continued, "they're after this jewel called Roseheart, which—"

The bookkeeper's eyes widened and then looked at the spider monkey.

The ugly, wound-faced creature turned toward the captives and growled.

"Oh, my apologies," Digfred said, looking at Igvard.

"What'd he say?" James asked.

"That they're gonna lock you up until their benefactor arrives to sort you out."

"Traitor," Igvard growled at him.

When James looked behind him again, he saw that Hadwin and Moffat had sat down at the table and were laughing with several other monkeys playing cards and drinking from the whiskey bottle. Moffat noticed him looking and raised his bottle in a toast. "Cheers, mate. I sincerely hope you are not fed to the murderous fish here. It'd be a shame to see you disappear under the murky water, as we'd never be able to see your beautiful bones!"

"Deal," Digfred was saying to the bookkeeper, who'd just finished making gestures and squawks. The skeleton turned around to look at them, fixing his head on his neck.

"What deal?" Igvard snarled.

"Scab-Eye here says we'll be fed and provided plenty of whiskey if we tell them all about you and your mission. I acquiesced."

"Why would you do that?" James snapped at him. "Why are you helping them?"

"For me bloody entertainment," Digfred said. "Why the bloody hell else?"

Though ratting them out was treachery on Digfred's part, it was, in fact, precisely what Quizlow had wanted. But James did not believe Digfred knew this.

He might have just saved our skin, though, James thought.

The monkeys with the spears were sneaking furtive glances at the table where the others had taken over their game, and now the leader pushed Igvard forward and grunted.

"That meant 'move,'" Digfred said. "I negotiated with Scab-Eye here to find the rustiest, coldest cage for you to stay in. Not sure if they'll feed you, so your bones will thank me after you've died of hunger and the maggots have scourged them clean.

"Now, if you don't mind, I'm gonna join me mates in a game of Underworld poker—cheers!" And he tipped his skull at them and walked off.

15
CAGED

There were no cages that were colder or rustier than the others. They were *all* cold and rusty. The one James shared with Cat was very cold because there was a draft blowing down from above. But they were lucky, because they didn't have to share it with one of the permanent residents—like Igvard. Igvard had been forced into the one beside them and his had old human remains. Its bones, dirt-colored from tannins stains, and brittle with hairline fractures, were swathed in threadbare clothes. Its arm dangled out of the cage with a tiny copper ring on its finger, and its skull had patches of rotting hair.

Cat figured their captors wanted them all together because it was easier to feed them, since they needed to bring only one bucket across the rope bridge that passed alongside them. The two dozen other cages were empty—at least of the living.

In order to discourage them from escaping, they were raised high up over strip of land—not quite as high as the fleet of boats, but high enough to break their legs from the fall. From there, they could see the hulls of the ships overhead covered in the glowing mushrooms oscillating on the large chains. There, the monkeys continued to work, clad in ragged, small tunics, and breeches held up by tight leather belts jangling with tools. Some of them wore outlandish helmets with small iron lanterns built into them, which allowed them to see as they leaped to ladders or ships. Some climbed along the walls picking the glowing mushrooms, while others worked tirelessly on the boats, scampering across wooden platforms dangling from cranes. There were blacksmith monkeys who toiled with anvils and hammers, making sparks dance from hammers, sawyers working the watermill, caulkers with their mallets and caulking irons, pouring hot pitch over oakum, and sailmakers in caves that served as lofts.

"I imagine they're preparing for war," Igvard said. He had taken off his traveler's cloak to give to James and Cat, and they were both huddled together under it.

Cat, who was looking at the activities below, gave a short snort. "War? In their state?" he said, looking at Igvard.

To James it wasn't *that* strange. He'd seen enough strange in the past month and a half. And clearly, they were still quite capable. But Cat had a point—how much of a threat could they be?

Igvard got up, rocking his cage, and repositioned himself closer to them. "You had the gist of it, James. I think they're cursed."

James shivered under the cloak and looked up at his uncle. "The Tomb of Forgotten Secrets?"

"Yes," Cat said. "But Quizlow said *some* of the Scathra pirates went there with Grisledor. So, why are *all* of them cursed?"

"Dunno," Igvard said. "You've heard what's been said of that place. A place of forgotten secrets. There are magics there so terrible the world shut them away to never see the light of day. They went there and were cursed with some unknown magic and—"

"It explains why the world hasn't heard a peep from them in ten years," Cat said. "But they hope to reemerge again. How?"

"My uncle," James said quietly, sniffling. His nose was still running. "He's going to the Tomb of Forgotten Secrets, isn't he? Maybe he knows how to break the curse. Maybe he made a deal with them." He didn't want to believe it, but he remembered the look on the simian bookkeeper's face when Digfred said "Roseheart." He knew about the fayling. The mercenaries were bringing it here, just as the Boneheads had said.

"I never thought it'd be my brother to betray your mother," Igvard sighed.

"What if it's not, though?" James said. "I mean, maybe the ogres took him as a captive as well. Maybe they're using him."

"Well, being manipulated into breaking his oath wouldn't exactly make him a *good* Spellfather, would it?" Cat said.

"It's unlikely my brother would put so much at risk—just to spare his own neck."

"Either he's corrupted, or he's a coward," Cat said, looking at him.

"It's the nature of our blood," Igvard said. "Corruption is something I'd believe. I never had faith in my family."

I can believe that, James thought, remembering how Igvard's whole family had pretty much betrayed him. He looked at Igvard. "He's a coward."

His uncle met his eyes.

"And I'm talking about your father," James elaborated. Igvard didn't speak, and James looked away, bringing his knees up under him. His toes were cold. "He left me, too, you know," he found himself saying. "When I lived in Urrd. He was taken to a—well—*dungeon*." He paused. It felt strange talking about the things in Urrd now—calling a psychiatric ward a dungeon. All the years he'd spent in Urrd seemed a strange dream to him. He couldn't even call it *Earth* anymore—and he'd only been here a month and a half. "He said it wasn't his fault, but maybe that was just an excuse. He wasn't there to take care of me. To train me." James looked at Cat. "Magic took the place of caring for me. He obsessed over it. In my world, he was a great magician."

Igvard lowered his gaze. "It's in his blood," he said at last.

James stared at his uncle. "Is it in mine, too?"

Igvard shook his head. "Don't know you enough. Maybe you got Penelope's wisdom."

"I bet they're alike," James said darkly. "Arthur and Oskar. Both have abandoned me for...magic." He tapped his foot on the bottom of the cage irritably. "And even if Oskar *was* threatened, it makes no difference. He's breaking his vow to my mother one way or another."

"Well," Igvard said, "I'm not waiting for Quizlow."

"Why not?"

Igvard rolled his head slightly toward James and stared stoically past him. "I want to face my brother. Look him in the eyes."

"Think you can talk him out of whatever he's plotting?" James asked.

"I'll make him see reason," Igvard said.

Why? Because you were so much better than him? He couldn't imagine why Igvard was suddenly taking the high ground. It wasn't in his character. "Why are *you* so bothered by his betrayal? What's in it for you?"

Igvard's eyes fell on James. "I *was* a bit selfish, James. I admit that." He rolled his head away contemplatively. Then said, "You know, now that I'm here in your life, it's...*different*. I feel *obligated*. Nobody ever expected anything of me. I was Igvi the runt. Nobody expected more from me than whoring and wallowing with pigs and goblin thugs. Your mother decided not to choose me as your Spellfather. I had a chance to do better, and she denied me that."

So, you see me as another chance to do better. His uncle didn't have to say it.

"Oh, please," Cat mumbled.

James ignored him, and said, "When we were in Cades, you told me he was looking for that Armagod—or part of one. Do you think that has anything to do with what he's plotting?"

"It could," Igvard said. "Rumor had it that a shard of the Poseidon Stone was still in circulation—after Jack destroyed the Motherstone."

"Motherstone?" James echoed.

"During the war, Grisledor had a piece of the Poseidon Stone in an amulet given to him by his father. Later, Jack found the Motherstone, which was the larger part of the stone Grisledor had. Grisledor took the Motherstone for himself, and added it to his amulet's power, thereby increasing it greatly—claiming it was his birthright. But before he was eventually destroyed by Jack, he hid it."

"Where?"

"One rumor has it he threw it in the sea. Another says he buried it. Still another says he gave it to someone. A woman."

"So, it's still out there," James concluded. "Maybe my uncle found it."

"And he's rallying Grisledor's army—apparently having formed a pact with them," Cat pointed out. "He wants to start up where Grisledor left off."

"So it seems," Igvard said. "But that's not like my brother."

"You said Dreadfuls are capable of anything," James reminded him, hearkening back to the time they were gathered on the boat a week ago.

Igvard smiled sheepishly. "Of course I'm going to play devil's advocate with you when you sing praise for my brother—a man you'd never met."

"So, you were just trolling me?" James sneered.

"Trolling?" Igvard looked slightly nonplussed by the use of the word. "He knew the dangers of the Armagods—about touching them. It would not be easy to corrupt my brother. That's why I want to look into his eyes. He was a Wicard for many years, working for the Office of Unusual Affairs.

"But after the war, he had to leave the Wozigod. Life is hard when your brother is the most hated and feared man in the realm."

James looked down at Hadwin, Digfred, and Moffat sitting at the table laughing and playing cards. He could understand what Oskar was going through. Having to bear the weight of the terrible things your kin did. *Or do I? How many people have I met in this realm that I've averted my eyes from—or hung my head in shame?* To tell the truth, he hadn't met many. Only that one lady in Akhret the day he came to Nobrocoso with Quizlow. *"On the Day of Pig, we cursed Dreadful's name..."* She was referring to the Glutton's sorcerer, who Jack Dreadful had turned into a skunk pig many years ago. Even after the sorcerer had turned back into a human, he'd had to endure the name Skunk Pig. The sorcerer had been evil, allegedly experimenting on the children of the city. But the lady had had as much hatred for the sorcerer as for his father—Jack Dreadful. He could only remember later thinking, *Dreadful, that's my last name.* It made him think—and feel a deep sense of shame inside himself. *Shame? You mean when I secretly admire him? That shame? Oh, but I'm allowed to admire him. It was not my dad who did those terrible things. It was Cowl.* Sigurd had said so. At least that was the working theory. He wondered if he'd learn the truth when he got to the Tomb of Forgotten Secrets. He felt, however, that his desire to prove it was Cowl controlling his father's actions was a way to lessen his guilt for admiring him, and it made him feel somewhat queasy inside.

~

Life in the cage was miserable. By the second day, Igvard had grown cold himself without his cloak and huddled in the corner of his cage, shivering. He'd gone so far as to strip the threadbare clothes off his roommate to use as a blanket. The activity caused the leg to fall out and clatter on the ground below, and this, unfortunately, caught Hadwin's attention. Maybe Hadwin was feeling a bit bored and wanted to have some fun, because he got up, yawned, and, picking up the leg bone, proceeded to torment them with it. "Oh, what a gorgeous fibula this is. Could you, perhaps, introduce me to your new friend, *mate*? We *are* mates now, am I right? Ah—so sturdy!" he moaned, whacking the bone on the table. "Always wanted to meet a nice sturdy marrow lass."

In response, Igvard took the skull and chucked it down at him and it clocked him on the skull.

"Oi—still has her hair!" Hadwin said, picking up the head and turning to the other skeletons. "Generous locks of richly spun molasses with hints of chestnut—and crawlin' with parasites. My goodness, she's a beauty! If only I'd a ring!"

But he soon grew bored of the charade, because the three of them found a new hobby of throwing the skull and hitting the bottom of Igvard's cage. It became annoying, especially when they tried to sleep, and Moffat would get up and throw the skull—*bang!* "Wake up, clots!"

Soon, there was nothing left of the skull and they couldn't throw it anymore. But next came bottles, rocks, and old moldy books. Igvard managed to catch one of the books. He tried reading it, but the words were blurred, and he passed it to Cat, who used it as a pillow.

When it was time to eat, their captors would scramble across the rope ladder that passed over their cages carrying two buckets. They'd lower them through the hole of the cages' tops, and James and Cat would grab theirs. But it wasn't anything edible—moldy bread, or cold, tasteless gruel. The other bucket had dirty water in it, and James and Cat drank it only when their thirst was unbearable. Igvard told them not to be picky about it and slurped his water and gruel down. He even ate the bread with mold on it. But James did not expect his uncle to be picky—he figured he picked up his unusual taste from all those years he spent living among "pigs and goblin thugs."

By the third day, Cat was concerned about whether Quizlow could even find them. He thought that perhaps the task was more challenging than the gnome had anticipated. Maybe the Scathra had continued to capture and kill the mice after the gnomes had left, and the mice were all in hiding. Or maybe Quizlow and Hatset were captured or killed themselves. It scared James to think about it and he tried to put it out of his mind. But it was a recurring fear, and he had to console himself, reasoning that Quizlow had survived Akhret where he was hunted by the Glutton's ferocious pjjin, who had a nose for smalls. If he could survive that, he thought, he should have no problem here in these tunnels.

He tried to sleep often. If he did, he would not feel the hunger or the thirst as much. The water hurt his stomach to drink, so he took only small sips. It was hard to sleep, and Cat let him borrow his soggy book to lay his head on, keeping it on the interior of the cloak so it wouldn't fall out. He dozed only when he was very tired, like he did on the first night. That night he had had a dreamless sleep and woke with a crick in his neck from the awkward position.

On the second and third night he didn't sleep as soundly. But he dreamed. He dreamed of the rocking sea and smelling the fresh scent of the sea air touching his cheek, blowing back his hair. He supposed it was the draft coming down from above that prompted that dream sequence—and was gladdened for it. He never imagined he'd yearn for those slow, boring days at sea, but feeling the sun on his body, and the breeze tousling his hair, tickling the skin on his forearms, felt priceless now.

The third night he dreamed he was falling. Falling and falling. The feel of the wind whooshed past his face and hair. The falling dreams were not bad—not terrifying, anyway. The terrifying dreams came later—when he dreamed of *him*. He could not say which *him* it was. There was a man with long black hair and citrine eyes, and a face half swathed in tattoos. Even in his dream he realized it could have been Jack. He'd never seen his father. But he knew, the way you often *know* in dreams. It was a strange sort of familiar, like a demon that lives inside you. He feared him more than anything he'd feared in his life. And he feared that he'd see his face.

But after some time, like in a dream, it became *not* Jack. In place of the man he feared was a badly burned face—burned down to the skull, the one eye socket a crater filled with the dark of the fathomless sea, or an endless night. The other was organic, alive, full of sardonic humor and murder.

He didn't know who he feared more. Jack, or this abomination.

But he supposed he had an equal terror of them both. Jack was a mystery.

But the one-eyed demon laughed and laughed until blood poured from his lips. And then he grabbed James by the arm. "'Ello, mate. Believe yer fallin' in love. Course, I'll need a ring for me betrothed. A ring soaked in the blood of yer clotting father!" He tried not to look into that one ugly eyeball, but he couldn't hide from it. Even when he fled into other dreams, dreams that were fragments of other places, other times, he couldn't hide from the laughter.

Slowly, thankfully, the fear bled away, and turned into a familiar, soft harmony playing behind the nightmare.

He didn't actually see her.

But he *felt* her.

He felt the sense of her there. *Dark hair, long tresses, and lovely eyes*, his grandfather had said. But to him, that description was moot. No, he only knew the look.

She had a knowing look.

Mother.

The music got louder. And now he could recognize it. It played over and over, like a TikTok on loop. It was old, recognizable, and he felt a strong sense of homesickness.

When he awoke, it faded from his ears, but his mind continued to play it. At first, he didn't know where it came from, but then he remembered Arthur standing in his old burned-out bedroom humming a few bars from the song. *It's that old lullaby of my mother's*, he thought. He found that if he tried, he could hum the whole song. He'd known it all his life, there was just no reason to recall it.

All morning he lay there, sharing the traveler's cloak with Cat, thinking about the song. He couldn't help but feel it had something to do with that mysterious look on his mother's face he'd seen in her portrait when he was at the Faugs.

~

On the sixth day, Quizlow turned up. James was so bored by that point, he'd begun to read the old mangy book Cat had been sleeping on. Cat was lying on the cage's bottom, relishing the sound of the strange words rolling off his tongue. James knew it was his peculiar Dreadful power that allowed him to translate most foreign tongues, and Cat had just stopped him at a particular word that didn't seem to translate well, when James noticed the mouse dash across the rope bridge and leap nimbly onto the top of their cage. He immediately stood up and took the mouse into his cupped palms. "Quizlow!" he whispered, crouching, and hoping his actions hadn't been too conspicuous. He set him and the mouse down in a fold of Igvard's traveler's cloak.

"How've you been?" Quizlow asked.

"We're being tortured," Cat moaned.

Quizlow's eyes widened, his face crinkling with concern.

But then Cat said, "Tortured by being in this cage! How're we supposed to stay cramped up here like rats?"

Quizlow's expression relaxed, but then changed to that of indignation. "Don't *joke* about that, boy!"

"Please, if we were tortured, you'd have heard James screaming all the way from Centrennia," Cat snorted.

Quizlow ignored this quip and turned to James. "I've been watching for almost a day."

"A *day*?" James looked at him mutinously. "And this is the first time you've contacted us?"

"Your captors are more attentive to smaller creatures than when they were human. I believe they're cursed, by the way," he said, sharing that his theory was the same as James's. "They're still very wary of spies, and it'd do you no good getting caught by your hairy turnkey because I ran into them while they were delivering breakfast."

"You're right," James said, remembering the amount of detail Quizlow paid attention to when springing them free from Argolhum.

"I'd been watching you, as I'd said. This is the most movement you've made in two days, so it's likely to draw suspicion from below."

James looked down at the Boneheads, who, surprisingly, had not moved from their spot at the table. He supposed it shouldn't have been surprising. Being dead might have given them a higher tolerance for boredom. Sometimes, he'd awaken to find them lying in pieces on the table. But then they'd come back together in the morning, stand up, and yawn like they'd just woke up.

"You have another mouse," Cat observed.

James noticed, too, now that Cat had said something. This mouse had darker, thicker fur and a slightly pinkish belly.

"Yes," Quizlow said. "This is Pasley. I recruited him because he can run this place with his eyes closed."

"I take it they liked your gift," James deduced.

"Oh, they were very happy," Quizlow said, petting Pasley's whiskers. "They'd never tasted blueberries. In fact, they hadn't even seen someone like me before. They thought I was very—odd."

"Why?" James asked.

"The older generations have died out. But Hatset vouched for me, and I made the offering with the blueberry. They think I am some sort of deity—producing ripe, delicious blueberries for them. They were more than happy to offer me Pasley here."

"Can you get us out?" Cat asked.

Quizlow sighed and sat folding his legs inside the collar of the cloak. "That'd be impractical. You'll have to stay here—at least for the time being."

"How much longer?" James moaned.

Igvard stretched his legs and slid closer to them, before snorting nastily. "James, you wanted to be here. Here we are. There's no going anywhere until my brother arrives." He turned to face Quizlow's voice now, leaning the side of his temple against the bars. "But what's the plan after my brother arrives?"

"Er—yeah," James said, looking up, but feeling a bit sheepish from Igvard's chastising. "What if we can't reason with Oskar?"

The gnome didn't answer right away. He went to Pasley and loosened a knot in the twine around his neck, where a small bundle was. "James, you're looking kind of peakish." He brought the bundle down and untied it, letting a blueberry roll out. "Here, I'll make you breakfast. Fresh fruit." As he did this, he laid everything he knew out for them to see. They were in a pretty grim situation. By now, their captors had moved the *Persephone*.

He believed they were considering turning her to scrap to salvage her parts, but they'd patched up the hole in her hull all the same so she wouldn't sink. Still, there was the problem of sailing the ship. Without a crew there was no way they could escape. Even if everything worked, and the water forced them out of Sarvelok and they were returned to sea, they'd be stranded.

"So, what are you saying?" Cat said. "Are we prisoners for life?"

"I'm working on it," Quizlow said as he muttered a spell under his breath, and the blueberries began to multiply.

"How long would you say it'd take for Formandible and his crew to arrive?" Igvard asked. "It's already been close to two weeks since they left the Realm of Shadows."

"I don't know the speed of a Harsler pirate ship, but it's manned by a strong crew. Their ships come out of Svasker and are lapstrake, so they will take longer to cover such distance. Even with smalls to provide them with food and fresh water, they may need to stop in Centrennia for some time—supplies, maybe some taverns. No reason for them to hurry. We may see them arrive in another week, more or less."

"Another week?" Cat cried a little too loudly. "We can't be here another week!"

Quizlow gave him a look that told him to keep quiet, and then said, "Oskar may arrive before that, who's to say?"

James shifted uncomfortably and stared listlessly out the cage. When he came here hoping to see his uncle it never occurred to him that he wouldn't be here. He didn't think they'd have to sit in a cage for two weeks being taunted by the Boneheads, using a bucket as their privy—*starving.* Aching.

I guess I am a bit reckless, he thought. "OK," James said at last, biting off a nail and spitting it out. He'd gnawed his fingernails down pretty low by now. "Promise us at least you'll visit us daily. Otherwise, we'll go mad in here."

"I will," Quizlow said. Then he hopped onto Pasley, leaped through the bars onto the rope bridge, and scurried off as quickly as he'd come.

16
QUIZLOW THE SPY

Even after he'd spent about a week in Argolhum, James never imagined how intolerable two weeks in the cage would be. His muscles cramped, his stomach hurt, he didn't eat, and his dried lips took on a raisiny texture from lack of water. By the tenth day (he wasn't sure anymore how long it'd been) his uncle insisted that he eat something, and Cat gave him his share of the blueberries Quizlow made while he ate James's gruel and bread. He slept with his head near the waste bucket, not caring about the stink, which he could barely smell, and the flies landed on his cheeks and crawled around. The tickling sensation was something to feel.

It was hard—or damn well near impossible—not to feel responsible for their current circumstance. James had told Quizlow before that he'd had no real hand in coming here, but he did not seem to believe him. *He knew I'd wanted to come. I didn't want to go home. I'd said as much. And she picked up on it—the* Persephone. She was a strange vessel, a weapon that had belonged to his father. She was dark and mysterious. *Like my father. All the playthings of my father are trouble. Do I really want to go to this lost, forgotten tomb full of his lost, forgotten baubles?* But now, just as he'd told Quizlow, he was being drawn deeper and deeper into the mysterious, blood-soaked magic his father wielded. *Ever since he brought me to this land, gave me my father's legacies, I've been following in his footsteps. Trailing his legacy of blood. I should not have listened to Grandfather that night he told me to call Galajitar. I should not have listened, and I should have...*

Stayed in Urrd?

He could not honestly say he wanted that. No more than he wanted to go home and live a peaceful life at the Faugs as he was intended to do. But perhaps his willful nature came from his father. Perhaps it was that nature that led him down the dark path he took. The hot-bloodedness. The wanderlust. The desire for power and magic.

Igvard did not seem to believe he'd been responsible for moving the ship. He had heard snatches of their dispute before they were swept into the Sarvelok, but later he'd brushed off the notion that James had controlled the ship's destination. "It was the Boneheads—that I can assure you," he'd said. "I didn't trust them from the start. And Stray is the only one who'd benefit from us being here. He knows we'll have to summon him. We could have sailed straight to Arupa without interference in the right conditions and he would've got nothing. He said we'd never get here, but he wanted us here all the same. She's his ship, and we were his prisoners from the moment he was summoned."

This seemed very likely to be true. And yet Quizlow still seemed to think he was at least *partly* responsible. At any rate, Igvard held no ill will toward him despite his suffering. It had almost seemed like he was used to confinement, which was probably true. He had spent two years as a lizard.

Quizlow's infrequent visits were the only things that kept their sanities. When he finally did show up, they were careful not to make sudden movements or noise when he hopped down on the floor of their cage, lest they raised the suspicion of the monkeys above or below. During that time, he made them dozens of blueberries, and was once nice enough to turn Igvard's water into ale, having gathered a few drops from the stash below by soaking his cloth with it. It wasn't just Igvard who enjoyed the ale, though. James and Cat drank their share—or as much as they dared—and enjoyed the buzz it gave them. Quizlow would not allow them to get completely tanked; he was afraid their captors would grow suspicious when they could only talk with slurred speech.

James's favorite time, however, was when Quizlow told them about his discoveries. Riding Pasley, he'd covered much of the lair, and also learned a lot about the mice living there. They had lived in the lair for over fifty-five generations. The mice knew the tunnels well, though some families were more familiar with certain sections of the lair than others. This meant that occasionally he had to switch mice. Whenever he came back this way, he used Pasley. Hatset was doing fine, having returned to the *Persephone* to be with his siblings, and some of the salt harvest mice—that's what he called them—had made the perilous journey to meet with them just to learn about the world. These mice were capable of drinking salt water, so they led the *Persephone*'s mischief to where the Scathra got their fresh water—an underground stream that came down from the mountain. Of course, mice could survive months without water, so it wasn't too much of a problem.

"Anyway, enough about mice," Quizlow said one day, his face reddening for a moment. It appeared he'd discovered something interesting today and wanted to tell them about it but had gone on too long on the topic of mice. He sometimes forgot that humans didn't care for the creatures half as much as he did. But James didn't care how long he rambled on about them. They had nowhere to be. Quizlow did, however, because he wanted to continue his exploring. Sometimes, James wished he was four inches tall, too, so he could go dashing about the place on a mouse named Pasley or Hatset. Gnomes didn't seem to have much trouble being imprisoned. But he supposed there was a tradeoff—they had to worry about being stepped on.

"I've finally located the sanctum where they keep the sea monster," he said, finally getting around to the important matter. He told them all about it.

Deep in the lair, down many tunnels, he'd found the well. And just as he'd told them before, a large iron cauldron filled with a very potent poison hung over it. But to keep it from accidentally spilling, the well had a hatch that closed. Wanting to investigate further, Quizlow spurred his mouse on. As it turned out, the mouse he rode—Tallow—knew the way and brought him to the cavern directly below it. Four of the canals led to this cavern—and it was probably the largest, because it had the largest pit he'd ever seen. The only thing he could see was its mouth, an enormous pit of teeth with rows of pharyngeal jaws that went all the way down into its throat. Quizlow estimated the creature's mouth was the size of a volcanic crater.

"How much water could this creature move do you think?" Igvard asked.

"My guess," Quizlow said, "is that it can swallow a whole fleet and still be hungry. After eating, it does regurgitate the refuse, but only after a month of digestion. It could flood the entire interior of the mountain in less than an hour," Quizlow projected.

"So, if you do poison the beast, it would most likely kill us," Cat pointed out.

"But at least it would stop the Scathra," James said.

"They open the floodgates to prevent the flooding," Quizlow explained. "But it takes a lot of work to open all those floodgates. I lost count after *twenty*."

"You weren't there," Cat said, "but we saw how slowly they raised the portcullises, which were not nearly as heavy as the floodgates."

"Their floodgates use counterweights," Igvard presumed.

"But it takes more than one person to turn the capstan to open one. Now that they're monkeys, and not as strong..." Quizlow said. "I'm sure they'll open the gates prior to making the sea monster sick. But if they wait until after—"

"They wouldn't have enough time to open all the floodgates," James realized.

"Then the lair would flood," Igvard finished. He mused on this for a while, before shaking his head. "If they open anything first, however, it would be the main door—Sarvelok's Maw."

"So, theoretically, we could escape," James said. "But we'd need them to open these gates—" He looked out across the shipyard.

"There are four floodgates in this shipyard," Quizlow said. "Also, note that they have raised their ships in the air."

"Why?" Cat asked.

"When the water is high, the boats cannot get out because they hit the ceiling. The water must be regulated."

"Escape seems less practical the more we talk about it," Igvard said dejectedly.

James sighed and looked at Quizlow. "So, you believe they've been cursed, too?"

"It's the only logical explanation. I was also shocked to see it. But I remembered what Arthur and Oskar had told me. Penelope had mentioned the Scathra falling under a spell before she fled Grisledor."

"I'm curious," Igvard said, "why the curse has affected the Scathra here."

"I, too, wondered that," Quizlow said. "But there are terrible magics in the world. Blood Magic."

"Yes," Igvard agreed.

James looked at his uncle. "You know of—"

"I know the Gralls put a lot of stock in hemomancy—Blood Magic— and that the Wozigod had forbidden its practice. Even the Spell-guardian rite is forbidden in some regions. Blood Magic can curse whole families."

"But what about an entire race?" Cat asked.

They were silent for a while. Then Quizlow said, "We know that Grisledor returned to this place after he left the Tomb of Forgotten Secrets, then. Probably unintentionally cursing the Scathra here."

"But he didn't return to Centrennia," Cat said. "The Scathra there have not been cursed."

"No," Quizlow agreed. "But now it's all starting to make more sense to me."

"Either Grisledor has come back to life, or Oskar is trying to break the curse and replace him as their leader," James said, beating him to it.

"Well," Quizlow said, "I know Grisledor hasn't come back to life. So, I suppose it's the latter."

17
OGRES GATHERED AROUND A TABLE

When Formandible's crew arrived on the eleventh day, Quizlow bore the news to them as quickly as he could. He'd been exploring the south end of the lair where the main door was when he learned of the arrival. In truth, he just wanted fresh air and sunlight, but he'd gotten to examining the mechanism that lowered the main door—the large chains that rove through hawseholes, the rusting pulleys, and the counterweights. It was all more complex than he'd imagined. He'd counted up to twenty Scathra monkeys operating in the loft, and they'd gotten languid and incompetent, just as they'd suspected.

He saw that they had ladders that led to the watchtowers, which peered out of each eye of Sarvelok's face. There were alcoves here, with seal skin pelts on the floor beside cast-iron cressets that burned with pitch. Below was the nose, which served as a machicolation—holes through which the raiders could lob hot oil to set passing ships on fire. Inside the nose, also, was a chamber where the rusted chains descended through, and a door that opened up to a long stone corridor lined with torches, braziers to heat burning coals, and even carts to deliver rocks for the murder-holes. The other two heads did not necessarily serve as lofts, but the eyes, noses, and mouths served as machicolations—death for any who came near the base there. He had looked below and seen the wreckage that had accumulated on the sides of the mountain's entrance—and that death would greet any survivors that managed to escape being sucked into Sarvelok's Maw.

It was when Quizlow had spurred his mouse into a storage chamber that he'd heard the commotion in the loft. The loft monkeys had spent most of the time drunk on their jobs, throwing bottles out the lookout holes, or climbing out to squabble on the nose. But now they had all scrambled to the capstan and were struggling to turn it. The familiar groan of the main door's deck lowering rankled Quizlow's nerves, and the frightened mouse scurried away until Quizlow gained control of him again. When he got up to the eyehole, he looked out at the gorge and spied the ship in the distance. At about that time, a deep horn blasted, resounding through the lair. Scathra raiders were scrambling everywhere. They had to lift the floodgates in certain areas and close them in others.

Even at a distance, Quizlow could make out the double-banked ship—it's lapstrake make, and lateen sails flapping in the wind. At this distance, he couldn't make out the device of the crossed battle-axes under a skull, nor the large mammoth skull as the figurehead—which would categorize it as an ogre's pirate ship—but he knew it was there.

"And you're sure it's them," Igvard said.

"A Seabeard's longship would be half the size and is square-rigged. And only ogres build longships with two decks like this one. They are noted for their large but less-sophisticated boats."

After telling them this, Quizlow disappeared again. The three of them could only wait for the inevitable.

It wasn't long before a second horn was heard—this time, two shorter blasts. Suddenly, hundreds of monkeys from below were scampering to stations, disappearing through tunnels. Then there was the sound of floodgates screeching open, while others shut. Cool sea air flowed through the tunnels and wafted out of some of the caves, smelling humid and earthy and stale. But the floodgates in the shipyard never opened, and Igvard said the boat must have been redirected to a harbor somewhere.

After that—nothing. James waited and waited for what felt like hours.

Eventually, he fell asleep—but was later awakened to the sound of a winch turning, and the sensation of being suddenly lowered. Disoriented from sleep, he clambered to the side where Cat was, rocking the cage forward. Below, he saw the large, burly shapes of the visitors—and one very large one, with a long metal-gray beard.

Formandible.

He thought it'd be a relief to finally be on the ground—that was until they unlocked the door and let them out, and James felt the blood rush from his head. Cat stumbled clumsily on his feet as well. His sprained ankle had healed by now, but his legs were weak from cramps. And even Igvard needed to grip on to the bars of the cage to steady himself.

A number of Scathra monkeys were surrounding them with pila and knives. James saw the ugly-faced spider monkey again holding his flail, and he directed the three of them toward the table that the Boneheads had occupied for almost a week. They were nowhere to be seen now. In their place sat Formandible, using a large chest to rest his haunches. Flanking him were two of his freebooters, looking tired with sandbagged and reddened eyes, and smelling like old, dingy leather and rotted fish— Gunter and Grease Mold.

When Formandible looked on them, he growled. His pierced ugly nostrils flared, and a thick lather of burnt-mustard saliva slipped from the corner of his mouth and dribbled into his beard, already crusty with spittle and mats of coagulated blood.

"No, there was not a second ship named *Persephone* in the harbor, you owe me a keg of malted imp gin, Grease Mold," Gunter said, taking a seat at the far end of the table on a barrel.

Formandible ignored this and instead stood up and strode toward Igvard, who had sat on a lopsided barrel, holding his lower back in pain for having sat awkwardly for over a week. "How?" he growled. Thick white slime oozed from the corners of his eyes; his nostrils were peeling from sunburn.

"*Traitor,*" Igvard countered, glowering at him.

Formandible looked him over, then spat at Igvard's feet. He turned to examine James, his snout wrinkling, his eyes showing displeasure. "Gunter," he grunted. "You right." He stroked the haft of his ax, an old, lanzones-colored nail slicing through smears of oil and blood on the ax head. "Boy worth something alive. So"—he turned to Igvard—"it good you brought him here, hooman. But you"—and he suddenly grabbed Igvard around the neck with one hand, the muscles in his tattooed forearm rippling like a whale's throat grooves—"you insult me for last time."

Igvard choked, his hands leaping to the one secured around his neck. But Formandible lifted him off the barrel and kicked it away from him. "When I ask, you tell," he barked, and shoved Igvard to the ground. He stood over him, his goliath form diminishing the man's as he stared down on him with pure violent rage. "How you get here, hooman?" He said the word *hooman* like a curse, and he stepped toward him, his hand moving to the ax at his belt.

Igvard edged away on his elbows until they touched water. "Mandible," he said, "Can't explain—dunno how—we flew—we—"

Formandible put a black, troll-hide boot on Igvard's ankle and pressed down, then crouched and grabbed him by the throat again. "Take me for fool, yeh do." And suddenly, he shoved Igvard's head into the water. Igvard struggled wildly, kicking, but Formandible lowered his knee on his legs, as the other ogres and monkeys watched on, laughing. "Lot o' fish in water here, Igvard. Think yer head 'nough to feed 'em?"

James lurched forward on feet that stabbed like pins, but Grease Mold stepped forward and elbowed him in the ribs, sending him stomach first into the table.

Cat jumped, but Grease Mold grabbed him by his matted hair and shoved him to the ground and kicked him. Cat tried to move, but then lay sprawled out, bewildered and in pain.

"Stop!" James retched.

The water rippled, and silver flecks darted through it toward his uncle's head.

Grease Mold knelt beside James and bared his rotting yellow teeth. "Skinners'll peel yer uncle's face right off and pluck out 'is eyeballs like li'l treats. Then, we gonna sit 'im here next teh you, let flies work on 'im. How's that, *flea*?"

James vomited the little food he had in him and clutched his stomach, gasping for air. Grease Mold shoved his head forward and rose to his feet.

Formandible yanked Igvard from the water, moments before the silver fish leaped at him. They danced across the rippling surface, scattering the wrinkles of light everywhere, before diving back in.

Igvard coughed and sputtered violently as Formandible, his teeth grinding, dragged him, cold and wet, to the table. "Think he ready to flap 'is fat lips." He shoved Igvard into a chair. "Now. Le's start over. How did yeh—"

"It's Jack's ship," James blurted out, grabbing the edge of the table and steadying his breaths. "She brought us here. She's—"

"Magic," finished Gunter. "Just as I suspected."

"Is this true?" Formandible growled, pulling on Igvard's hair.

Igvard was coughing, his face flushed and streaming. But he managed to nod, and say, "*Not—lying!*"

The captain stooped beside him and leaned into his face. "Good. Hate teh see yer face without skin. Heh-heh!" He looked at Gunter. "If boat can do this magic, it be good teh have. And boy of the wizard can teach us how teh make 'er fly."

James had gotten Cat up from the ground and sat down in the chairs at the table, his hand still holding his side. He glared at Formandible now. "Where's the stone? Where's Roseheart?" The last he'd seen of the magical gemstone his mother had given to Oskar was in the hand of Gunter.

Formandible rose and stepped over to him, breathing heavily. For a moment he expected violence. The leader of the freebooters always had an edge before. But now he could practically smell the aversion trickling out of his glands. Yet, the blistering enmity in his eyes regarded him with something different. *He knows my value*, James thought. But that didn't matter. Formandible looked capable of murdering the other two just to get at him.

Formandible turned to Grease Mold and signaled him with his thumb. The ogre walked off. "Yer precious stone," he said, leaning against the table, "*broken*."

James looked at him, not turning fully, but unsure if he believed him. He didn't want to meet that large nefarious gaze. "Whaddya mean?"

Grease Mold had returned from the bookkeeper's table carrying a padlocked coffer. It was cruder than the one he'd seen in Estyrmor, with a rusted iron hasp, bloodstains, dents, and flecks of tar and sawdust on it. He set it on the table over a leftover card from the Boneheads' game. Inside, James could hear a peculiar sound—like something was bouncing around. The coffer moved a few inches from the sheer force of it.

Grease Mold pulled a pair of iron cuffs dangling through his belt, and slapped one end over Igvard's wrist, and the other over Cat's. The second pair was for James, but Formandible stopped him.

Gunter looked to Grease Mold. "There was a box of whazzits and such over yonder. I'm sure there's an iron clasp there. Find it; we'll fit this table with it and reeve their shackles through."

Grease Mold grunted and went off in search of this, and Formandible reached for his belt and unfastened a ring of keys. There were only three on it.

"What's wrong with her?" James asked, looking at the coffer. He didn't understand what kind of problem they'd be having with her; he remembered that Roseheart had gone willingly to Gunter that night in Coven's Hall.

"She senses a disturbance," Gunter said. "She was compliant when she came to us, but it might only have been because you were sitting at the table. See here," he said, moving toward James. "I had every intention of bringing you, but Formandible was against it." He looked at the hulking beast beside him. "He only realized his mistake when we'd set sail and she asked us where you were."

James stared at him, but it was Cat who spoke up, rubbing the side of his cheek that was bruised now. "You bloody fool. You were supposed to take James, weren't you?"

"It was expected of us," Gunter said. "But as I said, Formandible here thought it'd be best if we sold her instead. You can imagine that this change of heart did not please her."

James recalled that his mother had chosen Roseheart to decide his Spellguardian because she could see through deceit—knew people's intentions. Well, Formandible's intention had changed, and that caused a problem with her, it appeared.

"Two o' me brethren jumped overboard and drowned," Formandible murmured, leaning a heavy, scabbed elbow on the table. "Her enchanted words curse our ears. I fear we not make it here."

James looked up into his eyes, but the beast was no longer staring at him. The corners of his mouth were pulled down in a frown as his eyes languidly examined the ale stains on the wood. "Even when put her in coffer—buried her in hold under chests o' pig iron, heaps o' aurochs and bear hide—she sing and talk, talk and sing. She drove brethren and me teh madness."

"Serves you right," James said.

Formandible's eyes returned to the moment and regarded him with a smoldering degree of rancor. "Make her stop."

James eyed the coffer budging forward as though making its way across the table.

"I don't hear her singing," Cat said.

"Nor I," James agreed. But she heard them, because a second later, a soft chuckle came from inside the chest, muffled, but articulate enough to understand. "Ahahoohoohoohooo!" she laughed. "Is that bloody moose still bleating like a mooncalf? 'E sounds like a whinging little girl who's lost her wimple. Did you know he cries big ogre tears? His meanness is all blarney. Behind it is an old goat who cries for an ogress that was skinned for want of a purse by a Gandanian merchant. His beard grows ever whiter with each passing moon. He mutters her name in his sleep, the baboon! Want to hear it? Indecipherable to intelligible ears. What's it, you spume-eyebrowed, goat-bearded, fly-herder? Ah yes—*Meyeshony*."

Formandible's eyes flared and flickered at the name, and his fists closed and struck the coffer's lid.

"Oh, I got it right this time? She's a pretty name for a grunting, squalid gnat-brain. Ayuh—but then men came along, with their magic and fire, and branded your hides and named you murderous animals that deserved nothing more than enslavement. And they gave her a name to match her filthy skin and flea-torn scalp tangled with goblin fetus fetishes. Gore-Lip was her name." She hooted again. "Did anyone think his heart could bleed, child? *I* didn't."

"Make her stop!" Formandible growled. His throat ground like a pestle on granite. "Or I crush!"

James took the key from his hand, slipped it into the lock, and turned. *Click!* He didn't need to touch the lid. The coffer sprang open, and out hopped Roseheart. She was like an ordinary mockingbird, except for her colors. Her breast was gold, but her back was lavender, her wingtips chased with beautiful shades of jade and turquoise. Her tiny eyes were glimmers of sapphire, and her beak was orangish-gray—like old metal in firelight. "Ah, fresh air at last!" She sneezed. "Or as fresh as it gets in the presence of these smelly japes."

"*Alyshyn Sigoris* are the words," Gunter muttered.

James had heard the words only once before—in the Coven's Hall after the gemstone had leaped out of ornate coffer from bursts of magic. The Ring Witch had said them, and had transformed the beautiful gemstone into a living, breathing, talking bird. She had talked and talked and had not shut up since. He was certain that saying them again would turn her back to her original state. He looked at her now, and Roseheart gave a hop and turned toward him. "My dear James. Certainly, you're not—"

"It's for your own good," James said, cutting her off.

"James," Igvard started.

"Stay your tongue, jackanape," the bird said, cocking her head at Igvard. "He's made up his mind long ago. He won't let the ogre crush me. His eyes say he knows what's in it for him. He'll risk me falling into enemy hands rather than to never touch a legacy left by his father." She cocked her head at James. "Am I right, boy?"

James just stared at her, mesmerized.

"Do it," urged Formandible.

"Before you condemn me, child, ask yourself if truth is the paramour you seek. Betrothed—inevitably you shall wed. But one day, you shall wake to find a shoat in your bed—hahahaha!"

"*Alyshyn Sigoris!*" James cried.

There was that shock of perfect light—the glistening of a web of pearl-strung rainbows that blinded him. Nothing more than that. No sound. Just a *clunk!* as the beautiful chrysoprase fell over on its side.

Formandible let out a long sigh, his fingers relaxing on the edge of the table.

James looked at him, expressionless. "When is my uncle coming?"

The captain regarded him with flinty eyes and chuckled. "You are fool, boy."

James bit his lip but refrained from a retort. "What did my uncle offer you to steal her from us?"

Formandible plucked the stone from the table and dropped her back into the coffer before shutting the lid. He locked it.

"His name is Rat," Gunter said, ignoring the question. "That is all we know of his identity. And it would do you good to remember that."

Grease Mold had returned to the table with some nails. He laid their chains through the clasp on the table, and then hammered it down with four nails, grunting with satisfaction when he was done. The third pair of manacles Formandible took and fastened one cuff over James's right wrist.

James was somewhat grateful they would not have to sit in the cage again. At least here at the table he had more freedom. "OK, then who is Rat?" he asked.

"He represents our benefactors. That's all I will tell you," Gunter said.

"Why?" Cat asked. "Who are you afraid will find out? We're stuck here, in case you haven't noticed."

"We have our orders," Formandible grumbled.

James noticed that when the captain said this, he seemed a little uneasy for the first time, and his eyes shifted warily to a large sack tied by rope to Gunter's belt. It held something in it about the size of a human head.

"What if we were to negotiate with you?" Igvard spoke up, shooting a skeptical glance at Formandible. He was speaking to Gunter directly now.

James could tell his uncle was trying to be coy. *He knows there's a power struggle between the two. I bet he's gonna try to use that to divide them.*

But Formandible pounced on the move instantly. "What you offer us, *hooman*? What you offer us our benefactors cannot?" he barked, stepping menacingly toward him.

Igvard flinched away from the lumbering ogre.

He's scared as a church mouse now, James thought. "You want what's in the Tomb of Secrets, don't you?" James spoke up. "But you haven't gone there yet. That means you need these benefactors. But I say, why not cut out the middleman? We can go there now. You won't have to split what you plunder."

Formandible laughed hard, sitting down on his barrel and tenting his fingers. His yellow nails poked through his beard matted together with residual fish oil. "Think yeh know benefactors, flea?"

"They need James," Cat said.

"Very clever," Gunter chuckled. "Well, let's put their wits to the test, shall we?" He looked at James. "What do you know about this Tomb of Forgotten Secrets?"

James looked down at the table, then sort of shrugged. He could feel Gunter's triumphant eyes watching him still. "Dunno."

"Right," Gunter said. "But the clever child could have at least said 'dangerous.'"

"I do know Grisledor tried it," James blurted out. He didn't mean to say it, but Gunter's gloating tone had begun to irritate him.

"Yes," Gunter said. "Grisledor tried it. A great and powerful sorcerer who took to the seas and humbled your father. Yet, he was nearly defeated by this place."

"There were other factors involved," Igvard drawled, not looking at him.

Gunter ignored this. "Our benefactors are very powerful and have invested a lot of resources into finding this place. And even more in learning how to avoid the same mistake Grisledor made."

"Why you?" Cat asked.

"Because they're expendable," Igvard cut in.

Formandible growled in his throat, glaring at Igvard. For a moment, James thought he would lose his temper again. "Expen'able? No, fool hooman." He leaned toward Igvard, narrowing his eyes. "Benefactors understand our kind. Understand the sufferin' hoomans have put us through."

"The same way Grisledor understood you?" Cat asked. "Didn't he send your folk to the front lines?"

"The Wozigod has held dominance over most of the world for centuries," Gunter said, ignoring Cat. "They've monopolized power through their oppressive magic and have spread their influence across the globe into an empire. The Wozigod claim to be the champions of justice by quelling the likes of us. But make no mistake, they crave the same thing all other bloodthirsty tyrannies crave: Complete world domination and the oppression of races and creatures whom they perceive to be a threat to their established regime."

Formandible snorted loftily upon hearing that Gunter's reply was far more eloquent than he could have ever hoped to make, and he took a knife from his belt and an oilstone from a pouch and began sharpening it, watching Igvard for his reaction.

"When our voyage is at an end, we'll have enough plunder and Wizard's Gold to fund a rebellion for our kind in Logres, who are all but slaves in our own land."

"What do you mean *slaves*?" James asked. He didn't recall his grandfather ever telling him about slavery in Nobrocoso.

Gunter looked nonplussed for a brief moment. "Right, you're from that place—Urrd is it?" He folded his arms, the corners of his lips turning upward in a slender sneer. "Our cruder brethren—the less articulate ones—are more inclined to violence, and therefore, often spend their lives in dungeons, or are sent to labor in mines, or quarries with little to no pay."

James looked to Igvard. "Is this true?"

Igvard raised his eyebrows like a shrug, casually dismissing this as trivial. Then he said, "But this lot—look at them, James. If left among themselves, they turn to war, or piracy. In the past, they've killed *many*. I'd spare my sympathy for others."

James noticed his uncle didn't seem quite so understanding now toward the creatures as he'd been over a week ago before they betrayed him.

Formandible chuckled as he hunched forward, elbows on his knees. "Wizard men fear ogre as one. Keep us stupid. Poor. Can't rise up."

James looked at Formandible. "So, you think joining the High Seas Syndicate will change people's perception about you?"

"No," Gunter said. "Being civilized will."

But Formandible just snorted as he continued to sharpen his knife. "Civilized," he scoffed. "Only thing hoomans understand—power. Blood. War. *Death*."

James remembered Cat telling him about his homeland Suniria being taken over by goblins. Here the Scathra were preparing for war. And now the ogres. What next?

"'Nother war's comin'," Formandible crooned, as though he could read James's mind. "Benefactors want teh be on right side."

"They promised you wealth," Igvard said. "Then why did you try to sell Roseheart? That would be double-crossing your powerful benefactors who want nothing more than to help your peace-loving race," he finished, his voice laced with sarcasm.

Formandible sat forward. "Because we not want war with wizard. We force men from land—our land. *Logres*. It blocked by magic wall for centuries. Now, we part o' Syndicate, and—and—"

"They'll see to it that your kind dies first on the front lines of their new war," Cat said. "So, you're just a bunch of pawns."

Formandible rounded on him, then drove his knife into the table where Cat's hand would have been had he not moved it. He glowered at the boy, who sidled away from him. But a moment later, Formandible was shaking his head. "Boy right."

"Then come with us," James said, leaning across the table to stare into the captain's downcast eyes. "You have my uncle Oskar—or Rat. He knows about the Tomb of Secrets. How else was he to take me there? Forget your benefactors and the High Seas Syndicate. If you take us, we will honor our original agreement."

"*No.*"

James looked up.

It was Gunter who spoke now, which was a surprise. Surely, he was the most reasonable of the ogres—and the most intelligible. If anyone could see reason, it was him.

Yet, Gunter turned his head toward Formandible, a nearly imperceptible frown touching the edge of his mouth. "Because," he said, and he undid the rope around his belt, before placing the sack with the head-sized object in it on the table, "our benefactors are not ones to *disappoint*."

It was a telling look. James could see that this had been a source of contention in the past...and that Gunter had won. He wondered, however, what was in the bag that caused Formandible discomfort.

Formandible pulled his knife from the table, and then, grunting and looking down at it, continued to sharpen it on his oilstone.

18

RAT

Gunter saw to it that they were treated well. *Marginally* well, anyway. They were permitted to wash, but they had to do so with one hand cuffed to the table. They were fed roasted fish and maslin that had been cooked on embers. Maslin was unleavened bread, with a mixture of grains scrounged from sacks of looted ships, but it was better than the moldy stuff left over from the kitchen. There was also the treat of apples and pears, which grew on the island.

Meanwhile, the bookkeeper continued to categorize the piles of plunder—a job James was sure would take a thousand years, even if they had a hundred bookkeepers on all the isles. Monkeys carried chests here and there, splashing through the shallow water, and there were coins everywhere. He hadn't noticed before, but the mud glittered with gold and silver. There were urlans, and poddies and yammies of all shapes and sizes. Large gold bars, small silver bars, corroded copper and bronze crudely shaped coins—some with strange hieroglyphs. And they all gleamed like tiny drops of mercury.

Regardless of how much treasure they had, however, the monkeys still squabbled over it. Tirelessly. That was to be expected. They were monkeys, after all—*and* pirates. But they also squabbled tirelessly over *clothes*. The raiders probably could clothe an entire city with the wardrobes they kept,

195

and it was no surprise that they needed all the beautifully made wardrobes and bahuts to store them. But it was a strange thing to see a dancing monkey dwarfed in a wedding dress, or another scarpering around in the mud flaunting an oversized dishdasha. Those monkeys were very drunk, of course. But soon he came to see that crossdressing was not the only thing they partook in. They had drinking matches and vomited, smoked pipes, wrestled, chased one another up great stacks of chairs, fought with knives, and entertained the timeworn monkey habit of throwing their feces at one another.

With all the commotion, James knew it had to be easy for Quizlow to get about unnoticed, and he wondered what the small was up to—or if he'd overheard what had been said at the table. He looked for the movement of a mouse that would indicate he was nearby. But either he was very good at hiding, or he never came back to watch them.

He didn't see a sign of the Boneheads either, and he figured they were best mates with the monkeys at the table and had slipped off with their simian companions for a bit of sightseeing before the ogres arrived. James imagined they'd found some cave somewhere where they could continue to play cards and pour lots of whiskey over their rib cages. At least they weren't here to torment them, he thought.

They spent the night chained to the table in the uncomfortable dampness, listening to the dripping of water, and breathing in the stink of mildew and mold from the stacked furniture and attire on clotheslines. Grease Mold sat at the end of the table and put his barrel against the back of a cellarette and propped his feet up, his ax resting comfortably in his lap as he drank from a flagon. But James could not sleep now—not with so much going on. He ended up staring off across the water where there were mountains of boxes and chests stacked up as high as three-story buildings. The water near the jetties were cluttered with dropped and forsaken valuables: Glittering coins, books, crates, an old rotting credenza sitting lopsided and unwanted. Gleaming plates—now mirrors for the skinners that darted over their reflections—and many more items.

Later that night, when he was finally getting drowsy, he saw Formandible and Gunter go aboard the *Royal Bitch* with the spider monkey. The *Royal Bitch* was the name of the boat that was half lying on her side. As it turned out, she was being used as a headquarters. He saw them go into the poop cabin, and they didn't come out until a few hours later, that sack with the head-sized object, tied on Gunter's other side this time.

Cat, who was only half-asleep, noticed this, too, and leaned over and finally whispered in his ear, "*It's a crystal ball.*"

James looked at him. The last time he'd seen a crystal ball was in Paris—and Quizlow had used it to access YouTube. He didn't know what crystal balls did in this realm. "What's it do?"

"Wizards use them to communicate," Cat said.

James looked back toward the ogres. Communicate? Who were they communicating with?

His uncle?

~

He fell asleep at some point and awoke with a splinter in his chin hours later. Grease Mold had left his place at the head of the table leaving mud where his troll-skin boots had been, and Cat was drooling on his own arm, one manacled arm dangling freely.

"G'morning," he heard his uncle say; the man was eating a cold, fried fish, leaving its bones in a neat pile on the wood, and washing it down with a bottle of ale.

Butt-sore, James shifted in his seat, and turned at the sound of—*twang!*—and saw that Formandible's entire company of freebooters had gathered beside the *Royal Bitch*'s hull. They were loosing quarrels at some old furniture painted with targets. A dozen open crates full of rushes—undoubtedly used for cushions—lay at the captain's feet; he sat on a large keg inspecting a crossbow that still had bits of sweet flag on it.

"Ogres have big hands," Igvard told him, wiping the grease off his lips and flicking a fishbone off his plate with his index. "The Wozigod made it illegal to arm them, so it's hard for them to come by crossbows with wider foregrips and triggers for the size of their thick fingers."

James could tell Formandible was pleased. It was the first time he remembered seeing the pitiless pirate smile as he ran his finger along the stock, which was decorated with beautiful mother-of-pearl and silver dragonhead designs.

He thought maybe his face would disintegrate from the exertion. The goliath loaded the crossbow and tested it, sending a quarrel whistling into the old credenza they'd pulled from the water. Of the company, two of the ogres were missing, he noticed. Scab-Jaw and Bandersnatch. He recalled Formandible's story about how his two brethren had drowned on their way here. *Well, that's two less we have to worry about*, James thought. *If only we can get rid of the others.*

Formandible was testing the string now, and he ran a finger along the flight groove, chewing his lip in absorption.

The bookkeeper demonstrated to him how to aim the crossbow, using his own smaller version, and soon Formandible was squinting down the sights and aiming more accurately at his target.

"I sense a bleeding heart."

James turned around to find his uncle eyeing him with a tired but clever smirk. "Whaddya mean?"

"Yesterday, Formandible touched you with his sad little sob story. The one about the oppression of his kind. *Enslavement*, he called it."

James resumed his spectating, folding his arms. He didn't exactly have a bleeding heart for them. "In the land of Urrd," he said, "we look down on slavery."

Igvard chuckled. "I've run into many ogres in my day. They mostly do mercenary work, and if they can't get that—they revert to piracy. I might not be for the tyrannical regime of the Wozigod, but I agree that these beasts need to be—on a leash."

"You were singing a different song the other day," James pointed out.

"You misinterpreted my view," Igvard said, gnawing on a fishbone. "I don't have any love for the wizards in Yofhemgad—they have no love for us. They pay bounties on the heads of witches, necromancers, and beasts, and have treated many species and races with unfairness. But stopping the ogres from forming armies..." He whistled. "Look at them," he said, giving James's chair a nudge with his foot. "Those crossbows are superior because of their strength, and they can wear armor twice as thick. No man wants to face an ogre army on the battlefield, nor an ogre pirate at sea. The only way we can coexist with these beasts is in the current state—near enslavement. Give them a little power, they'll wipe us out. Mark my word."

It was hard to disagree given his experience with them, but he felt there had to be another way. He was about to say so when he saw something scurry across the planks and dash behind a stack of crates. Just as he was about to mention this to his uncle, a deep horn blast resounded through the cavern.

"*Whaaa—*" Cat lurched awake with a snort and sat up straight.

The monkeys froze in their places, some looking up from roasting breakfast over small fires. Then all at once, they scrambled for rope ladders, and vanished into tunnels.

"What's that?" James asked, looking at his uncle.

"That," Igvard said, sitting up properly, "may very well be the man we've been waiting for."

~

More horns resounded across the lair. The last time this happened, the ogres' ship had come in through Sarvelok's Maw. But the horns that sounded this time were different. Creaking floodgates opened and water rushed through. A powerful mechanism could be heard turning inside the mountain.

Cat asked what the noise was about, and Igvard said he'd heard the sound before. "Once, I'd traveled to the Floating City of Yu. A truly remarkable place," he said. "They were an advanced city with flying ships and technologies I'd never seen before."

The noise of the rushing seawater got louder, along with the creaking noises of the mechanisms. James imagined they were the sounds of sluice gates opening, spindles, crown wheels, and wheel shafts turning after years of disuse. And then a sound, like a loud bark, came crashing from above, trailing on the heels of a horrible screech from iron sliding through rusted grooves. The next thing they knew, daylight was spilling into the mountain, followed by gusts of fresh air.

James couldn't believe what he was seeing—the entire top of the mountain had split open and was dropping inward, a pair of wooden doors held by oversized chains extending from tree-trunk-sized operating beams. For a few seconds, it rained on them—fresh, clean water from the sky that had accumulated on the outside of the colossal doors.

The boats dangling from chains oscillated in the wind that swept down into the mountain, catching most of the water, and their hulls and sails glittered with droplets, sparkling with rainbows in the beams of sunshine.

It did not take long to wonder why these great doors had been opened—a shadow was floating into view, blocking out most of the clear blue sky. They could not entirely make it out with the swaying fleet of ships blocking their line of sight, but they could see a grand lapstrake hull with beautiful, gilded trimmings, and the head of a gemsbok device painted black and gold on flapping maroon lateen-rigged sails. She differed from a sea boat only by the sails sprouting from her side like batwings, glittering gold and silver.

James could hear Cat almost purring with excitement. "She's a flying boat. Sandalwood planks inlaid with enchanted floatstones, and sails woven with skyweb silks from Wu'al's eight-legged queens, and dyed bronze-white with starblood. An arm's length of that sailcloth is worth a bar of gold on the Skystar market!"

Indeed, this ship carried the prestigious title of opulence. Gunter had said his backers were wealthy, and this proved it beyond a doubt.

She came down elegantly—a descending angel with mundane colors shimmering like miracles.

"That's her," Gunter said, having come over to the table. "*Skybester*, she's hight. Bought from an Imirizian prince."

There was a wooden dock at the very top, and she stopped to hover over this. A monkey had climbed to the dock there, where a gilded dock line had been thrown over the side of the ship. He took the line and tied it to the dock post. Then, from beneath the *Skybester*, a trap door opened in the hull and a rope ladder unfurled.

Formandible had also come over to the table, his crossbow slung over his left shoulder. He turned to his band and shouted, "Oi—played with 'em long enough! Take 'em teh the 'old, and get ready teh sail, swabbers!"

As he said this, a troop of a dozen or more monkeys had begun to climb down the unfurled ladder of the *Skybester*, followed by a man in a flowing cloak. The monkeys were quicker. As they got closer, James could tell they were dressed better. Some wore barbute helmets and hauberks under their finely made yellow-and-crimson-striped gambesons, but at least three of them wore checkered turbans, glass goggles pulled up to their foreheads, and tiny brown fingerless gloves. Small crossbows, like the one the bookkeeper owned, were strapped over their shoulders, and these weapons were wine-red, with silver and gold trimmings. Their leather belts held ivory sheaths for knives encrusted in gemstones.

One of the elite monkeys untied a rope ladder, bundled on the deck of the lowest ship, and threw it down. And then down they came, descending to the isle that was across from the spit of land.

"You wish to know our benefactors?" Gunter said, passing them at the table. "Here's your chance."

They watched as the group crossed over the jetty stretching across the water to the spit. The man was tall, and wore a hood, but as he approached, James could see he had an iron mask underneath with no mouth—only slits for the eyes. Vertical grooves ran down the forehead, but the cheeks were dented, as though someone had struck it repeatedly with a hammer.

In his velvet-gloved hand he carried a rosewood cane with a smooth globe of aventurine at the top, and a gleaming gold cap at the bottom that clicked on each plank of the jetty.

James leaned close to Igvard. "Is it *him*?" he whispered.

His uncle's face remained expressionless as he raised his shoulders and dropped them.

When they reached the spit, the monkeys flanked the man, and he stood there regarding the three of them silently. "Uncuff him," a muffled voice said at last under the metal, and he pointed at James. "And who's the other child?"

Formandible grunted, pulled his key ring from his pocket, and fumbled through them for the small iron key. "Brat the boy knows. Picked up in Arupan dungeon." He unlocked the cuff around James's wrist, and James pulled his hand free, rubbing the chafed skin there. When he looked up at Rat, the man was holding his glove open before Formandible.

"Stone."

Formandible unlocked the coffer on the table, and plucked the chrysoprase from it, then dropped it into Rat's burgundy velvet palm.

"Was it any trouble?"

Formandible's forehead creased repulsively, but Gunter shook his head, watching as Rat carefully examined the stone in his palm. "Though I'm still not sure why you could not have come to Islad and save us a journey."

"Told you before we don't want to risk exposure," Rat said. "The Wozigod has been vigilant. Besides, you know very well I do not care for that land." He looked over at the table and lowered his voice. "They should not be here."

"We did not bring them," Gunter said, deflecting the accusatory tone. "I told you they'd be here last night."

"I heard you," Rat said absently, and came toward the table.

James remembered seeing Gunter coming out of the poop cabin with the crystal ball. *He must be talking about last night.* "Are we spoiling your plans, Oskar?"

Rat flinched at the name, then took a step toward him, gripping the cane firmly. "Rat." He said it as though he abhorred the name and regarded James through the slits in his mask as he stepped toward him. James leaned forward trying to see the eyes behind them, but the shadows hid the gold he wanted to see.

"Oh, don't bother with anonymity," Igvard said. "It's been compromised. Wasn't hard to figure out it was you who hired these bravos to steal Roseheart back from the witches. I thought you were clumsy and forgot your nephew. But you didn't. You're just after his inheritance."

"And he's working for someone else," James said, before turning toward Rat. "Aren't you?"

Rat faced Formandible, ignoring them. "Take them with you when you leave. I'm going to send—"

Gunter stepped froward. "Leave? We're not *leaving*. You're taking us, remember?"

"That was deal," Formandible growled.

"I'm changing it, then," Rat said, lowering his voice again. "I give you my word that you will be paid in full. Choose three to go with us. But I want Formandible to take them back to the Faugs—"

"No," Formandible growled. "We not sail again. You take us—boat and all—"

"As agreed," Gunter finished.

Rat clutched his fist around the stone in anger as he considered their demands. "Things have changed," he said quietly, "and I need—"

"We don't take our orders from you anymore," Gunter interrupted tensely.

Rat turned and looked at him. "Since when?" He stepped toward Gunter menacingly. "This was *my* plan."

"But it is *they* who pay us," Gunter growled, though he wouldn't look at Rat directly. And he reached down and set the sack on the table and removed the object from within. There, sat a gleaming, mulberry-hued crystal ball.

"Who?" James asked. He could see Rat was nervous; he was turning to look over his shoulders before he stepped even closer to Gunter.

"Gunter, please—" Rat said.

"Why do you want us to leave?" James asked, standing up. "I bet it's because you don't want to look at me. *Coward.*"

Rat stiffened at the word, and he drove the tip of his cane into a plank hard.

"He's right, brother," Igvard said, frowning. "You are a *coward.* Penelope trusted you. She didn't choose me to be a Spell-guardian; she didn't think I was trustworthy enough. No—she trusted *you.*" He lifted his hand, his manacles clinking as he pointed at him. "Don't think wearing a mask or sending us away will ease your conscience."

"You don't understand. You're in more danger than you can possibly know," Rat said thickly, his lips touching the metal over his mouth. "You were *not* supposed to be here."

"Screw you."

Rat stepped back, looking at James.

"That's right," James continued. "I'm *here.* I'm here and I'm screwing up your plans. *Enjoy* it."

"You heard him," Cat said. "Enjoy it, *fetcher.*"

"Look at me." James tilted his head, hoping for an angle—or perhaps a glimpse of the eyes inside the mask. He realized he hated Oskar. He hated Oskar more than he'd ever hated Igvard. Even though they'd pretty much betrayed him the same way, this was a far greater betrayal—because his mother had trusted him. And, like his father, he'd looked up to him. *He was the man I was supposed to live with at the Faugs until I was eighteen. He was the man my grandfather told me stories about when I was young. The one with werewolf heads on the walls of his great hall. I never knew him, but I feel like I have...from the stories.* "Look at me!"

But Rat's posture had changed. He'd gone rigid, his head cocked to one side as though listening for something he dreaded. Then he raised a hand, taking a step toward him. "Listen—" But he never finished.

Cat gasped; something was rattling on the table—as though Cat was jerking his arm, and James turned around. But Cat wasn't making the noise. Instead, he looked aghast—as did Igvard. The pair of manacles James had been freed from had lifted into the air by itself—before striking at him like a python. The next instant, the cold iron cuffs had snapped around one of his wrists before he could pull away. "What is this?" James cried, outraged. He looked at Rat. "Release me!"

Rat's burgundy glove had tightened around the aventurine ball, and he turned around; James had a hair-raising feeling that he was looking for something he couldn't see. Something that made the air bristle with the mysterious magic that had possessed his manacles.

And then they heard it. The voice of a cold, cold person he could not see.

"Why is the child not restrained, Rat?"

19
WOLVES & RATS

The voice was not far off. In fact, it was close enough to hear without it rising in volume.

James looked around for the voice, but he could see no one close enough to have spoken. Formandible, with his crossbow slung over his shoulder, went still, a troubled expression folding over his face. His fingers moved toward his ax out of instinct, but then paused as if knowing better. Gunter, who had sat at the table, steepled his fingers under his chin and turned his head subtly in the direction of the voice. The bookkeeper's underlings quickly shuffled off into the shadows, abandoning their antics with the coins at the other table. The bookkeeper himself stopped, and set aside his quill, before nervously adjusting his spectacles. He then handed a book to one of his helpers and ushered him away. The helper jumped to the ground and scampered across the jetty with it.

"This Dreadful child is consequential to our task," the voice continued. "And it is quite dangerous in these caves. It would be unfortunate if he were to fall into the water by accident."

One of the jetty's planks gave a creak where nothing touched it, seconds before the monkey passed. Then, without warning, the creature went caroming over the side into the water before it could offer up a startled cry.

Lamplight glittered off shiny scales that flashed like gemstones under the water. At least a dozen of them came, fluted fins tickling the surface before shooting forward. The monkey grabbed on to one of the piles crusting with salt, his fingers scratching at it as he tried to pull up, but the glimmers in the water latched on to him and tugged him back under. There wasn't a scream, only bubbles and spume that turned crimson.

"Who are you?" James challenged.

"Name's Wolf," Formandible spoke, now standing beside him.

And he calls my uncle Rat. Why? Is that his rank? James wondered. It sounded like a lower rank. But of what? And was Wolf the one in control? Seeing as he was invisible, James felt there was some sort of difference in the power between them. He felt the hairs rise on his forearm. A cold front seemed to trickle through him. Suddenly, he knew the invisible man had something to do with his father.

Cowl?

No, he's not Cowl. He's something else. When his grandfather had told him about Cowl that night in the woods, he felt that the man was at the center of a web of dark conspiracies. *He's not a Wolf rank, unless Wolf is the highest of ranks. But perhaps this is Cowl's collaborator.*

By now, the presence had reached the spit of land, stepping on planks that led through the mud. James could see the planks bending where no foot had been set.

"Captain Formandible," the disembodied voice said. It was deep, slightly nasal, and bristling with coolness. "Are you ready to depart?"

"I am," the ogre growled uneasily.

Planks creaked; the presence drew closer to the table. "Then return to your ship and prepare for departure."

"Yes," Formandible obeyed.

As he and Gunter left, the phantom voice changed direction, coming toward Rat. Only an occasional plank groaned beneath the weight of the hidden being. "Do we have it, *Rat*?"

Rat reached into his pocket and pulled out the stone.

A creak told James the invisible man had stepped toward him. A moment later, the stone lifted into the air and vanished. "Good. He shall be pleased, *Rat*. He shall be very pleased. And he shall remember your service."

James turned toward the disembodied voice. "Who are you?" he asked again.

A chuckle floated close to his ear—closer than he expected—and he jumped, his heart pounding. He was certain he would have heard the footfalls so close to him, but he hadn't.

"He's like his father," the voice fleered, turning toward Rat. A gloved hand grabbed James by the jaw. "The eyes in particular."

James felt like a caged animal being appraised by a cattleman. He tried to pull free, but the hand held him fast.

"*Fire*," the voice continued to drawl. "Your father's eyes possessed that distinct *quality*. That is good. Fire is useful."

He knew Wolf was referring to the stories he'd heard of his father who'd burned cities with the stone Vulcana. An unsettling feeling grew in his stomach.

The hand let go; the flesh in his jaw pulsed with pain. "As you've heard, my name is Wolf," the voice continued in his ear. "But who *I* am is unimportant."

"Why?" James asked. He felt cold.

"We want to know who *you* are."

James held his tongue.

"The question is," Wolf growled, "are you the Dark Lord's son?"

James looked around for the voice. It had already moved behind him. "What do you mean?"

"You know precisely what I mean. Your father would have made an invaluable asset to the right people. During the war, he was more of a lone wolf. When he came to blows with the Pirate Wizard, he became more of a freelancer, which was unfortunate. He could have been so much *more*."

"You're trying to recruit me."

"I have a client."

"What client?" Cat asked.

"Who do you work for?" Igvard asked the air. "The Dark Cloth?"

"James." The voice was focusing on him now, ignoring the others. "You will become powerful...like your father."

"You mean the Dark Lord?" James broke in. "I'm going to hazard a guess. You're working for this Cowl person, I take it. That's your client. Not sure if you know this, but he tried to control my father some eleven years ago." James sat forward in his chair. "But he failed. So, since your client"—James made air quotes—"couldn't control my father, he wants to control *me*. He hopes I'll take my father's place as the Dark Lord so he can manipulate me for—what—the next great war he's drumming up?" James gave a short, abrupt laugh. "Come on, I'm not *that* naive."

The voice was silent.

Everyone was silent.

All James could hear was the trickle of water and the soft scuffle of monkeys in their activities. "So," James said, looking around for the voice, "apparently, I'm right."

"Unfortunately," the voice said, having floated around to his left now, "my client is not very *patient*."

The way Wolf said "patient" made the blood drain from James's feet. But James had no intention of joining Wolf in whatever it was he and his uncle Oskar were involved in.

But what if I refuse? Then what? They wouldn't kill me. I'm the son of Jack. Jack Dreadful.

Still, nothing in Wolf's voice implied his decision would be taken lightly.

Just then, Rat stepped forward. "James," he said, "you must join us."

James looked at Rat, and suddenly he was filled with rage. "My mother trusted you," he said, his voice thick with disgust. "How *dare* you try to recruit me?"

"Hate me all you want, James. But you *must*. You have no choice now. You should have stayed in the Faugs." He turned to look for the voice. "Listen, he was not part of the—"

"He was," the voice said, still near James. "He always was, *Rat*. That was why I countermanded your order to Gunter when I learned they'd come here. You tried to keep him away. And I daresay, our client will *not* be pleased you tried to deceive him."

"He is not what we've come for."

"Nevertheless, he's an irreplaceable asset, Rat."

"I'm not an asset, Wolf," James snarled. "And I don't want any part in your little *cult*. Rat might have been stupid enough to join, but you won't take me. Just as you didn't take my father."

Wolf laughed. It was a short, wheezy thing caught in his throat, like something dying. "Your resolve is admirable, child. But you're mistaken by something. You're an irreplaceable asset to us only if you're on our side, but a threat if you're not. My client has given me agency in deciding your fate, should the latter be the case."

"Wolf," Rat said, stepping toward James protectively. "He's only a child. There is plenty of time for him to change his mind—for him to be persuaded to—"

But the anger was too much for James to bear. "I *won't*."

Rat turned around and grabbed him by the arm. "You will do as you're told, boy!"

"Let go of me now!" James growled.

"Let go of him!" Cat shouted.

"You heard him, Rat," Wolf said coldly. "He's made up his mind. And you had your chance, Rat. Now, our client doesn't think you've had your heart in it. He observed that your allegiance was faltering." The voice floated away like a ghost. "I'll be fair now. I shall instead confer with our client before taking matters into my own hands."

James didn't know what he meant by this, but he felt the warmth departing from him all at once, making his toes cold. Was he going to speak with Cowl?

He didn't think Wolf was anywhere near him, but suddenly a swirl of fragranced, teal smoke whispered across the table, and a second later, a disembodied, gloved hand materialized out of it and placed something on the table. Then, just as quickly as it'd appeared, it slipped back into the strange smoke that seemed to make him invisible, and the smoke itself melted into the air, as though it'd never been.

James stopped looking and listened for the footsteps. There were none, not even prints in the mud, or on the planks near his feet. He turned his attention now to the object the hand had deposited on the table. It was a coin that looked like an old, corroding denarius, but it had something that looked like the Eye of Ra engraved on it. Something was peculiar about the eye, however. Even as he stared more closely at it, he saw the dirty copper imprint of the eye ripple with eerie movement, and then it *turned* to look in the direction of Rat. He scooted his chair back in fright of the accursed thing, and then saw a strange carnelian light pulse in the small, engraved iris. It looked horribly wrong—that greasy verdigris contrasting with the sickly blood light.

Rat, who'd stepped forward, raising his hand, stopped suddenly, and then stumbled forward, his hand jumping to the back of his neck in a reflex of pain.

"He is not of any use," a cold voice drawled, coming from the coin. As the tone emanated from the copper, a metallic noise resonated across the table; James saw that the thing was vibrating. "You had your chance, *Rat*."

"No!" Rat had stumbled to one knee, as though an unseen power had forced him down, but his hands were shaking. One hand still gripped the back of his neck. When it came away, James gasped. The skin there blistered, and a painful-looking imprint of the eye glowed that same sickly red on it as though the flesh were translucent.

"He says you are weak, *Rat*," the disembodied voice of Wolf said. "Now, you must prove your worth. Ever he watches. Ever he hears."

"Show yourself!" James shouted at the voice.

Almost as though on cue, he felt something thud on the table, and he looked at a small prick in the wood, which glimmered with an orange spark, slowly turning the area around it into orange webs of fire and blackened charcoal. The smell of burning wood prickled his nostrils, along with hot steel, and smoke had begun to spiral into the air. Heat brushed his nostrils and cheeks. Slowly, the magic smoke unwrapped, and before his eyes was a steel dagger, entwined wyverns engraved in its blade. The blade was also laced in flickering fire that did not seem to touch it; it had not turned orange hot. Then a dragonscale-design hilt emerged from the smoke, with polished mother-of-pearl.

"Dispose of the boy, *Rat*."

James looked around for the voice, pulling on the cuff around his wrist.

Rat remained kneeling, the imprint of the eye fading, but the blisters remaining. The red light on the coin vanished, leaving a soft curl of teal smoke.

Rat lifted his head, then grasped the edge of the table.

James looked around, his heart pounding. Several of Wolf's elite monkeys had gathered around the table and had begun to load their crossbows out of precaution.

"If you do not, he will die anyway, *Rat*," the voice drawled, circling the table, "and then *you* will die—*horribly*. Jack's son can only impede—"

"He can be turned," Rat insisted, standing up. "He can—"

"No," James said defiantly. "I know my father would have rather died than serve...your master."

Rat looked around. "Wolf—"

"The dagger, *Rat*," Wolf sneered cutting him off.

"But you know I cannot. I cannot because he is my—"

"He asks this of you *because* of who you are, *Rat*. Once you join, you have no identity. You are remade. Remolded. *Reborn*. Only by doing this can you truly become who we are. Do this, and you will no longer be a Rat in our ranks."

Rat grabbed the hilt of the knife and pulled it free. A web of orange embers had spread across the tabletop by now; smoke filled the air.

James looked at Rat, his silhouette almost vanishing through the cloud. The ghostly fire still clung to the blade, almost translucent. A plank creaked behind Rat, whose head turned subtly, as though he was noting the sound. His fingers tightened around the hilt.

Wolf is not standing behind him, though, James thought. *He must know that. Wolf can throw his sounds. If he tries to kill him, he will fail. I hope he knows this. Please know this. My life is depending on it!*

But James never found out what Rat's plan was, because, at that moment, someone stepped out from behind the crates holding a bottle of whiskey.

"Oi—what's goin' on here? Stealin' our seats? Just went off to take a leak. That was yesterday, mind you. But it's a big place here—privy's a mile away. Anyway, we're back, and just wanted to apologize to whoever runs this place. See, we sort of found this, um...*well*."

20
THE DARK LORD'S SON'S DECISION

Slouching against the cellarette was Digfred. Moffat stood beside him holding a pewter plate with a few biscuits and fish, his rib cage covered in crumbs and bits of the meat he'd chewed up. Hadwin stood just behind him, a fishing rod thrown over one shoulder. Digfred took a long draught of the whiskey and let the drink splash through his jaw and down through his rib cage to the planks under his feet.

Everything had stopped. Rat stood looking at the strange scene before them, unable to find a proper response to it, and there was no sound from Wolf at all.

"So, Hadwin here opens the well up and looks down and says, 'Oi, it's like lookin' at a giant arsehole with teeth, mate, have a look!' And then 'Achoo!' He sneezes and bangs his skull on that kettle hangin' over it—knocks it over." He took another swig in the pregnant silence, oblivious to everything. More whiskey splashed through his rib cage. "So, again—apologies, mates. Didn't mean to be such poor tenants. Anyway, I think the monster's uh—*sick* now. It's all Hadwin's fault, blame *him*."

For the time, the only sound was the whiskey splattering on the planks. Then James heard a whisper, and from thin air, bluish smoke materialized, a gloved hand, and outstretched fingers. Following that, a hiss and a yellowish substance burst through the air, fast as a jet of water, and struck

Digfred. The substance flowed with a strange, electric-glowing vapor, and clung to Digfred's bones, then erupted like a bubble, splattering the two others beside him.

Rat leaped away from them as smoke hissed from their bones, and Digfred gave a cry and stumbled backward. Droplets of the stuff flew through the air, some landing on the table, and James watched it eat into the wood, leaving bubbles of phlegm-colored foam there.

The skeletons tumbled into a pile, their bones smoldering.

"My bones," Hadwin cried out in pain. "They're disintegratin'!"

"Just when I'd found my clavicle!" Moffat groaned. "Oh the horror! The horror!"

Wolf's gloved hand vanished into thin air again, but the planks creaked. The next instant, the bookkeeper was jerked off his chair, and James heard the voice shout, "Why have you let those abominations wander about? Imagine if *this* had thwarted our plans?"

The bookkeeper kicked defenselessly in the air, clutching at his throat. Then he dropped to the ground, before a sudden force sent him flying into the water.

Even as the murderous fish pulled the creature below the surface, turning the water crimson, a growl echoed from deep within the lair. It sounded like the belly of the mountain had come to life.

"You've been granted a reprieve, *Rat*," came Wolf's icy voice. "But our client will not look kindly on your miscarriage of resolve. You shall remain a Rat." One of the planks creaked near the jetty. "Perhaps you shall die a Rat, too."

Rat moved toward the table raising his hand, but suddenly it stopped in the air. It appeared something had grabbed his wrist.

"*Leave* them."

"No," Rat protested.

"You will," Wolf sneered. "In ten minutes, this lair will be underwater." When he said this, his elite monkeys lowered their crossbows and scrambled toward the jetty.

"You should have chosen your allies more wisely," Wolf said, his voice aimed at James. "If you drown, you'll have cheated a far worse death than the one that plagues the dark waters of Sarvelok."

"Wait," Igvard cried, standing. "We can be of use. Tell him, Oskar!"

The ground suddenly trembled beneath their feet. Even the pewter plate on the table had begun to rattle.

Cat started, "No, you can't leave—" But he was cut off by a growl that thundered through the mountain like a Titan's fury. He clapped his hands over his ears as the lair shook beneath their feet.

This sent the monkeys into a turmoil, and they leaped up crates, or sprang for ladders.

"James!" Rat cried, turning toward the table. "You are the son of Jack. Do what he would do!"

James glowered at the man. *Do what Jack would do? What the hell does that* mean?

But Wolf grabbed Rat by the throat. "Move, *Rat*!"

Sarvelok's horn blasted twice, resounding across the lair. Hundreds of monkeys were scrambling to their stations; others rushed for piles of loot, hoping to salvage what they could.

The floodgates, James thought. *They have to raise them all in time, or this place floods!* But he wasn't sure if they could do it in time. Wolf certainly didn't think they could. He turned to Cat. "*Skybester*'s our only chance of getting out of here," he said. "We have to be on that ship when she leaves!"

"That's what I was thinkin'," Cat said, looking around for something. His eyes found the yellowish stain on the table, having eaten its way through the wood.

James saw it, too, and moved his manacle's chain into the foam. It didn't look like enough. It probably wasn't, but they had to try.

The ground beneath them shook again. This time it felt like the whole island was moving.

Do what Jack would do, his uncle had said. James looked up at Rat hurrying across the jetty, followed by a dozen monkeys carrying coffers over their heads. *What would Jack do?*

"It's not working," Igvard said, seeing what James was doing. "Chain's too thick."

James looked at him. "What did he mean 'Do what Jack would do'?" he cried.

Igvard looked at him with uncertainty. "You know what he means, James. But you said you wouldn't."

The plate rattled louder on the table. Now, a warm wind rushed through the cavern, bringing a horribly rotten stench with it.

Then it came.

They looked out across the cavern. A swarm of monkeys had scrambled up the piles of plunder on the islets farther away as a wave caromed through, foam glistening at its crest. It was the first wave, knocking loot into the water and pushing it toward them. When the wave reached land, it had mostly diminished, but struck the *Royal Bitch* with a clap anyway, and flowed around her, the sudsy water looking slightly yellowish. It glided past, engulfing their feet. Tiny bits of organic scum floated in it, coating their shoes in a thin film.

"No," James said. "There's still Quizlow." He remembered seeing him before his uncle had showed up. But now Quizlow was nowhere to be seen. And even if he did come, what could he do? Still, he looked desperately for a mouse with a gnome. If they could get out of their irons, they could get aboard the *Royal Bitch*. Perhaps the water would push them out. *No*, he thought, *if they don't get the floodgates open, we'll just drown on the ship!*

Another wave swept through, this one larger than the last. It came crashing across the spit and washed past their feet over their ankles.

Cat leaped up on the table, then grabbed James's wrist. "Hey," he cried. "You gotta do it, James! You gotta call *him*!"

The water flooded around the towers of crates. Some of them teetered, like trees in a storm. Boxes tumbled, crashing into the water. Monkeys waded past, arms holding coffers. They shrieked at each other, some strapping knapsacks to their backs and scrambling for the ladders.

"Get up!" Igvard commanded. "We're gonna lift the table!"

James didn't know what that would do, but he complied, and all three of them stood, then lifted the table and walked it across the planks away from the oncoming water. James looked to see Rat climbing the rope ladders. *The coward!* he thought. Anger surged through his veins. *I should call him. And I'd tell him to cut off that coward's head! I really should!*

More water came surging into the cavern. But by now they could hear some of the floodgates opening.

"That'll buy us some time," Igvard said. "I hope!"

"But where's Quizlow?" James shouted as he watched a troop of monkeys heading for the *Royal Bitch*. Undoubtedly, he was lost in all the confusion.

Another groan came through the tunnels in the walls along with a hefty roar of seawater. It pushed the shrieking monkeys out and flooded into the shipyard cavern. Piles of chests, crates, boxes, and chairs began to tumble over. Water frothed, splashing up over the planks.

They dropped the table and leaped on top just as the wave struck. Barrels rained down around them. One—an empty one—struck James, knocking him into the water. His wrist screamed in protest, pulling sharply on the cuff. Coming up out of the sudsy film, he looked around. A monkey had been washed into the water, squealing, holding on to another empty barrel. Seconds later, he was yanked under.

"The skinners are coming up here in the water," Igvard observed. "Get up on this table, quickly!"

James clambered back up onto the table and watched, his heart pounding, as the water washed backward past them, bringing with it squirming silver fish with beady, slag-black eyes and sharp cruel fangs.

"Hell, I'm not gonna die like this!" Cat screamed in James's ear. *"Call him—now!"*

A pile of crates listed, pulling taut on a clothesline attached to a dresser. The dresser, balanced precariously on the top, fell, tumbling down the pile, splashing in the water. More coffers fell, spilling open. Corroded coins, old goblets, and ingots of iron and steel fell in cascades around them, bouncing on the planks streaming with water and foam.

The caverns trembled again. A winding, eructation echoed throughout the lair filled with a clammy stench.

A beautiful coffer struck the table, opening and bursting with shiny gold yammies that bounced off the tabletop and went rolling off, dancing through the spume.

Now, the lantern hanging on the polearm crashed to a plank shattering, its flame guttering in the dark. And as it was flickering out, James saw a mouse scrambling over the wet planks, trying to avoid the water. On its back was—

"Quizlow!" James screamed.

The mouse dashed toward them, and James jumped down from the table and scooped up the mouse. "Quizlow," he shouted, "get us out of here!"

The wet mouse dropped on the ground and scurried away, and he was left holding the small wet man.

"Don't be ridiculous," Quizlow shouted. "I don't have the *key*!"

"What?" James roared.

But it would have been impossible to get the key. Formandible had it, and he had left. Where would he find another?

Igvard was desperately trying to pull the iron pad eye from the table now. "Call him, James," he shouted. "It's the only way out!"

"I'm NOT dying like this!" Cat screamed.

"But I'll owe him! I'll owe him something I can't give!"

"You won't have to worry about that, James!" Cat shouted back. "If you call him, we'll get to the Tomb of Forgotten Secrets. And then—then—*the Lady of the Tomb*! She'll—"

But Cat didn't need to finish. He knew what Sigurd had said. *Miasharun protected Jack... He pledged his soul to her. And his soul she took.*

He was protected from Stray.

But that's how my father got roped into this. He became her pawn. Now I will become her pawn.

"Quizlow!" James cried as darkness closed in around them. "I—"

"You came here because you wanted your father's weapon," Quizlow shouted. "So, you're already a pawn of hers, James. You were a pawn the moment you decided to come here!"

Then a pawn I'll be.

In the final flickers of light from the lamp, James turned away from him. Then, taking a deep breath and clenching his fists, he turned toward the darkness.

"Rekenhowler!"

21

THUNDER, SMOKE, & FIRE

He waited.

Nothing.

Water surged raw from the tunnels, plunging over the strip of land, washing over the cassoni and crates. Frothed around barrels, hissing, warm. Most of the monkeys had grabbed on to the ladders and were climbing up.

"Rekenhowler!"

The heated breath from the sea monster's mouth whipped through the lair, blowing out the remaining lanterns. Mist shot up like geysers from the rushing water.

Still nothing.

Louder, James thought, placing Quizlow on his shoulder. He cupped a hand over his mouth. *"REKENHOWLER!"*

They were knee-deep in foaming sea.

"Pull!" his uncle clamored over the crashing swells.

Hands towing on their binding chains, the three of them managed to clamber over tumbled crates and up onto the cellarette that had fallen behind them, hauling the table along.

"REKENHOWLER!" James shouted again. His foot slipped; foamy water exploded on all sides of him as he tried to keep his balance. Icy fingers

221

of terror seized him, eroding at his resolve like sulfuric acid. He tried to marshal his thoughts, but he was losing control. *My voice can't carry that far! We're too far from the ship!*

Seeing how fast the water was coming in, he knew the shipyard would soon overflow and they wouldn't be able to stay out of the water for long.

Another tower of crates had tumbled over, and Igvard climbed up on them. But one of them toppled, and Cat slipped. The fall yanked on James, and he fell backward pulling his uncle. All three of them fell, plunging into the warm swirling water. Quizlow, who'd been holding on to his ear, lost his grip and went hurtling off his shoulder into the whirling oblivion. Crates toppled over, crashing down around them. Something hit James on the head. Blinded from pain for an instant, he could do nothing but suck water into his lungs.

We're dead.

And then he heard a sound like the walls were collapsing above him.

Or exploding.

The mountain had begun to chortle. Great spells of laughter rolled from its abyss. Next, a sound like a meteor barreling through the mountain.

And then...

Fire.

He was marvelous at fire. It was an art. Like the sea pouring into the cavern, great gusts swept through the dark, igniting on piles of damp algae-covered chests. Igniting waterlogged books, and old cassoni. Chairs, wardrobes, and cabinets. It lit the water, rolling, gorgeous balls that licked up the walls, entwined around posts, and snaked along the planks. Glittering sparks spread through the air—small galaxies, twisting, flitting, and swirling. A million moths, their wings ablaze.

Then the conflagrant ship split the walls of the cavern, sending blocks of stone racing like shrapnel, some with tiny comet tails of wrinkly smoke in their wake. The *Persephone*'s hull sparkled, as though gemstones of fire were embedded in her, and her torched sails and bronze-and-orange-bespeckled masts sent gales of sparks streaming through the cavern. The hull crashed into the water, ploughing through towers of crates and barrels, moldering hutches, cupboards and cabinets. Her bowsprit lanced through lines of clothes strung up over chairs teetering on boxes, snagging jerkins and gowns, as her prow sideswiped stacks of coffers, sending coins shattering through the air. Steam burst from water that hissed and boiled with angry foam.

James pulled himself up onto a barrel, the cuff cutting into his wrist painfully, watching as the vessel smashed through the debris, setting them on fire. The air was filling with smoke, the glistening rubies dancing over the torrent. As James fought his way out of the water, now turning hot, he pulled the table with him, his uncle and Cat helping.

Slag-black boots, flecks of embers captured in the thick leather, landed in the water. James lifted his drenched face toward the burning figure. Whippoorwills of light throbbed in his vision; where Stray stood, steam hissed up from under his soles—the water had burst into a wild boil.

The smoking silhouette strode forward, then reached down and grabbed James by the back of his collar and lifted him from the water.

"Hoist the table 'n' bring her 'long," the apparition growled to Cat and Igvard, and, still clutching James, dragged him toward the *Persephone*, where a ring of fire had encircled her. The water was shallow here, but bubbling. Yet, as before, the heat did not burn their feet.

"Young Dreadful," Stray's sepulchral voice crooned as he let go of James and stood beside the boat.

James looked up to see the burnt face of the man from his nightmares— and the one organic eyeball sitting in his face like a red bioluminescent jellyfish in a tar pit.

"Rekenhowler," he said, coughing, and using a palm to get the water out of his eyes. He started forward, but his other hand was still caught on the manacle.

"Y'know," the demon growled, "I was beginnin' to think yeh wasn't gonna. Then yeh did." He chuckled and blew a stream of smoke from his nostrils. "But yeh were like, '*Rek-en-howler*,'" Stray said in a mocking little voice. "Like a bloody pocket mouse." He was grinning and scratching at the burnt flesh and coagulated blood on his chin. "Ever heard a bloody pocket mouse talk? It's like this—" And he stuck out his two blackened front teeth and a burnt tongue, and made a little peep, puckering his desiccated lips. "Pip pip." He thundered laughter. "That's 'ow yeh said me na-ha-ha-hame, Dreadful. Like a li'l *pocket mouse*." He gave James a shove in the shoulder, and snorted, before spitting in the water. A smoking chair grew out of it. Then he sat. He pulled the table toward him and leaned back against the *Persephone*'s hull, propping his feet on the top. He yawned, ignoring the water pushing barrels and crates out into the cavern as it gushed around the boat.

"What are you doing?" James cried.

"'F yer gon call me, James Dreadful, *call me*. Call me like a Dark Lord. Not a bloody pocket mouse."

James looked toward the rope ladders. By now Rat had vanished through the *Skybester*'s hatch, and the Scathra monkeys were lining up to get inside. "They're—they're—"

"Gettin' away?" finished Stray. "Oi"—and he turned to one of his scorched deckhands who'd come down the gangway—"'e calls me at the bloody twelfth hour and tells me they're gettin' away. In't he just like that bleedin' clotter—'is old man?" He returned to the matter.

"Say it."

James narrowed his eyes and dug his nails into his palms. Then, closing his eyes, he breathed out of his nostrils. He thought of Oskar—how he hated him and felt his blood boil with hate.

And fire.

Then his eyes flew open. *"Rekenhowler."*

"Well, tickle my goolies, that sounds like the bloody Dark Lord." His barbed wire smile sliced through his cheeks. "And it'll bloody do.

"Now, yeh fetcher, yeh gotta sign the contract." His head swiveled over his shoulder. "Oi, yeh shellback, gimme 'at 'air." He snapped his fingers, and a scorched boatswain stepped toward him, holding the human skin parchment. "Yeh still gotta put down yer bloody ink, mate."

"Stray, we don't have time—"

"Don't lecture me 'bout time, lass. Took yer bloody time callin' me. 'Um 'a take me bloody time, y'swine. 'N' I've got Satan's clot this time. Squeezed it into an inkpot meself this bleedin' morn."

He'd set a smoldering inkpot on the table with a quill. "Now, yeh li'l fetcher, put'cher ink down." He pointed to the bottom of the scroll where he'd unraveled it.

"Y-you'll save us?" James stammered as he took the quill in his fingers, his one wrist still cuffed to the table.

"You're not tryin' to trick us?" Cat cried.

"Jus' sign the damn contract, yeh clotter," Stray barked, flicking up his burnt eyelid.

James looked down at the parchment. He had no choice. It was soaked through, but the ink remained un-besmirched, and the quill, when he touched it to the parchment, did not smudge in the water.

He gritted his teeth and scratched out his signature as best he could on the rugged tabletop.

Stray leaned forward to look at the signature, blowing a puff of smoke on the parchment. The water cleared with the magic of his smoke, and he held a hand up, which lit up like a torch, shining light on it. "That'll do, Dreadful. You now owe me the soul of one bloody *Galajitar*." And he leaned back in his chair and gave a horrendous growl, like a beast, and there was a clap of thunder that was nearly drowned out by the raging sea around them.

"Well?" James cried, slamming his cuffed fist on the table. "What are you waiting for? Get Wolf! Get that traitor Oskar! Save us, goddammit!"

Stray chuckled and leaned back farther in his chair until it balanced on two legs. He howled and blew a perfect halo of smoke into the air above his head. Then he grabbed James by the collar and pulled him up to his face. That one organic eyeball glowered at him, the burnt lid looking like the flake of the charred end of a piece of toast. "Le's get somethin' straight, fool." He sat forward, dropping an elbow on the parchment. Boots came down in the water. Ash dropped from his chin and lit the contract on fire. As it burned up and floated away in tiny scraps, he twisted his cheeks in a lurid grin. "We may have a contract, boy, signed by the very stinkin' quill yer father plucked his goddamn *nose* with. But here's what yeh gotta know." And he pulled James's face until his slag-colored nostrils, hardened like a crispy cinder, poked his cheek. *"I ain'tcher bitch."*

Stray threw his head back and laughed. Blood rolled out of his mouth, down his cheeks, and a tongue of fire sprouted from it and blossomed like a bursting rose with golden angel wings.

At once, the sailors on his ship sprang over the gunwale, capes of flaming sparks dancing wildly in the dark, and landed on the ground in volleys of water and steam. Swords sang from sheaths. Morning star flails came out, battle-axes, and crossbows. They were nightmarish creations, like fiery scarecrows come to life. Scorched flesh burst, hissed, and bubbled under scarlet-hot chain mail and surcoats that had melted into skin. Scraps of skin clung to burnt fabric that floated off their bodies in curls of smoke. Their faces smoldered with leaves of fire springing from cheeks and foreheads, licking off charred ears.

By now, most of the monkeys had scrambled up the rope ladders. But Stray's champions moved fast, sprinting through the bursting whitecaps, their kneecaps turning the wild rapids into steam, grabbed on to the ropes, and climbed, hand over burnt-black hand.

Clang!

James's eyes bulged. Stray had sliced the manacles binding the three of them to the table.

They were free.

Stray rose to his feet, and growled, "Come along, pocket mouse." He started toward the rope ladder.

His fighters had reached some of the ships dangling from chains.

The monkeys had been tying large sacks of loot to ropes and lifting them up to the *Skybester*, but when they looked down, they saw the melted, eyeless nightmares clambering the lines. Shrieking, they threw their loot down and scrambled onto ropes.

Stray raised his hand and aimed a finger at the ladder across the jetty, before turning to James and grinning. "Give love teh yer father for me, mate. Fire is me art. And he made it so." Fire jumped from his hand in an arc onto the rope ladder, then raced up. Flecks of his flame sprang off onto the dangling boats, torching them, and then swept along their hulls, turning the luminous mushrooms into bits of crumbling slag. Sails glowed neon, sending luminous butterflies through the air, and they rained down on them like magnolia petals in spring. Monkeys caught fire, screamed, and fell, kicking through the air.

The old ships groaned, split. Boards and masts fell tumbling, flipping through the air, raining around them. A combusted sailcloth flapped in the dark like a raging phoenix, swirling down, smoke soughing behind it.

James took refuge on the *Persephone*, his uncle and Cat hot on his heels. "Where's Quizlow?" James shouted as Stray stood watching with a bloodlust in his one organic eye.

"Here!" A confused and frightened Hatset scurried across the burning planks toward them, Quizlow astride him. "Tell Stray we must leave; the shipyard's crumbling!"

Stray's marauders had caught up to the monkeys lined up on the ladder trying to enter the *Skybester*'s open trapdoor. They squawked and shrieked and threw their heavy sacks at them. But before the first of the demons could reach the top, the rope was cut from inside the *Skybester*. The row of monkeys screamed and fell—down, down, down they went into boiling seawater along with Stray's men.

"Hahahahahahahaha!" howled Stray as he waded through the water, his cloak of ghostly fire hissing in the breakers. He reached down in the water and snatched up one of the squirming monkeys. "Look at me face, yeh clotter. Look at it!" he growled.

And the monkey erupted into fire.

When Stray returned to the boat, he tossed something at James. "Now don't say I never done nothin' fer yeh, *pocket mouse*," he drawled.

James caught it and opened his hand. It was Orbis—the amulet the monkeys had taken from his uncle when they first arrived. He slipped it around his neck absently and looked at him. "They're getting away! We have to get after them!"

Stray's marauders had not yet returned to the ship before the *Persephone* had set sail again, her conflagrant sails billowing outward, as though a strong gust had come through the tunnels. The shipyard shook; the invading sea splashed up on all sides.

"Around we go!" Stray cried.

James and Cat stumbled across the deck and grabbed the gunwale. The ship swung around.

Behind, one of the boats dangling from the chains fell, crackling with wings of fire. It split apart in midair, bursting into splinters and boards. The transom left a scythe of smoke and flurries of sparks trailing in its wake. Then the halves crashed into the tumultuous water of the cavern, creating a massive swell that belted the *Persephone*'s hull, sending them all sprawling on the deck.

Out of the shipyard, the *Persephone* sailed, scraping the walls. James found himself rolling past a human torch who'd lunged over the gunwale, before springing for the ratlines, blade clenched tightly in orange-glowing teeth, heels leaving rosebuds of flame on the rope.

Water shattered against the hull as they were forced along, the blazing sails lighting up the tunnels like clusters of hellish ghosts.

"Hold on!" Stray growled.

The ship was close to the ceiling, the water was so high. The mast scraped it, clattering on one of the murder-holes. A flaming crow's nest fell, smashing to the deck with a bursting blizzard of sparks, which skated through the water, washing from larboard to starboard.

James gained his feet and looked ahead. On a tumultuous wave, the *Persephone* was bowling toward the opened main door where sunlight was streaming into the canal. The ride was so violent, James wrapped his fingers in the deadeyes' lanyards and hung on as she rose and fell.

The gunwale pitched at him; the deck groaned and spat flames and gushed salt water. Her bulwark scraped the walls, and then they struck the roof of the mouth and the mast of the mainsail snapped and fell backward, then was ripped clean off. Then, down they went, crashing out of the canal in a burst of spumy water.

"WHOOOOOOEEEEEEEE!" screamed Stray.

They rushed along through the gorge, and the mad demon was laughing. "Goddamn, what a ride! Haven't skinned me arse like that since yer damn old man!"

James held on tightly to the gunwale long after the ride had calmed. He felt his very bones had been jarred and wrecked, his whole body bruised. Cat was lying flat on his back, gasping, and Igvard still had his fingers gripping the backstay sheet, looking sick.

At last, James let go and fell to his knees. The world was spinning around him, and he thought he might vomit. Water blurred his eyes. His ears rang. He wasn't even sure he was alive.

Then he got up and stumbled toward Stray. "Where—where are they?" he demanded. "Where's my uncle and—"

"Look astern, mate," Stray growled, nudging his head in that direction.

James turned and stood with his mouth gaping. The beautiful *Skybester* had risen over the island from the smoldering mountain. Beneath her, another large ship dangled from hawsers.

The *Trollbasher*.

"How are you gonna—"

"Thar ain't no gettin' that ship, mate," Stray growled. "Ef yeh called me sooner, I'd've stormed the island long ago, and I'd've killed this Wolf o' yers. But yeh called me too bloody *late*, kid."

"But that was the deal," Igvard said, making his way midship, fighting vertigo. "The deal was—"

"That I save yeh from a watery grave," Stray growled with a snort, "and defeat yer enemies within me powers. However, I can't act outside of me capabilities. And a demon can't tarry long in the land of the livin'. I got burnin' lakes teh sail and burnt daisies teh pluck. Las' I remember, I was winnin' a game with ole Deleculio, who's a flesher. 'E's gonna owe me a pound o' flesh." He strolled along the deck, his cloak of ghostly fire turning into creases of smoke as he looked at the splintered stump where the mainmast once was, now bits of smoldering wood.

The fires burning on the deck were much smaller now, and so were the flames burning on his sailors.

"That was not the deal!" Quizlow said, riding up to him on Hatset along the gunwale.

Stray gave a puff of smoke and snorted. "I changed the deal, scamp. Not me fault he didn't read it before signin'. Next time don't wait till the skinners are humpin' yer toes to sign a deal with the devil.

"Now listen here. Yeh called me and I came, and yer skins are yer own now. I held up me end of the contract. Now yeh'll deliver the Galajitar wizard to me—all five-hundred and ninety-eight leaves of that book. I'll come three times." He held up three fingers. "Three bloody times, mate." He looked at James. "And ef yeh don' have it by the third." He laughed. "Well, I need a bloody swabber fer me deck. It'll be fun teh see what a century of burnin' can do teh yer pre'y li'l face—*pocket mouse*."

By now, the fires on the *Persephone* were all but extinguished, and only ash drifted heavily in the air.

"Aren't you even gonna sail us to the Tomb of Secrets?" Cat cried.

"I ain'tcher skipper, mate," Stray growled. "Me time in the mortal world's up." And he tipped his cavalier's hat at them and his body turned into a cloud of smoke.

Around them his sailors gave sobs and cries of torment, and then they, too, dissolved into refuse that floated away on the wind.

The *Persephone* groaned, and then smoke wafted up from all around them, filling the air and their lungs, and making them cough. She moaned, the wood pulsing beneath their feet.

James grabbed on to the gunwale, shutting his eyes for a bit. Creaks and groans resounded everywhere, as the ship began to repair herself in the clouds. Squinting, he peered through one eye, then the other, seeing the torrents rolling off the taut sheets in the wind. And then he heard the wind belt against sailcloth with a roar and looked up to see a silhouette of the mainsail in rays of mercury sunlight penciling through the smoke.

But when the haze had all cleared, she was not new. She floated on the sea, her masts were all intact, the crow's nest was where it'd always been. But she still smelled of rot and mold, her sails still needed repairing, and the worms were still at the bilge. And now, only a thin layer of ash had settled on the deck to indicate that the Dog of Hell had once stood at her helm.

22

JAMES'S REVELATION

"So, now that you serve him, what are you going to do?" the gnome asked. His small, round face looked exhausted in the sunlight. He stood on the starboard's gunwale with Hatset, his matted hair sticking up in tiny spikes from the wetness. There were small puffs below eyes pink from tiredness. He'd spent many sleepless nights in the lair curled up with Hatset to keep warm, but what had truly kept Quizlow up was worrying, and his spiky hair showed it; a few strands of gray had grown into it as well as his eyebrows.

He was worried now more than ever.

"Dunno," James answered.

Quizlow looked at him and then gave a lengthy sigh. "I was thinking about what you'd said earlier."

Igvard was inspecting the sails, walking up and down midship, running his fingers over sheets and shrouds, wondering if they were completely there. Cat was leaning against the gunwale, both elbows on the wood, staring off at the open sea. He looked in shock still, with the adrenaline finally starting to leave his blood. His tunic was torn, showing the bruises and cuts he'd sustained.

James himself was sitting, arms folded around his knees in a small pool of water that kept washing from one side of the ship to the other. He no longer felt it on him; he was thoroughly drenched all the way through anyway. He was looking down at the fingernail that had broken off over a week ago, examining the hardened, strange pink flesh where the nail had been. Everything that had happened over the past week felt like an odd lucid dream, and yet his aching—and this torn nail—was evidence it hadn't been. He looked up at Quizlow now, silhouetted against the light of the sky, the wind buffeting the small wisps of hair sticking up as Hatset sniffed around him. "What'd you say earlier?"

"Before we entered Sarvelok, you said I'd brought you back too soon. That I'd given you your father's heirlooms and set you on this course."

James touched the amulet Orbis Stray had given back to him before they escaped Sarvelok's Maw, and then said, "Hell, I—"

"It wasn't fair," Quizlow cut in. "What I'd said before...about your grandfather."

"Whaddya mean?"

"When I said your grandfather should have given Wizizorkus the book that night—that he was the cause for us to return too soon. But what about myself? If I'd been more astute, I would not have heeded your mother's wishes. That was the only reason I gave you your father's heirlooms. I didn't look at the you—the you as a person. I didn't ask you if you wanted to return."

"What would his alternative have been?" Cat asked, though he continued to stare out at the water.

"I could have allowed the goblin to take your father's grimoire. He would not have come after you. You could have lived the rest of your days out in Urrd."

"Don't be ridiculous."

Quizlow looked at James, nonplussed. *"Huh?"*

James got up. "You think I wanted to live a safe life in Urrd? Going to ball games, colleges, and having a career in what?" He gestured at the sea flippantly. "Law?" He snorted. "Quizlow, coming here to this land? This was the best thing that ever happened to me. I wouldn't trade it for the position of a—a CEO of some tech company, or...some stockbroker on Wall Street...or anything. Now stop moping and feeling guilty about dragging me into this. My grandpa told me it'd be like this, and I'd be disappointed if it wasn't."

Cat smiled and then gave a hoot of laughter. "Y'know, Prince. You're not so bad for an Urrdling. Still a fetcher, though."

"Did someone say fetcher?" a voice said. The hatch door from belowdecks had opened up, and Digfred climbed out and stood yawning in the sunlight. "Oooooooh, the sun's tickling me funny bone," he said as Hadwin and Moffat came out behind him, chuckling about something.

"You're back?" Igvard said. He'd taken off his white argyle-patterned doublet, which was torn and stained yellow under the armpits. It was a shame they couldn't have swiped some new clothes when they were in Sarvelok. There were thousands of tunics, doublets, and jerkins they could have worn. His bare chest was flabby, his arms emaciated, and he had quite a few black-and-blue bruises on him—possibly where Formandible had roughed him up.

"Thought it'd be that simple to get rid of us?" Hadwin asked.

"Thought we told you," Moffat said. "Wherever the ship goes, we go."

"Oh dear," Digfred moaned, sitting on the deck, "all that violence has made me nauseous. I long for those good days when it made me all giddy inside to see someone decapitated, eviscerated—or both. Me poor eyeholes are sick right now. I think they're vomiting."

"And we're in *this* depressing place again," growled Moffat. "And the four-poster bed's gone—along with everything else. Terrible—especially that wardrobe that belonged to Penelope. Was wonderin' how long your uncle here would go wearin' that old rag before he'd consider a blouse. I was lookin' for a spell of entertainment while we drift along on the sea."

As it turned out, it was Quizlow who'd told the Boneheads about the well in the cave above the sea monster. And after he'd overheard the conversation with Wolf and Rat, he sent the Boneheads to help them. Digfred, however, had taken it upon himself to make their act of treachery *convincing.* He was of the mind that the three "clotters" could not have reacted authentically had they known the Boneheads were putting on a mummer's act. "I take my job seriously," Digfred genuinely said.

"But Quizlow could have only told you *after* Captain Formandible arrived," Cat pointed out. "So, you were putting on an act the whole time, right?"

"Uh—*surrrrrrre,*" Digfred replied.

~

Belowdecks, the cabins were still full of water that sloshed around as the *Persephone* sailed, so Igvard had the Boneheads go below with buckets and scoop the water out. It would be a long, tedious process, which they could have decided *not* to do, but Igvard wasn't particularly convinced that the Boneheads throwing a skull at the bottom of his cage was all an act. Digfred agreed that the whole "find them the coldest and rustiest cage," or throwing his hand at them, or having the monkeys piss in their drinking water ("What?" James, Cat, and Igvard cried at once) was part of Quizlow's plot, so they humbly (or at least as humbly as they could convincingly be) agreed to go belowdecks where there were still skinners and bucket out the water.

There was only one chair left and a barrel, which James and Cat sat on. The rest of the barrels were belowdecks, and Igvard was not going to risk going for it until the water level was lower to get one to sit on. Quizlow made blueberries for dinner as the sun came down, and the breeze flowing over the bulwark was cool. James hung his clothes over the gunwale with Cat's, shivering in the air. He wished he still had the bearskin, but he supposed it was floating somewhere in the sea now. He looked at Igvard, who'd sat down with them, then Quizlow, who sat on the gunwale near a sniffing Hatset. It was time to find out what was going on. "Who is Wolf?"

Quizlow sighed, then stared over James's head. "It's complicated. Author never elaborated on his theory about...*them.*"

"When you say *them*," started Cat, "you mean—"

"The Wozigod's dark branch: The Office of the Dark. That was what they were called many years ago." Quizlow focused on James now. "The official office today is called the Office of Unusual Affairs, and hunt down monsters and evil spirits. But that's not the *them* we're talking about."

"Then who's *them?*" James asked.

If there was ever a time Quizlow had a graver expression, James couldn't remember. "The Office of the Dark's purpose was to eliminate undesirable bloodlines from existence: Werewolves, vampires, witches, forgottens—blood that contaminated mankind," Quizlow began. "One of these bloodlines happened to be the ancestors of the now known Dreadfuls, which was why they fled to Morrfir and came to settle in the Islad province.

"Anyway, as the war with Grisledor was ending, the Office of the Dark was dissolved, its members purged."

"When you say purged—" Cat started.

"Killed," Igvard confirmed.

"The leadership in the Wozigod wanted to deny they had any involvement with the Office of the Dark. Much of the High Seas Syndicate's propaganda was that the Wozigod was corrupted at the very core and were killing off certain bloodlines—even seers—so that the whereabouts of certain weapons could remain hidden."

"But those in the Office of the Dark who escaped the purge later formed a new cult that was not under the Wozigod's supervision. And they were called—"

"Phantom," Igvard said. "But this is only just a myth."

"So Phantom is *them?*" Cat said.

"I'd hoped they were only ever just a myth," Quizlow said.

"Igvard seems to think so," James said. "But why? Why is it so hard to believe? I've seen a lot of things harder to believe than that in the past month."

"I've heard rumors," Igvard said, "that this cult had managed to infiltrate the Wozigod at high levels. That they even have contact with the Underworld. That they're poised to take over the entire realm of mortals. Y'know, it's a bit far-fetched."

"Tsk," James said dubiously.

"There's no proof that they exist," Quizlow said. "There are no living witnesses who've seen them. They leave behind no clues—nothing. That's quite a feat, even for a dark, all-powerful cult."

"Maybe because they're *invisible*," Cat pointed out.

"Or hiding in plain sight," James said. "If they've infiltrated the Wozigod. Do you think Wolf is from this cult?"

"Perhaps," Quizlow said. "Or he could belong to the Dark Cloth."

"What's that?" James asked.

"Mercenaries who use stealth magic called Slything," Cat said. "They're known mostly in the Morhun region but have been seen all over the world. Or *not* seen."

"The Office of the Dark allegedly used the Dark Cloth for their clandestine operations," Quizlow pointed out.

"Which would explain Phantom's continued use of them," Igvard said. "And why Wolf is a Slyther."

"You mean he was recruited from the Dark Cloth," James said.

"Maybe," Igvard replied.

"But this is speculation. For all we know, Wolf belongs to the Syndicate and Phantom really *is* just a myth."

"How would that be any less dangerous?" James asked.

"If Wolf belonged to the alleged Phantom," Quizlow said, "we'd be dealing with a former branch of the Wozigod with powers far more dangerous than we could possibly imagine. The Office of the Dark had a history of acquiring dark magic to study. If they ran off with many secrets and have taken over many positions inside the Wozigod, we could expect to face a most insidious adversary with deep resources."

"And they're trying to recruit me," James said.

"That was a most disturbing development," Quizlow agreed. "It seems apparent Oskar got mixed up in the cult and they were hoping he'd be able to turn you, James."

James felt a small chill slip along his spine like a ghostly finger. If that was true, then perhaps it was best he hadn't come home six months ago. Oskar would have tried to convince him to join Phantom. Oskar probably realized he wasn't returning and decided to kick off Plan B, which was enter the Tomb of Forgotten Secrets without him. "What do you think Phantom promised him?"

"Power," Igvard said absently.

James had to agree with that. If Oskar was anything like Arthur, who couldn't resist using magic in the land of Urrd, Oskar probably fell for the same temptation. Only here, he had a chance to become as great and powerful as his brother Jack. Of course, there was only one thing. He looked up at Igvard. "But Jack *wasn't* evil."

Quizlow looked at him strangely.

Even Igvard scratched at his beard, raising a curious eyebrow. "How so?"

"Sigurd said that Cowl had mind-slaved my father when he committed those atrocities," James continued. He took a deep breath. He found he was trying to avoid Quizlow's gaze when he spoke. He realized that he hadn't shared Sigurd's theory with him yet, and now he realized he was afraid of what he might think.

"No, James," Quizlow said. His voice had a weight of finality to it. "Penelope told us what she envisioned before your father died. She told us how he went there and was mind-slaved by the mystery man—but nothing of how he'd experienced mind-controlling sorcery prior to that fateful night."

"She did not tell anyone else," James persisted, "because she couldn't prove it. But Jack told her that there were times he'd lose control of his willpower."

"And Penelope wouldn't tell Arthur this—why?" Igvard said.

"I dunno," James said, confused. "She wanted proof of it—proof Jack wasn't lying to explain his actions." James looked at Igvard. "Anyway, how did the Wozigod explain my dad's death, if they don't believe in Phantom—or Cowl?"

"They say he tried to use the Armagods, but they were too powerful for him and ultimately destroyed him along with the stones," Quizlow responded.

"So—no Cowl?"

"No," Quizlow said. "Listen, I believe he exists. I even believe he controlled Jack on Risegar as your mother said. But Jack was—troubled, James. He grew up in the Realm of Shadows. He sided with Grisledor. He was—he was—*not good.*"

James clenched his fists in frustration and sat stolidly for a bit, feeling their eyes all on him. He could hear the Boneheads joking as they worked tirelessly, passing the bucket of water up the ladder to one another, and Hadwin chucking the water overboard. He felt like he was grasping at straws. *But I'm not. I'll just have to prove it. I'll have to prove that Dad is not a monster. I have to prove that it always was and has been Cowl.* "He was no monster," James asserted. "All those times he burned and murdered. It wasn't him. It was Cowl." He looked at Quizlow. "And Cowl is responsible for why Oskar is the way he is, too. He's doing the same thing. *Cowl.*" He stood, balling his fists. "If you don't believe me, I'll—I'll just have to *prove* it."

"What do you have in mind?" Quizlow asked, narrowing his eyes.

"I'm going there. I'm going to the Tomb of Forgotten Secrets." He turned challengingly toward Quizlow. "So, either help me, or get out of my way!"

Quizlow just stared at him before a look of realization settled over his face. He knew what James was implying and his eyes hardened with defiance. "No." He folded his arms, scowling. "It's too soon. If you go there without the proper training, James, you will meet your fate—as Jack did. You are not ready to meet the Lady of the Tomb yet. So—no. I will not help lead you down the same path your father took."

"Because I wasn't trained by Spell-guardians?" James snapped. "But look at the ones I had. Both were not exactly guardians I could look up to." He didn't mean to disgrace Arthur like that, but he was tired of being disappointed by guardians. Tired of being told he was not ready when he'd proved he was. Maybe it was time he had faith in himself. Like Cat said—trust no one. "I must know the truth about my father." He straightened himself, strengthening his resolve. "So you won't help me? Fine, I'll just do it myself."

"Just curious," Igvard said smugly. "How do you plan to get to the Tomb of Forgotten Secrets when we are stranded at sea?"

James turned to his uncle and laughed. "*I'm* not stranded."

23
CARPETS - THE HORSES
OF HEROES

"*I still* expressly forbid it!"

Standing on top of the barrel, Quizlow reminded James of an angry leprechaun with a Napoleon complex—what with his hands pressed firmly against his hips, and the stern scowl scrawled over his pudgy features.

It was the following morning. The Boneheads had dumped enough water into the sea so that Cat could go below and bring Rimbecella back to James, and Quizlow had just finished making them breakfast. But James had hardly eaten. He had laid the carpet out on the table, careful to brush away the crumbs before an astonished Igvard. She had been stashed away in the hold in one of the sacks full of pole rings, fairleads, and old sailcloth.

"I know," James said absently. "But I've no choice." It did not frighten him anymore to think of flying her. Not when he'd flown all the way from Akhret with Cat and Quizlow holding on to him. He believed now that she'd stopped working simply because she'd run out of magic. He'd flown her for quite some time, and then continued to fly her day in and day out when he was at the Faugs castle. He supposed she got tired after a while, like any other thing. You couldn't drive a car without stopping to fill it up with gas—or ride a horse without stopping for a break and to feed it. *I think she just needed a long rest is all.*

Of course, that was what he was *hoping* was the problem. If he was wrong, he'd have a long way to swim. But he tried not to think of it that way as he looked her over, and then lifted her from the table, shook her out, and then put her on the deck. "I'm going to the Tomb of Forgotten Secrets. It's...it's my destiny." It felt right to say, even though he knew Quizlow would object.

"It's not!" Quizlow said predictably.

But Cat was with him this time. "I'm not going to try to stop him. Hell, he could have walked around the boat calling her name, and I bet she would've flown to him just like that," he said, snapping. "So, I probably *didn't* stop him, anyway. But he didn't because he knew how we felt about her." He snorted. "She's like a girlfriend we all hate. Anyway, the kid knows his heart. If he wants to fly her and call it his destiny, I'm not standing in his way anymore. In fact..." Cat stepped toward him. "I always said I'd go with you to the end of the world. If you're going to a watery grave, I guess that's kind of like the end of the world."

"You're both being ridiculous," Quizlow said. "Now stop this foolishness and put her away."

Igvard continued to stare at the carpet and shook his head. "Wait, so you had a flying carpet all this time?"

"It's complicated," James said, rolling his eyes.

"She's fickle, as all sorcerers have found out when they flew them. One day, he may fall to his death. Well, he fell into the sea, so he was lucky," Quizlow said.

"He's right," Igvard allowed. "You're not my brother, James. Jack could fly them because he understood them. What do you know about her?"

"I know enough," James said stubbornly.

"Oh, it's all Blood Magic," Hadwin said as he stomped past holding a bucket of water. "The boy can fly it because his father could. Runs in the family." He reached the gunwale and heaved the bucket of water over the side with a grunt.

"What do you mean?" James asked. "What do you know—"

"About flying carpets?" Hadwin said. He stood upright, holding the bucket at his side, and pretended to wipe sweat off his brow. "We traveled with your old man, mate. Think we didn't hear about his flying carpets? Anyway, heard a story your old man told us about 'em." He looked down at the carpet and ran a toe along the Tree of Life design. "There was an old king who had a flying carpet. Liked to show off to the world just how special he was. Each time, he put more on her back. Y'know. First, he'd fly his fat old lady. Then his fat brothers and cousins. Then his servants, concubines, even his bloody horse. Then one day, he put his whole bloody kingdom on her and flew her."

Cat glared at him dubiously. "His *kingdom*?"

"Tall tale, mate," Hadwin said, emptying the last bit of water out at his feet and making to put the bucket over Cat's head. Cat scowled and knocked it away. "Anyway, the kingdom fell—*smash!* Smashed to smithereens. Houses and smashed stuff and roads, broken horses and clotters—everywhere. A big bloody quagmire. You see, king dungface found out that day—shattered skull, crushed ribs, and dyin' on the ground—that it wasn't magic she ran out of." He bent down and scooped up some water as it washed over his feet, then flung it overboard. "It's bloody patience, mate. She doesn't fly you to the bloody market for a heel of bread and a ruddy pint. For that she'll dump you on your bloody arse and make sure the dray cracks your spine in the street on its way to the palace."

"Oi, where'd yeh go?" Digfred called from belowdecks. "Bring that bucket down here *today*. We're losin' our bloody rhythm, yeh marrow."

Hadwin turned to head back to the hatch, saying, "The lesson your father learned, James, was that flyin' carpets weren't horses. They were bloody angels. Modesty will take you to the end of the bleedin' world—if that's where yeh want to go."

～

Hadwin's words were the bit of inspiration he needed to drive home his resolve. And when he said her name this time, his voice seemed to crackle with power. No, not power—*confidence*. It was a far cry from when he stood in those woods with his grandpa staring at the fluted bark of that tree trying to coax a petulant wizard out of its roots. Yes, she was his, but he was also hers. *She* is *kinda like a girlfriend*, he thought.

She leaped into the air, hovering, her silky fabric floating like a strange, beautiful mist, the beads of white pearl water droplets rolling off her fabric as though it was slick with grease.

The Boneheads came above to watch and slouched against the gunwale like a bunch of middies, drinking salt water out of a skin to slake their thirsts after a night's work dumping water and singing like slave miners in Nome. After watching the "spectacular boy flying the rug" they were going to fall apart belowdecks for some shut eye, they said.

James looked at Quizlow, who was still standing on the barrel looking stubborn as ever. "Still out?" He felt Quizlow would change his mind when he saw he was determined to go, but the gnome looked tired, not just stubborn. *He blames himself for all that's happened to me.*

Quizlow gave a wry, sad smile. "James, this is your journey. I was not chosen by Roseheart to guide you."

"But—" James faltered. "You know so much. You—"

"Indeed," Quizlow said. "And that wisdom tells you not to go. Not to seek the power of this woman. Like everything else, the carpet, the book, the *Persephone*—they've all come to you. And where does it all lead?"

You're wrong, James thought. *Because my father was not the man you believed he was.* "I wish you would reconsider." Perhaps it was unfair for him to say that. Quizlow had done so much for him already. The tiredness in his eyes spoke it all. But Quizlow had become such a part of his life, he felt naked without him. *Well*, he thought, *I'll have to learn not to rely on him so much.* "All right," he said at last before going over to the gnome. "We'll be parting ways, then."

"You don't have to," Quizlow said gloomily.

"I do." He looked down at his feet. "When I first saw you in that shop in Paris, you thought I was some dumb Urrdling who didn't know anything about the Old World."

"You've grown a bit since then," Quizlow said. "I have to admit, you are passionate. But you're not wise—not yet."

"What do you mean?" James asked, looking up at him.

"In wisdom, James, you understand how little you know, and humble yourself to all that you don't understand about the world. You also understand the dangers of reckless behavior."

Little do you know, it was my grandpa who taught me to be reckless, he thought. *And reckless behavior was what saved us when I escaped the Glutton's palace.*

Still, he could not help but feel ashamed from the rebuke. As Quizlow had said before, Arthur was by no means an ideal guardian. Perhaps he shouldn't be taking the old man's advice. "You're right, I guess," he mumbled, and then looked up. "Hey, thanks for everything you've done for me—for us."

Quizlow's smile was somewhat bashful, yet still sad. "I won't be there this time to help. You'll be on your own," he warned.

"I know." Acknowledging this filled his stomach with unpleasant worms.

"What's your plan?" Igvard asked, leaning against the gunwale.

James looked at him. "I have her," he said, nodding toward the carpet. "We can get there before Oskar and Wolf. When they do arrive, we'll be waiting for them. Two words is all I need to say—*Alyshyn Sigoris.*"

"You'll call your mother's guardian," Quizlow said, raising his eyebrows in surprise. James could see that even he thought this was clever.

"My Spell-guardian will be there with Roseheart," James said. "She'll open the door for me." This, of course, was the extent of his planning. He had no idea what awaited him at the Tomb of Forgotten Secrets, but he felt confident with Rimbecella—his angel.

"Wait." Quizlow stepped toward him scratching his head, and James turned around.

"If you ever need to contact me, do it through the Jimungi."

James knit his eyebrows. *"How?"*

"Pgwick," Quizlow said. The word sounded like a squeak. "It's an old countersign. But even old countersigns will get attention if you tell them who you are—James Dreadful, son of Penelope Farrow."

"Why?"

"She was well-loved by smalls," Quizlow said, smiling.

"Pgwick," James repeated. "I'll remember that."

"I'll be the one to remember it," Cat said. "I'm the *smart* one."

"Ha," James said, as he went over to Rimbecella and lifted her by the edge. Then, holding her with one hand, took Cat by the arm. "Take that other edge."

Cat didn't know how—and grabbed it awkwardly with fumbling fingers. "But how are you going to find this place?" he asked.

"Told you, it's my destiny," James replied, pulling the amulet Orbis from around his neck. "Show me the way to the Tomb of Forgotten Secrets," he commanded.

Almost immediately, the compass's needle began to spin. It spun and spun, never stopping. Without waiting, he stepped forward and leaped into the air.

Cat gave a cry, holding on to the carpet's front with all his might, the veins popping out in his forearms. And just like that, they were gliding across the deck, past Hadwin and his Boneheads, Cat kicking his legs and flailing his arms like he was trying to swim.

Then, closing his eyes, James thought—*speed*—and when he opened them again, they were flying.

Cat was screaming, his eyes tearing, too afraid to close them.

"Whoooowheeeeee!" James cried. He doubled back, and swooped low to see his uncle duck, an expression of disbelief and a little fear on his face, and Quizlow now standing beside Hatset on the gunwale. He swore he saw a ghost of a smile on the gnome's face, even as Hatset leaped frightened to the deck.

"We'll meet you back at the Faugs!" James shouted down to them. He wasn't sure if they heard him or not, but he was sure they'd know that this was the place he'd return to when this was all over.

Cat slipped, and James grabbed him and pulled him closer. "Now let's really *fly*!"

24

FLIGHT AT LAST!

He'd forgotten how fast she could go. In seconds, the *Persephone* had shrunk to a speck on the sea and Rimbecella had soared with them into the clouds, her fragranced cloth bunched up in his fists, and the back of her flapping wildly against his ankles. She rippled beneath him, boffing his knees, her frills kissing his knuckles, chin, and eyelashes.

Cat was rigid; the last time he'd been on her, he'd clutched him around the legs for dear life. It was understandable that he didn't know how to hold on to her correctly now. He pulled Cat toward him and shouted, "Loosen up. You don't have to hold on so tight!"

But Cat looked sick as he peered down at the clouds and occasional glimpses of the sea. "I can't. It's—I can't explain it. It's amazing, but terrifying!"

They banked, shooting through a stack of clouds. Her fabric folded over his knuckles, her warmth countering the growing cold in his hands. When he leaned into her, he could smell her sweet incense-like aroma, and her heat comforted his cheeks already numb from windburn. Looking around, he saw that they were surrounded by a serene whiteness, like great billowing mountains of snow. After over a week in captivity, this was such a blessed sight that even the cold fresh air felt like freedom glancing off his skin. It tickled the hairs on his forearms, whipped his head back, and burned into his eyes so that he had to squint. Even as the lobes of his ears turned numb, he couldn't help but laugh. It was all so invigorating. So rapturous.

He noticed how she sometimes bounced on the wind, as though the wind offered wave crests to slip over, while at other times she seemed to swim smoothly ahead, piercing clouds like a needle, scattering vapors into artistic swirls.

"Are you following the compass?" Cat shouted.

James pulled the compass out from around his neck and let the metal warm his fingers before opening it. "What the—" he started, scrunching up his forehead.

The needle was still spinning.

He repeated the location several more times, but nothing seemed to make it stop in any one particular direction. His heart fell. He was sure the needle would have stopped spinning by now. "It just spins and spins," he said finally.

"*What?*"

There were times when he'd messed with the compass before, telling it to point to some fictitious place—like Oz—and the compass had spun indefinitely. It worried him that it was doing the same now.

"What do we do?" Cat asked.

"Dunno." He was almost sure Orbis would have come through for him. Quizlow had told him it pointed where he desired to go, but never told him of its limitations.

"Turn her around," Cat said. "We have to go back."

Halfheartedly, James agreed. He leaned into a turn.

The cloth didn't respond.

His heart skipped a beat. *What's she doing?* He tried again, this time more violently, twisting his body to the right. But the only result was her fishtailing. "Cat—she won't—"

"What's going on?" Cat cried. "Turn her around!"

"I'm *trying*," James snapped, and tried again. Still to no avail. "She's not—" He looked down at the sea. Certainly, this was much farther than when he'd fallen from the sky the first time. *We'll both die from this height. Sea or no sea beneath us.*

Or perhaps dropping them into the sea was not her intent. Perhaps she was planning to fling them into a bottomless pit, or a volcano. *Quizlow was right. I know nothing about her!* He didn't realize that he'd tensed up until he looked down and saw his trembling fists full of cloth.

She's not a horse. She's an angel.

He loosened his grip and let out a breath of air from his lungs. He'd begun to feel a strange sense of serenity, so much so, that he let go of the cloth. "Don't worry," he said at last. "We're on the right course."

"Are you sure?"

He didn't answer, but he gripped Cat's forearm and held it tightly.

∼

For hours they drifted through the clouds listening to the wind buffet the clefts of their ears. It was the only sound. Cat had buried his face into the cloth to muffle his whimpers, and it reminded him of that poor prisoner Qasif before they escaped the Glutton's palace. He'd tried his luck with Rimbecella but was thrown out the window and to his death.

She's an angel.

It had never occurred to him that they should bring food and water—not until now. Flying to the island could take a long time, he realized. But he'd left so quickly, he hadn't thought about it. *Quizlow would have thought of it.*

His lips were dry and cracked now, and his stomach growled. And what if they couldn't find anything on the island to eat? If only he could regain control of her, they could stop somewhere. Then he realized how ridiculous that sounded. *It's not like we can just stop at the local KFC!*

He tried to remain calm and lowered his chin onto the cloth. Then he shut his eyes against the beating wind and tried to relax.

~

He might have relaxed too much, because the next thing he knew, he was awakened by the slap of a burst of wind. It scoured through his locks, yanking his head back. Opening his eyes, all he could see was the top of Rimbecella flapping in his face. Along his body, she was rippling wildly, almost frenziedly.

"*Shit!*" Cat cried.

A pile of dark clouds swam toward them. James twisted his head around; dusk had fallen. The horizon sported a burnt orange décor. But smoldering gray and dirt-white clouds were flowing across the sky around them, unfurling like gunmetal breakers. In seconds, they had penetrated the thunderheads, shot through them blindly. Cat grabbed his wrist so hard he lost circulation there, and cried, "*Where's this bloody bitch taking us?*"

But he couldn't see anything—only pockets of shadowy whites, creasing and widening.

And then, distant flickers—like electric fireflies through clots of wet cotton. Again and again—sparkles—even as the wind grew more turbulent, snapping the frilled edges of Rimbecella. She mounted a strong gale, then plunged, and James felt his stomach leave him.

A wild centipede of light arced through the thunderheads, smaller legs branching out around it.

BOOM!

The sky gave a withering response and sent it rolling past their ears.

Cat screamed.

"Hold on!" James shouted.

Then the rain came. Blinding. Falling like a sheet over them. More lightning streaked, lighting up the fluid, tempestuous sky. Rimbecella's frills flapped loudly and wetly in James's ear. Again, she plunged—

violently—caught in the temper of the element. She slipped fast through the rain like a beam of light. She zigged; Cat's grip was making his right hand even number by now. She zagged. Her zag threw James this time, and his hand slipped off of the cloth. The moment it did, the carpet went into a spin. He managed to hold on and pull himself toward her, but Cat had not been prepared. With a yelp, he vanished into the folding clouds. It was only after he did this that James heard him scream.

He acted quickly and grabbed the flapping corner of the carpet, screaming, "Rimbecella!"

She seemed to struggle with him; the wind was batting her against his face, and he could see only the flapping half in a streak of lightning. He realized suddenly he was falling, but he raised his legs, bent his knees, smoothed out the sides as best he could—even as he turned upside down, falling straight into oblivious storm clouds—and brought his legs onto her. Lightning ripped, and thunder clamored through a patch of cloud in front of him. He let himself straighten out and fly—*down*. His eyes failed him. Only lightning scratched through the blurred vision of the rain.

But after the rolling thunder, he could hear the long wail of Cat, and homed in on it, flying as fast as he dared.

Another flash lit the darkened sky; he saw, quite clearly then, that they were no longer at sea. Land was beneath them, with trees and mountains. He spotted Cat spinning around in the air like a ragdoll and shot toward him. He caught up and thrust out his hand. But Cat was twisting. James grabbed the cuff of his pants with his right hand, but it slipped out. He lost control himself and tumbled, holding only on to a corner of the carpet, before he could throw his legs back on. Then he swooped down again and crashed into him. The carpet puckered up, but he grabbed on and held Cat close as they both spun.

"Hold on!"

Cat grabbed a corner and clung to her. The weight of his body caused them to fishtail once more, as Cat's legs flew out behind them. They ducked low, skimming the tops of trees.

It was a jungle island, full of mountains with lush trees and brush, and he glimpsed several smoking volcanos in the distance. There were giant idols covered in thick moss and ivy, and an ancient temple drowned in flora. But the carpet continued, sailing over all these, the wind still whipping at her wet frills, flinging sprays of water in their eyes.

The sun peeked out of the clouds, dashing the land with light, and a rainbow blazed from the thunderheads, striking a mountain ahead of them. But it was no ordinary rainbow. As they drew closer to it, a glint of lightning danced from the clouds and speared it, sending a spray of emerald sparks. Then it danced off, the lightning full of rainbow colors, and struck the carpet right at the tip.

She erupted like a sunburst, blinding them, scattering lilac sparks in the wind. James felt the fire strike his eyebrows, but it wasn't hot—it was cold. Very cold.

Still, Rimbecella's front edge snapped into a weird fire of blazing amethyst, emerald, ruby, and sapphire colors, and it sent her into a spin.

James felt vertigo.

The fire spread down the corner to Cat's hands, and he leaped. But James caught him, holding on to the one small corner of her. His feet danced on the wind; the carpet spun him around and around. The mountain loomed in front of them. He saw a small window—tiny—like an arrowslit in the Faugs. And then he was blinded by a spear of light. A shock of lightning pervaded his whole body, and then rainbow smoke suffused his lungs with incense-sweet fumes.

Everything was a blur from spinning. But he held on to Cat, who was screaming, even as they spun, impossibly—

—through the tiny window in the mountain.

Cat was still grasping his hand, his eyes shut.

The next thing they knew, they were falling toward a strange floor inside a cold, empty crypt full of dark, cold, stone faces.

They struck the floor almost gently, but rolled all the same, limbs flailing, grunting, until they stopped and lay still.

James did not ache—he felt only his eyebrows burning, and he rubbed them and opened his eyes. He saw something peculiar—or perhaps the strangest thing he'd ever seen in his life. A spear of brilliant light pierced the window, and the wind howled against the arrowslit, blowing specks of glittery dust through. And there was Rimbecella, lit with the strange rainbow fire, flapping about in the dark—a mystical, opal phoenix.

But then she evaporated, turning into a thousand moonbeam gnats, which glittered in the multicolored smoke. The gnats formed something of a Tree of Life image in the air, and he heard a strange spiritual music that he forgot almost instantly.

And then she faded entirely from existence.

25

THE FORGOTTEN SONG

"How did we—" Cat had regained his feet and was looking up at the narrow arrowslit window penetrated by the sunbeam. "How'd we fit through *there*?"

James didn't answer at first; he was checking himself for severe disfigurement. He thought he would hurt more, having fallen from so high up. He felt his legs, then his arms and elbows. He was intact. Rainwater rolled down from his face, dripping from his nose. Strangely, the only thing hurting was his right eyebrow, which he now began to massage. *Is my face still there?* By now, he'd begun to feel a numbing sensation taking over half his face, and it was beginning to alarm him.

Cat said, "Look how high it is—and narrow—*James!*"

James got to his feet and looked up at what Cat was pointing to. Indeed, the arrowslit window was only a few inches in width, if that much. "Dunno how we got through, Cat. But she's a magic carpet. She also *flies*, in case you haven't noticed." Rimbecella bringing them in through a two-inch-wide window wasn't the most amazing thing he'd seen in the past month or so. "I'm more concerned about where she is. Did you see?" He lowered his hand from his face. "She vanished. Like *really* vanished." He wasn't sure what he'd seen. His mind had gone numb for a moment as it tried to grasp the reality of what happened, and chunks of his memory were missing. *Did* he see her turn into glowing specks that morphed into a tree? Did she evaporate in fiery smoke? Somehow, he felt like something wonderful, yet terribly sad had happened. Like the death of an angel? Could flying carpets die? If they lived, then certainly they could die. Or did angels not die? He didn't know. He didn't know what the sign she left in the air meant, or what the strange lightning that glanced off the rainbow was.

First Quizlow, now Rimbecella, he thought. He felt like he was being abandoned by the guardians who had watched over him and it gave him an unnerving sense of isolation.

Cat, however, didn't seem to care. He was walking around, staying close to the beam of light on the floor, looking at their surroundings. He was probably too bewildered to hear anything James was saying. Right now, he was looking up at a row of large statues of what appeared to be mythical beasts carved out of limestone. "Did she bring us to some dungeon?" he wondered aloud.

"The window as narrow as a balist—balistr—what was it?" James asked.

"Balistraria," Cat contributed. "An arrowslit."

"Yeah, that's what he said," James confirmed, still remembering his first voyage at sea when the ogres and Igvard were plotting to acquire Roseheart. Gunter's description was quite accurate it turned out.

"And the beam of sunlight," Cat recalled. "Yes. I remember that. I didn't think it was true."

James gave a chuckle. "My uncle said something about becoming a shapeshifter. I wonder if the sunlight is enchanted?"

"Dunno," Cat said. "But this must be the Tomb of Forgotten Secrets. I can't believe it. We're—we're just *here*." He turned around to look at James, folding his arms. He was shivering and water dropped from his bitten earlobe and fell out of his hair. "Thought she was taking us to our deaths. The storm, the lightning. Felt like the wrath of Pzuwa."

"Wrath of what?"

"Nothin'," Cat said, and took fistfuls of his hair and squeezed to wring the water out. He pulled off his shirt and then his pants and squeezed the water out of them, too. "I've been too wet, James. I've spent too much time"—he hopped up and down on one foot while fingering his ear—"trying to get water out of my bloody ears!"

"And I've seen you naked more times than I'd care to," James said, watching as the water ran into small cracks on the floor.

"Don't pretend you don't like it, Prince."

James barely heard him because for the first time he noticed that the travertine floor had strange carvings that reminded him of Adinkra symbols. Each tile had different ones. He supposed he needed not wonder anymore if his inherited power to understand all tongues included ancient symbols. It was like Braille to him.

"So, you want to know how we'll get out of here without your flying death rug?" Cat asked, wringing out streams of water from the cuff of his pants.

"We're stranded," James said, crouching and running a finger over the stone tiles. "We also have no food or water."

"Good thinking, Prince," Cat said, and then decidedly squeezed the remaining water from his pants into his mouth.

James stood and went to stand in the light piercing through the window. He hadn't expected Rimbecella to abandon them like this. What were they to do now? He'd told Quizlow he'd meet them back in the Faugs.

"We only had a humble breakfast this morning," Cat said. "Has it been a day? I can't feel the hunger anymore. I've just been feeling weak." He looked down at himself. "That's another rib I can see. I'll name this one Solemi."

"Put your clothes back on. If there are ghosts here and they murder us, you'll die naked."

"I'd rather die naked than cold," Cat said, and stubbornly went to investigate their surroundings. "This is some sort of hall," he observed, padding on the cold stone in his bare feet, still wringing out his clothes. "You know, I'm glad your little mistress left you. It was a terrible relationship. She ditches you over and over, and you just keep coming back to be ditched again. And when I woke up on the hard deck this morning in a puddle of water, I didn't know that one of the most important lessons I'd learn today was that flapping your arms a thousand feet in the air does absolutely noth—" Cat's voice broke off suddenly, and James whirled around. His friend was barely a silhouette in the dark. "James!"

He came quickly, his shoes squishing noisily, droplets of water running down his face. "What is it?" In the dark, he didn't know what he was looking at—only a large object standing away from the giant chimerical creations. He couldn't see so well; he'd been standing near the ray of light too long. But Cat's eyes had grown more accustomed to the dark.

"It's a—a statue."

"So?" James said.

"But it looks like—"

James squinted. As his eyes adjusted, its contours came into relief. "Formandible!" James breathed.

Cat gave the stone a prod with his finger.

Solid stone.

James touched it, too. The ogre was turned entirely to stone and was poised with his ax in the air.

"They're here already," James muttered.

"What do you think happened?"

James looked around the hall, but it was too dark to see anything that might be a threat. "Something attacked him?" He thought surely they'd be ahead of the *Skybester*. The carpet seemed like she could outstrip a flying boat on its best day, even if they were a day behind. But now he supposed he'd underestimated the speed of the ship.

"How are we going to get in without Roseheart?" Cat asked.

"Dunno, Cat." His entire plan had revolved around Rimbecella and getting here before the others. Now he was at a loss; apprehension began to worry at his resolve. "Let's go," he said, lowering his voice out of precaution.

Cat put his clothes on, and they moved toward the opposite end of the hall. His face was still pulsing with pain, and he rubbed at his eyebrow again. At the end of the hall was a doorless threshold. The wall around it was covered in the same hieroglyphs, beautifully carved, reminding him of the walls in the Egyptian pyramids. There was a torch there, and Cat took it from its sconce and whispered, "*Igra!*" This time, the fire immediately caught.

"Getting better," James noted.

Cat blew on it gently as the fire picked up, crackling and spitting. "Hey," he said, staring at James's face in the light. "What happened to your *face*?"

James felt along his eyebrow, imagining, horrified, that it'd swollen up and turned purple or something. "What's the matter? It's all tingly."

Cat stepped closer. "Your eyebrow turned silvery. Just that one. And the skin's all red there."

"That strange fire hit me—dunno."

"Hope you're not cursed," he said. "Still burns?"

"Yes."

But Cat was looking past him, and James turned his attention there. The torch had lit up the entrance. Broken cobwebs floated languidly in the corners, but the light stretched through, exposing more walls with hieroglyphs on them. Something else, however, lurked in the dark beyond the door—sighs like air tickling over lips, or slipping across tongues, seemed to rise out of the dark. Never before had a sound made his skin slide with fright.

"Hear that?" Cat whispered, shining his torch through the door.

"Ghosts," James ventured. "This is a tomb."

"Yeah," Cat said, and shivered. "What do we do about the ghosts?"

James felt his bones shaking and wished he'd wrung the water out of his clothes like Cat. "Where's that loudmouth I first met who accused me of wetting my britches?" He'd never forget how Cat had bullied him that first time they met in Argolhum.

"Called you a pisser. It was a well-deserved title. But you forget I'm street bred. I always hide behind the brave idiot, so—you first."

James moved forward, Cat following close behind. They came to a case of stairs and stepped down them. The walls were covered in moss, but he could still see hieroglyphs beneath them carved into the bricks. As they made their way down the stone steps, chipped and broken from use, and matted with moss, he brushed aside a thick cobweb full of insect husks that had come loose and was flailing in the slight breeze wafting through the dark. Water dripped from the ceiling and ran down the stone walls.

The whispers came again; he wondered if mummified horrors were sending curses over desiccated lips toward them. As they went farther, an arched entrance met them leading to a smaller chamber with moist, stale air. Cat's torchlight spilled across columns slick with wet moss and the exposed breasts of a cracked sphinx's bust sitting in a grooved niche. She rested on a stone plinth with faces carved into it. Old, cracked mustard ewers with ugly half animals' heads collected dust in corners.

So, my father came here a long time ago. I'm standing where he stood—my mother and Sigurd beside him. But not just that. This is also where Grisledor stood with my mother years later! Maybe even where he stuck her with the poisoned knife! It felt strange standing where his parents had been. *If only I knew what they knew!*

Ahead was a wall lit by an unknown source; it had a silvery moonlight glow about it. Pictograms were carved into its surface. Something about it drew him, and he went toward it while Cat crept over to inspect a wall covered in pictograms. *But without Roseheart, how are we going to get in?*

Nevertheless, he was curious. As he leaned forward, still feeling his face tingling, Cat scoured away some of the moss with his fingers by the other wall.

"Can you read these?" Cat asked.

"No," James replied, passing his hand just inches over the stone he was studying. These pictograms had seemed more important, he realized, because the light seemed enchanted, and no moss grew on it. It was almost as though the light was preserving the wall. "I think this is some sort of enchanted panel."

"James, listen to these walls," Cat said. "I think the whispers are coming from *them*."

James joined Cat and put his ear to the wall there. But the sounds did not seem any louder. "Doesn't seem like it."

Cat shined his torch around, looking for the source again. "Where are you coming from?"

James returned to his wall with the enchanted light and stared at it, hoping that his Dreadful power to understand language would change them into words he could understand.

"Hey," Cat said.

"What?"

"These symbols. They're hieroglyphs, right?"

"What about 'em?"

"Well, they're mostly animals."

Cat was right. The symbols he was observing were mostly birds, in fact. "I dunno," James said.

The whispers came again, floating through the chamber like a gentle breeze. This time, he tried to listen to what they were saying. The words were quiet and inarticulate, but he swore he could hear the soft sigh of a melody behind it.

"They seemed to be infatuated with animals," Cat continued. "Look— bears, wolves, birds, *apes*. Like the curse of the pirates."

"*Shhh*," James said. He'd begun to pace, contemplating.

"I can interpret this," Cat said after a while, still touching the wall with his fingers. "Look here. Walk...man...house...dead...return (I think)... spirit...*Asabwa*?" He looked at James. "Asabwa is the god of beasts," he explained. "That must be why all their pictograms are...animals."

James continued to listen to the whispers. This time, he was certain they were louder and more articulate, but they were still indecipherable. And he was sure it was music he could hear.

"To tread in the house of the dead...a man must walk as spirit," Cat continued to translate, his fingers tracing along the pictograms. "And wait—here—*to return to his skin, he must have the...*" He frowned. "Not sure if I understand that last bit. Umm—*wait*—in Suniria the Shadow Walkers, who travel to the spirit plane, need a powerful *ashra* to return to the land of the living."

"What's that?"

"I dunno, a sort of object or thing that connects them to the physical world. I know their *ashras* are sometimes torcs, or rings, or something you can hold on to."

"A stone?"

Cat shrugged. "I suppose it could be a stone." He scrunched up his forehead. "What are you thinking?"

"It's a key, isn't it? A key that allows you through a door back into the realm of the living."

Cat thought about it. "You're right. It would function as a sort of key. To open a door. But—" And then he realized what James meant. "You mean—"

"Yes," James said. "Roseheart. She's the key. She's what allows us to traverse the house of the dead. Only...why do we have to traverse the house of the dead?"

"We're in a tomb," Cat pointed out.

"But you know what I mean. Why do we have to traverse the spiritual plane?"

"It's a way to keep its members exclusive," Cat speculated. "There's no way through these walls—"

"Unless you have the right key," James finished.

Again, the whispers. They were much louder now. And so was the music.

James stood looking at the moonbeam wall staring at the pictogram of the bird. "*Key*," he said at last.

Almost at once, two of the hieroglyphs lit up as though a ray of moonlight struck them. The whispers and music grew louder like they were seeping out of the walls.

"Something's happening," James said.

Cat joined him and looked over his shoulder.

Of the pictograms there were three birds, and two of them were glimmering on the wall. One of them remained dark. The first bird stood on a triangle.

"Mountain," Cat pointed out, touching it.

The other stood on a tree they saw because it was a line with quotes on each side. The unlit one stood on an *S* with an odd *B* character. Cat figured it was a flower. But he had no sooner finished observing this, when he cried, "*James!*"

James turned. Smoke had begun to pour out of the pictograms on the walls around them. A strange, eerie, silvery smoke. He knew it was cursed—that it would transform them just as it had Grisledor's army of raiders.

"Let's get out of here!" Cat shouted.

But James grabbed him by the arm. "Don't even bother, Cat. The only way to escape this is through here."

"But we don't have Roseheart!" Cat cried, pulling his wrist away and turning to run.

"I think we do," James said, not moving from his spot.

Cat rounded on him. "What do you mean *we do*?"

He could hear it coming from all around now—the beautiful soft refrain. "Faylings can take different forms, but my mother made this one shaped like a bird. Look—the pictograms are birds. My mother gave the key to Oskar. She didn't give it to Arthur because he already had it." He wasn't sure if he was trying to convince Cat or himself now. But it was all starting to come together.

"Your grandfather's dead, James."

"You don't understand. He passed it on to *me*."

The wisps of silvery smoke rolled across the mossy travertine tiles, curling toward their ankles.

"And you didn't know?"

"No," James said. "Because I didn't realize what sort of key it was. It was a key, all right, but a *musical* one."

The lullaby.

His mother had given him the enchanted mobile which his grandpa had brought to Urrd and had put in his bedroom. And Arthur had played it over and over until it was a part of his grandson's subconscious.

A part of me.

Now he could not mistake the song coming from the wall for anything else. It was the song of the mockingbird who guarded the entrance to the tomb. She guarded it with the lullaby his mother had given him.

And by now, the song was no longer a whisper:

To whom do I grant this entry,
Into the Tomb of gods?
To whom do I allow to plunder
Coffers, crowns, and rods?

Magic here hath slept, not astir,
For seven centuries
Magic here hath slept, not astir,
For seven centuries.

It was the first two stanzas of the lullaby. *My birthright,* James thought. *The song is the key to my birthright.*

James pressed a finger to the pictogram of the darkened bird on the rosebud—*like the rosebud on my chamber pot*—and closing his eyes, hummed the remaining stanzas. When he did, the bird lit up with moonlight, and now the whisperers through the walls continued the song to completion:

Only I, the heir of crypts and

Dark, with a key to shine the way.
To walk among secrets that have
Not seen the light of day.

The missing stanza.

"James!" Cat cried as the smoke wrapped around their ankles.

James knew, almost by instinct, to grab Cat's wrist. He felt the song course through him, and then a sensation that seemed to tickle his insides. All around him, the silvery smoke flowed, wrapping them in strange wispy lights. Then he looked down at his hand—the one not holding Cat's wrist—and saw it dissolve into smoke. It was a strange, peaceful sensation. The music suffused his body, rippling through him, filling him with light. And then he was moving, floating through the air, along with the silvery smoke.

Only I, the heir of crypts and
Dark, with a key to shine the way.

He was not corporeal, he was only a soft, rolling gas that shimmered like moonbeams glancing off clouds. Around him, he saw shapes in a steady stream of smoke. Shapes that became fish, giraffes, coyotes, snakes, bears, or other animals, which dove out of the smoke and vanished like glistening sea creatures.

Down they went, passing through dark crypts, a flood of cloudy magic, rippling with the souls of beasts and fowls. Down, down they went. Occasionally, they passed small arrowslit windows, and puffs of smoke escaped from the sides and became howling creatures, dashing down the mountainside into the jungle. Or they passed facets of water that spat out salmon, or flounder, or mackerels, exploding into the air in glistening droplets, fins glinting in sunlight to fall in streams dashing through waterfalls. Down, down still they went, through the mountain, sending a volley of parrots of emerald-green with cherry napes squawking into the wild.

And then the stream of smoke pushed into a chamber through the nostrils of an old brass statue of a many-armed and -legged god that sat in an old dusty corner of a long dark hallway.

Still clutching Cat's wrist, he looked at him. "We made it—" But he stopped midsentence, and his eyes grew wide.

There, in front of them, stood Gunter, holding an ax.

26

THE TOMB OF FORGOTTEN SECRETS

For about three seconds James and Cat huddled there, waiting for the ogre to turn around. Then Cat took a step forward and gave him a poke. "He's stone, James. Just like Captain Formandible."

James also tried. When it didn't budge, he let out his breath and looked around. They were in a dark corridor with arrowslit windows. Light filtered through from outside. Old chests stacked along walls, tall ceramic ewers, and brass oil lamps cluttered around a table heaped with ancient, cobwebbed tomes and scrolls. Cat lifted one of the brass lamps from a stack of tomes— *"Igra!"* In the light, he examined Gunter more closely and snorted. "Turned into a lump of granite."

"Think we're in danger?" James asked. "Maybe a basilisk?"

"Can't say," Cat replied. "We should be cautious at any rate."

James came around to see Gunter's face, but the rough contours of it did not betray an expression he could read. However, it appeared he did not have a chance to raise his ax. "It doesn't seem he was trying to defend himself."

"*Wolf*," Cat said at last. "That scum would backstab anyone."

James looked at him. "But that would mean he allowed Wolf to petrify Formandible."

Cat put his hands on his hips and stroked the stubble on his jaw.

"Gunter and Formandible had their differences," he pointed out. "And Formandible didn't trust Wolf from the start."

It was true. Formandible had wanted to sell Roseheart so that they wouldn't have to do deal with Wolf. "But then why'd Wolf betray Gunter?"

Cat shrugged. "Front lines," he said, and James figured he was referring to the statement he made to Formandible—about ogres being expendable. "Come on. So much for the kindness of their benefactors. But if they thought someone like Wolf represented kind, considerate—" He stopped because he heard a sound coming through the dark archway that led into the corridor. Almost immediately, he whispered, *"Imwa!"* The lamp extinguished, leaving them in dark again. For a minute, they just stood listening. Something rattled. Something else thumped. As James crept forward on Cat's heels, he began to realize the dark in the tomb was alive with sounds. Lots of them. For a horrific moment, he thought the place was infested with bats because he heard flapping. But then the sound became more distinguishable. They sounded more like a storm of pages whispering in the air. But how could that be? Cat stopped at the side of the arched entrance and hunkered down on the balls of his feet, thief-like, and listened intently. Someone somewhere was murmuring—and occasionally chuckling. And something else hooted. Another something chimed—pinged, and crashed and broke. James didn't know what to make of the sounds and the mystery of it all haunted him. When he looked over his shoulder at where they'd come through—the many-armed and -legged Kali-looking statue—he knew there was no way out. *We're stuck here as far as I can tell*, he thought. *Entombed, with the rest of the world's deadliest secrets.* "Come on," he whispered, taking the oil lamp from Cat. "It's creepy, but we can't stay here."

As he stepped out of the chamber, Cat whispered, *"Igra,"* and the lamp lit up again.

Light spilled into a hallway lined with cabinets and tables. At their feet was a long rug that stretched to the end. Together they moved down the hall. The cabinets had bottles of potions, jars—they even saw a skull tucked in the corner of one, swathed in cobwebs. There were alchemical ingredients and recipes, books, and scrolls. Chests lined with bottles, jars filled with creatures and organs preserved in vinegar. They passed a door leading into a chamber lit by rush candles—and heard someone counting something that went *clink, clink!*

James tried the handle, but it was locked, so he peered in through the barred window. All he could see was a room full of coffers and a table with a long scroll unfurled to the floor. A quill moved all on its own, scratching ink on the scroll, and the voice continued to mutter.

Was it a ghost?

They continued on.

There were many chambers filled with mysteries, they found. In one, a looking glass showed the reflection of a beautiful woman combing her long auburn tresses, and when she saw them, she smiled. Yet, there was no one casting the reflection. Still farther, they spied statues of maidens, brass animal busts, fancy chests, and coffers of jewels.

Finally, they came to a stairwell that led to a large hall and halted.

Oh jeez, James thought. They had discovered, at last, where the strange sounds of flapping pages were coming from. Here were shelves stacked up to the arced ceiling, and most of them had books. But these books weren't the type to sit around on the shelves. They chattered and flapped around like birds. And the tomes were all unique in their own ways, with old covers made from leather—and with buckles to fasten them shut. But they flew about like odd-shaped sparrows, flapping their covers like delicate wings. They prattled among themselves like great philosophers, and their voices made it sound like a lecture hall full of pompous professors.

As they went down the stairs, they saw hundreds of them. *No doubt this is the place my father found his book—Galajitar*, he thought. Of course, that book only talked inside his head.

There were not just bookshelves, though. There were piles of...*stuff*. That was what he called the treasures they passed as they strolled down towering aisles while ducking the flapping tomes. There was so much, he could not even hope to list all of it: A breastplate engraved with glimmering runes. An enchanted ax burning with green fire. A brass globe of the world the size of a bedchamber on a plinth. A life-size gold elephant breathing smoke out of its trunk. Large, beautiful, rolled-up carpets. Stacks of extraordinary paintings. A cage with a giant squawking skeleton bird. Glass jars with exotic colorful insects trying to get out. A crystal dove that flew into the air fell shattering on the floor, pieced itself together, and flew off again. A locked casket that glowed from within. A crystal ball sitting on a fancy cushion with a frightening laughing face encased within.

And much, much more.

The place was large, but the area they were exploring was where most of the treasures were. Beyond it, the bookshelves seemed to stretch farther into the hall.

Finally, they came to the end of it and a clearing in the large assortment of treasures that had been stashed on tables, shelves, and cabinets. Cat stopped and, folding his arms, leaned against a table with an open coffer full of old coins that stood in the middle of in the space.

"What do you think?" James asked, having stopped to take in his surroundings. "This place is huge. We could search for hours."

"But most of the rest seems to be bookshelves," Cat said, examining the coins spilled across the table. "We could go another way, but this is where all the stuff's at."

James set the lamp on the table and walked around. "OK, but don't touch anything."

He'd just finished saying that when suddenly, a voice shouted, "Hands off, thief!"

James spun around to find Cat dropping one of the coins back onto the table, looking startled. "Told you not to touch anything!"

Cat shrugged. "I'd already picked it up."

James looked around for the voice, but Cat nudged his head toward the table, and said, "It's the *coin*."

He stared at Cat and then looked down at the table where the small copper coin lay. He saw nothing unusual about it—just the imprint of a head marred by greenish-blue verdigris.

Then the face on the coin moved.

It reminded him of the coin Wolf had, and he felt a chill go through him. "That—that coin. It—"

But before he could finish, the coin stood upright on its own and began to twirl along the table as if to balance on its side. When it did, it began to roll with a thin teeter. "*I'm the property of Emperor Mitsutshi*," a small voice barked angrily. *"So, you've no right touching me, outlaw!"*

Cat's eyes opened wide and he turned his head to look at James. "It can *talk*!" he said with a laugh.

"Of course I can talk, you pillock," the voice continued as it gyrated and fell flat, facing up. The head on the coin moved under the layers of verdigris. "We are Mitsutshi's magic coins."

"Magic coins?" James repeated, standing over the table and folding his arms. "Why would anyone need *those*?"

The small head under the patina moved toward him. "*Why?* What ignorance! Our emperor was ahead of his time. Thought it'd be a great idea to make a currency that could claim its earner. Couldn't be stolen, cheated out of, or misrepresented, because we'd cry, 'Thief!' 'Fraud!' or, 'You didn't earn us, you lousy layabout!'"

Cat sat in the chair beside the table and set his elbows on it. "Sounds like a good idea, come to think of it," he said as he palmed his chin.

"Course it was," another coin with a woman's voice and blue-green verdigris covering the coppery face chimed in from the pile.

"But it was never meant to be," said the first coin.

"Why not?" James asked.

"The life of a coin under such financial botherations is very stressful," spoke another. He had corrosion in splotches over the back of his head and sounded like a professor of heavy proportions. "It could drive one to drink."

James thought immediately of Moffat when he heard this and snorted.

"So, even you scobs can get stuck on the old sauce?" Cat asked, trying to hold in laughter.

"*Scobs?*" the professor coin objected and jumped up to roll around in fury. "Nay! But we could spend ourselves on a good pint and watch our masters drown themselves in their troubles."

"And we made bloody sacrifices," the woman-sounding coin said.

"Threw our brothers away on 'sound investments,' we did," the professor coin said proudly.

"And when our kith and kin were linin' the pockets of mountebanks," said the lady coin, "we'd sing our requiem for 'em as we'd clink into the alewife's palm."

"Wow," Cat said, fingering the scruff on his chin. "Didn't know coins led such interesting lives."

"Aye, but you can't go about ruining your masters' financial lives without repercussions," the professor-sounding coin said. "And soon society turned against us. So, we ran off."

"Ran?" James echoed.

"*Rolled*, mind you. But they hunted us down. Many of us tried to lay low. Pretended to be your usual inanimate coins."

"There's the real tragedy," the woman coin said. "*We* knew what our worth was, even if the blockhead who owned us didn't."

"Mitsutshi made us too perfect!" continued the professor. "We knew when our worth was being squandered by stupidity. The endless baubles! Depressing! We couldn't stay silent."

"So, what'd they do?" the woman coin went on. "I'll tell you what. Too afraid to melt us down, they were. We were a *curse*. Even as scobs we were a threat. So, they did the only thing they could. They locked us up."

"Maybe someday they'll let us out—when people have learned their ways around a coin purse, but who knows," finished the professor.

"I'm—sorry?" James said.

"What are you apologizin' for, lad?" the lady coin said. "'Twas a thousand years ago. You weren't even a twinkle in your mother's eye."

James scratched his head. "Anyway, you wouldn't, by any chance, have seen someone come through here?"

"Someone?" the lady coin said. "'Tisn't a caravanserai, child! Someones don't come strollin' through here. Come to think of it, what are *you* doin' here?"

"They're bloody tomb raiders, I'll tell you," the professor cried. "Come to nick a few treasures, aye?"

James took Cat by the arm, nudging his head for him to follow. Cat got up and came with him. "If they didn't see them," he said, ducking several conversing books engaged in a heated discussion on politics, "maybe they're not here."

"Let's look around a bit more," Cat said, pulling out of his hand. "We could wander around here for a long time and find nothing."

He was right, he supposed. And after having heard the stories of the strange sentient coins, he wanted to know the stories behind more of the enchanted things here. It hadn't occurred to him before—he was too engrossed in the strangeness of it all for the more refined curiosities to intrigue him. Now he had time to acknowledge them, and he completely forgot about the Lady of the Tomb for which he had come. He stared, mesmerized, at stacks of chattering books on the floor, their covers jabbing like lips, and an odd clockwork machine whose only purpose seemed to puff colorful smoke. As he wandered away from the coins—who'd begun to roll around on the table talking with one another—he came upon three objects that sat under blankets. They were adjacent to a large map that depicted the land of Urrd, an enormous copper dollhouse, and a weird set of furniture. The furniture drew his attention more immediately because they had clawed feet, squamous fabric, and creepy eyes that were closed. He had never seen anything like them. There were odd-shaped chairs, an unusual couch, a bizarre ottoman, and an insidious-looking chiffonier. Cat had also begun to inspect them with a sort of morbid fascination, but soon, James's attention had returned to the mysterious objects beneath the beautiful blankets. These blankets had interlacing gold floral designs, and he imagined whatever they were hiding was even more beautiful.

Before he could touch them, however, Cat gave a bark of fright and sprang away from the chiffonier, which had suddenly opened its pair of large, bulbous eyeballs. They were staring lazily at Cat, and a low growl vibrated from somewhere inside its throat. One of the clawed feet moved forward.

"Yikes!" Cat said.

James agreed with "yikes," but he could not pretend he was surprised anymore—there were flying books and talking coins, what was a walking chiffonier? Seeing that Cat was not in any danger, he turned his attention back to the blankets.

"James, look. It's a walking—" Cat paused as the chairs, ottoman, and finally the couch began to crawl around, making animal snorts.

"I see that," James said. But there was only one thing in the Tomb of Forgotten Secrets—as far as he could see anyway—that was covered up. *A secret among secrets*, he thought. He felt a strange tingly sensation, as though his skin was prickling from a shiver.

At last, he reached for the sheet on the left of the three objects. But before his fingers could touch it, he was interrupted again. This time by a voice:

"I wouldn't if I were you."

He spun around, looking for it. It wasn't one of the coins. They had tiny voices. This voice, however, came from one of the many shelves nearby. Of the odd things on the shelves, he saw only a peacock made of purple glass, an old brass bust of a king, a set of gold weighing scales held up by a porcelain mole, and a fancy copper dollhouse. "Who said that?" he asked.

Cat was too busy following the walking couch as it padded across the red carpeted floor to notice.

When nothing spoke up, James reached for the blanket again.

"Don't touch that!"

It was a different voice this time.

"In fact, don't touch anything."

By now, he could tell the voices were coming from the large dollhouse built like a fancy copper palace. At least he had *thought* it was a dollhouse. Now he saw it was an elaborate cage, and there were three different-colored weasels living inside.

"Cat, come here!" James yelled.

Cat was still examining the strange livestock, having determined they were not dangerous. They were wandering around, nudging tables and shelves and snorting like cows at pasture. He looked up, his eyes full of wonder, and came over to join James beside the beautiful cage. The weasels had come up to the entrance and were watching them with curious, beady eyes.

"They talk, too," James said. "But they're like—" He paused. Undoubtedly, the voices communicated a sense that they *knew* stuff. Not like the coins that just seemed silly.

"Hello," said a green-and-yellow-polka-dot weasel. "I'm Poppy."

"Zippy," said a purple-and-pink-striped weasel.

"And Dippy," a third orange, striped, and spotted weasel said.

James folded his arms as Cat stepped back, looking impressed. "Who are you?" James asked.

"Consider us your advisors," Poppy said.

"Advisors?" Cat grimaced.

"We advised you not to touch that," explained Zippy, pointing at the blankets.

"Why?" Cat asked.

"Because everything is in here," Dippy said.

"For a reason," Poppy finished.

"Very dangerous," Zippy told them.

"I see," James said. "Why do you speak like that? Why does Poppy speak first, then Zippy, then Dippy?"

"Why does winter turn to spring?" Dippy asked.

"Spring to summer?"

"Summer to fall?"

"Fall to winter?" finished Dippy. "Oh—no need to answer, it was rhetorical. Now, could you do us a favor?"

"Could you let us out of here?" Poppy asked.

"Mighty boring for incredible geniuses," Zippy started.

"Such as we," Dippy went on.

"To be locked up for centuries," finished Poppy.

"No," Cat said nastily. "You just told us not to touch anything. How dumb do you think we are?"

"Did we?" Zippy asked.

"Oh, yes we *did*," said Dippy. "But it is OK to free *us*. We're your advisors."

"Dangerous we are not," finished Poppy.

"What he said." James nudged his head at Cat. "You're forbidden, aren't you? Maybe it's because you're talking weasels."

"Or those strange colors," Cat pointed out.

"I thought our colors might have had something to do with these bars," Zippy admitted.

"Ah, but there are so many things that are forbidden here," Dippy said.

"Great works of philosophers and intellectuals from all over time. Poems and works of literature," Poppy rambled.

"Spells created by great—or terrible—wizards," Zippy elaborated.

"Is there a difference between great and terrible?" Dippy asked.

"*No*," Poppy said.

"Or recipes for the most sumptuous desserts," said Zippy, and smacked his tiny pink lips.

"Curious—where's that recipe?" Dippy asked.

"It's crumpled and stuffed between one of the yellowed leaves of a taciturn tome," Poppy answered. "'Tis a cheesecake, I heard one of the tomes say."

"Tickles the palate in such a way, you feel as though you've discovered a most agreeable afterlife," Zippy said.

"Once you taste the cheesecake, you are doomed," Dippy said.

"If you are forced."

"To abstain," finished Zippy.

"Gluffors were not afraid to eat it," Dippy told them, "but they ended up waging a war for the secret ingredient."

"For a thousand years," Poppy reflected.

"The ingredient is powdery bliss," Zippy said.

"And then there are the creations," Dippy continued.

"Terrible ones like that rongleblaster," Poppy explained, nudging his head toward something across the hall.

On a pedestal and encased in glass, was an odd-looking instrument that looked frighteningly similar to a rifle.

"The pinderbogle," Zippy said, nudging his head at a glass tank that had tubes connecting to a jar with a brain in water.

"And worst of all, the Zjkakgfpadupfhl." Dippy nudged his colorful head at the stone box on a top shelf across from them. It had a glass screen. "Took us ten years just to properly pronounce that. It channels evil from the darkest recesses of hell—a world of senseless drivel and lackadaisical drama of the poorest tastes that can melt your brain into soup. A whole generation watched these things a thousand years ago. The descendants of those inhabitants now reside in Logres to this very day—and they are called ogres."

"OK," James said. "But what's under the blankets?"

"Oh, you don't want to see *those*," Poppy said. "They're boring."

"Old," said Zippy.

"Mirrors," Dippy finished.

James stepped toward them, and before Poppy could speak up, he threw the sheet off the first one. "Won't mind if we look, then," he said.

It was *not* a mirror. Not one that he had seen, anyway. First of all, the top of the mirror had a gold face belonging to a woman. The face had the serenest expression, and the work was gorgeously done—a masterpiece for sure. The whole frame was gold, with ornate jewels embedded in elaborate designs, and the whole thing stood on gold clawed feet. But the beauty of it was not what stole his eyes—what stole them was the image *in* the glass. It wasn't a reflection at all. It was the bottom of a sea.

It *had* to be enchanted. The sea looked *very* real, with fish swimming through the water past the glass, and the view being from atop a coral reef.

"*Whoa!*" Cat said breathlessly.

James took a step back from it. It almost seemed as though there was no glass in front of it, and that he could reach into it and touch the water.

"Mesmerizing, isn't it?" Zippy said.

"Now I'll bet he'll do something *really* clever," Dippy said. "He'll *touch* it."

"Maybe he'll jump into it," Poppy added with a giggle.

Cat pulled the blankets off the other two. They were made similarly, but these scenes were vastly different. The one in the middle led to a ledge that stood over an active volcano. The other, however, led to the tranquility of outer space, which Cat was gazing into, his mouth hanging open as his eyes reflected enchantedly on the billions of stars.

James stepped toward the volcanic one and raised his hand toward it. He felt heat bristling on the palm of his skin.

"You can step into these things, can't you?" he asked, looking back at the three weasels.

"Of course you can," Zippy said.

"But you said they were just ordinary mirrors." James's tone had turned waspish now.

"We said that," Dippy admitted.

"That's quite ordinary to us," Poppy pointed out, "seeing as we've been looking at them for so long."

"How long have you been here?" Cat asked, looking at them.

James turned toward them and felt another chill go through him. There was something about these creatures that was more unsettling than any of the things he'd seen. Even the cage with the large undead bird, or the crystal ball with that wild, horrid face in it. "Are you some sort of—" He paused, not knowing what to call them. "What *are* you?"

"Advisors," Zippy said innocently.

"Whatever," James muttered, giving up. "Anyway, we're looking for a woman called the Lady of the Tomb. Would you happen to know where we could find her?"

"Try one of the mirrors," Dippy said.

"Your advice is rubbish," Cat growled. "James, throw the blankets over the cage."

"I agree," James said.

But Poppy said, "All right, we'll tell you. Two of the mirrors lead to death."

"One of them leads to the Lady of the Tomb," finished Zippy.

"Now, are you going to let us out?" asked Dippy.

"Or leave us here to die of boredom?" Poppy said.

"Dunno," James replied, picking up one of the blankets. "Which one leads to the lady?"

"Oh, clever!" Zippy said. "The boy's trying to bargain."

"Our freedom," said Dippy.

"For the lady."

"Well?" James said, still holding the blanket. "You can either help us—"

"Or shut up," Cat said.

"We'd love to help," Zippy started.

"But we don't know *which* mirror is the right one," finished Dippy.

"So you're useless," Cat surmised.

"That was insolent," Poppy said.

"They're always insolent."

James was about to put the blanket over the cage, when he stopped. "What do you mean by that, Zippy?"

"The last man who came through here had a tongue on him, too," said Dippy. "He called us useless."

"Very upsetting," said Poppy.

"*Who?*" Cat demanded.

"The man with a mask," said Zippy.

"A cloak," said Dippy.

"And a cane," said Poppy.

"Oskar." James looked at Cat, before turning back to them. "OK—answer me carefully, or"—he stepped toward them—"or you'll get the blanket. Where did he go?"

"Through the mirror," Zippy said.

"*Which* mirror?" James demanded angrily.

"The—uh—middle one," Dippy said.

James turned to look at the middle one. Certainly, if the weasels were lying, they'd step into a burning crater full of lava. He looked back at Dippy. "Are you sure? If you're lying—"

"We can't come back and release you," Cat finished.

"I'm sure," Poppy said.

Cat grabbed James's arm. "I should go first—just to see—"

But James shook his hand off and looked back at the weasels. "You're lying, aren't you?" He didn't know which one to look at, so he looked at Zippy.

"Me?" said Zippy. "Oh—I'm not lying. It's the left one, for sure."

"You said it was the middle!" Cat shouted.

"*I* said it was the middle," Dippy said, "but I wasn't sure."

"But I *was* sure," Poppy said, "that it was the one on the right."

Cat just shook his head. "Forget it, James. We'd better—"

But at that moment, they heard a voice echo across the hall from the direction they'd come.

"Touch nothing."

It was Wolf.

27

CURSE OF THE FAYLING

There were plenty of places to hide. They sought refuge behind an out-of-the-way table with brass, patina-stained candlesticks, and a cracked statue of a chimera made from alabaster. The tablecloth's frilled edges dropped to the floor, and when they crouched, they were afforded a view of the small clearing by lifting a fold of it.

Just as they'd begun to hear sounds of someone approaching, Cat remembered the light, and scurried out of his hiding spot. He snatched the oil lamp from the table where the coins had fallen silent, and, scampering low like a mouse, slid back under the table again. *"Imwa!"*

James reached out and stilled the moving tablecloth. "Thought they were *ahead*. So, Oskar gave them the slip?"

Cat's response was to slap a hand over James's mouth.

Seconds later, footsteps echoed in their immediately surrounding. A tall man had followed the trail through the piles of treasures, along with a dozen monkeys in helmets, yellow-and-crimson-striped gambesons, and their miniature crossbows strapped over their shoulders.

Lying flat on his stomach, James could look up high enough from under the tablecloth to see the man. He figured it was Wolf, judging by his sharp tone, and he saw that he was no longer invisible. He wore a dark-green robe and a hood that was thrown off. His ivory skin was a motley of tattoos—the most distinctive being a centipede that was inked along his left cheek, its mandibles stopping at the chin, and he had piercing, steely eyes—eyes that were looking now at the three wondrous mirrors.

"This misadventure has delayed us for too long," Wolf growled.

James heard Cat snort quietly beside him. Apparently, Cat had come to the same conclusion: something had happened to delay Wolf, which wasn't a surprise—he'd brought a troop of monkeys with him.

"*Luros,*" Wolf murmured, gesturing with three fingers in the air. Almost at once, cast-iron wyverns that James hadn't noticed before that were holding old candles in their mouths came to life, rattling on chandeliers above him. They crawled along it, tails flickering, before taking to the air. Flapping iron wings, they swooped down to stand on the table with the coffer.

One of the monkeys was startled by this and raised his crossbow, but Wolf knocked the weapon from his hand. It clattered on the floor. Meanwhile, the candles in the cast-iron wyvern's mouths had burst into flame. Once this had happened, the creatures turned back into statues with tiny ruby eyes.

"Do not *shoot* anything either," Wolf drawled, looking at the monkey going to retrieve his crossbow.

A short way off behind them, they heard another monkey screech. Wolf paid the noise no heed as he turned to the mirrors and strode toward them, slipping a hand into his robe's pocket. A few moments later, a monkey skidded into view looking harassed. On all fours he scrambled up onto the table with the coffer of coins and looked behind him, hissing.

James could not figure out why he was behaving this way until he heard a small sound—like tiny metal rods clicking on the floor. The troop of monkeys turned their heads toward the sound expectantly—*click, click, click*.

James leaned forward more to see what it was. It was a copper stool with long, spindly, penny-colored legs, trotting like an old mongrel. It stopped at the table, its plated seat twisting and turning to look for where the monkey had gone, and then raised its two front legs up to the table.

The monkey turned and shrieked at Wolf, who stood gazing into the enchanted mirrors.

"Stop your griping, Groop," Wolf snarled, pulling an old book out of his pocket. "Told you not to touch it." He came back toward the table and set the book on it as his troop of monkeys spread out, examining their surroundings. As he leafed through the pages, Groop kicked ineffectually at the enchanted stool.

"We're near the sanctum," Wolf said, fingering through pages and stopping at an earmarked section. "*Oros Mirrors*," he murmured at last, turning around.

Oros Mirrors, James thought. He remembered his grandfather had one in the attic of his old house. Quizlow had used it to transport himself from Paris to them in an instant. Of course, he should have recognized them! But the one he'd seen was cracked and showed only a reflection of himself.

One of the monkeys made hand signals to Wolf, but Wolf only shook his head. "Rat knows which mirror to use. Unquestionably, that was his plan when he crossed me." Wolf dug a thumb into the book until his pad flushed brick-red.

Groop stumbled backward and fell on the pile of coins. At that moment, several voices cried, "Unhand us, you simian cutthroat! You haven't earned us!"

Groop was so startled by the voice, he sprang off the table, sending the coins scattering across the floor.

Almost immediately, the copper stool darted after him like a joyful pup, and the corroded coins bellowed, "*Thieves! Thieves!*"

"Enough!" Wolf shouted. He grabbed Groop by the throat as he was scampering past, chased by the enchanted stool. "One more sound out of you—" he growled. The stool came scurrying up to him, and he gave it a vicious kick, and sent it tumbling across the floor into a pile of chattering books. The commotion toppled over a brass bust of a woman wearing jewelry. He threw the monkey, who landed on his feet and rushed under the table in the middle of the clearing, clutching his throat.

"Already we're farther than Grisledor," Wolf said. "I won't let a damn mirror stand in my way. There must be some clue as to which one he chose."

One of the monkeys, James assumed was some sort of lieutenant, gave an unintelligible squawk, and gestured wildly at the blankets on the floor.

"No doubt he pulled them all off to deceive us," conjectured Wolf.

Funny, James thought. *That wasn't our intention.* Though now that he thought about it, he supposed Oskar had slipped under the blankets without removing them for the very reason Wolf mentioned.

The lieutenant tapped Wolf's elbow and Wolf looked down to find him pointing at his pocket. "Yes," he said, understanding. He went over to the table with the coffer and placed the book on it. Then he reached into his pocket, pulled out the beautiful chrysoprase stone, and set her on the book.

He's going to use Roseheart? James was confused. *How?* He was just wondering this when he saw that enchanted stool jump up out of the pile it had been kicked into. A string of pearl necklaces from the bust dangled off its metallic corner.

This frightened one of the monkeys, causing him to leap away from it. He ended up banging into a chair, which sent him tumbling sideways and rolling into the leg of the table James and Cat were hiding beneath.

The boys flinched and crept backward, but James's heel nudged against an easel behind him where an oil painting had been positioned.

The upset painting toppled to the floor.

This caught the monkey's attention, even as the copper stool bolted, yelping like a terrier and vanishing into the vast hall. James and Cat held their breaths as the suspicious primate hobbled toward them and pried aside the tablecloth with a questing finger.

"*Alyshyn Sigoris*," Wolf said before he could go any farther, and the monkey turned away and scampered back toward the table where Wolf was.

Almost at once there was a flash of beautiful light, and the living mockingbird stood on the book in the place of the stone.

"—me back to stone!" she cried.

Relieved as James was for not having been discovered, he was still shocked by this new development. Surely Oskar knew the song, but how was *Wolf* able to use her? Then he remembered Quizlow telling him that the Wozigod had ways of getting past the Blood Magic. Certainly, Cowl had ways, too. *So, the only reason Wolf needed Oskar was to know which mirror to enter?*

"Fowl," Wolf said coldly. "Despite your efforts to stall us, we've made it here."

"I thought you didn't need me, you bloody platypus. The song was all you needed, and you forced it out of me. So now, why don't you fall on a hippogriff's horn and let me be?"

Groop giggled from under the table.

"Tell me about the Oros Mirrors."

"You may know how to make a lady sing, my dear, but this disposition you shan't temper."

Wolf reached into his robe's pocket and pulled out a small bottle. He uncorked it and poured a drop out onto his finger and held it up.

"So, you possess a drop of Dreadful blood. My allegiance doesn't waver, you grunting wildebeest. Music can be teased from a stone, but what you want is submission, which I shan't give! The blood is useless from here on, yeh mooncalf. Haven't you figured it out yet?"

Wolf's hand turned into a fist. "I'll—"

"Hurt me? Please do, you smelly tapir. Do your bloody worst! Surely even a fool like yourself would know not to smite a fayling. Go on, smite me and find out."

"*Alyshyn Sigoris*," Wolf said.

"I'll turn," she cried with a sardonic laugh, "but only so I don't have to look upon your minotaur face!" And with that, she turned back to stone.

Wolf picked her up and dropped her back into his pocket. Cursing, he wandered back to the mirrors again, followed by the monkeys. At last, coming up with an idea, he turned around and barked, "Groop—here—*now*!"

Tentatively, Groop came out from under the table and approached him.

Wolf pointed to the mirror on the left. "Go."

Groop stepped back and shook his head.

Wolf was about to take a step toward him, when a voice spoke up. "Won't work, anyway."

It was Poppy.

Wolf looked at the copper cage. "You talk," he said.

"We talk," Zippy agreed.

"Did a man come through here?"

"A man did," said Dippy.

"Which mirror did he go through?"

"A good question," Poppy said.

"And we'd like to answer that," Zippy said.

"But you should set us free first," Dippy suggested.

"Yes, perhaps then we'd remember," taunted Poppy.

"Doubt that," Wolf said, turning back to the mirrors.

"That seems to never work," Zippy moaned.

"You'd think by the third time today we'd have some luck," Dippy sighed.

Wolf was about to turn back to Groop, when he stopped and looked at them again. *"Third?"*

"Oh yes. Three times," Poppy confirmed.

"First time it was with that fellow with the old, dented mask," elaborated Zippy.

"We told him where to find a better-looking mask in exchange for our freedom, but he just ignored us," said Dippy.

"What was the *second* time?"

"With those two raggedy beggar boys," Poppy giggled.

"They're hiding right under there," Zippy said, nudging his head toward the table with the cloth draped over it. "Jumped under that there table soon as you arrived."

James and Cat had begun to slip away, but in seconds, the monkeys had sprung up onto the tabletop, scattering the candlesticks, and pointing their crossbows down at them.

Putting their hands on their heads, they came out of hiding, flanked by their captors. "What happened, Wolf?" James spat. "Finally got stabbed in the back by one of your own?"

Wolf just scowled at them as he advanced on them. "How did you get here before us?"

"Flying carpet," Cat said.

Wolf slapped him across the face, and Cat tripped over his feet and fell. "Silly me," Wolf said, turning to James. "You have that accursed ship of your father's and her magic. That means your uncle is here, too." Wolf grabbed James by the arm, squeezing tightly, and pulled him toward the mirrors. "Which one did he take?"

"He's—" James started.

"He took the left," Cat said from the floor, holding the side of his face.

James paused, seeing that Wolf was watching him intently. "*Yes*," he said decisively. "*That* one."

Wolf let go of his arm and turned, lowering his eyes toward Cat. His hand had slipped back into his pocket where it was fondling the fayling there. "Suniri native, eh? Magic's inherent in your blood." He squatted beside Cat now. A hand tattooed with a wolf's head on it reached out and took his jaw into strong fingers. "Suniri blood's powerful. Used to have Jalfar trash like you abducted off the streets of Pyaret. Blood of a Jalfar was worth three basilisk tongues on the shadow market. Eyes fetch a good price, too." He took Cat's wrist then and lifted him from the floor. "Come, young Jalfar. Let us see if you are telling the truth."

"But I—I—" Cat stammered.

"No you don't!" James hissed, stepping toward Wolf.

The monkeys were on him instantly, one of them grabbing his arm. James pulled away from him and aimed a kick at his belly. His foot connected, and the monkey shrieked and went down.

He heard a whisper from Wolf, and when James turned around, he saw that Cat's body had gone limp.

Wolf pirouetted on the balls of his feet to face James, his lips pursed thin and purple with violence. *"You're trying me, child!"* As he said this, his fingers stretched out toward him, and James saw the air there ripple, like a heat wave— *"Voltaris!"*

James stumbled back, expecting to be scorched by fire. But instead, Wolf's forearm twitched—the tattoos moving eerily over the skin and illuminating with pulsing red light. Wolf stepped toward him and his fingers clutched James by the jaw. He gave a cry of pain. The fingers clamped viselike over his skin, almost crushing his bone. Gritting his teeth, he struggled to free himself, but it was like trying to pry stone from his face.

Wolf's lips twisted upward in a cruel smile, tremulously, and he shoved James back toward the table with supernatural strength. "Think you're clever?" Wolf said as he strode toward James, cloak sweeping out behind him.

Behind Wolf, James spied his friend lying lifelessly on the floor, but Wolf seized him again, pulling his jaw up toward a heavily inked face drawn up in a dark scowl. The forearm continued to pulse with the flecks of red embers in his veins, lending him the unnatural strength. *"Look at me."*

He looked into eyes that had turned reptilian. The arteries creeping up his throat pulsed with the same fluid in his forearms. "If you want to live, make yourself useful," he crooned in his ear.

James mumbled, but was barely able to make his jaws move. He tried to work words out of his throat.

"I 'ill," James mumbled.

Wolf slackened his grip.

"I'll obey. I swear."

"You'll obey all right."

"I'll obey." He paused, feeling the pulse crescendo in his throat against Wolf's fingers. "As much as my father did." He saw the smile ebb slowly from Wolf's centipede jaw.

"*What?*"

But James gave him no more time to deliberate on the meaning. "*Alyshyn Sigoris!*"

"You—" But something had begun to struggle in Wolf's pocket. The mage had just enough time to register what it was, when the bird shot out of his pocket and into the air over his head.

Wolf held on to James then, sneering, whispered, "Nice try— *Alfars!*" He thrust three fingers on James's forehead as he said it.

James felt suddenly drowsy.

But at that instant, he heard Roseheart cry, "Oh no you don't— *Cratos Aros!*"

Wolf's fingers had suddenly slipped off James's forehead, as though his hand had been deflected.

Even as James slid from the table to the floor, Wolf stumbled forward into it, cursing. Regaining his poise, he whirled around to confront Roseheart, who was circling above him.

"*Matra Sabotulia!*" she cried.

Suddenly, the cast-iron wyverns sleeping on the table awoke, their eyes glittering with burning rubies. Squawking, they hissed, and spat tiny bursts of fire at Wolf.

The monkeys shrieked, leaping out of the way, as a rosebud of fire caught on Wolf's cloak.

Wolf clapped the flame out with his hand, then aimed at the wyverns. "*Sutros!*"

One of them burst into bits of shrapnel, but the others took flight.

"*Matra Sabotulia!*" Roseheart cried again.

And all at once, James could hear whispers in the hall coming from everywhere. He turned on the floor, feeling sensations coming back into his legs, and looked for the source of the sounds. Some of the books chattering on the floor had jumped up and were flapping through the air now.

"Forced me to sing, did you, you poison-tongued pangolin," the fayling shrieked. *"I'll learn you!"*

More books were flying off the shelves. And still more were swooping down through the air toward Wolf.

"You will beg to die when I'm through!" Roseheart screamed.

Wolf leaped aside; a flock of tomes sailed over him. He reached for the hilt of his sword. But before he could draw it, he was belted over the head by the same swarm of books that had spun around and come back. At the same time, a wyvern sprang onto one of his sleeves and set it on fire.

"Alyshyn Sigoris!" Wolf shouted, shaking the creature off and clapping out the fire.

"Fool!" Roseheart cried, having settled on top of a bookshelf high above him. "The child's claim is stronger. So, blow it out your arse!"

Wolf towed his sword from its sheath. Like his knife, the sword burned with fire, but the fire was only visible an inch off the silver. He swiped at the tomes circling overhead and a breaker of flame swept through the air catching dozens of them. They flapped off, howling, while some fell burning to the table, pages turning black with crusting embers eating over their words.

"Matra Sabotulia!" Roseheart shrieked again, sailing past him.

Now the coins hurtled off the table, crying, "Thief! Thief!"

"Matra Sabotulia!"

The chairs, couch, table, and chiffonier growled and charged toward Wolf, bowling him over.

James peeled himself off the floor and began crawling toward the unconscious body of his friend. *"Cat!"* His tongue felt like lead.

Monkeys were shrieking around him and scampering everywhere. *Twang!* Quarrels sang through the air, piercing the chiffonier, causing it to roar. One monkey scrambled onto a bookshelf. Two loosed their quarrels at a swarm of books flying after them before being struck and knocked over, their crossbows clattering across the floor.

James reached Cat and grabbed his arm. He pulled open his friend's eyelids, but he was completely out. *Have to get him out of here*, he thought frantically.

Chaos was rapidly unfurling in the hall. Wolf had leaped up onto the table and swiped at the attacking furniture, sending streams of fire at them. The flame danced over the table like a conflagrant plastic sheet and caught on the galloping chairs. They gave wild growls and ran off, sending embers dancing through the air.

One of the monkeys had leaped onto the chiffonier that was prancing across the hall, knocking over a bust of a king and a beautiful golden harp. But when the creature roared, the monkey screamed and jumped off, tumbling to the floor, and was trampled to death.

During all of this, the weasels in their copper palace were leaping around shouting with joy and clapping their paws.

"Exciting!" shouted Poppy.

"Thrilling!" hooted Zippy.

"More! I want more!" cried Dippy.

Wolf was huddling beside the table now. He slipped the enchanted knife from his belt, and spying Roseheart flying by, hurled it at her. As he did, he whispered a spell, pointing his three fingers. The fiery blade shot through the air, riding on his whisper. It channeled the knife, guiding it true, and pierced her breast.

"*Matra Sabotulia!*" she shrieked one last time. Then she fell on to the table, having returned to stone form, bouncing twice, thrice—the fiery, ornate blade still penetrating her.

Finally, she went still.

As the tomes took flight again and the cast-iron wyverns turned back into statues, James watched as Wolf cautiously went over to it.

Is she dead? he wondered. But then he remembered what she'd said before. *Surely even a fool like yourself would know not to smite a fayling.*

But certainly, the worst of what she could do was over, he thought.

He climbed to his knees and stared at the stone on the table. But before Wolf could reach it, it split in two. The mage halted dead in his tracks, his ivory complexion turning pale. The two fragments had begun to spin rapidly, like two tops, creating a high-pitched whir. Then they flicked off the table in different directions, ricocheting off the bookshelf, an old chest, smashing several antique plates, pinging off of a king's bust, and shattered a ewer full of ash.

Wolf had dropped to the floor as the whirring pieces continued to boomerang around the hall like bullets. Finally, one of them struck the mirror beside the copper palace-cage. The sound of the shard striking the glass was loud, yet musical.

James could only imagine what magic the fayling possessed to maintain such power, even after being broken by Wolf's magic dagger. But it came to an end. They fell to the floor, having lost their magic, yet continued to spin and spin for what felt like minutes, before finally stopping.

After a while, Wolf got up, walked over to it, and kicked the pieces with his foot.

James got his own feet beneath him. He could move them now. Cat had begun to stir beside him, but his face looked numb. "James," he murmured, "what's—"

But his voice was cut off by a loud crack. Something had splintered. It was a sound loud enough to drown out the screeching monkeys still clinging to the bookshelves.

Slowly, James turned toward the sound. It was coming from the mirror the fayling shard had struck. The mirror of the sea's bottom. A large crack was spreading across the glass.

Wolf turned toward it, too, his eyes growing with alarm.

Then it burst.

A deluge of water poured into the hall.

Wolf backed away from it, cursing.

The monkeys shrieked, climbing the bookshelves higher, dropping crossbows and daggers.

It's Sarvelok all over again! James thought wildly, and grabbed Cat's arm as water gushed around him.

"James," Cat said sleepily, "we have to go. Can't stay!"

Tomes were flying away in huge swarms, all jabbering at once. Their combined covers looked like a cloud of smoke. Inanimate books were falling off the shelves, splashing in the water. Some opened up, emitting jets of flame, while others howled like banshees and sent wintery blasts like ice spells. Still others burst into colorful fireworks, like eruptions of rainbow-dappled light that sent wildly spinning comets through the air with trails of purple and pink smoke and burst into emerald fires. The beastly furniture roared and galloped through the hall, knocking over objects and shelves. A flock of screaming tomes, some having caught emerald fire, raced past, giving off acrid orange smoke, and then swooped down, gliding through the mirror leading into the erupting volcano.

It's the middle one, he thought. It was just speculation, but somehow, he knew the books that had resided here for perhaps hundreds of years would know which mirror to go through. "There!" he cried. "We're going after them!"

By now, water was up to their knees. James lifted Cat, getting his arms around his neck. "Come on, you've gotta help me walk, Cat!" he cried.

Cat moaned sleepily but put his weight under his feet.

Hearing a cry, James turned partially. There was Wolf, fighting off an angry couch, which had just bitten him. He tumbled off the table he was standing on into the water.

Bracing Cat, he waded toward the mirror. *Please be the right one!* he thought, feeling the heat bristling his skin. *Please be the right one!*

"James!" Cat moaned. "Hope you know what you're doing. Don't want—"

But before he could finish, James stepped through the mirror.

28
TRUTH & REFLECTION

He thought there would have been glass because he'd seen it crack on the other mirror. But when his hand moved to touch the enchanted surface, he touched only air.

It goes away when I try, he thought briefly. For a second his hand was immersed in something icy—and then he felt a gentle tug. Next— weightlessness. That, and stillness. He was as still as time. Yet he moved faster than light.

Light.

Light like the sun. *Perfect* light. He never could properly define *perfect* light—only that he'd seen it when Roseheart transformed and that it was beautiful. Now he knew that it was very bright—so bright it could kill his eyes. But it didn't. He could stare at it for all eternity and not blink.

Am I dead?

He didn't know he'd closed his eyes—not until he found himself standing in another hall, his arm still thrown around Cat's shoulder as he held him up. He checked his surroundings. He didn't know if the light-place he'd been in was all a strange dream or not. But here he stood, facing tonalite-brick walls covered in algae. The walls climbed to a ceiling he couldn't see, dappled in stains and hairline cracks, chipped and faceted and inscribed in strange runes. Rusted, cast-iron braziers had been ignited along them, wafting the odor of cooking pitch and other peculiar substances, and they gave off an artichoke-green that reflected everywhere.

The hall smelled like the sea. It was wet like the sea, too. Water leaking from the walls had swamped the floor, but it didn't rise past the mudguard of his shoes.

Something crackled along the wall above them and he looked toward the sound to see the books that had flown through the mirror. Like flitting moths, they were darting across the walls as though looking for a place to escape.

Dead ahead, something caught his eye—a large head like a Moai statue had been carved into the wall there, glowering with a vicious frown.

Cat's legs had all but given out now, and James felt he could no longer hold his weight and lowered him into the shallow water. "Cat?" he said. Even though he'd said it quietly, his voice carried across the hall.

Gently, he rolled Cat on his back. Then, crouching, pried open one of his eyelids. He couldn't properly make out if his purple irises contracted in the dark or not, but he pressed his hand on his chest and felt him breathing. He was just out. Out cold. He'd be fine if he lay there. His own drowsiness had left him even though his feet still had pins in them, but his legs still felt cumbersome. Wolf's spell had not had a full effect on him—probably because Roseheart had interfered.

From his crouched position, the mirror came into view. It was reflecting only the hall back at him, which wasn't consistent with what the other side had done. He noticed something near the statue's head behind him from the reflection and turned around. It had eluded him before—the sight of the hall was majestic, almost overwhelming with its size. But now he made out a dais at the far end.

And a figure standing over it.

He stood. Then, sloshing through the inch-deep water, approached it. The musty odor of algae crept under his nose; the water-soaked tonalite brick was slippery under his shoes. Four braziers standing on copper legs surrounded the dais atop stone plinths; only two of them were lit with the emerald fire.

If I find him, I don't know what I'll do. He was unaware he'd been clenching his hand into a fist until he felt a sharp pain where his nail had once broken off leaving the quick raw there. *He'll have to face me.* He knew the man dreaded to look at him—the mask was his shield. *When he looks at me, he sees his betrayal. But I'll force him to look me in the eyes!*

The water at his feet got shallow until he trod on wet, mossy stone. The plinths with the braziers had runes inscribed on it, like the walls, and faces of what he suspected to be gods appeared to gloat at him, their tongues lolling out. The figure had his back to him, but he'd taken his cloak off and had thrown it over one of the braziers he hadn't lit. The cane lay against it, too—its aventurine orb shiny in the jade light.

"Oskar." He didn't need to shout. He was only about a hundred feet away, but his voice bounced everywhere.

"You should not have come." The man hadn't turned to the sound of his voice. His shoulders rose; his head was hunched low.

James could tell sensation had come back to him—his toes were cold from the water sloshing around in his shoes. Yet, another coldness had begun to settle, sliding through his thighs down to his feet.

Then the man turned. The old gunmetal mask with the slits for eyes and hideous gashes was still on his face.

James grimaced. He was close enough now so that the green light could expose the resentment he was feeling. "Who do you think you are?"

Rat reached for his cane and enclosed his gloved hand around the ball. "James—"

"Who the *hell* do you think you are?" This time, his voice was thick, his stomach tensing with visceral hate. "You were supposed to be my *Spell-guardian*. My mother entrusted that duty to you—and—and you just left me to—" His teeth clenched; his flared nostrils contracted, pulling his forehead into hateful ripples.

Silence.

"Why?"

"James," the man said quietly. "I did not betray you." He took a step down the stairs. "I'm *saving* you."

"Saving me?" He folded his arms. "Take off your mask. Take it off and look at me."

"Very well." Rat laid his cane down and unfastened the ugly mask that'd been pressed against his face. Then he pulled it away.

James took a step back, his lower jaw hanging.

The ugly plate of gunmetal iron clattered on the steps of the dais at the man's feet.

The icy sensation had stolen over all James's limbs by now. He was paralyzed all over. He dropped to one knee, the breath having departed his lungs, as he stared into familiar citrine eyes.

"Grandpa?"

29
THE LADY OF THE TOMB

He no longer wore the long white beard he was so accustomed to scratching. Nor did he have that long, bedraggled, white hair, its greasy locks twisting down his back. But he had that familiar liver-spotted hawk nose and the same citrine eyes, though the glints of mischief had long seemed to have waned into old sadness.

"I—I—I thought you were—"

"It worked out that you thought I was," Arthur said, stepping off the last step.

"Why?" *No, I know why*, he thought. Wolf had pretty much said back in the Sarvelok's shipyard. *"You've had your chance."* The finger with the broken nail pulsed with pain as his nails dug into his palm. "In Urrd, during those years we were apart"—he came toward his grandfather, his eyes not leaving the old man's tallow skin impressed with the lines of the mask—"you were supposed to *turn* me."

"James," Arthur said, holding up a hand, "I—"

"The man who killed my father—he *bought* you, didn't he? You went to Urrd to convince me to join him. To join Cowl." It all began to make sense. "The darkness inside you. The sinister influence you'd had on me when I was a child. Raising me to be like your son, the Dark Lord. Cowl had instructed it.

"But you failed. You were sent away for nine years. And I'd grown up with a normal life. Away from the influence of—of a monster!"

Arthur was silent for a moment staring at him with those citrine eyes. "I know that's how it looks, James. But...you have it wrong." Arthur took a step toward him. "I don't want you to join Cowl." He took another ungainly step toward him. James could see his hand tremble as he picked up the cane again. "I want you to *kill* him."

James felt his feet turn into icicles. Not from the outside, but from the *inside*. He stared at the old man—a man he no longer recognized. Here was this man he thought he knew—wise, gentle, the man in his bedroom who told him he needed to learn respect.

James circled him in a sidestep, eyeing him distrustfully. "Is that supposed to win me over, or something?"

Arthur gave a small snort. "This isn't a fairy tale, *boy*," he growled, grabbing him by the arm. "Not some bloody parable you learn in Sunday school. You either kill him, or he kills you."

James wrenched his arm free. "It's that easy, is it?" he snarled.

"You're right. I was supposed to turn you when we lived in Urrd."

"For Phantom?"

Arthur raised an eyebrow, apparently surprised he knew the name. "So you've heard."

James said nothing.

"After your father died," Arthur went on, "Phantom, which was in its infancy, wanted you."

"What's so special about me?" Over the past month and a half he'd been in Nobrocoso, he hadn't done anything *particularly* special. Flying carpet aside—he hadn't cast any spells or kicked anyone's ass like his father had.

"You are the son of Jack Dreadful," Arthur said. "The Wozigod was so terrified of you they sent assassins to murder you when you were a *child*. They fear what you will become, James. And rightly so. I had dealings with the Office of the Dark, and your mother wanted me to stay connected after they were dissolved. Keep your enemies close, she said. But when we went to Urrd, I was sent away for many years and I never was able to—"

"Indoctrinate?"

"Turn you," Arthur finished. "I never intended to make you into a Dark Lord for Phantom. I wanted to—"

"Turn me into your own weapon against Cowl," James finished.

"You could use the Lady of the Tomb just as your father had. You'd be powerful. Protected.

"But when things didn't turn out the way I'd planned, I couldn't expect you to—to kill him. So, *I* had to do it. That was why I came here. I came here hoping I could summon her myself. If Wolf could do it, so could I."

"But she didn't come?"

"No," Arthur said, turning to face James. "That's why you must do it. Only you."

"So," James said, "you told them you'd turn me. But you said back in Sarvelok that I wasn't part of the plan."

"No," Arthur said. "When I returned about a month ago, I told them I hadn't managed to turn you. But I could get them the Lady of the Tomb instead. I was hoping you'd still be at the Faugs hidden from Phantom— that you'd stay hidden. But when I heard that you'd gone to Sarvelok..." He tightened his grip on his cane. "I thought I'd convinced them to leave you alone if I brought Wolf to Miasharun. I was wrong."

"Why does Cowl want her anyway?" James asked.

For a moment, Arthur seemed distant, as though he were imagining a past James could not understand. Then he turned his attention back to him. "It was your father's weapon. The one thing that made him seemingly invincible." He walked back to the dais, the gold tip striking the stone on the step.

James saw the altar where a familiar symbol had been scrawled in blood.

Grootslang.

James was about to speak again, when he heard a small sound on the floor.

Arthur turned toward it, but he was too late. A hand reached out of suddenly visible smoke and touched the back of his head. Arthur gave a small gasp and stumbled forward.

James caught him in his arms but fell under his weight. By the time he'd pushed his body from him, he was aware that someone was standing behind him.

Wolf.

Getting his feet under him, he pushed himself up and faced him. "What did you do to him?" James demanded, taking a step backward.

Wolf had appeared out of the whirl of teal smoke that had clothed his body. He was holding his sword, fire licking silently along its length. "He'll be unconscious for an hour," Wolf said. "He won't be able to interfere." He sheathed it and took a step toward James. "We knew the fool's intentions all along. But he was useful—we had no idea the key to the Tomb of Secrets was a *song*."

"You used Roseheart."

"I did."

James looked nonplussed.

"I knew about the curse, and I knew Arthur would trigger it to prevent us all from entering. I'd learned from the monkeys how Penelope had tricked Grisledor, so I brought a talisman to protect me from the curse. The two ogres were not so lucky as to have one. I cursed both of them to prevent them from transmogrifying, but as my spell was taking effect, Gunter thought better and rushed toward Rat and grabbed him, realizing he needed to touch him to prevent the curse."

"They're dead?"

"It's reversible," Wolf said.

That was how Arthur took Gunter with him, James thought. "So, once you learned about the song, you made Roseheart sing it using Dreadful blood?"

"Your mother infused the magic of the song into the fayling stone,"

Wolf said. "Arthur gave us this information so that we'd trust him."

"So, you're clever," James said sarcastically. "What do you want from me?"

Wolf was running his hand along the altar where the Dreadful blood symbol had been drawn. "I expected your grandfather would have called her by now. He did not anticipate that I would have followed him here."

"You mean the Lady of the Tomb."

Wolf looked at him. "What do you know about her, James? What has your grandfather told you?"

"Nothing," James said. "Only that Cowl wants her."

Wolf laughed.

"But you won't get her," James chided, smiling. "What is she, a sorceress or something?"

Wolf continued to laugh. "Oh, *James*. I suppose nobody thought to inform you. The Lady of the Tomb is not a sorceress." Wolf passed his hand over the altar, as though trying to detect magic there. "They'd wanted to know Jack's secret for a long time—the Wozigod," he said. "Yes—they feared this Lady of the Tomb was a powerful creature. A fire-breathing beast your father could unleash to lay waste upon the land.

"A clever scholar who'd spent a great deal of time researching her learned that she was as terrible and powerful as the legends claimed. When she awoke, the mountains would rumble. With a sweep of her claw, she could change the shape of the world. Move continents. Great men would fall. Small men would rise. Empires would crumble, and new ones would ascend from the dirt.

"But she was not the terrible beast they feared her to be—all scales, fiery breath, and earthshaking roar. No, James, she was not this at all. The Lady of the Tomb, hidden in the Tomb of Forgotten Secrets." He wiped the blood symbol from the altar. "She's a *sword*."

A sword?

"A *sword*?"

"What made Jack Dreadful the most dreaded sorcerer of all time? He had the secrets of Galajitar, and a sword that made him nigh impossible to kill."

James was still reeling from this when Wolf looked up at him. "Now you're going to call her."

"Go to hell."

Wolf chuckled, the sounds ringing off the cold, wet walls. "Perhaps I ought to call *you* wolf—the bite you have." His eyes were cold and as steely as ever. He stared down his nostrils at James. *"Choose."*

James glowered at him. "Choose what?"

"I usually don't put my marks to sleep," Wolf said, moving down the steps of the dais. "I am a Qo'atyni Silencer—I kill. But I did not kill your friend. He will sleep for days. But he's *vulnerable.*" Wolf stopped. "Still, why him? Your grandfather—Rat—has outlived his usefulness." He reached into his belt and pulled out the burning knife. "With this Aclari steel, I could cut clean through his flesh like a surgeon," Wolf said, his smile cutting through his face, "and I'd still have your friend for later."

An icicle of fear cut through James. "What do you want me to do?" he asked quietly, his body going still.

"What you intended to do when you came here, James." Wolf seized him by the arm and pulled him up the steps to the dais. As he did, he muttered a spell, and the fire on his knife flickered out. An instant later, the silver flashed in the green firelight of the braziers, and James jerked his hand away. He didn't feel pain—at first. When he looked at the palm of his hand, however, it was welling up with blood.

Wolf grabbed him by the wrist and dabbed his finger in the blood streaming out. Then he scrawled the symbol of the Grootslang on the altar. "Even my client thought your grandfather's blood would suffice. No, it's clear now that only his son will bring her. Now—*call.*"

He'd felt that she would come to him. The Lady of the Tomb. She'd come and save him. She'd save him from Stray and his gruesome contract. She'd save him from Cowl. And now, he thought she'd save him from Wolf.

But she was only a sword. The Lady of the Tomb was just a *sword*. How could a sword help him?

He had no choice but to call her.

He closed his eyes.

"Miasharun."

He could feel his hot blood flowing from his hand and dripping onto the altar. *Maybe she'll appear in my hands. I could strike Wolf down where he stands.*

Wolf's hand gripped his shoulder tightly. "Again."

"Miasharun."

He remembered when he stood at the tree with his grandpa—that night in the woods. He'd called Galajitar.

Galajitar had answered.

"Again."

"Miasharun."

He said it with all the conviction in his heart.

"Again!"

"Miasharun."

Rimbecella, too, had answered his call.

Do not control, Galajitar had said.

"AGAIN!"

"Miasharun."

The hand gripped his shoulder so tight now he was beginning to wince in pain. "You disappoint, *child*."

"I can—I can call her," he said desperately. "I know I can. I was *meant* to."

"I thought so, too," Wolf said. "But you are not your father. No." He pulled James around until he could look into Wolf's ugly inked face. "Only the Dark Lord's son can call her. But you are not he. She will not serve you. You are pathetic. Weak. Your grandfather was supposed to make you worthy. But he is weak and pathetic like you."

"You don't know him."

Wolf bent low into his face. "He came to us because he was weak and pathetic. Don't you see? His mother cursed him so he could not use magic. Her fear of the Dreadfuls' powers made him weak, feeble, *pathetic*."

"You do not know him!" Hot fluid had burst from the corners of his eyes; he balled his hands into fists as he stepped away from Wolf.

"You've done nothing but prove your uselessness," Wolf growled.

James could sense it in the man's voice. It was thick with the kind of violence that kills. *He's going to kill me*, he thought. His pulse quickened; his eyes flitted to the hilt of his enchanted sword quickly—and he remembered in a flash his training with Cat. *I only have one shot at this!* He shut his eyes, even as the pulse of fear began to overwhelm him. *Use it*, he thought. His eyes flew open. Wolf had taken a step toward him, his gloved hand reaching for the hilt.

James stepped back again.

"Faal!"

His teeth bit into his lower dry lip, and his tongue glanced off the roof of his mouth with sharp pronunciation.

He sent the breath from his stomach.

The sword was unlit as it sprang from Wolf's scabbard.

Wolf's eyebrows knit in momentary confusion as his hand clasped over thin air.

Right hand outstretched, James reached for the hilt. *I have to catch it*, he thought as he leaned toward it.

But the sword flew past him, and cartwheeled down the stairs, finally clattering on the floor.

Wolf looked up at James, stupefied. *"What—"*

James turned to make a lunge for it, but Wolf lurched forward, grabbing him before he could.

"Voltaris." The rage in Wolf's eyes as they turned reptilian could have almost melted James. The skin on his forearms pulsed redly; arteries snaking up his throat throbbed like struggling worms. He held James with hands that clenched him like stone. "Pathetic child." His hands reached

his head. James knew his face was slowly being crushed under the steel fingers. His own hands grabbed at them wildly—his feet kicking. But Wolf had lifted him clear off the dais, reptilian eyes burning straight into his.

"Faal!"

James could barely hear it with the hands over his ears—but Wolf heard it clearly because he let go. James's foot struck the edge of a step, and he stumbled and fell to the stone floor.

Wolf had whirled around, arteries throbbing in his neck and face.

There, behind him, stood Cat. He was holding Wolf's unlit sword in his hands, having conjured it from the floor where James had dropped it.

Wolf sneered at him, stepping backward. "Jalfar scum," he chided as he came off the steps, eyes locked on the Suniri's. "Think you know the secrets of Aclari steel?"

Cat approached him and raised the sword until it was aligned with his face. *"Mehrun ehayl sweyen,"* he said in a tongue even James couldn't understand. "Djinn can wield Aclari steel out of the womb—*jackass!*" And he sent a whisper like a breath onto the blade—*"Igra!"* Green fire licked up the silver.

Wolf looked to the altar where his knife lay, but Cat stalked toward it, blocking his path.

"Fool child. I am a Qo'atyni Silencer. I will murder you with my eyes shut." As he said this, he reached into his robe and pulled out a small vial of liquid. He'd managed to only uncork it before Cat flicked the blade at him.

Wolf tried to sidestep the attack, even as he ingested the liquid from the vial. But the flash of green caught his cloak. Bursts of emerald fire spread across him, and he gave a cry. The teal smoke began to consume him even as the tongues of fire did, too.

Then Cat sprang forward and thrust the blade into Wolf's stomach.

Emerald fire erupted from under his cloak, bursting out of his sleeves and sending whippoorwills darting to the floor and dancing along the wet surface. A finger of flame snaked up his body to his face and lit it up like a gas lamp as it vanished in the teal smoke, and Wolf stumbled to the ground, screaming. As the smoke turned him into the color of air, the green sparks continued to spring from his clothes, forming burnt embers honeycombed in the flesh. Smoke swirled into the air. Sparkling green lights outlined his face, showing his mouth stretched wide in pain. He began to claw his way toward the shallow water, and when he reached it, it hissed, steamed, and bubbled. All James could see, however, was the water moving as a million pinprick glimmers of green reflected over the disturbed reflection.

Smoke had filled the hall. It smelled awful.

James turned to look at Cat still holding the sword with the emerald flame in hand. "I thought you were out for days."

"Like my mother said, 'only one sorcery can subdue a Jalfar—and that is death,' James."

30

AN UNFAIR PARTING

"**G**randpa." James was crouched over the old man. Cat stood over him holding the Aclari steel. It was still lit with waves of heat that wrinkled the air. "Grandpa."

"He'll be out for a while," Cat said, squatting down beside him and setting the sword on the floor. The wisps of scorching peridot flame crackled loudly on the wet tonalite stone, sending steam curling into the air. James checked his pulse on the wrist, but Cat said, "Are you feeling his pulse? My aunt was a healer—" He reached for Arthur's neck and put two fingers on the carotid artery there.

James rocked back on the balls of his feet, wrapping his arms around his knees.

"He has a slow one." Cat shook the old man. "But it's there."

James got up, found his cloak still thrown over one of the unlit braziers, and returned to put it over him before resuming his posture. It was cold, even though he could feel the heat coming off the sword. He stared at it now. The fire had dried a larger section of the stone floor and tiny green embers flicked along in webs of burnt algae. "He's my grandfather," James said. "Not my uncle."

Cat looked at him, baffled. "Was wondering why you called him that."

James told him everything. When he was finished, the fire had turned

308

the stone hot with flecks of embers, and Cat was shaking his head. "So, your grandfather's a traitor."

"No." James was still looking at the fire on the sword. "I dunno."

"He left us to die in Sarvelok, James. What was his excuse? What was his excuse for seeking out Phantom?"

"He did it on my mother's orders."

Cat stood and looked down at him. "It's your mother again. Always comes back to her. You're here because of her. She wants you to clear your family's bad name." He heaved a sigh. Then he went over to the Aclari steel, picked it up, and looked it over. He threw it. It landed in the shallow water, and the water began to bubble. He stood there looking at it silently, the green fire cooking underwater. "That was my first time."

"What?"

"Killing someone."

James looked at the back of his head, rising. "You—you said—"

"Know what I said." He turned around. "Couldn't do it before. They wanted me to. You know, in Arupa, you could make a few yammies doing it. Child assassins. Blow darts. A poisonous knife. If you were good, you could float poison into a man's tankard without him knowing with your *haas*. But that wasn't my cup of tea—no pun. I was a survivor, not a killer." He looked James in the eyes. "My mother would've never wanted it. I thought about that when I was on the streets. What my mother wouldn't have wanted to see me do. You see, if your mother Penelope really cared about you, she would have wanted you to stay in Urrd. She wouldn't have forced her husband's ugly legacy onto her son. To hell with legacy."

"Maybe you're right," James said quietly.

Cat came over to him, shoving his hands into his pockets. "Yeah, I killed for you, Prince. But this one—I'll sleep well tonight. Don't you worry about that."

James gave him a half smile, but it was more genuine than anything he'd ever done. "I'm grateful."

"Sure, Prince."

"James."

They turned back to the old man. His parched lips had moved.

"Grandpa."

Arthur's eyes opened slowly and stared at him for a long time, his breaths coming soft and shallow. "James?" He blinked and licked his lips. Slowly, he got up, holding his head. Then his eyes were alert. "Where is he?"

"Dead," Cat said.

The old man didn't seem to hear, because he scrambled to his feet, looking around. He turned toward the boiling water, the steam wafting across the hall, and scrunched up his brow, squinting at it in confusion. "What's—" When he realized it was the sword, he turned back to James. "How'd he die?"

"I killed him," Cat said.

Arthur looked at him, eyes moving from head to foot. "You're Eastern, child?"

"Jalfar."

"He saved me from Wolf."

Arthur's eyes hadn't moved from Cat. "That true?"

Cat looked down. "Wasn't going to let him kill my friend."

"Good," Arthur said. "My grandson and I are eternally grateful and are in your debt." He went to retrieve his walking stick and turned around. "I didn't expect Wolf would make it this far. Didn't expect you either, frankly. How *did* you get here? No doubt you used my son's ship?"

"We used a flying carpet," James said.

His grandpa raised his eyebrows. He was thrown. "You *what*?"

"It's a long story," James said.

But Arthur continued to fix his citrine eyes on him. "What is that on your face?" He stepped forward and pressed his thumb's pad to James's eyebrow, smoothing it out.

"What's wrong?" James asked, feeling it.

"It's silver."

"I know."

"Like your father's."

James gaped up at him, bewildered. "What do you mean like my father's?"

"Your father had silver eyebrows, too. He never told me how he got them. But he never told me anything, he was so resentful toward me."

"It was the flying carpet." He couldn't explain it. "She vanished."

"Those women—they'll do that, you know," Arthur said. "Jack had a hard time with them, too."

"Them?"

"There were more than one in his life, James. More than one."

"What are we going to do about the sword?" James asked. He'd already told Cat about the sword, and the boy had been relieved it wasn't something more mysterious. He wasn't sure what he thought the Lady of the Tomb was. A fairy, perhaps, or some sort of goddess. Either way, she seemed more devious, mysterious, and even frightening than a sword.

Arthur looked at him. "What about her?"

"She never came to me. She was supposed to protect me. I called her like Wolf had demanded. But she never came."

"I should think not." He squatted and retrieved his cloak, then put it on, slipping his arms through the wet sleeves. "I warned her to stay away."

James gaped at him.

Arthur sighed. "When I could not summon her, I realized the danger I'd put her in. I feared Wolf would find a way—perhaps using you." He went to stand beside the altar. "Penelope said that when Jack stood at this altar and dripped his blood on it, he heard the voice of Miasharun. And she looked into his soul and decided that he should serve her."

"So, he could summon her with blood?" James said, remembering the vial of blood he saw Wolf had.

"It was possible." Arthur turned his hand over, looking at the palm that he'd slashed. "But when I used my own blood, I was rejected. Just as I'd been with Galajitar," Arthur said, lowering his voice as his eyes fell uncomfortably on Cat, "she looked into me and turned me away."

James looked up into his eyes. "Should I try her now?"

Arthur had a cold smile. "No."

"But—"

"Not today," he said, wincing slightly as he put his bleeding hand on James's shoulder. "You were only supposed to meet her when you turned eighteen—and after years of guidance."

"But you told me it had to be me."

"And it does. Just not *yet*."

It left an empty feeling inside James. And a growing fear.

"But—I need her now."

"Why?" Arthur asked, stopping to look at him closely.

"Because...I want to see... I have to know the truth about..."

Arthur gave a chuckle and leaned heavily on his cane. "About what, James?"

He wasn't sure if he should tell Arthur about what Sigurd had said or not. But somehow, he knew Arthur would not believe it. And it wouldn't be fair to give him that kind of hope...to know that his son was not the Dark Lord. What if it was not true? What if it was just a way for Jack to excuse his unforgiveable behavior? It would open old wounds—wounds he could see still hidden behind Arthur's citrine eyes. Perhaps the old man deserved it.

Or maybe...just maybe I *don't want to know.*

"Nothing," James said at last. "Just...nothing."

"Very well, then. Let's get out of here."

"About that," Cat said. "There's a bit of a complication."

～

This time, he knew the light was not a dream. He realized it was pleasant, traveling through the Oros Mirror. But when they reached the other side, he came out into a wall of darkness and icy cold water. He got a mouthful of salty sea and panicked. He could only see from the light of the erupting volcano reflecting in the mirror they'd come through, and the warmth of it still touched his skin. But he immediately swam into the darkness, past bits of dirt, glittery dust particles, old wet tomes, burnt pages, swirling soggy scrolls, and fish caught in small whirlpools.

Up, up, up he swam, wishing he'd taken a deeper breath when he'd stepped through. The surface seemed forever away from him, but at last he broke it, gasping for air. About fifteen feet below, he could see the fiery glow from the mirror, and it spilled some light into the hall. Things bumped into him as he coughed. He was wondering how they'd get out when he heard a moan and felt himself being swept toward an object limned in the faint light. Then a hand grabbed him. "Take my hand." It was his grandpa.

James found his hand, and it pulled him up onto something warm, breathing, and hairy. He struggled, his hands grabbing on to matted hair. Underneath, he felt like it was a seat. Gripping the hair, he knelt with one knee down, the other up.

"Yes," his grandpa said. "You made a complete wreck of this place—I agree."

Cat had reached the surface and was shouting out for them. As they continued to float—Arthur's hand wrapped in a lock of the thing's hair—James realized the object beneath him was the beast-couch.

"Gramps, get Cat!"

The old, wet man said a quiet spell; the aventurine globe lit up with sapphire light. "Over here, boy. Is his name Cat? Like tomcat? Swim, Tomcat! I know you have it in you!"

The creature was paddling toward Cat's voice. He saw now that it sported a quintet of eyeballs, and had scaly hide, and that his grandfather was holding on to its wet mane that fell down its backrest and arms. It still stunk of burned hair. It continued to paddle through the swirling water, grunting. A moment later, Cat grabbed on to the creature's welt, and James and Arthur took his wrist and pulled him up onto the scaly seat.

Cat, breathing hard, collapsed against the hairy backrest, coughing and rubbing the streaming water from his face.

"What is this creature?" James asked.

"A beast from the land of Naqod," Arthur said. "Esteemed teratogenesist, Parsinicus, was obsessed with monsters of all sorts and made some spectacular creations—all of them benign, of course. Unfortunately, most of his creations were banned. But admirers and connoisseurs hid some of his creations on a secret island known as Naqod. I suppose some are here to prevent the spread of them—though they are pure works of art."

There were so many questions about the secrets here that this was just a drop in a pool. But they had other pressing matters at hand. "How do we get out?" James asked.

"I'm not entirely sure," Arthur said. "The hall is mostly underwater. My son was in a similar predicament when he came. The two of you continue to show a striking resemblance to one another, I'm afraid."

The Naqod couch was still swimming in circles. Only the tops of the bookshelves came out of the water, and dozens of enchanted tomes were still flying around. Arthur set his cane down and caught one; it flapped wildly in his hands, spraying water in their faces. "Maybe one of our intellectuals can tell us. They've lived here for hundreds of years." He was only being funny though; he tossed the book back into the air, and it flapped away, muttering.

"Over there," Cat said, pulling his knees up and shivering.

James looked and saw something in the water floating toward them. He took his grandpa's cane and held it up to see better. The light was reflecting off the side of a ewer bouncing along in the water. It was halfway full so that it was poised enough to not tip over. But that wasn't the strangest thing. Balancing over the ewer's top was a painting. He'd seen a number of them before, lying around on tables, or propped against chairs or desks. He was wondering how this one managed to be propped up in such a way when he saw the three small creatures. Two were clinging to the neck of the ewer with their paws holding on to the frame, and the third creature was hiding inside it and holding the painting with his mouth.

"It's those talking weasels," Cat said.

"Oh—not them again," Arthur grumbled.

"You got out," James said.

"We got out," agreed Poppy.

"*Arrr-shrr-shrr-shrrr*," mumbled Zippy, who had the painting in his mouth.

"Roseheart," Dippy said.

"She was kind enough to open our cage before she died," Poppy said.

"*Chr-sh-k*," mumbled Zippy.

"What?" James frowned.

"He said 'tragic,'" Dippy supplied.

"How do we get out of here?" Cat asked.

"Sorry, but we're much too busy to talk about that," Poppy said.

"*Wher-shring—*"

"To keep this painting—"

"From falling," finished Poppy.

"Just drop it!" Arthur blurted out, scowling.

"*Ook—is-ish-shi-i-an*," mumbled Zippy.

"Whom we told where to find a better-looking mask," Dippy finished.

"Can you tell us how to get out?" Arthur growled.

"Might you do us a favor first?" Poppy asked.

"What?" James said.

"*Chake-chish-hrr—*"

"Priceless painting—"

"Before we—"

"*Shrpit—*"

"In the water."

Now that James was close enough, he could see it was quite a handsome oil painting of a ferocious-looking boat floating on the sea. "What is it?" he asked.

"A painting." Dippy said.

"Why is it here in the Tomb of Forgotten Secrets?" James asked.

"'Tis a beautiful painting, no?" Poppy said.

"Yes—but why is it in *here*?" Cat asked.

"*Hshrshrsh-ish-sh-ashusha-shi-shroshen-shin-shysh*," enlightened Zippy.

"*What?*" James and Cat cried together.

"Precisely," Poppy said. "Now make sure nothing happens to it."

They had to make several tries as they passed the ewer with the three weasels floating by shouting at them. Finally, James took his grandpa's cane and pulled the ewer closer, and Cat reached over and grabbed the painting, almost falling off in the process.

"Now what was it you were saying about the painting?" James asked.

But Poppy said, "Now, for the magic words." And the three of them sang, "*Izog-bozog-fozog!*"

Suddenly, there was a loud rumbling across the hall, and the wall groaned and split, then crumbled away. Daylight penciled through like beams of molten bronze. Instantly, the water began to rush out, splashing over the stone wall. A fresh breeze swooped in.

They snagged on the side of the stone wall that had crumbled away beneath them, and streams of water flowed past and gushed down the mountain. A pile of debris gathered behind them—old books, scrolls, and the bodies of some monkeys. The other Naqod creatures had assembled around them, too, balancing on the stone ledge, ululating like uncanny hippopotamuses.

As this happened, a sudden gust of wind whipped through the hall, followed by a quiet voice, gentle, like the breath of a lover.

"*Ashar Itola.*"

"What was that?" Cat asked, looking at James.

"Dunno," James said. "What language was that?"

"I do not know," Arthur said.

"It appears," said Zippy.

"That the Lady."

"Of the Tomb."

"Is at last free," Zippy finished.

"Free?" James looked at them. He tried to recall what the mysterious words were—and wondered if they were even meant for him.

"Let her go," Arthur said at last.

The echo swept through the hall, and then, all at once, dashed out, like a crescendo of enchanted music, and the stones crumbled away before them. James held on to the beast's mane as they were swept out of the hall along with the three weasels in the half-filled ewer. In the sun, he saw the ewer in plain light for the first time. It was a strange color he'd never seen before. He could not describe it, nor could he recall it when he looked away.

It was a water ride that could not have been replicated at any amusement park. Down they went, the water flowing and splashing—*magically*. James could only describe it as magically, because the water dashed down the mountainside in controlled gushes, almost *floating* over rocks. The Naqod couch swam with it. Flecks of water shot into the air, pierced by a vibrant sun, and made rainbow auras that dashed in their eyes. They continued down the mountain in the wild torrent of water that changed—with a wondrous spell shouted by Zippy—into galloping crystalline impalas that smashed into droplets when they hit the stones. All the time the Naqod creatures moaned and paddled and kept the three of them balanced so they didn't plunge to their deaths. Behind, the chairs bounced on crests, whinnying like small foals, the table kicked, and the chiffonier tumbled about, its drawers opening up to swallow mouthfuls of sudsy water.

"Whoooo!" Arthur cried as they rushed past craggy rocks, the stubble on his chin catching flecks of the diamond droplets splashed by diving impalas breaking on boulders, or overturning pebbles.

They reached the bottom of the mountain, and the impalas went prancing through the jungle, forming a racing stream ahead. Some of the watery impalas burst into foam and sprang into the foliage, gathering dirt. They didn't keep their form far from the source, however, and dissolved into rivulets and puddles.

Now the river broke in two, cutting around a large hillock with stones and tangled large trees, with snakes, parrots, and lemurs. James, who was holding on to the side, wiping the water from his eyes, while holding on to the painting, watched as the magical ewer, with the un-rememberable color, was swept away along with the leaping impalas in suds and dirt.

"Perchance—"

"We shall—"

"Meet—"

"Again," the weasels cried, before they vanished in a cloud of mist glowing in sunbeams.

Meanwhile, the three of them plunged down another cliff, James clinging tightly to the beast's mane, and at last came to a calm stream in the middle of the jungle. Surrounding them were ferns, flowers, and snakes of liana.

The Naqod furniture-beasts were clustered together, grunting and swimming and lapping at the tucks of clear, fresh water.

"Well," Arthur said, turning to lounge on the couch, his wet robes clinging to him, "this isn't all *too* unpleasant."

The Naqod climbed out of the water and began to clamber up a bank and into a thick forest of bamboo. Knee-high ferns sprawled over the ground, dappled in glittery lights from above. The whinnying chairs followed, dripping water off wet manes. Their mouths and eyeballs were on the back, so when they grazed, nibbling at the fronds, they bent over with their front legs sticking up. The chiffonier waddled about like a chunky, square penguin, its drawers full of water, opening and closing like mouths.

Still holding the oil painting, James hopped off the Naqod couch onto some rocks, followed by Cat. But Arthur stood gracefully using his cane and gave the couch a pat with his hand. "Good day to you," he said pleasantly. He stepped ashore stumbling a bit on a pile of unstable stones, before scrambling up the bank, his cloak catching in spike-rush. A forest of bamboo awaited him, and he took off his wet cloak. He looked up at the sky. "It'll be dusk soon," he said. "Let's build a fire."

Cat and James set out, breaking down bamboo, as his grandfather disrobed down to his smallclothes. When James and Cat had returned with armfuls of bamboo, he had cleared a place in the ferns, and had set rocks and kindling down. His bare, liver-spotted arms caught bands of sunlight that filtered through the bamboo.

They piled the bamboo up, and Cat lit it. *"Igra."* Fire caught on the stalks. Cracks, pops, and bursts like gunfire rang out as Arthur squatted by it, warming himself.

James and Cat pulled off their tunics, too, to dry them.

"My goodness," Arthur said, stepping away from the fire to inspect James's bare arms covered in scrapes and bruises. "You've so many scars already." He took James's hands in his, examining them. They were full of blisters, and he ran his thumb over the flesh where the nail had been torn away. He looked at James's face—eyes hollowed and sandbagged, nose still peeling from sunburn, lips chapped and split, and the one silver eyebrow. "I bet you don't remember what it's like to sit on a toilet." He turned the hand over.

"How did you survive?"

The bamboo fire cracked obnoxiously behind them; Arthur gave a small chuckle, dropping the hand. "The goblin snatched me up and took me to an old cave." He went to stand by the fire as it continued to blast. Cat returned with another armful and chucked it on. The Naqod were still in sight, moaning and walking through ferns and bamboo. "He tied me up. I had to reason with him."

"What about Galajitar?"

Arthur eyed Cat, who'd sat beside the fire to warm himself. The fire cracked and popped some more, and Arthur led him away, finding a stick of bamboo to help him along. He'd left his cane lying beside the fire. "The goblin was gloating that he'd gotten it from you. I convinced him to take me to a place." He stopped a good distance away from the fire near the chiffonier sniffing at a fern and leaned against a firm stalk.

"So, you never got the book back?"

"It was wise to leave Galajitar with the goblin," Arthur said. "My client would find it powerful and useful. The object is to kill him, not give him more weapons."

"But I need the—" He stopped. He was getting so used to saying "I need." Was that how Jack fell into his pit of darkness? Needing things like books and swords, boats and enchanted stones? Yet, he'd already taken the first step. He had to commit now. "When you left us in Sarvelok, I called Stray. I signed his contract. I owe him that book, or it's my soul. It's either the book or the sword."

"Listen," Arthur said, paternally taking him by the shoulder. "The Tomb of Forgotten Secrets has been opened and the Lady of the Tomb is free. She will come to you before Stray can claim your soul."

"How do you know?"

"You are Jack's son. She will not abandon you."

James hesitated, wondering if the explanation would suffice. Then he said, "Did you know I would call him?"

"I was informed of your expedient arrival. The ogres contacted me through that crystal ball. I figured out you'd met *Persephone*'s beast. You are very much like your father, as I've said."

James stared at him accusingly. "We almost died."

"I told you to do what Jack would do."

"That was reckless!" He'd just imagined Quizlow's rebuking look, the judgmental disappointment in his eyes. "You're reck—"

"What did I tell you before in the woods?" his grandpa suddenly snapped. "Where are your *balls*, James?" He grabbed him by the arm, his hands leaving marks on the already bruised skin there, and pulled him around to face him. "Do you think your father became great without sacrifices? He didn't balk at using a demon. He had the balls to play with fire."

"And he got burned." Cat was standing behind them, bare-chested, arms folded. "Where's his precious balls now? Well-done, I should think."

Arthur regarded him almost distantly, through clouded eyes. "You wouldn't understand, boy. You're no Dreadful." He let go of James.

"I know what it's all about," James said, his voice dropping to a chilly note. "Galajitar turned you down. But you want to be great." His eyes narrowed. "Like an old man with a second chance to bring meaning to his life. But you couldn't be more than mediocre, could you? So, now you hope *I* can." He stared into the old man's citrine eyes. "But there's something you don't know. My father was mind-controlled by Cowl. That's why he did those terrible things." He stepped toward him, scowling. "Now, tell me," he growled, the broken-nailed index hurting as he pressed into it, "what's *your* excuse?"

Arthur stared at him, then leaned on his bamboo stick. He gave James an old familiar grin but sighed. The fact that Arthur did not seem to register the depth of what he'd just said about his son showed how little he cared.

Or he just thinks I'm ridiculous!

Arthur turned and walked back toward the fire. "Your hate is justified. When you were a little boy, I filled you with the darkness that was in me."

James and Cat followed, arms folded.

The old man picked up his clothes and put them on. They were warm, but still damp. Then he stopped and stared at the fire. *"I can't."*

"You can't—what?" James asked.

"I can't, James." He had turned to look at him now, the sadness he'd seen before was there, as though James had reminded him of it.

"I'm with Phantom. Unless I wish to live here on this island for the rest of my life, I must return to them. Once you've been branded, nowhere is safe from them." He touched the place on his neck where that strange eye had appeared burned into the flesh. "This is the only place I can hide. It is hidden from all eyes." He looked around at the bamboo and saw a bird fly past. Or maybe it was a chattering tome.

"Then stay here," James said, his voice gentler, and sat by the fire.

"I cannot. There is too much to do."

"For Phantom?" James cried, his hackles rising.

Arthur gave a tired laugh. "James, there are other forces at play here. Forces I cannot tell you about." His eyes darted to the oil painting. "Don't play with that. There's a reason it was in that place." He'd finished putting on his clothes, and now he wrapped his cloak around him. Then he turned and started off through the bamboo, picking up his cane along the way.

"Where are you going?" James shouted.

He stopped. "Do not go down that road with me, James. This one I must travel alone. Go back to the Faugs. When you're older, find the Lady of the Tomb." He turned and continued on his way.

"I'm sorry, James," Cat said. "I—"

"Fetcher!" James suddenly leaped to his feet. He didn't remember moving his legs, but the next instant, he was running toward the old man. He didn't know what he was going to do when he reached him. He just knew he was full of rage. "Don't you *dare* walk out on me again!"

Arthur heard his quick movements—saw the bamboo rustling.

Crack! Pop! Crack!

The bamboo exploded in the fire.

And suddenly, the old man spun around.

James caught a glimpse of something in his citrine eyes—a sparkle of the magic that had always been there—sleeping. There was a shadow in his grandfather's face, too, like the one he saw when he was just five—as he stretched out his hand—and that fireball had burst from his fingertips, hot, crackling, burning, and killing the dark in its path.

Like the day Arthur had set the house on fire.

A whisper.

"Exciperi."

The next instant, James was thrown back, as though he'd been struck by a baseball bat—or a cudgel wielded by Formandible. It didn't hurt. The blow just sent him flying through the bamboo stalks that cracked and splintered. He struck the ground, and bounced head over heels, and rolled until he went still. If he was any more bruised than he already had been, he wasn't aware of it. But dazed—that he was certain of. The world swam. His vision blurred.

"I'll watch over you, James," a voice floated to him through the jungle.

All he could see were the tops of the stalks oscillating in the late lights, turning into blurs of green and blue.

"But don't you ever try to find me."

When he picked himself up to his knees and looked around, Cat was standing over him. He brushed him away and climbed to his feet. He looked, and looked, and looked.

But there was no sign of the old man with the citrine eyes anywhere to be found.

About the Author

Alan Creed fell in love with storytelling after seeing *Star Wars* for the first time as a child. When he was ten years old, his tutor asked him to write sentences containing three words: Ocean, Desert and Jungle. Instead of sentences, Alan wrote a 103-page story entitled Journey through the Desert. That's when he knew he wanted to be a writer. His 103-page story served as the source material for the *Dreadful Series*. Alan is currently working on the next installment in the series.

To learn more about Alan and the *Dreadful Series*, visit www.jamesdreadful.com.